A HOUSE IN THE HILLS

JOHN SUMNER

 New Generation Publishing

AUTHOR'S NOTES

This book is a work of fiction. Names, characters, businesses, organizations, places and events are the product of the author's imagination and are used fictitiously. Any resemblance to actual persons, living or dead, events or locales is entirely coincidental.

The narrative by the character 'Ross' is a true story, and permission has been given for it to be used. The names and places mentioned have been changed but the final outcome is pure fiction.

John Sumner
Spain 2007

ONE

As he was standing waiting for the bus, the sound of car horns made him turn round. He saw a small pickup truck cross the road in front of two cars travelling in the opposite direction, and pull up outside a shop that sold wall and floor tiles. He realized that it was a British vehicle when the only occupant, a lady, got out of the right hand door.

She was about one hundred and seventy centimetres tall, with short, light brown hair, and dressed in jeans and a sleeveless denim jacket covering a red shirt. She looked nervously around as she went into the shop, and moments later came out again with the owner, waving a letter, speaking pidgin Spanish, and pointing at her motor. The owner walked across the road to the storeroom as the lady undid the tailboard of the pickup, and then followed her inside. They emerged with a bag of tile adhesive each which they carried to the motor, placed them on the tail end, and gave them a push. Neither bags moved very far over the tailboard, but they both went back to the store for more. The same thing happened again, two bags on the tail, a push, and back for more. On the third trip, the shop owner gestured to the vehicle and said something to the lady, who shrugged and looked as if she was going to burst into tears. They turned and went back to the store, presumably for more bags of adhesive.

Unable to contain his curiosity, he walked towards the vehicle and climbed over the tail onto the flat bed. He picked up a bag, carried it to the cab end and laid it straight. He had three bags neatly lined up, when the two ladies came back from the store.

"How many bags are we going to load?" he asked.

"Well," said the lady, "I considered ten bags of

adhesive, and as many boxes of tiles as I could get on. They were ordered some time ago, but I've only just got back from France. When I got home, there was a letter waiting for me, telling me if I didn't pick my order up, they would sell it, so here I am."

"Do you want to come up here and load while I carry," he asked, "or would you prefer I loaded?"

"You load, please, and thank you for the help."

Less than half an hour later, the rear of the motor was almost filled with the ten bags of adhesive, several boxes of wall tiles and some larger boxes of floor tiles.

As he jumped down, he turned to the lady and said,

"I hope there's someone to help you unload all this lot."

She stood with her mouth slightly open, then answered,

"No, I never thought about unloading until you just mentioned it. With three of us loading, I was carried away until the motor was full. It's going to take me hours to unload these on my own, and I'm afraid my order might get sold if I don't take everything today."

He turned to the owner and spoke to her in reasonably good Spanish. She nodded a couple of times, and answered, pointing at the lady.

Turning back to her he said,

"I'm sorry, I seem to be the go-between here, but the Señora says she will save your order for a few days, provided you make another payment now and the balance before you pick up the last load."

"That's no problem." she said, "If you don't mind, would you tell her I'll pay for the whole order now and pick up the balance as soon as I can."

He passed on the message, and the owners eyes lit up. What he didn't know, was the size of the order, but he was soon going to find out.

She went into the shop, and came out a few minutes later with her receipt.

"Where are you taking all this?" he asked.

"Up into the hills," was her reply.

"If we leave now," he said, "we could unload this lot, and then come back for some more after lunch."

"I can't expect you to come home with me and unload all this." the lady replied in surprise.

"I'm not going to unload it all," he replied, "you're going to help."

She smiled, nodded, and said,

"I asked for that one didn't I?"

He lifted and secured the tailgate, pulled a canvas sheet over and tied it at the corners. As he was doing it, he said to the lady,

"I'm Ted, and I live in the apartment up there, the one with the plants on the patio."

"I'm... well, my name's Rosalinda, but I'm mostly called either Ross or Linda, you can take your pick."

"I'll call you 'Ross', as long as you don't turn out to be a frozen fish steak."

"That's definitely a new one; I don't think I've ever been compared to fish before. I dread to think what you could come up with if you knew all my names." she answered with a laugh.

They got into the pickup and Ross started the engine. Before pulling away said,

"I've made arrangements with the shop, and they're going to leave the rest of my order by the store room door, and I can pick it up when I'm ready. I need to turn round, is there anywhere further down the road?"

"When in Spain, do as the Spaniards do," Ted told her, "make a U turn here at the junction. There's nothing behind, clear in front, go for it!"

She turned the motor round and drove back through

the village. There was a roundabout at the road end where she went straight ahead, and a few minutes later, turned onto a concrete track that climbed gently up the side of a hill. After about ten minutes of careful driving, they came to a sharp left hand bend, but instead of following the road, Ross took a right hand turn onto another rising track. The track swung left, before levelling out, and coming to an abrupt end overlooking a valley. On their left hand side stood a single storey house with an almost flat un-tiled roof. Behind them was a door-less stone building, which could have been a store room or a garage.

"Welcome to my home." she said, "We can store the tiles in the building behind, but I'm not sure about the adhesive."

"The adhesive can go in there as well, it's not likely to rain heavily until October at the earliest, and you should have used it by then. Before we start unloading, would you like to show me round? I'm intrigued with such a small house up here in the hills."

"This isn't the only building. If we go round to the other side of the house, you'll be able to see the layout much easier."

They walked round the house onto a large almost circular, flat area, where another building, which was as big as the house, stood on their right. As he looked, he could see that both buildings were set at a slight angle. At the nearest point, they were about twelve metres apart, widening out to maybe thirteen or fourteen metres at the furthest point.

The area between the buildings was randomly littered with pallets holding all kind of building materials. There were several pallets of breeze block, a couple of pallets of 'ordinary' brick, some facing bricks, and many balustrade bases, tops, and pillars scattered around.

He slowly looked around the area, and in a hushed, almost silent voice, just said,

"Wow."

"Not bad is it?" Ross answered.

"It's just about the most fantastic place I have seen. It's so quiet, yet there's the sound of nature all around. It's clear and clean, and the view over the hills to the sea is nothing short of spectacular. How long have you lived here, you lucky person."

"I don't live here yet. I only bought it recently, and decided to finish building it before moving in, but there's quite a lot of work to be done first."

"How long do you think it will take?"

"If I have to do it on my own, I've thought about two years, at least."

"If I gave you a hand, I think we could finish in one year…. and eleven months."

Ross smiled, and said,

"I couldn't ask you to come and do all that work."

"Ross, you aren't listening to me. You aren't asking, I'm volunteering, and I'm not going to do all the work, you are going to do some as well."

"Are you serious? You haven't seen inside yet"

"I'm deadly serious. I'd love to come up here regularly, and help you restore this…. finca."

"What's a finca?" she asked.

"It has several meanings, but the meaning for this building is 'country house'."

"So I have bought myself a finca, which is a little more than a year old. The previous owners built this house and that…. well, what could it be, a barn, maybe. I haven't ventured inside it yet, and there could be anything in it, living or dead. There are windows at the rear, but they're boarded up. They overlook the valley, and the distance between the drop and the wall is rather narrow, so I'm afraid of falling if I try to remove the boards myself. The previous owners ran out of cash long before the project was finished and had to sell it or go bust. It was for sale at a good price, but I put in a lower offer, and it was accepted. I hate to brag, but I'm going to, this project was quite cheap and I was able to pay for it in full. There is no need to worry about me not finishing it either, I've enough money to finish the house, with plenty to spare. Enough about that for now, let me show you the interior."

They went back around the house again, and in through a door on the side.

He stopped in amazement. The floor sloped from about half way along the room down to the wall on their right and was covered with large, red unevenly fitted tiles.

"I don't mean to be rude Ross, but I hope this isn't your work, and all these tiles are going to be replaced."

"You aren't being rude Ted. This is how I bought the house, sloping floor complete with uneven tiles. Wait until you see the kitchen walls though."

At the top of the room, slightly offset to the left was a door leading to what Ted presumed was the kitchen.

Ross opened the door, and with a slight bow, said,

"After you, please."

He took two paces into the kitchen, and stopped.

"My God," Ted said in a horrified voice, "who the hell thought up that revolting mixture?"

On the left hand side was a 'wet room' set up for a washing machine and room for storage cupboards. The wet room and the kitchen floors were evenly laid with very nice 'café-au-lait' coloured tiles, but the kitchen walls were partially covered in a complete muddle of small, individual, purple and pink tiles. It looked as though they had been aimlessly selected, and stuck haphazardly onto the wall. There were gaps in the corners where whole tiles wouldn't fit, and round the inset of the windows was still bare concrete.

"Do you still want to stick around and help?" Ross asked.

"On the condition there's to be no more hideous decoration, yes." Ted answered.

"There's no more tiled walls. The walls in the other room are painted, as you saw, and the only other room is the loo, and that's still unpainted concrete. Be honest, Ted, do you really want to help me, now you've seen it?"

"You were obviously going to start in here because we've just brought wall tiles back from the village. I just hope you've more colour sense than the previous builders. Without being sexist, those colours weren't chosen by a woman."

"I bought this from two men, so say no more."

"You can't say things like that, it's not politically correct." Ted answered with a smile.

"Bollocks!" Ross replied. "This is Spain, not bloody England... sorry, it's just that I get so mad with all this 'you can't say this or that, because it may offend someone'. It offends me, but then I'm only British, and that doesn't count."

"Spoken like a true patriot," he said, "that is one of the reasons I'm here in Spain, I couldn't stand it either."

"I'm here for personal reasons. I may unburden myself sometime, if I need to, and if you'd like to listen to me."

"No problem, we can talk while we work."

"Some of the things I'll tell you would probably be better said when we were resting, say during our lunch break."

"That sounds serious." Ted answered, giving Ross a

11

worried look.

"It is," Ross replied, "but let's not talk about it now, we have a truck to unload, and another journey to make to the village for more tiles. I have a lot more things to order, so if you're going to help me, could I ask your help with planning? I've only got ideas in my mind, and if I don't get those ideas written down, or something, I'll forget what I want to do. Somehow I have to plan two bedrooms and a bathroom to go over the top of here. It sounds easy, but where do I put the stairs, and more importantly, the plumbing and the electrics?"

"No problem. I have a computer disc that can be used for planning. It has so many things on it I can't start to describe it. All we need is the inside and outside dimensions, window and door sizes and positions then we fill in from there."

"That sounds brilliant. With that, I could change my mind as often as I want to."

"Not if the tiles are on the wall, you can't."

"I didn't mean... I can't tell if you're joking or not. I suppose I'll get used to it if you're going to help me.

"Come on, let's get the truck unloaded, and go back to the village." Ted said, "We can have a sandwich in my apartment if you like and have a brief look at the home designer disc while we eat. Do you know the room size?"

"The house measurements are written on a pad in the pickup." Ross replied.

It took a while for them to unload and stack the boxes and bags in the store room. Ted had found some pallets at the rear of the store, and the boxes and bags were stacked on them to keep them off the ground. By the time the pickup was empty, they were both sweating heavily, and their shirts were stuck to their bodies.

"Is there any water in the kitchen?" asked Ted, "I

could do with a cold drink."

"I'm not sure." Ross answered, "I know there's no mains water, only a well. At the moment though, it doesn't work, and I can't get any water."

"That is something we are going to have to sort out before we start building. We'll need drinking water when we are working, particularly when we get to the hottest part of the summer, but we will also need water to mix the concrete. Leave it for now I'll take a look round for you when we get back with the next load. Come on, back to the Pueblo and we can have a sandwich and a nice cool drink."

She turned the pickup round, and drove back towards the village.

"Can we do a slight detour?" Ted asked, "I was on my way to do some shopping, when I met a maiden in distress."

"It's a bloody long time since I was a maiden." she laughed. "Of course we can, any supermarket in particular?"

Ted directed her to the one he wanted, and showed her the best place to park. They both went inside and emerged twenty minutes later carrying several bags of food. They drove back along the coast road, before turning inland towards the village.

"You know," said Ross, "I've been in the area for several weeks, and I've not been down here. I didn't know about these shops, and I've not even seen the sea or the promenade."

"Paseo!" Ted corrected her, "A promenade in Spain is called the 'Paseo Marítimo'. When we get some time to spare, if you like, we can come down here and take a walk. There are plenty of cafés and restaurants so you may even be invited to have a drink or a meal, you never know your luck."

"That's a date, thank you. You may not have any time off for the next twelve months, though."

"That's the best rejection I've ever had." he said with a laugh.

"No Ted, that's not a rejection, it's just... I'll explain some other time. I would love to have a walk and a drink, but let's start working on the house, I need to be able to use it as soon as possible because.... well there are several reasons. I don't like renting an expensive house in the village when I'm only sleeping there. I would be better just renting a room somewhere, but haven't been able to find one yet. Don't get me wrong Ted, I have enough money to see the project through, but I don't like paying out money unnecessarily. There is another reason, but that's something that will have to wait."

"You are a real lady of mystery, aren't you? I think I'll call you 'The Mysterious Maiden'."

She laughed, and shook her head.

"I'm getting used to your silly comments, they're not offensive and at least make light of things."

As they had been talking they arrived in the village and when they eventually found somewhere to park made their way to Ted's apartment.

Her gave her a quick guided tour, and then said,

"I'll make some sandwiches if you turn the computer on. The disk is in the rack there and while we're eating, I'll get it ready for us to work on."

Ted brought the sandwiches into the living room and they sat together at the computer to eat them. He put the disc in the disc drive and started the process by entering the house dimensions on to the plan. He made a duplicate to represent a second floor, and was looking at the 'add on' section for bathroom and bedroom, trying to find the best position for them.

"I'm not sure really how this is supposed to work." he said after a while, "It was a free gift with a building magazine, and it's never been used, apart from an initial play around the day I got it. I think it may be better if we left it for now, and I'll have a good search tonight, when I've got more time."

"I don't want to take up your leisure time." Ross said

"All my time is leisure time since I had to retire," Ted replied. "When you bought the project, were there no plans included? Officially, neither building should have been started without any plans being passed, showing what their intended use was."

"I've not seen any, and the estate agent never mentioned them when he gave me all the legal papers. I know there is a licence to build so I've not worried about anything else. I'll contact him when I get a chance and see what he has to say."

Ted switched the computer off, and while they finished their sandwiches, they told each other a little about themselves.

Ted was from the North of England, near to Lancaster, while Ross came from the South, not far from Guildford. Ted said he had worked as an accountant for a very large building company before he had to retire early on medical grounds, but Ross would only say she had worked in a family business. There was a little reluctance for Ross to give her age, but admitted to being 'over thirty nine, but less than forty five'. Ted had therefore no hesitation in saying he was probably four or five years older than she was.

After lunch, Ross drove her pickup to the tile shop store, where outside the doors stood six piles of large boxes. They got out of the vehicle, and went to look at them.

"I think those are all for us." said Ross quietly,

looking at the details on the box sides.

"Bloody hell woman," said Ted, "are you going to tile the road up to the house as well?"

"I think I may have overestimated the number I need."

"I think you could be right! What are they for anyway?"

"The re-laying of the long area once the red tiles are taken up, and hopefully the bedrooms as well. I measured the room length and width and multiplied the two measurements together to give me the area. I doubled it to allow for the upstairs and gave the lady the figures I worked out."

"It looks as though you gave her the dimensions in square feet and she took it as square metres. I can have a word with her sometime and ask if she will take any full boxes back and credit you with them. We won't be able to take them all in one journey."

"I think they'll all go on the back without any problem." Ross said.

"Maybe they will, but think of the weight in the boxes. The pickup would struggle to get up any hills, let alone the driveway up to your house."

"I never thought about that. It's a good job I met you."

"Tell me that in twenty years' time when we've just finished the house, and about to dig a hole for the swimming pool."

"Twenty years! I was hoping more like twenty months."

"Ross, I hear what you say, but we have to plan this out properly, decide the priorities, and stick to our decisions. We cannot, for example, start work in the kitchen, and then move on to a bathroom. It just won't work."

"I said earlier that I have to get away from the house I'm renting. It's costing me unnecessary money, and if I'm going to be working at the house in the hills all day, it's something I could do without."

"In that case," Ted replied, "I think the priority is the only two rooms available. If we get the kitchen walls tiled, then the floor in the lounge finished properly, you could rig up a camp bed or something, and 'slum it' until we can get a bedroom done."

"That makes sense. Let's work on that idea for now. Kitchen wall tiles first, then I can buy some cupboards, work surfaces and a cooker and get them fitted."

"Don't forget a fridge for our cold drinks." Ted added.

"We need the water first." Ross reminded him.

"I'll have a look when we get up there, it can't be much of a problem." Ted replied.

They had been loading the boxes as they talked, and Ted was watching the back of the truck sag as they put box after box on the flat bed. He asked Ross to stop for a minute as he re-counted the number of boxes.

"That's enough Ross. We have a third of them loaded, let's leave it at that. We can get this lot unloaded, and time permitting, come back for some more later, and leave the rest until tomorrow. Before we leave though, I'm going back to the apartment. I have a cooler that we can keep some bottles of water in. We'll certainly need some when we've unloaded all this lot."

Ted filled his cooler with bottles of water, and put it on the floor of the pickup.

Ross drove away from the store, and up the hill out of the village.

"This feels strange," she said, "the front end seems to be in the air, and the steering feels light."

"Then don't go too fast. The weight of the boxes has

lifted the front end slightly, and the speed is nowhere near as good as it was earlier. As a matter of interest, are you in two or four wheel drive?"

"Two, I think. I'm not sure how to change it over. I don't like this Ted. If I pull over, will you drive it back to the house?"

Ross pulled into the side and they changed seats.

Ted showed her how to change to four wheel drive, and they set off again.

"It's certainly running a bit smoother." Ross said, "How does it feel to steer?"

"It is light, but if I keep the speed below ninety there should be no problem."

Ross looked at Ted with a smile, and said,

"I think the only way this vehicle will get up to ninety with this load on, will be if you drive off the road at the top of my drive, and down into the valley."

Ted returned the look, and said,

"Who's the one coming out with daft comments now? I hope we're not going to be fighting to see who can come up with the worst jokes are we?"

"I hope not, but I can see we both have a daft sense of humour though."

Ted drove to the house and reversed the truck up to the stone garage.

"After we finish the necessary building work, we could look at possible altering the road slightly. If we make the top corner wider, you could drive in a larger circle, straight into the garage, head first. To get out, you would reverse straight back, and then drive into the corner and down to the other track."

"That is a good idea, but for much later on. Let's get these tiles sorted, but before we unload, could you have a look for the water? I need to use the loo, and I don't like the idea of not being able to flush it afterwards."

"OK, I'll do it now. I've not seen a pipe in the kitchen, but I take it there is one somewhere and hopefully one in the loo. Do you know if there are any more around, because, providing I find the water pump, I don't want to turn it on, and find water gushing all over the house."

"Don't worry about that, please, just find some water."

"If I hear you scream I'll know the pipes haven't been connected." Ted said with a laugh.

Ross rushed away to the toilet, while Ted went round to the other end of the building. Under one of the kitchen windows, he found a metal box, and inside it was the water pump. It was connected to a 'temporary' electrical circuit and as he switched the pump on, was rewarded by the sound of running water. The problem was though, the running water was inside the kitchen!

He hastily turned the pump off again, and went inside to inspect the damage. He saw a big puddle of water near to the right hand corner. There was about four centimetres of pipe sticking through the wall and Ted realised that it was the main water supply to the house, but he would have a struggle to fit a tap on a piece of pipe that length. He found a small tub in the opposite corner and placed it under the pipe. As he went outside, intending to turn the water on again, Ross was coming round the corner from the loo. Ted could see that her hair and shirt was slightly wet.

She was laughing as she said,

"I was sat on the loo, when suddenly a spray of water came from the pipe that's fixed to the cistern. I'm glad you turned it off quickly though, I could have been soaked by the time I'd finished."

"I think a look at the fittings is all that's needed," answered Ted. "The pipe in the kitchen has been cut so short, no junction piece or a tap can be fixed to it. Once we get the tiles off the wall, we will be able to do something with it. Let's get those tiles unloaded, and we can go back to the village for some more. I can pick up my tool box and a mop from the apartment before we come back, and maybe I can tighten the pipe so you don't have a shower next time you're sat on the loo. Just as a point of interest, there is no meter fitted to the water pipe, which proves that there isn't mains water, but your own well water. You are going to have to get that checked out and find out where and how big your water deposit is."

They unloaded as quickly as they could, and after a cooling drink, drove back for their next load of tiles. When the tiles were on board, Ted went to his apartment and got his tool box, a mop and a bucket and loaded them in the cab.

Back at the house, they carried the tile boxes into the garage, and stacked them with the others on the pallets. The second set unloaded, they spent the next ten minutes getting their breath back and cooling down with more drinks of cold water.

Ted took his tool box to the toilet to see where the water was leaking, and as he opened the door, could see immediately why. The nut connecting the water pipe to the cistern was cross threaded, and therefore loose. He carefully unscrewed it, wound some UPVC tape around the threads on the pipe, and tightened the nut up, straight.

"There, that should be right, but I'm afraid the kitchen will have to wait, because I've nothing to fit that diameter of pipe."

"I'll ask at the tile shop if they have anything." answered Ross.

"With due respect to them, I think we should be

looking around at other places. If we make a full list of everything you need, we could go and look round a large DIY store just outside Malaga. It's similar to an English B&Q, but has more variety."

"That's a good idea. We could make out a list later if you like, and in the morning, go and price things up."

"OK, that's tomorrow sorted out. Meanwhile, let's go and mop the kitchen floor. I could possibly clamp the water pipe closed so we could use the water elsewhere if we need it. With not having a tap on the pipe, as soon as the pump is switched on, water will flow. If the pipe is closed, water will only flow where any other tap is opened. After I've done that, we could have a look at the other building and maybe open a window or two, even if it's only to let light in. If we see any animals inside, we can leave the door open for them to escape."

"Or let more of them in." Ross said with a laugh.

"I never thought of that." Said Ted. "We could start a mini zoo in there."

It didn't take long to mop the kitchen floor, and by using two pieces of wood and two clamps, Ted sealed the water pipe. They went outside, and Ted showed Ross how to switch the water on so that she could flush the loo whenever she needed to. Ted picked up his tool box again, and they walked over to the other building.

"There are two doors," Ross told him, "one at each end. They are locked, but I have two keys on the ring that look as though they fit an ordinary sort of lock."

Ross put one of the keys into the lock, and it turned with no hesitation. She put her shoulder to the door, and gave it a push, but it would not open.

"It feels as though there is something stopping it from opening." she said. "Here, you have a try, you're supposed to be stronger than me."

"What do you mean supposed to be? I bet I can open

that door with one hand tied behind my back."

"Bet taken. I'll hold one hand, and you can try to open it with the other."

Ross got hold of Ted's hand and held it away so he could not use it. He reached out, took hold of the key, and pulled the door open!

"Easy when you know how," he laughed, "the thing that you thought was holding it closed, was the door frame. A lot of doors in Spain seem to open outwards."

"Know all!" Ross laughed, "Come on, let's find out what's inside. You can go first, age before beauty, as they say."

"That's another politically incorrect statement," Ted replied, "I could sue you for that."

"Do you remember what I said this morning about PC comments?"

"I think you used the word 'bollocks'" he replied, laughing.

"Same word applies now." Ross told him.

Ted pulled the door open wide. It was very dark inside, and they could see very little beyond the doorway. Ted was feeling his way along the wall on his left when his hand found a gap, and he almost fell into it.

"I've found a window," he said, "well, a window space. From what I can feel, this wall is thicker than usual as well. Ahh! There is a bolt though the wood that covers the window frame, and passes through a piece of timber here over the gap. There is a nut holding them together and if I can undo it, we can remove the window cover, which will give us some light. I'll need a spanner from my tool box."

"I'll get it." said Ross, "It's only just outside the door."

She was back in seconds and handed it to Ted. He selected an adjustable spanner, and gave the nut a turn. It moved fairly easily, and he was able to use his fingers to undo it further.

"Come and get hold of the wood here, please Ross and I'll see if I can shift the outer piece."

Ross came to his side, and got hold of the wood where he asked her. Ted then knelt into the window gap, and took hold of the bolt.

"Can you unscrew the nut with one hand, and hold the wood as you do it"?

"It's fairly loose now," Ross said, "do you want me to take it off completely?"

"Yes! I'm holding onto the bolt, so remove the wood as well. If you squeeze in next to me, we'll see if we can twist the outer piece of wood and bring it in through the gap where the glass should be."

"I don't think there's enough room for me to get in there with you, and even if I did get in, I don't think either of us would be able to move."

"OK. I'm going to keep hold of this bolt, and lift it up a little. The wood over the frame will lift as well, so when there's a gap at the bottom, get hold of the wood, and slowly twist it to the right, and at the same time, pull it in towards you. If we have it right we should be able to bring the wood in at an angle through the window frame."

It was a struggle, but eventually the wood cover came through the frame, and it was leant against the wall.

"While we have the momentum going," said Ted, "let's get the other covers off. We can worry about fitting the glass later."

It took about half an hour to get the six windows uncovered, and it was amazing how much light shone through into the building. They turned together, and looked around to see the whole area was filled with a jumble of building materials and implements.

"My God," gasped Ross, "what is all that lot?"

"That, my love, as far as I can see, is a lot of necessary things for us to be able to continue with your project. See, near the door, a petrol generator. If we can get that running, we can use it for making electricity to run the cement mixer that's stood next to it. There are bricks and breeze blocks galore, a large bag that looks like it contains sand, and other things hidden that we can't see at the moment."

Ross wandered away to look at what was leaning on the opposite wall, and Ted went between two pallets of brick to find out what was behind them.

"Ted, where are you?"

"Don't worry Ross, I've not deserted you just yet." he told her, "I'm behind the pallets of bricks. What have you found over there?"

"They look like patio doors, four sets, not all the same size, but all complete with roller blinds. I wonder what they were bought for. Have you got anything interesting?"

"Would you like to rephrase that remark?" Ted replied.

"No." Ross replied, laughing.

"Right, I won't start to brag then. I've found the glass for those windows we just opened, complete with the plastic inserts. We can fit them when it's convenient. Just as a matter of interest, when we go looking for your kitchen, have you a colour in mind?"

"No, not really. I'm the sort of person who sees something, and says, 'that's what I want'. Why do you ask?"

"I've just found two, three and a half metre lengths of work surface, in grey marble effect, and beside them, what looks like a complete kitchen in flat pack boxes. There are floor cupboards, wall cupboards, a set of drawers and a stainless steel sink. Did you know any of these were here when you bought the house?"

"No." answered Ross. "I never actually came in here, I was only shown inside the other building."

As they'd been talking, Ross had come round the pallets, and was looking in awe at the units Ted had found.

"Can you see what they're like, you know the design or the colour?"

"I can't see the design without opening the boxes, but on the end of the pack, it says 'white lacquered', so I presume that's what they are."

"Are they all white?"

"Perfectly, the boxes are stacked neatly on top of each other."

"Idiot! I meant... you know bloody well what I meant. I think I'm going to have problems with you. While we're talking about silly comments, what's with this 'my love' thing you came out with a few minutes ago?"

"Yes, well, sorry about that. It's the sort of thing I often come out with. I hope I didn't offend you."

"No, not at all, in fact I say the same sort of thing. I'm sure we both know that anything we say like that, you know, like 'love' and 'dear', is only meant in a friendly way, not romantic."

As Ross was speaking, Ted was looking around the building.

"Am I talking to myself?" asked Ross.

"No my love, of course not darling, I heard everything you said about friendship and not romantic. Something has just occurred to me though. Look at this building. It's as near as damn it to the size of the other one, and I reckon, with a lot of hard graft between us, we could probably build three double bedrooms in this block."

"That is brilliant thinking Ted. You know, it does make sense, three bedrooms and a bathroom in this area."

"I was thinking of en suite bathrooms for each room."

"Could we do that?"

"I think so. I've already said, it's going to be hard work, so are you prepared for that, if we can plan it out properly?"

"I am not afraid of hard work as long as there is something worthwhile at the end of it."

"You know Ross, I'm sure this block was meant for the bedrooms. There must be some drawings or plans somewhere. I said at lunch time these blocks would not have been built without submitting plans. We are going to have to work on this together Ross, and I don't want you to agree with everything I suggest. It's your house, and if you say you don't like something, say so. I'll sulk for a week or two, but I'll have to come round in the end. I suggest we accurately measure the width first, and then the length wall to wall and sit down with some paper and sketch some ideas. There are a couple of tape measures in my tool box, a pencil, and I have some scrap paper in my pocket. If we measure up now, we could put some ideas into the computer, and see what you think. Making this block into bedrooms will be a hell of a lot easier than trying to fit two bedrooms, a bathroom and some stairs on top of the other block."

"I agree with you on that, Ted. I have an A4 size pad in the cab. I'll go and get it now and you could sketch your ideas, and if I like it, we can plan ahead. If not, we keep re-designing it until a compromise is found. Does that sound OK to you?"

"That's fine by me," Ted replied, "but the final decision will be yours. There's no need to get the pad now, let's measure the width and length, make a note of it, lock the door here, tidy round where necessary, and get back to the village. There's nothing more we can do today, we can make an early start tomorrow."

"How early is early?" asked Ross.

"I don't think we need to be here at sunrise", replied Ted, "but when we have to do any heavy work, the earlier we start, the cooler it will be."

"That makes sense," said Ross "but we said we could go and price up things in Malaga tomorrow, so we won't need to be up here anyway."

"That's true." said Ted. "Don't think I'm being pushy Ross, but if we go back to the village now, we could get washed and changed and take our note pad down to the Paseo. We can find a restaurant doing 'Menu del Día', where we can sit, eat, drink and draw. How does that grab you?"

"That is a nice idea," said Ross "I'll treat you for helping me out today."

"No you won't," argued Ted "I asked you first."

"I insist." laughed Ross.

"OK," said Ted, "no more arguments, I'll pay for your meal, you can pay for mine."

"You're an awkward sod," Ross said, still laughing. "If you pay for our meal tonight, it's my treat if we go out together any other time."

"Thank you," Ted answered, "That is fine by me."

They drove back to the village, and Ross arranged to be outside Ted's apartment an hour later, showered, changed and ready for a meal together.

Ted was waiting outside the apartment when Ross arrived. She asked him if he would drive to where they were going, then she could see the direction they were taking. He drove down from the Pueblo and onto the main coast road. He took a left at a roundabout, then right towards the sea. Ted knew he would find a parking space at the end of the road, and pulled into a vacant spot. He locked the pickup, and guided Ross towards the steps at the top of the Paseo. They had taken a few steps down, when Ross stopped, looked down the length of the walk, and said,

"This is fabulous! It looks so... natural and inviting, the sea is calm, and it's almost like being in a picture postcard."

They started an easy stroll along the Paseo, and had not gone very far, when Ross slipped her arm into Ted's. He glanced at her, and the look on her face was a real picture. She realised Ted was looking at her, and quickly pulled her arm out of his.

"Sorry Ted," she said, "I wasn't thinking."

"Ross," Ted replied, "put your arm back where it was. If you are comfortable holding my arm, that's OK by me."

Ross put her arm back and they continued their stroll, stopping at various restaurants to look at the menus.

"Is there any particular type of food you prefer?" Ted asked, after they had looked at several.

"Not really" Ross replied, "I like all types, Chinese, Indian, and Thai. I don't know about Mexican, but I do love a good chilli-con-carne."

"In that case," Ted answered, "I think I know just the place. There's a restaurant a bit further up that's called 'The Mexican Ranch', and I am sure they'll do chilli."

"What are we waiting for then, lead the way."

Five minutes later, they were at the restaurant, and sure enough, chilli was on the menu. They sat next to each other at the only table for two that was vacant, which also looked out over the sea.

A waitress came to the table, handed them a menu and asked what they would like to drink.

"Red wine for me, please," said Ross.

"Dos vinos tintos, por favor." Ted said.

(Two red wines please)

They looked at the menu and decided which starter they wanted, followed by the chilli-con-carne. Their wine arrived, and after the waitress took their food order, Ted put the pad on the table and started to tell Ross his idea for the bedrooms.

"Since we measured up, I have been thinking about this. There is a combination of ways we could do it, but as I said earlier, you have the final say. We could build three very big bedrooms with en-suite bathrooms, or two normal size rooms and two a bit smaller. The standard size rooms could have full en-suite bathrooms, and the smaller ones, a shower room. My personal preference would be the latter. If I use this page as the whole building, I can show you both designs. The building is nine and a quarter metres wide and almost fifteen metres long. If we make the master bedroom and the one next door four metres wide, then the other two three metres wide, making allowances for the thickness of the walls, that uses up the length of the block. Each room could be around eight metres in length, the two main rooms being eight metres by four metres, and the smaller ones eight by three. At the top left hand corner of the main bedroom, as we look at it, we build a bathroom two metres wide by three metres long. We could fit a bath with a shower over it, a toilet, bidet and a wash basin. If the bedrooms are eight metres long, it leaves a corridor outside running from one end of the building to the other which would be about a metre and a quarter wide. Are you OK so far?"

Ted stopped talking just as the waitress brought their first course. They sat in silence and enjoyed the cold Gazpacho soup with extra finely diced onion, tomato and cucumber. Neither spoke until their bowls were empty.

"That was delicious," said Ross "I don't think I've ever had cold soup before."

"It's a typical Andalucían dish," Ted answered. "In the summer months, it can be a tasty cooling dish at any time, not just a starter."

"Before they bring the chilli Ted, I'd like to say that I can't fault the layout the way you have drawn and planned it. Except possibly the bidet. I don't know how to use one, so do I really need one?"

"Well I have one in my apartment, but I've never needed to use it, although I'm not sure about a lady. They apparently can be refreshing and efficiently cleansing at certain times of the month, and especially after sex."

"I don't need one for that particular activity! It's quite some time since that happened. OK let's leave that for the time being."

Ross looked back at the drawing, and then said,

"What about doors, and light, as in daylight?"

"A door on the bathroom side of the bedroom would lead onto the corridor. I thought the patio doors could be built into the end walls. They would almost cover the entire wall, giving each room plenty of light."

"The whole layout looks good, but you've given me the dimensions in metres but I'm not all that sure about metric and don't know how to convert it."

"You don't." Ted replied, "All you do is use one measurement, and use it all the time. The building materials we use for the walls are metric, and so are the doors."

At that moment, their chilli arrived. There wasn't a word spoken, except for an 'mmm' from each of them, as they tasted their meal.

Ten minutes later, they sat back in their seats, their plates clean.

"That was just about the nicest chill-con-carne I've ever eaten," said Ross, "with one exception though, I think I make a better one."

"In that case," said Ted, "when we finish your house in the hills, you can invite me to sample it. If its flavour is better than this one, I may propose to you."

Ross just smiled, but Ted thought it a weak one, one that hid something that wasn't quite right.

Ross picked up the drawing again, and looked it over.

"This looks as though it was drawn by someone who knows their job."

"Well," admitted Ted, "I told you I was an accountant with a large building company, so I picked up plenty of tips and ideas. I know how to build a wall without it falling down, and how the doors and windows are fitted into a building. I've seen plenty of drawings for hotels and houses, and this idea comes from a motel that the company built a few years ago. You could imagine the passageway from one door to the other door as a motel corridor, with doors leading into the rooms."

"I like it, Ted, it looks so complete, but I can't imagine the drawing in reality, if you know what I mean."

"I think I do. Next time we're at the house, we can lay a row of bricks on the floor to the measurement of the main bedroom and bathroom. That will give you a visual of how big each room will be. I am not going to do this on my own, I would like you to help, and then anything you want altered can be done before we start joining the bricks together."

They broke off their thoughts for a moment, as the waitress asked what they would like for a sweet. They both opted for ice cream.

Ross was looking towards the sea, seemingly concentrating on what Ted had just told her. Ted could see her nodding, probably agreeing with what they had just been discussing.

After eating their ice cream, Ted asked Ross if she would like a coffee.

"Yes please, black – or am I not allowed to say that?"

Ted laughed, she was catching on fast!

"In Spain, a black coffee is 'café solo' and is served in a small cup. If you prefer a large coffee, you add 'grande' after the 'solo'. Ordinary coffee with milk is 'café con leche' or 'café sombra', for one not quite as strong."

Ross was gazing out to sea again, with a look of delight in her eyes. The sun was starting to set, and the whole area was bathed in a bright red glow. Ted rubbed one of his fingers over the back of Ross's hand, and she turned to look at him. Smiling broadly Ross declared the spectacle as 'breath taking'.

"I don't mean to be rude, Ross, but how long is it since you've been to the...err... seaside?"

"Not all that long ago, but it was strictly a business visit and I had no time to admire the views. Prior to the last visit..." Ross though for a moment or two, and continued, "A long time ago Ted," and then added wistfully, "many years, in fact. This though, makes up for all those lost years."

Ted asked for the bill, and paid for their food.

"How much did all that cost us?" asked Ross, "in pounds I mean."

"Just over eight pounds each," Ted answered.

"For all that we've eaten and the wine and coffee, eight pounds. Bloody hell Ted, we'll definitely be back again."

They left the restaurant, and started the walk back to the pickup. Ross linked his arm again as though it was a natural thing for her to do. They stopped walking just as the sun was about to disappear, and watched as it sank below the horizon. Ross squeezed his arm, looked at him, and in a quiet voice said,

"Ted, I have known you for just one day, but during that time, you have shown me a lot of things that I've missed. I now have much more enthusiasm to get my house built, because I know the direction I'm going. You've shown me this beautiful area, with more food establishments than I have ever seen together in one place. If we work as well together as we have relaxed tonight, I am going to have a house in the hills to be proud of. Once we have finished it, you must not forget me. I would like you to be a regular visitor, because we both seem to have a sense of purpose in life. Much of my life has been horrendous, and I am in Spain to change everything. Thank you again, and I'm sure you won't take this the wrong way."

She leaned forwards and gave him a gentle kiss on his lips, and a hug that Ted took for real friendship.

Without another word, they walked slowly towards the pickup, and drove back to the village.

Pulling up outside Ted's apartment, Ross thanked him again for all he had done.

"What time shall I pick you up in the morning?" she asked.

"Shall we say ten o'clock?" he answered. "The rush hour traffic will have gone by then."

"Ten o'clock it is fine by me," Ross replied, "see you tomorrow then."

Ted got out of the pickup, and Ross drove away, waving to him from her open window.

TWO

Spot on ten o'clock, Ross pulled up outside his apartment block. She slid over into the passenger seat, inferring that Ted should do the driving, and as he climbed in, he wished her a cheery 'good morning'.

"Good morning Ted. I really am looking forward to this and I would like today to be as good as yesterday, and tomorrow to be the same. I have suddenly found a new lease of life, thanks to you, and I hope nothing will dampen my enthusiasm."

Ted drove the pickup back through the village, and on to the Autopista towards Malaga. It took just under an hour to reach the store and Ted parked her pickup almost outside the front doors. As they got out, Ross looked the store over and said it looked ten times bigger than any B&Q she had seen in the UK. Ted picked up the A4 pad with the previous night's drawings on it and they made their way to the store entrance. As they went through the doors, Ted took Ross by the arm, and said,

"I suggest a coffee first, so we can list what we need, and leave space to make notes and prices."

"Coffee sounds good to me." said Ross, as she looked around the vast showroom.

Ted led the way to the cafeteria, got their coffee and sat down at a table. He put the pad down between them, so they could decide what they wanted to price.

Ross started to write the list, and said,

"If we build two main bedrooms and bathrooms, as you have suggested, we want to price, two baths for the main rooms and two shower units for the smaller ones. Four toilets and four washbasins, but I'm still unsure about a bidet. Is a bidet difficult to fix, Ted?"

"No." he said, "In fact they are almost as easy to fix as a washbasin. The bidets are fixed to the floor instead

34

of the wall, that's basically the only difference."

"OK then," Ross said, "we can price them anyway. We aren't buying anything today, so I still have time to think."

Ted nodded in agreement, and then said,

"I was thinking about you in bed last night...."

"Would you like to rephrase that please?" Ross interrupted with a laugh.

"I think I'd better." Ted answered with a grin. "What I was thinking about while I was in bed last night, was tiles. I said yesterday that there were many more tiles than you need for the floor in the.... shall we call it 'the living block'? If that's so, we could use what's left to tile the corridor from door to door in the bedroom block. I'm only guessing at the moment, but working on the measurements we have, and allowing for any cutting I think you should have enough for the corridor and maybe one room."

"Fine, so now I have to find tiles to go in three bedrooms. That's a lot of tiles to buy in one go."

"You were going to have to buy something anyway to put on the floors, either for the bedrooms or corridor. They don't have to be the same design in every bedroom though, and you don't have to buy tiles for all the rooms at the same time."

"I know, but I hope I can find enough tiles that I like. When I lived at home, if Mum got fed up of the colour scheme in the house, she bought some new wallpaper and a carpet, it's much easier that way."

"What about wooden flooring?" Ted suggested.

Ross looked up from the drawing, and said,

"Now that is something I hadn't thought about. We can look at the price, and compare it to tiles."

"It's not just price," Ted replied, "tiles can be cold to the feet, especially during the winter period. Wooden floors tend to be warmer, and you can match your bedroom furniture to the wood if you like."

"You're not just a good looking fella' are you, you have brains as well."

Ted grinned, slightly abashed at Ross's comment.

"They're not my ideas," he replied, "these are tips I picked up from the building planners at the company I worked for. Shall we go and have a look round?"

They left the café and walked into the store. The first section they came to were the bathroom displays. Ross stopped walking and looked in amazement at the variety on offer. She had decided in advance that all four rooms would be fitted in the same design, so she took hold of Ted's hand and pulled him from display to display until she found some designs she liked. Ted made notes of prices and picked up some brochures so they could remember which designs she preferred. Ross was like a child in a toy store, rushing from one section to another, and Ted followed, enjoying the enthusiasm she displayed. As they walked around, Ross would either hold onto his arm, or on occasions, held his hand. Ted took this, not as a gesture of love, merely friendship, and possibly a touch of security.

Almost three hours later, they emerged from the store, and the enthusiasm had not left Ross, as they walked arm in arm back to the pickup. Ted opened her door, and closed it once she was seated. He walked round to his door and as he got in, Ross put her hand on his, and said, with a smile,

"You must be one of the last true English gentlemen. I don't think anyone has ever opened a car door and let me in first."

"I don't know about gentleman, but I was brought up to show manners and respect to people. My attitude now is, if the respect is appreciated, I will continue to show it.

If it is not, then sod them."

"Ted, I for one appreciate it, in fact I appreciate everything you have done for me, yesterday and this morning. I think you and I are going to work together on my house as good companions."

"Do you know Ross, your joy, last night and this morning must be infectious, because I cannot remember enjoying a night out and a shopping trip like this for many years. The way you were in the store, holding my hand and pulling me to something you wanted to see, made me feel like a young newlywed, looking to fill his house with good things."

"I held your hand?" asked Ross in amazement.

Ted turned towards her and nodded, smiling at her question.

"Ted, I'm sorry, I didn't... I mean... I... Ted... I... I."

"Ross please," Ted interrupted "you did nothing wrong. I haven't taken it as a show of affection, so please don't feel embarrassed. Shall we change the subject? It's lunch time, and I know there's a tapas bar just up the road here. Are you hungry after all that shopping?"

"Yes, I am, but before we go, I'd like to say again I'm sorry if I got carried away in the store."

Ted said nothing, started the motor and drove the short distance to the tapas bar. Once inside, he showed Ross what there was to eat, and explained some of the dishes she wasn't sure about. She was undecided about two, so Ted ordered both, and one for himself, together with two glasses of red wine. He led Ross to a table to wait for their tapa to be brought over. They sat opposite one another, and after a sip of his wine, Ted reached across the table and gently took hold of Ross's left hand.

"Now young lady," he said in a low, friendly voice, "let's get something straight. Last night, on the Paseo, you got hold of my arm as we walked. Today, you did the same, and held my hand as well. You must feel you trust me, otherwise you wouldn't have done it. I have no illusions about it being a romantic gesture, so if you feel comfortable holding or touching me, please do not restrain yourself because you think I may get the wrong idea."

Ted took Ross's ring finger in-between his fingers.

"Are you newly divorced, or just separated?"

"How do you know I'm either?" Ross asked.

"I can feel the groove your ring has worn on this finger. I felt it earlier today, when you held my hand. The groove on my finger hasn't quite gone, and I haven't had a ring on that finger for a few years."

Ross looked at her finger, and in a hushed voice, answered Ted's question.

"I suppose the answer is, I'm separated. I've left my husband, although I know he probably won't have noticed."

Ted asked no more questions about her marriage, it was nothing to do with him, but if she wanted to talk to him, he would be there to listen.

"I don't want to see you unhappy, Ross. Some of the comments you've made since we met, make me think you have been neglected in complements, manners and possibly other things as well. If I pay you a complement, please take it as well meaning and without an ulterior motive."

Ross looked at him for a moment, smiled, and said,

"Thank you Ted, and I will take your comments as well meaning. In the two days, well, one and a half, that I've known you, you've made me feel relaxed, and that's good. Your offer to help me with the house is, I assure you, very, very much appreciated, and bringing me to that store was an eye-opener. If you are sure you don't mind me holding your arm or hand, then I'll not be embarrassed about it again."

Ross smiled again and Ted could see her sadness and worry had disappeared.

After finishing their lunch, Ted got the drawing pad out again, and looked it over.

"Is there anything else we need to price today?" Ross asked.

"Not right now." Ted replied. "We will have to think later on about taps, plug holes, pipes and things like that, but we won't need them until the walls are built. Then we will have to think about the electrics. Lights, plug sockets and things. One point about electrics. I am not fully competent about the making of circuits. I can do most connections, but the actual ring mains and connection to the power supply, I cannot do."

"In that case, when the time comes, we will have to get an electrician to do it for us. What about bricks and other building materials?"

"There are a couple of builders suppliers in the pueblo. They may charge a little more than they do here, but when you add carriage to the cost, there won't be much difference."

"What's the 'pueblo' mean? I've heard you and other people say it, but I've not tied it in with anything yet."

"'Pueblo' simply means 'village'. If you live down by the sea you are on the 'Costa' and where your house is, you are in the 'Campo', which means 'countryside'."

Ross sat looking at the drawing again, and as she read the notes, yawned.

"Oh, I'm sorry Ted, that wasn't a sign of boredom, I just suddenly feel a bit sleepy."

"You must have acclimatised yourself to Spain. It's siesta time, and I'm sure you don't need me to explain that word."

Ross smiled,

"No, I learned that word within a few days of arriving in Spain. We're quite a drive away from our homes, so I may fall asleep as you're driving us back."

"I was hoping you were going to drive home." Ted answered with a straight face, "Then I could have a sleep."

Ross looked up from the drawing at Ted's face, but try as he may, Ted could not keep his face straight.

"You rotten thing," Ross laughed. "Seriously though, I do feel tired."

"We can sit in the pickup and recline the seat backs slightly, leave the window open a bit, and nod off for an hour or so".

Now it was Ross's turn to keep her face straight.

"We've know each other for less than two days, and already you are asking me to sleep with you."

Ted smiled, and said,

"I promise to behave myself."

"Why?"

"Your husband may come looking for me and do me some serious bodily harm."

"Please, don't spoil the day by using bad language."

A little bit of fun between two friends, as they made their way back to the pickup. To prove a point, Ross got hold of Ted's hand, and held it tightly.

Once more, Ted opened the door for Ross.

"Thank you kind Sir," she said.

"A pleasure my lady," he replied, giving an exaggerated low bow.

Within minutes of them reclining their seat backs, they were asleep.

They were wakened about an hour later when a couple of teenagers on their exhaust-less motor scooters came roaring past. The noise must have disorientated

Ross, as she grabbed Ted's arm, and cried,

"What the hell was that?"

"Two Spanish teenagers being typical Spanish teenagers." he replied sleepily. "They probably drive round the car park every day, just to waken those who are enjoying a siesta. Now you are awake, do you feel better for your sleep?"

"I'd rather have woken up normally," said Ross, stretching, "but yes, I do feel better for it, thank you."

"When we start work on your house, I suggest we take sandwiches or something similar to eat at lunch time. After we've eaten, we lie in the shade and have a siesta, like we have now. That way, we'll feel more like working later when it's cooler."

"You'll say anything to get me to sleep with you," said Ross with a laugh.

"I'm going to have to think before I speak." Ted replied, shaking his head. "I don't know about you, but I need the loo, and another drink. Shall we go back to the bar, and freshen up?"

"Yes, please. As much as I want to get my house built, I am enjoying today's break. Once again, Ted, Thank you very much."

"That's no problem. Today we relax, tomorrow we start work on your new home."

Ted drove back to the tapas bar, where they used the facilities, and had another drink.

Ted started the drive home, but after just a few kilometres on the Autopista, he turned off, and drove the rest of the way back on the old coast road. He did a few detours to show Ross some of the sights and at one point he parked the pickup outside a café. They went inside to have a drink, but mainly to use the loo again. Arriving back at the village, Ted pulled up outside his apartment, but before he got out, said,

"Where in the village do you live? Don't get me wrong, I'm not going to be rushing to your house every night."

Ross laughed, and answered,

"To be quite honest Ted, I can't pronounce the name of the street. If you go up here to the roundabout, the first road up the hill and round the other side of the village, there are some small side roads. The third one, and as you go down it, the road narrows. At the end, there is room to park the pickup, and some steps go up to a little square. There are three houses round that square, and the one I'm renting is number twelve. Don't ask where the other eleven are, I've no idea. It's very small and just about big enough for two people. Still, if we get working on my house, I won't need to worry about the size of it for much longer."

"I've always been told size doesn't matter," said Ted, almost seriously.

"Will you behave yourself please, you should not be talking like that to a married woman," Ross answered with a laugh, and a slight blush.

"What are you having to eat tonight?" Ted asked her, changing the subject.

"No idea yet. I'll find something in the freezer when I get round to it."

"I've two pork chops in my fridge, some potatoes to bake and a Ted special salad waiting to be made. How do you fancy helping me eat it?"

"No, Ted, I... I..."

"Ross, I'm not trying to get you into my bed. I'm just offering you an evening meal, but if you say no, I won't be offended."

"Thank you Ted, but no, not tonight. Another night maybe, it's just that I've got something important to do later. What time shall I pick you up in the morning?"

"Is eight o'clock too early for you?"

"No, eight is fine. I started work at the same time when I was in England, so I'm used to being up and about. What are we doing about food and drink?"

"I'll make some sandwiches tomorrow and we can share them, and I'll put some bottles of water or something in the cooler. We can talk about other day's lunches tomorrow."

"Right, thanks once again for today's trip. I can look at the list and the prices and all those brochures, and maybe come to a decision over tiles or wood floors. Right, I'm off, see you here at eight."

Ted made his way inside, suddenly feeling deflated after such a hectic day.

THREE

The church clock had started to strike eight o'clock as Ross drove round the bend and stopped where Ted was waiting. He got into the pickup, and they wished each other a good morning. Ted put his cooler on the seat beside him and strapped himself in as Ross turned the motor round.

"I'm sure you drove up to the bend in the road, and waited until the church clock struck." Ted joked. "On the first stroke, you drove round the corner to make sure you were here at the time you said."

"Nothing quite so obvious, Ted." Ross replied. "When I dropped you off last night, I checked the clock, and noted how long it took to get home. It was just about five minutes, so I walked out of the house just before five to eight, and here I am, spot on time."

"Are you a morning person Ross, or would you like me to shut up?"

"I'm not too bad in a morning, a lot depends on how... certain things... and..."

"The time of the month." Ted finished for her.

Ross blushed slightly, and said he'd hit the nail on the head.

It took just over ten minutes to reach the house, and during the drive, they decided the first job was to start removing all the tiles from the kitchen walls. Ted suddenly realised they would need to hire a skip, because not only was there the kitchen tiles to remove, but the living area floor tiles as well. During the renovations, there would be a fair amount of waste and rubbish to dispose of, and there was nowhere to put it all at the moment. He mentioned his thoughts to Ross, who agreed with him, and said they could sort it out the following day.

"We could, on the other hand dump it all on the corner of the track. It will give us a base when we get round to widening it."

"Good thinking." Ross replied, "That will save me having to worry about skip hire, particularly as I don't speak much Spanish."

Getting out of the pickup, Ted looked around again, taking in the views. He turned to Ross and commented about how far they could see in the clear morning air. He glanced upwards at the house, and a sudden thought occurred to him.

"Ross, now we've agreed to make the other block into the sleeping area, you are going to have to get this roof tiled. The other block has already been done, so this should be done to match it. I'm afraid I have no idea how to fit those semi-circular tiles to the roof though, and I'd rather not attempt it and end up making a mess of your roof."

"I'll have to find someone who knows how to do it," she said, "we'll have to look in one of those free newspapers, there's bound to be at least one advert for someone who can tile roofs."

Before going into the house, they went to the bedroom block, where Ted had seen a thick plastic sheet. Between them they carried it to the kitchen, folded it lengthways into four, and laid it along one wall. It made a cushion for the floor tiles so they would not get damaged by the falling tiles as they were knocked off the walls.

Ross suggested they started at opposite corners, and meet in the middle of the same wall. They both had cold chisels and a soft mallet, but as Ross was about to start, she pulled at one tile with her hand, and to her surprise, it came easily off the wall. She told Ted what had happened, and he examined the adhesive on the tile. He

45

rubbed the surface, and to their horror, it crumbled into powder. Ted took hold of another tile, gently pulled, and it came away as easily as the first.

"Those tiles could fall off the wall at any time." Ross said in horror. "We could be hurt if any drop on us."

"We are going to have to be careful now." Ted replied. "I think it would be better if we started at the top and worked our way down the walls. In the other block are two metal frames, and if I put a double plank of wood on the rungs, we can use that to reach the ceiling. I can start at the top, and clear to half way down, and then move across the wall and do the same there. You can then clear the bottom half, following me along."

They set up the frames and the wood, and it didn't take Ted long to clear his top section. The step was moved along the wall, and he started again on the upper part. Ross made a start on the bottom half of the section Ted had just cleared.

Because the adhesive was so poor, the whole clearance took just over an hour. They loaded all the tiles into a wheelbarrow and dumped them onto the track outside. Ted used a sweeping brush on the walls to clear any loose debris, thinking they would be able to start putting on the new tiles straight away. When the room was clear of dust, Ted took a closer look at the wall.

"It's no wonder the adhesive crumbled," he said, "the wall hasn't been prepared. They put tile adhesive on top of the skimmed wall, and the two dried out together. There needs to be a barrier between the two, so the tile adhesive holds the tiles in a sort of suction. We are going to have to paint all four walls with something we call 'size' in England."

"We're back to size again, are we." Ross asked.

"Behave yourself, a married lady should not be talking about things like that."

Ross smiled, knowing he was getting his own back for the remark she made the previous day.

"What happens now?" Ross asked.

"Let's go and have a look in the other place and see if there is anything we can use. At a pinch, we could put a coat of paint on, but that is not as effective. Alternatively, we could go to the tile shop in the village, and buy some size, or whatever it's called in Spain."

"Never mind searching, we can drive down there to get it and be back here in about twenty five minutes."

They got what they wanted, plus two paint buckets and brushes, and were back at work within half an hour. Ted made up the size, divided it into the two buckets, and each of them gave the walls a liberal coating. It would have to be left to dry overnight before they could start the tiling.

"That's a good start." said Ross in a dejected tone.

"Not really a problem," Ted answered, "we'll be able to start the tiling as soon as we get here in the morning. I've checked the walls with a plumb line, and the corners are surprisingly straight, so there shouldn't be much cutting in on the corners. We can go and fit the glass into the window frames in the other block, and afterwards, mark out the walls of the main bedroom and en-suite bathroom."

The clips were easy to insert into the frames, and it didn't take them long to have all the six windows glazed.

Before starting on the bedroom walls, Ted asked Ross if she wanted the dividing walls built in brick or breeze block.

"What difference does it make?" Ross asked.

"Well, if we use a double row of brick, it will take longer to do, and cost quite a lot more, but breeze blocks are wider and larger so in theory, we could get the walls built reasonably quickly. On the down side though, if we use breeze block, anyone in the next room may be able to hear you when you are in the throes of an erotic sensation."

"There's no chance of that happening, so we can use breeze block.

"We could use a double row if you wanted."

"I'll leave the decision to you Ted."

"OK then, a single row of breeze block." Ted decided. "Don't forget, there will be a skim of concrete over the blocks on either side, so the room sizes will be slightly smaller than the drawing says."

"That's no problem as far as I'm concerned, after all, I'll only be sleeping here."

"We will have to build a row of brick inside the bathroom, where we can secure and cover the water and waste pipes, so we'll have to make allowances when we measure the walls."

Ted found some chalk in his tool box, and with Ross's help, accurately measured the first bedroom and bathroom areas. They double checked to make sure the figures were right, before outlining the room with chalk.

"Ross dear, come here a moment please."

Ross stood in front of Ted with a puzzled look on her face. Ted took both her hands in his, and looked at her palms.

"Nice, soft skin," he said, "I don't think you should be carrying bricks and breeze block around, or you'll end up with your hands as rough as...."

"....a bears arse." Ross finished for him with a laugh.

Ted opened the base of his tool box, and took out a pair of strong work gloves for her to wear.

They each carried a couple of breeze blocks and laid them along the chalk line. They repeated this until there was a line of breeze block all the way round the 'room'. Ted looked critically at them, removed some and altered others, and then placed a second row on top. He looked it over again, before saying he was happy with it.

"Right," he said, "we are in the corridor outside your bedroom. We go through this gap, which will be the door."

As he spoke, Ted led Ross by the hand through the gap. He carried on describing the layout.

"We are in a short corridor, or hallway, and here on the left, is the door to the bathroom."

He led Ross inside, and pointed to different sections.

"The bath goes lengthways at the top here. On the right we could have the wash basin, with the toilet and bidet, if you decide to have one, on the left. We go out through the door again, and turn left into the bedroom proper. On that far wall, we can fit one of the large patio doors, and for this room only, you could if you wanted, have a window fitted into the left hand wall."

Ross looked about her, taking in the layout Ted had described.

Ted was amused to see Ross stood with her head slightly on one side again, nodding slowly as she looked about.

"I like it Ted." she said, "simple, but effective. My decision is, we build them all like this. There is just one thing I'd like though. It's been one of my dreams to have a sunken bath, would that be possible in this room?"

"You are determined to make me work for my money, aren't you?" Ted answered.

"Money?" she said, "what money?"

Ted smiled, and told her a sunken bath could be possible, but a lot depended on the thickness of the concrete floor, and if it was practical to line up the bath plug hole to the main drain, wherever that was.

Ross put her hand on Ted's arm, and giving him a pleading smile asked if he would consider it.

"I will consider it Ross, but not right now. My watch says it's lunch time, so let's go and have something to eat."

They took off their gloves, and as they walked into the sunlight, Ross grabbed Ted's arm and said,

"You haven't got a watch on, so how do you know its lunch time?"

"My stomach's rumbling." he answered.

Ted dragged the tarpaulin out of the kitchen, and spread it out it near to the house wall, just out of the sun. He put his cool box between them, and said,

"Help yourself Ross. There's cheese ones, ham ones, and to be different, ham and cheese ones. In the cool box, there's mineral water, or bottled iced tea with peach."

They sat in the shade and enjoyed their lunch and when all the sandwiches had gone and they had drunk what they wanted, it was time for their planned siesta. They settled themselves on the canvas, and it didn't take long for either of them to fall asleep.

They both awoke almost at the same time, as the sun turned their shade into an oven like heat.

"What time is it?" asked Ross, still with her eyes closed.

"Nearly three thirty," said Ted looking at the clock on his telephone. "That sleep has done me a world of good. How about you?"

"I feel refreshed and ready for the next step, if I knew what the next step was."

"Let's go and see if we can get the generator running, and check out the cement mixer. I noticed there were a couple of bags of cement by that big bag of sand, so we could mix a batch, and lay the first line of blocks for your bedroom and bathroom. The concrete can dry overnight, and when we get here in the morning, we can start in the kitchen, and then we can come back in here and start on the bedroom walls."

"You are determined to make me work for my money, aren't you?" said Ross.

"Money, what money?" Ted answered, and they both burst into laughter.

"Thing is though," said Ross, "I can pay myself as much as I want, but you are working for love and you get your payment in kind."

Ross suddenly realised what she had said, and started to stutter and blush.

"Ted I... didn't... sorry... Ted I...I... mean... don't take... oh hell what... shit... I'm..."

Ted was laughing as Ross stuttered and tried to cover up her poor choice of words. He reached out, and held her by the shoulders, and said,

"Ross, slow down and cool it, there's no problem."

Ross looked at Ted with tears in her eyes. He took his handkerchief out of his pocket, and gently wiped the tears away.

"Ross, oh Ross, what am I to do with you?"

Ross gave a weak smile, and shook her head.

"Ross, we've been through the 'love' and 'dear', the arm in arm and holding hands, as well as size, and sleeping together. Those comments have been taken as a joke between ourselves, and we have laughed at them without taking them too seriously. We are two mature people, enjoying a laugh with each other and at each other. Your slip of the tongue, 'payment in kind', would have got an answer from me something like, 'I should be so lucky' or 'promises, promises'. Please Ross, don't be upset if you say something that may have a sexual innuendo, because I'll laugh, and try to give a suggestive answer in return. I hope you'll do the same as well, so please, get over being embarrassed when you talk to me.

I have a broad mind, so please feel free to say whatever you like. Now my lecture is over, so let's dry those tears and go and get the generator working."

"You really are a nice, kind person Ted," Ross told him. "Thank you for reassuring me and I'll try not to get embarrassed at the daft comments I make. I'm not used to working closely with anyone, but I'm getting used to being with you Ted, and as a working companion, you give me the drive to keep going. I gave you a friendly kiss the other night while we were on the Paseo, and I'm going to give you another one now."

Ross lifted her head, and gave Ted a gentle kiss.

"That's for everything you've just said, and for being such an understanding person."

"I'll be as understanding as you want, if I get more kisses like that." he said with a smile.

"Behave yourself," Ross answered returning the smile, "remember I'm a married woman, at least on paper I am."

Ted purposely took hold of her hand and led her to the bedroom block where the generator was. He pulled it outside into the open air, turned to Ross and said,

"Right, married lady, shall we see if there is any petrol in this thing to get it started."

Ted unscrewed the tank cap, and looked inside. He could see a reasonable amount in the tank, so he put the cap back on, turned on the fuel tap and watched as fuel flowed into the carburettor.

"Right," he said, "if I get hold of this toggle, and give the cord a pull, in theory, it should start, but knowing that it has been stood idle for some time, it probably won't."

Ted pulled the cord, and the motor just turned over. After a number of pulls, Ted could smell petrol. He gave the cord a sharp pull, and the motor caught, but after a few coughs, cut out again.

"Let me have a try," said Ross, "I'm usually successful when I pull things."

Ted smiled at her remark, and when Ross saw his face, she smiled herself, and said,

"I've done it again, haven't I?"

"Yes, Rosalinda... whatever your name is, you have. A married lady should not be bragging to a stranger about her capabilities."

"Rosalinda Jones.... and that's all you'll get until I know you better. I was bragging, because I had to mow the lawn at home, and we had a petrol mower. That's all I was bragging about, Ted... whatever your name is."

"Hall, Edwin Michael Hall, the Edwin was shortened to Eddy and then to Ted. Mum told me that if I had been a girl, my name would have been Edwina Michelle."

He paused for a moment, and said,

"Go on then, see if you have the touch."

Ross, who was stood on the opposite side of the generator, took hold of the toggle. She pulled it once, slowly, then a fast one immediately after. The motor fired up, almost died, then it caught and continued to run with a steady beat. There was a gauge on top of the outlet sockets, showing the amperage that was being generated. It rose slowly until it showed full charge. Ross smiled at Ted, and said,

"Who's got the touch then?"

"You have Ross, and that gauge proves there is electricity between us."

"That's not a very funny joke Ted, so don't give up the day job."

"If I give up my day job, you'll be back to renovating the house on your own."

"And probably talking to myself without getting any stupid answers back."

"You'll miss me when I've gone."

"Edwin Michael Hall, you are not going anywhere, because you promised to help me for the next year. And if I think you're going to escape, I may have to restrain you to keep you working."

"Tied to the kitchen sink without trousers, as my ex used to say."

"Don't know about the 'no trouser bit', I keep reminding you I'm a married woman."

"Shall we see if the cement mixer works."

"Good idea."

Ted unravelled the wire, and checked it for any breaks or cracks. He made sure the switch was in the off position, and plugged it into the generator. He gave the switch a quick on and off, and the mixer started to revolve. He turned the switch on again to make sure everything was working properly, then switched it off, and allowed it to stop.

"Do you know how to mix concrete?" he asked Ross.

"I've used ready mixed before, just adding water as per the instructions on the bag, but mixing from scratch, I've no idea."

"Well, for what we need now, it should be four parts of this sand to one part of cement. Then we add water until it looks the right consistency. Further up this room is a large drum, the type the English would call a 'forty five gallon drum'. If we fill that with water, and keep it topped up, we can fill a bucket from it to wet the mixture."

"Where are we going to get the water from?" asked Ross.

"Just inside this door, and the one at the far end, there's a pipe with a tap fixed to it. I'll check them out in a minute, I just hope they have been connected to the pump. I'll bring some hose pipe from home, and fix it to the tap, so we can have our own supply of running water. For work use only, no drinking it until we know its source. The wheelbarrow we used this morning can be used for carrying the mixed concrete to where we are working."

"How should we work this Ted? I have no experience in brick laying or concrete mixing, so what's our plan of action, so to speak?"

"If it's OK with you, I suggest we work like this. The first mixing we do together. I'll wheel the concrete to where the blocks are, and start the base layer. You come with me and I'll show you what I'm doing, and maybe let you lay some blocks. When the concrete is almost used up, and if we have time, you can come back here and mix the next batch. How do you feel about that?"

"That sounds a good idea. Show me the way now, and I'll try on my own for the next mix."

Ted picked up a shovel that was leaning on the side of the sand bag, took a generous shovel full, and put it into a bucket.

"To be accurate," he told Ross, "it is better to use buckets. A shovel of sand piles high on the blade, but cement slides off, therefore you don't get the true ratio."

He had only put four buckets full in, when he said,

"I think we should move the mixer closer to the sand and save all this walking with full buckets," said Ted, "otherwise you could end up with muscles like Popeye."

Between them, they moved the mixer closer to the bag and finished loading it with sand. Ted broke open a bag of cement, and added it to the sand, letting the dry ingredients mix while he got the water ready. Showing Ross where the tap was, he filled a bucket, added it to the mix, and went for more. When Ted judged the mix was of the right consistency, he tipped it into the wheelbarrow, and pushed it to where they were to start building. He went back, and threw a bucket of water into the mixer, letting it wash round for a minute or two, and while it was still going round, tipped the water into the large drum. Swinging the mixer half upright, he turned it off.

"We'll not mix any more just yet, we need to know how far this mix will go. Come on down here and let's make a start. The blocks for the first wall have to be moved back, before I can lay any concrete on the floor, but I need to mark on the wall where our new rows of blocks are to join it."

Ted marked the wall with a pencil line, and knocked the concrete out until he was down to bare brick. He took some string from his tool box, and stretched it tightly along the floor where the edge of the blocks would sit. Together they moved the blocks back, and Ted spread a thick line of concrete on the floor. He went back to the wall end, and started to place the blocks on top of it. He cleaned the loose concrete from the floor at both sides, put it back into the wheelbarrow and continued laying right down the line. Their first mix was enough for the base of the whole room, plus some for part of a second row on the main wall. Ted decided they had done enough building for one day, so he scraped the wheelbarrow and the cement mixer, making them ready for the next time they were used. The petrol tap on the motor was turned off and the generator pulled back inside. Ross locked the door, and they walked back to the kitchen to make sure the size was drying properly. Everything seemed to be in order so Ross decided to call it a day. They got into the pickup, and as Ross started the engine, she asked,

"What's for the evening meal tonight?"

"You or me?"

"Us. That is, if I'm invited tonight."

Ted smiled, and replied,

"Well, it could be chicken or pork escalope, with boiled, baked or roast potatoes and the usual Ted's special salad."

"Sounds nice, so am I invited tonight?"

"Seeing as you asked me so nicely, yes."

"Please may I ask you a favour?"

"You can ask, I may not agree though."

Now it was Ross's turn to smile, as she replied,

"Could I possibly use your shower, because the one in my house won't work properly, it keeps running cold."

"Of course you can," Ted answered, "you can have your shower while I do the tea."

Before they got to the village, Ross turned off the main road, and drove to her house.

"I won't be a minute," she said, "I just want to get my clean clothes."

Ross ran inside, and left Ted to turn the pickup around. He had just pulled up outside the house, when she came back out again with a bundle of clothes in a plastic bag.

"Home, James." She said, fastening her seat belt.

When they were inside the apartment, Ted filled a pan with water, so there would be no drop in pressure while Ross was under the shower. He gave her a bath towel and left her to it as he started the tea. He had the potatoes peeled, cut and simmering in a pan, when he heard the shower cut off. He was putting the salad together when he heard the sound of bare feet walking towards the kitchen.

"Have you seen a half-naked woman before, Ted?" Ross called before she reached the kitchen.

"Not for a long time and never in this apartment," he asked, "Why?"

Ross poked her head round the kitchen doorway, keeping her body out of sight.

"I'm only half dressed, but I wondered if you have such a thing as a hair dryer."

"Oh, God, yes, somewhere. I think it's in one of my boxes, and I'll have to look for it."

"No, Ted, don't bother, I'll use the towel."

"If you don't mind me seeing a half-naked married woman, I can get it for you in a moment, it's only on top of one of the three boxes in the spare bedroom."

Ross walked into the kitchen wearing only her bra and a pair of very pale pink bikini briefs.

"Here you are Ted, a half-naked married woman."

"Thank you Ross. I'm not sure my eyes can stand the strain." he said, looking her over quickly.

"As long as it doesn't affect your heart," she said, "or anything else for that matter." she added with a laugh.

"There's a name for women like you," Ted answered, smiling, as he left the kitchen to find the hair dryer.

He soon found it, and handed it to Ross, who had followed him from the kitchen and was standing in his bedroom doorway.

"There's a plug to the side of the wardrobe, and enough flex for you to be able to use the mirror on the door. I'm going back to the kitchen to take something before I have an attack of some kind."

"I'll have a red wine as well, that'll cool us down."

"Do we need cooling?"

"I don't, but I'll still have the red wine, please."

Ted went back to the kitchen to finish making their tea. He had the wine poured and the food on plates as Ross came into the kitchen, now fully dressed.

"Feel better now I'm dressed, Ted?"

Ted smiled, and pretended to tremble. He picked up his glass of wine, shaking it, and holding it with two hands.

"This is my third glass since you walked half naked into my kitchen in your white bra and pink briefs."

Ross laughed at his antics with the wine.

"Just for your information, the briefs are actually white but accidentally got washed with my red shirt."

"Sit down, married lady. I don't want to hear any more about your underwear."

"You're not complaining, are you?"

"Ross, we have known each other for five days, and suddenly you are walking around half undressed as if we've known each other for years. No, I'm not complaining, rather the opposite. You have a nice figure, and it does a man no harm to see forbidden flesh. Now get your salad eaten before it gets cold."

Ross started to eat her meal, and after a few minutes, declared it very nice.

"You'll make someone a good wife one day." Ross said.

"So will you Ross. I'm not prying into your marriage problems, so don't take it the wrong way. I genuinely hope you can solve whatever problems there are, and you'll end up living happily ever after."

"Not with the present one." Ross replied. "There are too many problems. I may tell you about them one day, but not right now."

"Change of subject, then. Your shower in the house running cold. Have you checked the gas bottle? If it is low on gas, there is not enough pressure to keep the flame high enough to heat the water while you are showering."

"I'll check it when I get back. Why the sudden interest? Anyone would think you didn't want me to use your shower again. Afraid of seeing me undressed are we?"

Ted smiled, shook his head and continued to eat his tea.

When they had finished the meal, Ted offered Ross a choice of yoghurt or ice cream for her afters.

"Yoghurt, please," Ross answered, "it's less fattening than ice cream."

"You are going to be too busy building a house to get fat. You and I will lose some weight while we build those walls, that's a promise. Would you like a coffee or tea now or after I've washed up?"

"I'll wash up, you made the meal." said Ross forcefully.

"You're a bossy bugger!" Ted replied with a laugh.

"Someone needs to be. Do you eat like this every night when you're on your own?"

"Yes. I have a change of meat, you know, pork fillet, or steak, chicken or turkey. I always have potatoes, very occasionally chips, salad during the summer, fresh vegetables at other times. And of course, a glass of red wine with the meal."

"How long have you been looking after yourself?"

Ted looked upwards, and thought.

"It must be fifteen or sixteen years. I was divorced when I was thirty one, so it can't be far off that."

"Have you been entirely on your own all that time?"

"Without a woman, you mean? No, I met a lady and had a very passionate affair with her. It lasted a few months, until she told me she was pregnant. It wasn't mine though, that I can guarantee. I met another lady and we went out for a few years on and off, more off than on though. It was an odd relationship, and I may tell you about it sometime."

"Do you miss her?"

"Not anymore."

"You miss female company?"

"Not any more" Ted repeated, smiling as he answered.

Ross returned his smile.

"You know Ted, you and I enjoy each other's company just by talking, don't we?"

"As the TV advert says, 'it's nice to talk'."

"Do you have any children?" Ross asked.

"No" he replied sadly, "I'm afraid not. It was one of those things that weren't meant to be. Would you mind if I explained the reason another time, it's rather complicated?"

"Not at all Ted. I can see it makes you sad so we can leave it for now. Do you mind me asking about your marriage?"

"Not at all. How are we to get to know each other if we don't ask questions?"

"I think you know I've had problems in my marriage. If you're able to talk to me about yours, it will help me to overcome some of my doubts. Do you mind doing that for me?"

"Ross, if I can help you in any way, I will. All you have to do is ask."

"Thank you Ted. I have a feeling I've met a good man who can help me build a future."

"Shall we finish the washing up? I'll make a brew, then we can sit in the lounge and talk."

When the kitchen chores were done, Ted made a pot of tea which they took into the lounge. They sat together on the settee, and Ted asked Ross if she wanted to watch anything on the television.

"Is there anything interesting on?" Ross asked.

"Not really, I tend to watch the evening news at seven, and then there are the soaps. Things like that keep me interested for a while, and I often switch off by ten o'clock."

"Then what?"

"At the moment, I think about tomorrows work. What needs to be done in what order, and what the next step should be."

"What would you do if there was someone here with you?"

"I'm not sure Ross. I've been on my own for so long, I've not needed to think about anyone else. If you were a regular visitor, for example, I would have to think what two people would do together. Like chat about our lives, or maybe watch some TV, I even have some games on my computer that are for two people. Or, if you were agreeable, we could go and have a drink together, have a walk, even have a drive round the area. I don't think we would be staring at the walls in silence all night."

"Do you care what other people think of you?"

"No." He replied, "I'm not the sort of person who wants everyone to love me. There are some who think I'm odd, but they don't worry me."

"I'm not one of those Ted. I pride myself on being able to make a judgement on a person quite quickly, and I find you a generous person, willing to help other without pushing yourself on them. I also like your attitude. You treat me as if you've known me for years, and I like that in a man. I think that's why I was able to walk around this apartment half dressed, I knew you wouldn't take it the wrong way."

"Without being rude, I think I know the difference between a half-naked lady asking for a hair dryer, and a half naked lady wanting me to make her a fully naked lady. You are too nice a person to want me to do that after only knowing me for such a short time. I would never take advantage of a vulnerable married lady either."

Ross got hold of Ted's arm with both hands, and said,

"When would you take advantage of me, then?"

Ted smiled as he looked at Ross.

"You, young lady, have invited yourself for your evening meal, sat cuddled up to me on the settee, and ask me a question like that! Rosalinda whoever Jones, I have told you before, I would only take advantage of you either when you are not a married lady, or when I knew without doubt you seriously wanted me to take advantage. For now though, you are safe."

"If you truly mean those words Ted, I have nothing to fear from you, but if you let me down, you'll be sorry, believe me."

"I do believe you Ross. Besides, I don't want to miss out on those nice, soft 'understanding' kisses I get occasionally."

"You like them, do you?"

"Yes I do. There is a difference between a soft friendly kiss and a full blooded 'I want sex' one. At least anyone with any understanding of ladies should be able to tell the difference."

"There are some of us who haven't had a proper kiss of any kind for years." Ross told him sadly.

"You are joking, aren't you?" Ted asked, aghast.

Ross shook her head, and whispered,

"I can't remember when my husband last kissed me as a friendly gesture. I didn't even get kissed the last time he had sex with me."

"It hurts to say things like that, doesn't it?"

Ross nodded her reply, a tear running down her cheek.

Ted took hold of her hand, gave it a squeeze and said, "Shall we forget your marriage for now, and go back to mine?"

"Do you mind doing that?"

"No problem. Where would you like me start?"

"Where did you meet her?"

"At one of the local Saturday dances. We were all rocking and such things, and one particular night, I was stood, 'eyeing up the talent', when she walked over to me and asked if I would dance with her. We danced a few times and when the night finished, before she went off home with her mate, asked if I would be there the following week. I said I would, and we agreed to meet outside. I met her and her friend outside for the next couple of weeks, and then the third week she said she had come on her own. At the end of the night, she asked me if I would like to take her home. I had a little car at the time, and it was then I found out she didn't live far away from where I lived. That night, we had a kiss or two in the darkness of the car, and being a randy teenager, I had a feel of her breasts before she decided it was time to go. We arranged to meet the following week, and the whole thing blossomed from there, so to speak. After about two months, we were bonking like crazy when we got the opportunity, and if we weren't bonking, we were having sex in other ways. She wasn't a virgin, and admitted to having three other men. I wasn't a virgin either, and admitted to five other girls. I lied, it was only two!"

"Why did you lie then?" Ross asked.

"Typical fella! Wanted to be the all-knowing man. I'd been going out with girls since the age of fifteen, but when I met Tina I was nineteen. Prior to Tina, I was going on seventeen, when I started to date someone I thought a bit special. Her name was Anne, and we had been seeing each other for a few weeks, when I tried it on. I got a slap on the face and a knee in my conkers for my trouble. It slowed me down, sexually, and from then on I was afraid to touch anyone in case I got turned down again. You could say my ego was deflated, as well as something else. Believe it or not, it was about a year later that I lost my virginity to the same girl. I had a number of girlfriends over the years, but only had sex with one of them. So when I had sex with Tina, she was my third one, and although I pretended to 'know it all', I was in fact quite green."

"Did your girlfriends make you use a condom?"

"They didn't make me, but I used them anyway. I'm a bit old fashioned in that respect, and thought it the man's job to make sure nobody got pregnant.

"Did you always use one?"

"There were occasions with Tina when we did it without, but I managed to pull out on time, so there were, I'm glad to say, no scares of pregnancy."

"What were you doing, work wise when you met?"

"I was preparing for my final accountancy examination. Tina was just finishing her 'A' levels at school, and had decided to go to a technical college for three years."

"When did you get married then?"

"We were going out together for seven years before we got married. We had been engaged for six. If I was honest, we should never have got married. I knew and I'm sure Tina knew as well that things weren't working properly. But all the arrangements had been made, you know, date, church service, cars, photographer and flowers. The reception had been booked and the deposit paid, so I suppose it because of that, we went ahead and got married. About eighteen months before the wedding, I got a promotion and had to move away. Tina wasn't very happy, but accepted that it was better than being out of work. She was about to leave the college, looking for a job near where I was working, and was offered a job two days before we got married."

"Where was the honeymoon?"

"Italy, Rimini to be more accurate. We had fifteen days in the resort, decent hotel, good food and then a twenty four hour delay getting back because of an air traffic controllers dispute. When we got home, we moved into a rented house, which was close to work for both of us. We could walk when it was fine, and use the car when it was wet. The day I returned to work after the honeymoon, I got some ribbing of course. The lads thought I should only have a sun tan on my back, from the sun shining through the bedroom window."

"Typical male comments! Why should the man always be on top?"

Ted laughed at Ross's remark. She had moved down the settee, and had her head on Ted's shoulder.

"Are you comfortable?" Ted asked.

"Very, thank you. You're not complaining again, are you?"

"No Ross, I'm not. To tell you the truth, I feel more comfortable with you being here than I have for many years."

"Don't get too comfortable with me, remember I'm a married woman."

"I know, you keep reminding me. So, married woman, why are you in another man's home when it's well after midnight?"

"Is it? I'd better go home, or I'll be the talk of the wash-house tomorrow."

"It's a long time since I heard that remark."

"Thank you very much for my meal Ted, I enjoyed it, and the nice talk afterwards."

"My pleasure, Ross. Same tomorrow if you like, just tell me which meat you prefer, and I'll get it out of the freezer ready."

"Are you sure, I mean... well that's nice, thank you Ted, I will. Can we have some turkey, it'll make me

66

think it's Christmas."

"Turkey it is then. Drive carefully, and I'll see you in the morning."

Ted opened the door to let Ross out, and as she got alongside him, he said,

"Come here married lady."

He gave her a soft kiss on her lips, and as he pulled away, said,

"That's just a friendly kiss to say thank you for today, and good night."

"It should be me thanking you."

"You already did, now go home, before I forget myself."

"See you at eight," Ross laughed as she went through the door and down the stairs

As Ted started to clear everything away, he realised he missed some company, especially female. He had no other thought in his mind that the relationship with Ross could be anything other than good friends and work mates, unless as he kept reminding her, she stopped being a married lady.

FOUR

The next morning, Ted was waiting outside when Ross arrived. He got into the pickup, wished her the usual cheery good morning, and fastened his seat belt.

"Where are we going to start today?" asked Ross as she drove away.

"Kitchen tiles first. If we can get all of them on today, we can grout them tomorrow. When the grout has dried, we could bring the boxes of cupboards into the kitchen ready for erecting."

"I only asked for today, and you've given me the next three. Men!"

Ted laughed, and asked,

"What's made you so cheerful this early in the day?"

"I think it could be the company I'm about to have. It's quite some time since I've looked forward to doing a hard day's work."

"You may not be saying that when we start to build those walls in the bedroom area. That will be hard work. I keep telling you that we will sweat from carrying the breeze blocks about, and mixing and laying concrete."

"I'm going off work, sick."

"No you're not, it's your house, and you have to make sure I don't make a mess of things."

The little bit of fun between them lasted until they reached the house. They went straight through to the kitchen, and checked the walls were dry and ready for the tiles to be fixed. Ted looked round the room and said,

"Before we start tiling, may I make a suggestion?"

"No, I'm a married lady."

Ted shook his head, and answered,

"Not first thing in a morning, please Ross. If I may, I'd like to suggest that there should be a door in here. To get in and out of the house, there's only one door.

Imagine, you've done a load of washing. You take it out of the machine in the wet room, walk through the house, out of the door in the lounge and back to this end of the building again to hang it out to dry."

"You're right, I'd never thought about that." Ross said. "Where do you suggest it should go?"

"Either side wall really, but if this were my house, I'd have it on this right hand wall because it's nearer to the open space where a washing line or a rotary dryer could go."

"OK by me. Where would you put it?"

"I think it should be in the middle, but making sure there is enough room for whole tiles up to the frame edge. If I measure the distance from the wall end, I can mark the first line. The tape measure's in my tool box here, so let's do it now."

"Too early in the morning."

"Married lady, keep your mind on the job. Kitchen door job, that is."

Ted measured where the edge of the doorway would go, and then drew an outline on the wall. With a cold chisel he tapped a groove around the pencil marks he had made, tapped out two corners, passed the chisel to Ross, and asked her to remove the concrete within the grooves.

"It won't take you long to do that, meanwhile, I'll start to bring in the tiles and adhesive from the store room."

Ted brought some boxes in and left them just outside the kitchen door. After three trips, he looked into the kitchen, and saw that the 'doorway' was clear of concrete, and Ross had cleared the rubbish up off the floor. Ted asked her if she would bring two of the large buckets out of the bedroom block while he brought the rest of the tiles in.

Eventually, all the kitchen tiles were inside, and they

were ready to start work. Ted mixed the first bag of adhesive, and spread it over half of one wall, starting at the top. He used a notched scraper to score the adhesive, and started to set the tiles. The first wall he did was backing on to the rear of the lounge, because apart from the door, it was a full wall. There was half a tile to cut into the corner and therefore it didn't take long for him to fit three rows of tiles down the wall, followed by a line of 'dado' tiles to break the monotony. While he was busy tiling, Ross mixed another batch of adhesive so he could fix the next section, just two whole tiles, and the bottom line left for cut tiles to be fitted later. They managed two walls and quarter of another, before they stopped for lunch.

Sitting in their usual place, they ate the sandwiches and had plenty of liquid to drink. Ross turned to Ted, and said,

"Do you really need a siesta today?"

"It's always a good idea, it's bloody hard having to work when the temperature is in the twenties. It's even hotter indoors where there's no breeze. Why do you ask?"

"I just thought, if we go back to the kitchen instead of having a siesta, and finish the walls, we could bring the boxes of cupboards inside, and get them ready for putting in place. We may get an early finish again, you never know."

"We'll finish tiling up to the doorway today anyway, but we can't do anything else until the tiles have been grouted. I suppose we could bring some of the boxes in and erect one or two cupboards."

"No erections, I'm married."

"You really are enjoying making these innuendo's since I told you not to be embarrassed when you talk to me."

"Ted, I'm enjoying every second of it. I have never been able to say things like this before, I've thought them, but if I'd spoken out loud, I'd more than likely have got… into trouble."

Ted put his arm round Ross's shoulder, kissed her forehead, and said,

"I will never take a sexual innuendo seriously, it will be a joke between the two of us."

"If you take my comments as a joke, how will you know when I'm serious?"

"By the look in those lovely eyes of yours. When I met you, they were flat and non-committal, but recently, they have been clear and sparkling. I hope they stay that way."

"If we can keep working and laughing as we are now, they may sparkle for ever."

"OK Twinkle, let's go and finish the kitchen walls. When we've done that, the flat packs can be brought in, and if time permits we can…."

"OK, OK, I give up. Let's go and have a sleep."

Ted smiled at Ross and said,

"Now you're beginning to see things my way. Just for once though, I'll bow to your request, and finish the tiling. We'll have to go back to Malaga very soon, and find an outside door for the kitchen."

"We could go tomorrow morning, before coming up here."

"We could, but at that time of the day, the traffic into Malaga is horrendous, two or three lanes of almost stationary traffic. When we finish the tiling, we could go this afternoon, it will be much easier to drive there and back."

"That's a good idea Ted, come on then, let's get to it."

Ross started cutting and fitting the bottom tiles, while

71

Ted knocked a hole in the wall where the door was to go. It didn't take him long, and once the gap was right, he gave it a coating of concrete, then smoothed and squared the edges. The concrete would be set by morning, and he would be able to fit the door frame, and finish the tiling round it. He found a piece of boarding, and used it to cover the hole in the wall.

Two hours later they had finished. Ted cleared the floor, and put the tiles and the bags of unused adhesive in a corner ready for morning.

Ross had just finished sweeping the floor, and turned towards Ted.

"Is that it for now?" she asked.

"I think so, twinkle, but before we go to Malaga, I think you should go and get another 'T' shirt."

"Why, is it dirty?" Ross asked, looking down the front.

"No, it's not dirty," Ted answered, "it's transparent with sweat. You may as well not be wearing one and you a married lady flashing at your workmate."

"You've seen a pair of boobs before, haven't you?"

"Yes Ross I have, but never when I've been working. If you keep walking around like that, I could easily fit the door upside down or in the wrong place."

"I don't think so Ted Hall, I'll make sure you put everything in the right place."

"Ross Jones, you get worse."

Ross laughed, a long happy laugh, eyes sparkling.

"I've no clean shirts at home. It's washing night tonight, but tomorrow I'll have to wear my red shirt and that's thicker and warmer than a 'T' shirt."

"I haven't worn my shirt since this morning, so you can wear that now, and I'll get a clean one from home. You can take a couple of mine home with you, I've got plenty. Take that wet one off, and put this one on."

Ross started to take the 'T' shirt off, but it was so wet, she was having difficulties.

"Ted, can you help me please?"

He told her to lean towards him, with her arms straight in front. He took hold of the hem at either side, and pulled it over her head.

"I think my bra is as wet as the shirt, but I'm not taking that off, because you haven't got a spare dry one."

Ted smiled, and in an effeminate voice, said,

"How do you know where my spare bras are?"

He picked up an old towel he'd brought from home, and passed it to her.

"You can dry yourself with this before you put my shirt on."

"I'm not drying myself or putting the shirt on until we are ready to leave." she told him.

Ten minutes later, they were ready, and went out of the front door. Ross handed Ted the towel, and asked him if he would dry her back. When she was happy it was dry, she turned round, and in a sexy voice, asked him if he would like to dry the front.

"I think, young lady, you should do your own front."

"Why, do you think I'm tempting you?"

"You are very tempting, Salome, and I'm afraid of getting carried away, and losing a friend."

"Salome, Twinkle, what next?"

Ted smiled at her and said,

"I'll think of something. Please will you get dressed. I admit to admiring the scenery as much as I did last night, but the scenery is out of my reach, as you well know."

Ross drove back to the village, and for a change, easily found a parking space. They went up to Ted's apartment and into his bedroom, where he found a clean 'T' shirt, and gave Ross three of his spare ones.

"I'm just going to change my shorts before we go to

Malaga," said Ted, and then added "haven't you got any shorts to wear while we're working Ross?"

"Sadly, that's something I haven't got." she replied.

"I haven't got any that will fit you," Ted answered, "they're all far too big."

"No problem Ted, I can buy some next time I go shopping for clothes."

"Are you going to stand there while I take my shorts off?"

"It doesn't bother me, so why are you asking?"

Ted had no reply, so took off his work shorts and only in his underpants, calmly got another pair of shorts from the drawer and put them on, followed by the clean 'T' shirt. They left his bedroom and went into the lounge. Ted got a tape measure, and a pair of scissors from his cupboard, and said to Ross,

"Right, married lady, get those jeans off. In five minutes time, you'll have a pair of shorts to work in." He put up the ironing board, and plugged his iron into a socket.

Without hesitating, Ross took her jeans off, and handed them to him. He got the tape measure, and asked Ross how long she would like the legs to be. She pointed down her leg, and indicated the length she wanted them. Ted measured the length, added an inch, and went to the ironing board. He measured the length again and then with a large pair of scissors, cut off each leg where he had marked. Then, using some 'wonder hem' turned the legs up, and handing them back to Ross, said,

" Here you are Ross, try that for size."

"How many more times have I to tell you I'm married?" she answered with a straight face. Her eyes gave her away though!

She put them on, and declared them a perfect fit.

"Ted," Ross said, "do you really not mind me

74

standing around your apartment wearing only my underclothes?"

"Ross, you have got a lovely body, one that any hot blooded man would appreciate. I have seen you twice in your underwear, you have seen me once, and neither of us made a grab for the other on either occasion. We have both been married and obviously seen naked bodies in the past. I have told you before, as far as I'm concerned, until you stand stark naked in front of me, and you make it clear that you want me, I will never make a pass at you. I may kiss you when I feel the moment is right, but that will not be sexual. I may also give you a hug or a cuddle, which also will not be sexual. At the moment, we are working very well together, but when we start on those bedroom walls, we will sweat more than we did today. If your clothes become 'see through', I won't be stopping work to stare at you. Do you understand what I am saying?"

Ross took a step towards Ted, put her arms round his waist and said,

"I've said this before Ted, you really are a nice man. You've been so at ease with me, I sometimes forget myself. When I got married, I made those vows, and the most important one I personally believe in, is 'forsaking all others'. In other words, don't commit adultery. I will always believe in that until the day I become widowed, or divorced. We have both said, in different ways, that neither of us would take advantage of each other, unless I wasn't married. I do admit to liking you kissing and hugging me, because it gives me a feeling of security. Please, don't stop doing that, but as for sex, right now Ted, that is not at the top of my agenda. I'm aware that my husband has committed adultery on many occasions, but that doesn't mean I'm going to do the same just to get back at him. You do make me feel good when we're together, that's why I can hold your arm or your hand without any misunderstanding. Without this sounding wrong, I hope we can continue our friendship for a long time, because I rather like you, and I wouldn't like anything to split us up. Now we both know where we stand with each other, shall we go to Malaga and buy a back door?"

As she stopped speaking, Ross leaned forwards, and gave Ted a kiss.

The following day, as soon as they arrived at the house, Ted removed the wood from the gap, and started to fit the door frame. It didn't take long to do, and just before the final pins went in, he asked Ross to mix some tile adhesive.

"We can leave the door off for now," he said, "it will give us a cooling breeze while we finish tiling round the frame and finish this wall off."

"Why do we want a breeze? I thought you would like to judge the Miss Wet 'T' shirt competition."

"I think I'll be doing that regularly when we start building the bedroom walls."

"If it's going to be that hot, couldn't we put the patio doors in first and leave them open while we work?"

"No. The dividing walls should be built first, and then we can measure the exact centre of the wall. After we have marked where the patio doors will go, a line of brick may have to be taken from the top, and a concrete lintel built in. Only when the concrete has dried round the lintel, will we be able to knock out the bricks below."

Within an hour and a half, they had finished tiling the kitchen. Ted looked critically around the walls, making sure there were no obvious errors. He turned to Ross, and said,

"They look straight and level, I think we can say we've done a good job. I suggest we leave the grouting until tomorrow when the tiles round the door are properly set. We can leave the door off until tonight so that the air can circulate round the room. There is a box of tiles left over, plus three single ones. If you take the full box back to the shop, they may credit you for it. Do you still want to bring the cupboards in now, or wait until we finish grouting tomorrow?"

"Will it make it difficult to do the grouting if we have some of the cupboards built up?"

"Not really, although we can't put them in the position you want. I suggest we make up the sink unit first. Now that I've fixed the water pipe, we can put the sink in the right place first, and build the rest of the cupboards round it when we are ready. The wall cupboards can go on later when the tile grouting is properly dry."

Ross nodded, and looked round the room.

"I'll accept what you say about the sink, so shall we go and bring it in?"

"Ross, are you all right? Where's the twinkle gone?"

Ross gave him a weak smile.

"I'm not fully with it this morning. It's... err... you know..."

"The wrong time of the month." Ted finished for her.

"Right. Let me tell you something, which I hope won't embarrass you too much. In the past I've.... err.... had some problems and I'm getting to the age when I have to start thinking about the 'change'. Every month when I'm due, I get the usual symptoms, but recently some months, nothing happens. When it does, it's quite heavy, and I just haven't the energy to do too much work. This month is going to be one of them."

"That isn't a problem to me, Ross. If at any time you feel as if you need to rest, tell me, please. Don't keep going because you think you have too, it isn't worth it. If

I need a rest, I'll stop, so you must do the same. You are the boss in this house, and it's up to you to say how we work. Do you want to carry on, or shall we have the rest of the day off?"

"I'm not used to being the boss in my own home," Ross answered, "I've usually had to do as I was told. If we bring the sink unit in, and maybe a couple of other cupboards, you can put them together while I watch and pass you the things you need. If we work until our usual lunch time, see how I feel, and decide whether we work this afternoon, or take it easy. I'm sorry..."

"Don't you dare say sorry Ross." Ted interrupted, "It's one of the things a woman has to endure, and I know ladies differ in the way it affects them. Any time you need to slow down or stop, you tell me. Now I'll bring in the cupboards, and between us we can put them together. When you've had enough, we stop."

"Thank you Ted, I'm glad you are such an understanding person. I dread to think what it would be like if I was working with my husband, no, with my ex-husband. Well one day.... hopefully."

Ted went to where the cupboard flat packs were, and found the sink base unit was on top of the pile. It was quite heavy, but with a struggle managed to get the box over to the kitchen. He left the box in the middle of the floor, and went back for another one. He decided to bring the tall base cupboard and a normal base unit, because he wanted to see which would fit better between the sink unit and the wall.

Between them they opened the first box, and checked its contents. Finding everything was correct, he started to build, following the enclosed instructions. Ross watched, and handed him a screwdriver or an Allen key when he asked. The first one didn't take too long and was left in the middle of the kitchen, ready for putting in place when the area was ready. The other two cupboards were built up in next to no time and left beside the others.

"That's it for today Ross, I can see you are almost asleep, so no arguing with Ted. I am going to fit the door on to the hinges, lock it, and we're going home."

"I'm not going to argue," Ross replied wearily, "I feel as if I could sleep for a week, and as for eating my lunch, not right now, thank you."

Half an hour later they were inside Ted's apartment, and he walked Ross straight to his bedroom, pointed at the bed, and said,

"There is my bed. Get into it, and go to sleep. I don't care how long you stay there as long as you feel better when you wake up. If you haven't woken up by the time it's my bedtime, you will find me next to you in the morning. No arguing, bed... now."

"Yes, Sir." Ross answered with a smile and a mock salute, but without another word, took off her shorts and 'T' shirt, and got into bed. Ted left her and went to the kitchen to eat his lunch. He looked in on her about an hour later, and she was fast asleep.

Late that afternoon, Ted was doing some work on his computer, when Ross walked into the lounge. He looked round, and said,

"Hello, are you feeling any better after your sleep?"

"A bit," Ross replied, "but I need to go home for a tampon and some clean knicks."

"Knicks," echoed Ted, "I don't think I've heard that one before."

"My.... the daughter of a very close friend calls her knickers, 'knicks' and the word has stuck."

"It's different, I admit, the sort of thing a young girl would say as she learned about dressing herself."

"True, but I need some. Would you run me round to my apartment to get them, then I can have a shower and get changed before tea."

"If you trust me with your key," Ted told her, "you can tell me where the things are, I'll go and get them for you and you can stay here and rest."

"It's easy to find my clothes. They are on the chair at the side of the bed and the other things are on the shelf in the bathroom. Do you mind going for them, honestly?"

"Not in the slightest. You still look tired, so go and lie down until I get back, then you can have the shower. Would you like me to make you a drink before I leave?"

"No, thanks Ted, I can wait until you get back."

Ted drove to her house and let himself in. He noticed how much colder the house was compared to his apartment, and thought that Ross would be more relaxed if she were warmer, particularly at the moment. He found the clothes she wanted, picked up the box from the bathroom, and made his way back home.

As he went through the door, Ted saw Ross, still in her underwear, sat on the settee. She had a mug of coffee in front of her, and Ted's mug was on the table next to it. He smiled as he went into the lounge, and said,

"Now that's what I call room service."

"Don't bank on it too often, I'm only a visitor here."

"You are the only visitor who's ever sat on that settee in her underwear."

Ross smiled at him, and replied,

"As I've just said, don't bank on it too often."

"You seem to be a bit brighter, are you feeling better?"

"Not really. I need a shower, well at least I want to wash myself.... down there but I haven't the energy to get in the bath."

"You could use the shower unit in the small bathroom, or you could give the bidet a try, see how it feels."

"Now that is a good idea! You describe how it works, and I'll give it a go."

They went to the bathroom, and Ted verbally demonstrated how a bidet works. Leaving her to it, he went back to the kitchen to make their evening meal. He had forgotten to take the meat out of the freezer that morning, so had decided on an easy 'egg, chips and beans' tea. He was almost finished when Ross came into the kitchen to join him.

"You were right about a bidet being refreshing," Ross said, "I've decided you can fit one into the main bathroom in my house."

"I'm glad you approve. Are you feeling better now?"

"Refreshed, but still tired, thank you. If I have a good night's sleep, maybe I'll feel better tomorrow, ready for some work."

"It's Sunday tomorrow, so you can have another day off to help with your recovery."

"I've lost track of the days this week. So, if it's Sunday tomorrow, why don't we go to a restaurant for our lunch. I've seen many adverts for Sunday Lunches, but never tried one. It'll give you a break from cooking as well. Have you any suggestions where we could go?"

"I do know of a very nice restaurant in Nerja, called 'Sloans'. They do a three course meal for a very good price, and serve beef, pork or chicken, but you can have a slice of all three if you prefer. There is usually a fish dish if you prefer it. The restaurant also has an outside terrace, so you can decide where you like to eat. I've been several times, and would recommend it to anyone."

"That's settled for tomorrow's lunch, but now I'm ready for tonight's meal."

"One egg or two?" Ted asked.

"Just one egg, but plenty of chips and beans."

A few minutes later, they were sat at the table

enjoying their evening meal.

Afterwards, they took a mug of coffee into the lounge, watched the television and caught up on the latest news from the UK.

Ross was sat close to Ted, her head on his shoulder. He looked at her a little later in the night, to see she was falling asleep again. He gently touched her hand, and in a soft voice, said,

"Come on Ross, I think it's time you were back in bed again."

"Can you drive me home, and pick me up again tomorrow?"

"No, Ross, you are going nowhere until you are feeling better. You can go to bed now, and you'll probably be fast asleep when I get there. Don't argue, you know nothing can happen, so you are as safe as your house in the hills."

"Thank you Ted, but are you sure…?"

"I'm absolutely certain. You can use the spare bed if you prefer."

Ross got up, gave Ted a kiss on his cheek, and said,

"I'll sleep in your bed, I know I'm safe with you."

Ross was fast asleep when Ted went to bed, and didn't even move when he got into the bed beside her. He looked at the sleeping lady, and thought, 'if only, Ted Hall, if only…', and fell asleep himself.

Ted awoke the next morning and remembered who was in bed with him. He turned and looked, but Ross had her eyes closed and seemed still to be asleep.

As quietly as possible he got out of the bed, went into the kitchen and switched the coffee machine on. He left it to percolate and walked back to the bathroom. He was just finishing shaving as Ross walked past on her way to the other bathroom.

"'Morning Ted," she called as she passed his door.

Ted waited until Ross came back towards the bedroom before answering her.

"Morning Ross", he said, walking out of his bathroom, "did you sleep well?"

"Yes, thank you, and I'm feeling a lot better this morning. Not quite a hundred per cent, but getting there. I think I'll manage a shower later on before we go out for lunch. I'll go and make the coffee while you finish getting dressed."

"Too late, the coffee has brewed and waiting to be poured into the mugs."

"Oooo, proper little domestic aren't we? You'll make someone a good husband. I wish I had one!"

They were stood in the bedroom doorway, both wearing their underclothes. Ross looked Ted over and said,

"We're like an old married couple, stood here almost naked, and we ignore the fact."

"Who's ignoring it?" asked Ted, "you've just looked me over as though I was a prize calf at the market."

"By the look of that bulge, it's more like a prize stud."

"I think I'd better get dressed," said Ted, "before I forget my promise."

"I think we'd both better get dressed, although it would do you no good if you were to forget your promise or have you forgotten my condition?"

Ted put his arms on her waist, and said,

"I could get used to you being around my apartment. You give me things to think and talk about. It really is nice to have a companion."

"Companions don't hug each other in their underwear, do they?"

Ted stepped back, and said,

"I'm sorry Ross, I didn't mean…"

"It's OK Ted," Ross interrupted with a smile, "I wasn't complaining."

Ted went to his wardrobe, took out a dressing gown, handed it to Ross, and reaching back in, took another one out for himself.

"Now we can go and have a coffee and something to eat before getting ready to go out later."

"I need to call at the house in the village later to get a clean pair of jeans and T shirt. I can't very well go into a restaurant in my working clothes, can I?"

Later that afternoon, after enjoying a well-served Sunday roast, Ross and Ted were slowly strolling arm in arm along the Paseo. Ross stopped abruptly and pulled on Ted's arm.

"Turn round, quick." she said.

"What's the matter," Ted asked as they did a complete turnabout.

"I've just seen one of Brian's mates with his wife and children down on the beach. I hope they haven't seen me because that really would be asking for trouble."

"I take it that Brian is your husband." Ted asked.

"Yes he is," Ross replied, "and I don't want him to know where I am."

They had come to a curve in the Paseo and were heading towards the next beach, when Ted slowed Ross down and asked her if she could point out the person she had seen. Hiding slightly behind Ted, she pointed out a family back along the beach. The adults were still sat looking out to sea and the children running into the waves and back again. Neither parent was taking any notice of anything but their children.

"I'm sure they didn't see you Ross," Ted said, "otherwise they would be looking around or even on the telephone. Under these circumstances, and to be on the safe side, I think we should stay away from the more popular holiday beaches for a while."

The chance sighting had shaken Ross, so they made their way back to the car, and drove towards the village.

"It's too nice a day to be going to my flat," said Ted, "I'd rather be sitting outside under the shade of an umbrella."

"We could go to my house in the hills, but I haven't got anything to shade us." Ross said.

"I have," Ted answered, "in the upstairs storeroom, I have four almost new loungers, and an umbrella with a metal stand. We can get two loungers and the umbrella, take them to your house, and sit in the warmth of the sun. They can be left there for us to use at lunch time when we're working."

As he was speaking, he had pulled up outside the apartment. They went up to the store room and found the items still in bubble wrap. It took two trips to get everything they wanted in the motor, including some bottles of water. Twenty minutes later, they were setting the things up in the area between the two buildings.

"We are not going into that house this afternoon Ted." Ross said, "Today we relax outside and enjoy the sun."

Ted sat down on his lounger, and took off his shirt before stretching out in the shade. Ross was lying on her lounger, only the large umbrella between them.

After about twenty minutes Ross sat up, and turning to Ted said,

"It's all right for you, lying there without a shirt while I have to sweat in mine."

She got hold of the hem of the shirt and lifted it over her head.

"Look at me Ted," she said, "I'm going to take my bra off. If we are going to sweat like you say, I'm going to work topless just like you. I am not coming on to you, neither am I asking you to touch me. I want you to look at me now so you can get used to seeing me bare breasted."

Ross undid and removed her bra, and then sat up straight allowing Ted to have a good look at her.

"Ross, I've said before you have a very nice body and showing me your bare breasts proves the point. I'm glad you trust me enough to see you like that, so if you're determined to work topless, I promise you faithfully I'll not stare, neither will I try to touch you."

"Thank you Ted. Now I'm going to lie back on this lounger again and enjoy the sun, just like you."

Later in the afternoon, as Ted turned over to let some sun onto his back, he glanced at Ross, and thinking she was asleep, noticed her body was looking rather red.

"Are you asleep Ross?" he asked.

"Just dozing." she answered, "What's wrong?"

"You're looking a bit red, just be careful because the last thing you need is sunburn."

"Are you offering to rub some sun tan lotion onto my body Ted Hall? Before you ask, the answer is no!"

"I didn't even think of it Ross, especially since I haven't any sun tan lotion anyway, here or at the apartment."

Ross looked down her body and said,

"I am a bit red, aren't I? I'll turn over and do my back for a while and then I'll put my T shirt back on and hide myself from prying eyes."

"My eyes are closed Ross. I told you before I wasn't going to stare at you so don't try and make me out to be a fibber."

"I'm only pulling your leg Ted. I've been having an occasional peek at you out of the corner of my eye, and as far as I know, you haven't looked at me since I took my bra off."

"I've got a photographic memory." Ted answered, his eyes still closed, "Why do you think I've turned onto my stomach?"

He got a slap on his back for the cheeky answer.

Ross sat back on the lounger and turned over. She stayed on her stomach for about half an hour, then sat up and said,

"I think I should cover myself up, I can feel my skin is tight and starting to burn slightly."

"In the apartment I have a bottle of after sun lotion which I can spray on before you go to bed. It doesn't need to be rubbed in, just a light spray, let it dry and will take the burning feeling away. Shall we put the loungers and umbrella in the kitchen? We can bring them outside in the morning, use them when we have our lunch and siesta and put them away again when we finish work."

Early next morning they were hard at work building one of the dividing walls of the two main bedrooms, and by late morning, they had reached halfway between the floor and ceiling.

"I think that's enough on this wall." said Ted, climbing off the wood on the frames. "We can let the concrete set up fully before we put the next rows on, so now we carry on with the bathroom walls, and with a bit of luck they will be the same height by lunch time."

They were, and Ted decided the walls should be left for at least twenty four hours before building any higher.

"What shall we do after our siesta then?" asked Ross as they started their lunch.

Ted thought for a moment or two, and said,

"We could have a look at the tiles on the living room floor. If they are as firmly fixed down as the kitchen wall tiles were, it could take less than an hour to clear them. Once they are all off, we can look at how we can level the floor before putting new tiles down."

"Is it going to be a problem levelling the floor?"

"I'm not sure," Ted answered, "a lot depends on the height difference between the kitchen end and the far wall. If it's not much, we may have to get some hard core in and re-lay it. Let's wait until we measure it before making a decision."

The floor tiles were fitted a little better than the kitchen wall tiles, but they were still taken up and the floor swept clean in a very short time.

A string line was run from one corner of the room to the other, and using a special spirit level, the difference in height from each corner was measured at both sides.

"There is a difference of fourteen centimetres," said Ted, "that's around five and a half inches in old money. The drop starts about half way down the length, so if we put concrete down to make it level all the way along, the doorway will have to be re-aligned, and the fireplace will have to be built up higher."

"That seems drastic Ted, is there no other way to do it? If we altered the door, it would mean fitting steps on the outside."

Ted looked the floor over before saying,

"I'll have to think this one over Ross, there must be an easier way to sort it out. I wish we could find the plans, because there is no way anything like this would have been passed by the Ayuntamiento."

"The who?" Ross asked.

"Sorry, the town council. They have to approve all building plans and issue a license before anyone can start work. Did you say the previous owners ran out of money? I think that happened sometime before they actually got out. They must have had professional builders to help with the two blocks. In both, the corners are square and the walls straight, the kitchen floor is level the tiles are laid properly. I cannot understand though why this floor slopes so badly. The floor should have been level before the building of the walls started. I suspect they were running out of cash after those kitchen tiles were put down, so they got rid of the builder and tried to do it alone. You can tell that by comparing the kitchen tiles and the ones we have just taken up. Look at all the building materials inside the other block and spread around outside. If they hadn't bought all that at once, they would have had more cash to see this floor right."

"Is it going to cost me a lot of money to sort out?"

"I don't think so, you know my hourly rate isn't very high." Ted answered.

"Can we do it between us Ted?"

"Probably, but I'm not sure yet just how to go about it. Let's measure the full length of this room and I'll try to come up with a solution. Can you remember a few weeks ago, we were using my computer to try and make two bedrooms and a bathroom to fit on the top of this building? I'm glad you decided to use the other block for the bedrooms, because it gives you a lot more room to live in. There is one thing that puzzles me though. Why has the loo been built at the rear side of the main house and the door facing outwards? I would have thought the door would be better in here. Imagine in a year's time, sitting here watching the telly and you need the loo. You have to go out in the dark and round to the other side, then back again when you've finished. It may be all right in the summer, but in winter or if it's raining….. need I say more?"

"Maybe it's something to do with the level of the floor in here." Ross said, "if the floor here is higher or lower than the loo floor, the doors may not fit, or a step up or down would be needed."

"That could be true, Ross. You're not often wrong,

but you're right this time."

"Bloody cheek!"

Ted grinned, and said,

"We've got all the necessary measurements of this floor, so I think you should cover up the forbidden fruit, and we can go home."

"Forbidden fruit? That's a new one. I don't think I've heard anyone call a pair of breasts 'forbidden fruit'."

"They are very nice breasts Ross, but to me they are forbidden."

"I think you're right, it is time to go home before I get compared to something else that could be frozen."

That evening after their meal, they were watching the television when Ted suddenly sat up and exclaimed,

"That's it, I know how we can do it."

"How many more times? We can't do it because I'm married."

"I might have known you'd corrupt the conversation somewhere along the line. Sadly I'm not talking about what you think I'm talking about, but the floor in your living room."

He got up, picked up a pencil and found some paper he could draw on.

"This is the floor from the kitchen end," he said as he sketched the room. "If we draw a line across the room, roughly where the floor starts to slope and break the concrete along it, we can then dig down and level the floor from there, making a fourteen centimetre deep step to divide the room. The top half you could make into a dining area plus, say some display cabinets and, if you like even a computer desk. The bottom section can be the lounge with chairs and sofas, television, music centre, maybe a DVD player. A log fire in the fireplace will keep you warm in the winter while you sit on your sofa and watch the telly."

"You're a genius Ted Hall, what would I do without you?"

"Hire a builder to do the work and pay the earth for it, where as I have to put in my time, knowing I'll not get paid for the graft I've lovingly tended on your house in the hills."

"Don't get sarcastic with me Ted Hall, you know you'll get your reward sometime."

"That's what I'm afraid of, sometime."

"Let's get back to this floor problem. Will it really work, and will there be any other problems."

"It can work, but it's going to be time consuming digging out by hand. We are going to have to dig about thirty centimetres, which is around a foot in old English, down from the top of the step, and level the ground before laying more concrete. For the time being, I think we are going to have to work on this in between jobs, until we have more time to spend on it. Tomorrow, we'll measure the floor to find the point where the floor starts to drop. We can mark it across, draw a line and see if it's possible to break the concrete with my cold chisel. If it won't, then we will have to hire a hammer drill. After we've checked the concrete, we go back to the other block and finish the bedroom walls."

"You're a hard taskmaster Mr Hall. The way you're pushing things we could be finished by the end of the month."

"You wish, Mrs Jones, you wish."

"Smythe-Jones if you don't mind!"

"Ohh! Aren't we posh, a double barrelled surname. Do you remember the word you used when I was talking about 'political correctness'?"

"You mean 'bollocks'?" Ross asked.

"Exactly!" Was Ted's answer.

Ross nudged him in the ribs with her elbow, and said,

"Watch it you, that's my name you're degrading. Well that's not true is it? It's partly Brian's name, and you can degrade that as much as you want.

"Shall I revert to Mrs Smith then?"

"You know that word I've just used?"

"You mean 'bollocks'?"

"Yes! So if you want yours to stay where they are now, curb your language."

"You're in a good mood tonight, are you feeling better?"

"I've almost finished, and nowhere near as tired as I was last week."

"I'm glad to hear it. Does that mean you're going home at nights from now on?"

"Are you trying to get rid of me Ted Hall? You'll miss me when I've gone."

"It'll be safer though. Just imagine what would happen if Brian found out you were in my bed."

"He wouldn't believe nothing had happened. He'd just bloody kill me." Ross replied in a sad low voice.

"Then kill me afterwards. See you in Heaven?"

"I doubt it Ted, some of the things I've been thinking about recently would disqualify my entry."

"Oh yes! Am I allowed to ask what they are?"

"Not right now, but maybe at a later date. Can we get back to our original conversation?"

"I thought we'd finished discussing the living room floor."

"I'd like to tell you some of the things I've thought about. I'd like wooden floors in the two large bedrooms and I'd also like us to concentrate on those two rooms to finish them as soon as we can. How long, in your estimation, would it take to finish them and be ready for furnishing?"

"Bloody hell Ross, that's some question to throw at

92

me. Your bedroom walls will be finished tomorrow, two days for the other dividing wall and bathroom, two or three days in each room for skimming the walls, two days each for fitting the floor, and about the same for finishing the bathrooms. We need at least another five or six days to do the patio doors. I reckon at least six or seven weeks, depending on how we work things, and providing that nothing goes wrong and holds us up. To be on the safe side, call it two months. It also means that I can't build you a sunken bath. I still need to find if any drains for the block exist, and if there aren't any, add at least another week to our total. On top of all that, we need to allow time for the electrician and a plumber to do their work, so add another two weeks at least. My final estimate is around three months."

"You're determined to keep at it aren't you?"

"There's no point in slowing down Ross, you're the one who wants the work finished as quickly as possible. I've already outlined our next moves, but I'll make a suggestion. Tomorrow morning we get the walls in the main bedroom finished. If there is any concrete left over, we can start to lay the base line in the second room. If we get an outline down, we can leave it to set up while we go to Malaga for the flooring. I can do the wall, while you put down the underlay for the main room."

"Will I be able to do it on my own? Putting the underlay down, that is, before you corrupt the conversation."

"What else could you be doing on your own if you weren't talking about the floor?"

"There is something I could do on my own, and there have been many times recently when I've wanted to, but never have done."

"If you talking about what I think you are talking about, are you being serious Ross?"

Ross nodded, staring into space as though thinking about the past.

"Are you saying Brian neglected you that way?" Ted asked in a low voice.

"For many years. I don't want to talk about it right now Ted, maybe some other time, OK?"

"Of course, Ross, but I'm sorry to hear you had a problem like that. I'll not mention it again, that's a promise."

Ross weakly smiled at Ted and said,

"What were you saying about the floor?"

"If we go to the store in Malaga and get the wood and all the fittings necessary, you could cut and fit the underlay while I build up the other dividing walls."

"We need some more bags of cement sometime soon." Ross told him.

"We can get some when we pick up the flooring. I think it's time we went to bed we seem to have made ourselves a lot of work tomorrow."

They had been in bed for a while, when Ross turned towards Ted, and said,

"Are you still awake Ted?"

"Yes Ross. Is something wrong?"

"I'm just thinking, and I'm getting myself in a right mess. To be honest Ted, I've got used to being here with you. I don't mean in bed, but our work together and our meals and the things we say without taking offence. We work hard and enjoy ourselves but I don't want you to read anything into what I said earlier, you know, the 'doing it myself' bit."

"I hadn't thought about it since it was mentioned Ross. I've already promised not to take advantage of you, and whatever you say to me will stay in my memory but not taken as any hint or hidden meaning. I've said before Ross, you are safe with me while you are married, so stop worrying and go to sleep."

"Thank you Ted, but I will start going home at night now I'm better, but I hope I may be invited to stay again if the same need arises."

"You can stay here whenever you like and for as long as you wish. Use the spare bed if it makes you feel any easier."

"No thank you, I'm quite comfortable in this one for the time being. I think I'm ready for sleep. Thanks for the reassurance, see you in the morning."

Ross leaned forward and kissed Ted. Afterwards he thought it was a little softer than usual and lingered slightly longer. 'In your dreams' he thought, as he nodded off to sleep.

FIVE

A couple of weeks later while having their lunch, they took stock of the way their plans were working out.

Ted had finished building the walls for the two main bedrooms and bathrooms. The final skimming on the master bedroom was setting nicely and he was almost ready to start the second coat on the other room.

Ross had cut and laid the underlay in the bathroom of the first bedroom, and had reached halfway down the main room. She had stopped there at Ted's suggestion, and covered the whole of the room with the tarpaulin sheet. This would prevent any brick dust or chippings getting into the flooring when the wall was knocked out to fit the patio doors. Ted had read the fitting instructions for them and found there was no need for a lintel, as the door and the shutters fitted into the full height of the wall with their own built in lintel. He had marked the area and removed the concrete, leaving bare brickwork ready for knocking the wall through. He would start on that when he finished skimming the wall in the second room. Ross had contacted an electrician who was coming out that afternoon to look at what was needed and to give them a quote for the job. A plumber had already been to see the house, and had promised to phone them with a price the next day.

Ross had 'covered up' when the plumber came, and said she would have to do the same when the electrician arrived. She had got used to walking around the site topless, Ted hardly giving her a second glance as they worked. Strangers were different though, Ross said,

"I only show my body to trusted people. The only ones to have seen me like this is Brian and you. The only persons to see me in my underwear are Brian and you, and only Brian has ever seen me naked."

96

The living room floor was proving to be difficult because the concrete base would not break with a cold chisel or a standard hammer drill. Ted was now contemplating hiring a heavy duty drill and compressor to do the job at a later date.

Initially, Ted had planned a gas water heater fitted to the outside wall of the block, one at each end, each heater supplying two bathrooms. The plumber has suggested to Ross that he fitted solar panels to both blocks for the hot water supply, and they could be used for heating each block if she wanted it fitting at a later date. There would be a small secondary tank fitted in each block with an electrical heater in case there was insufficient sun to heat the water through the panels. The plumber mentioned that the Andalucían Government were offering a grant towards the cost of fitting solar panels, so Ross, Ted and the plumber sat and discussed the proposals. Before leaving, he offered to write a quotation for fitting solar panels and the original with gas water heaters.

Ross said she thought the idea of solar panels was good, but would wait and see the difference in the cost before making her final choice.

They sat in the shade waiting for the electrician to arrive, and as soon as Ross heard a vehicle coming up the hill, grabbed her T shirt and put it on.

"You may get an extra discount if you leave it off," Ted said.

"I only allow you to see me like this because you give me a generous discount for the privilege, and therefore I have no need to pay you a wage."

"You'll tell me anything to avoid paying me." said Ted.

"Stop complaining, I'll take the T shirt off again when the electrician has gone, and you can stare at me all afternoon."

They had no time to continue with their bit of fun because Ross had to go to the front of the house to meet the electrician.

He was shown round the two blocks and he wrote down his recommendations, ready to price up. He made a few suggestions, but the main comment he made, was that the job itself would be relatively easy. He offered to tie everything up with the electricity company, making sure they could press a switch and have lights once he had completed his work.

About an hour later, he was ready to go, and promised to phone the following afternoon with his price. They thanked him for coming, watched as he drove away, and went back to work. Ted had mixed some concrete to put a final skim on the second bedroom wall before the electrician arrived, and was ready to start on the wall, when Ross walked into the room minus her T shirt.

"Do you want a hand?" she asked.

"I wouldn't mind," Ted answered, "if I skim, you can put the concrete on the board ready for me to use."

"Fine," answered Ross, "it's some time since we did anything like this together."

Ted climbed up on the platform he had built and took a board of concrete off Ross. He skimmed from the corner at ceiling level and worked down and across until he had used up all concrete on his board. Ross had put some more on another board, ready for Ted to keep up the momentum. One wall finished, Ted moved the platform to the next wall, which was the bathroom. They worked quickly and had got almost to the last section of wall when disaster struck! Ted had finished one board, and was reaching down to take the other off Ross. She passed it up to him, but before he could get hold of it, the board slipped in her hands, tipped backwards, and most of the concrete slid off and onto Ross's breasts and down her body. She screamed in fright as the cold, wet mix slid down her and onto the floor. Ted couldn't help it, and started to laugh. Ross glared at him for a moment then suddenly saw the funny side of it and joined in the laughter.

"That's a new slant on a mud bath." she said. "I'd better not go out in the sun though or I'll have a statue of myself."

"You need to get that off you quickly Ross, there's lime in that mixture and it could burn your skin. Go over to the water container and wash it off."

Ross rushed away, followed closely by Ted. On reaching the water, Ross got a handful of water and splashed it on the top half of her body.

"Bloody hell, Ted, that's cold." she gasped.

"If you bend over the water barrel I'll splash the water on you, while you wipe your breasts until it has gone."

He stood opposite Ross and put his hands into the water. He took a double handful and threw it over her breasts, while Ross vigorously scrubbed with both hands to wash the concrete away. It took five or six hands full before Ross decided she was clean, and taking one of the towels hanging beside the water butt, briskly dried herself.

"That feels much better," she said, "That's one thing I'm not going to try again in a hurry."

"Do you feel all right to carry on?" Ted asked her.

"Yes, thanks Ted. I'll be OK when I warm up a bit."

"Come on then," said Ted, "there isn't much more to do, and when these walls are done, that's it until you want the other bedrooms finished."

"The other bedrooms are not urgent right now. There

are more important jobs to finish. When do you think we can fit the patio doors to this room?"

"I can knock the bricks out in the morning, and tidy the edges up, but I'll have to build a square pillar at each side to give the wall extra strength. The edges will have to be squared off and the gap accurate before the door frame can go in. It will have to be left to set, and the frames screwed to the walls before the doors are lifted into place. I would guess, well it's Tuesday today, so we can probably fit the doors on Saturday morning."

That is exactly the way it worked, except it was Saturday afternoon before the doors were in place and secured. Ted lowered the shutter blind, and they left the house for the rest of the weekend.

"I'm sorry if I keep pushing you, Ted," Ross said the following Wednesday night after their evening meal, "but what have we to do ourselves in the bedrooms?"

"Finish the underlay and fit the wood in the main bedroom and bathroom, and fit the whole lot in the other room. Once the electrician and plumber have finished in the bedroom block, they have to start in the living area. We'll have to tidy up a bit when they finish in the bedroom block, but as soon as the flooring is finished, you will be able to put the bedroom furniture in. The doors will have to be fitted as well, but there isn't much point in being able to use a bedroom though if the living area is uninhabitable."

"What should we do next then to keep the momentum going? We can't do anything in the bedrooms while the electrician and the plumber are working there."

"We'll have to work round them. While they are in the bedroom block, we work in the living area, and we move over there when they move into the house. I think we could get all the boxes of cupboards into the kitchen ready to make up when they've finished in there. The plumber can connect the taps and fit a pipe, tap and waste pipe for the washing machine. The order we do things is up to you though."

"I'm in your hands Ted….."

"A married lady should not say things like that."

"Keep your mind on the work, please Mr Hall," Ross told him with a laugh. "As I was saying before I was so rudely interrupted, you decide which way to work, and I'll be happy to follow your instructions."

Ted thought for a moment, and then said,

"I think we should get all the kitchen cupboards and the work surfaces into the kitchen. When we decide to start work in there, we won't want to be running across to the other block and back again. When the electrician has finished in the second bedroom, we can then fit the underlay. The wooden floor sections can be fitted when the plumber and electrician have finished completely. In the meantime, we need to go and buy some lighting for the ceilings in all the rooms. The electrician has told you how many lights you need, and where he will fit them. I suggest tomorrow, we start moving the kitchen cupboards, and when the electrician and the plumber arrive, we leave them to it and go and buy your lights. While we are there, we can hire a drill ready to start on the living room floor. As you said earlier, we are going to have to work round them for a week or two."

At eight o'clock the following morning, Ross and Ted were opening all the doors ready to start work. They started by taking the worktops from the bedroom block into the kitchen. After the second one was safely taken over, they had a brief rest before tackling the boxes of wall cupboards and the remaining floor units. Ross decided she could carry the smaller boxes, and proved her point by picking up the first box and carrying it out of the door. As she picked up the box, Ted saw something drop off the bottom and onto the floor. He took no notice for the moment, as he picked up the larger box containing a floor cupboard, and followed Ross to the kitchen. As they went back for more boxes, Ted said to Ross,

"Don't go rushing off for a moment, I want to look at something, and before you corrupt the conversation again, it's nothing to do with your body, or mine."

"Why would I think anything like that?" asked Ross in a 'butter wouldn't melt' tone."

Ted smiled as they went inside the building. Reaching the pile of boxes, he bent down and picked up what had fallen from the box Ross had carried. He found some folded papers and thinking they were the fitting instructions, opened them up. He looked at them and his eyes lit up.

"Eureka," he yelled in delight, "Ross, it's the plans for this block and the other."

He took the plans outside into the light so they could read them better. Ross was close behind him as he laid them on one of the pallets of bricks. He examined the floor plan of the bedroom block with interest.

"They were going to use this block as bedrooms," he said, "but nothing like the way we planned it. I'm sure this will interest the plumber though because there is a drain pipe running the full length of the block, and out at the other end, where it joins the drain from the house and into the septic tank. That is going to save a lot of work, especially when we get round to completing the other bedrooms. It will also make it easier for the plumber to fit the waste pipes from all the bathrooms. The problem is though, how does he get to the waste pipe when it's buried under concrete?"

Ross was looking at the plans and running her finger along dividing walls.

"They were making this into three double bedrooms," she said, "one bathroom and a small store room. It's nowhere near as neat and compact as your idea."

"Our idea," Ted said, "I only made suggestions."

"And you've been making them ever since." said Ross with a big smile.

Ted shook his head in disbelief, before saying,

"I don't know why I don't think well ahead before I speak to you. Many years ago, I heard somebody change a well-known phrase into, 'He who laughs last, has found the dirty meaning'. I think that applies to you!"

"I don't always think of a dirty meaning, the remark I just made wasn't dirty, it was an opinion. Shall we get back to these plans? Are these blue lines where the water pipes would have gone?"

"Yes, that's right, but we should leave the plumber to make the decision of the right pipe route."

Ted opened the other set of plans, and looked it over.

"Ross," he said in an amazed voice, "look at this."

"What am I looking at." she said.

Ted pointed to the side view of the house.

"The floor plan shows a step down from the kitchen into the living room. It seems as though the previous owners decided to level the living room floor to that of the kitchen, and stopped when they ran into problems. Why they laid the tiles on top of the slope doesn't make any sense, it would have been better to leave it bare concrete."

"They must have got to a state of panic, and decided to try and cover up their mistakes."

Ted nodded in agreement, then said,

"Talking of cover ups, I can hear a vehicle coming up the hill, so it must be time for one of Ross's famous cover ups."

"Pity really, because I'm getting used to working like

this, and I'm getting a good tan as well, don't you think so?"

Ted smiled, but said nothing in reply.

Ross picked up her T shirt and put it on, before saying,

"What are you smiling at Ted Hall? I'll bet you've thought of a dirty meaning to what I just said."

"Nothing dirty at all Ross." Ted answered.

"Then it must be some silly remark, otherwise you wouldn't be smiling like that. Come on, tell Ross, then we can go and meet the plumber."

"All I was thinking when you mentioned your tan," Ted said "was how well the forbidden fruits were ripening in the sun."

Ross laughed and said,

"Don't you dare start squeezing them to find out how ripe they really are."

"Would I do a thing like that?" asked Ted innocently.

"Given half a chance, Ted Hall, I'm sure you would." Ross replied, walking rapidly towards the plumber as he got out of his van.

The fittings for both bathrooms had been delivered the previous week, and had been placed in the position where Ross wanted them. The plumber had told them the way he was going to work, and would stand the toilet and washbasin on some strips of wood until Ted and Ross were ready to fit the floor.

The electrician was coming the following day to start his work making grooves in the ceilings and walls so he could run wires to each room and to the switches and plugs.

Ted showed the plumber the floor plans he had found, and he in turn was glad to see there was a drain under the flooring. He too wondered how they would get to it, but said that could wait until later that week.

During the drive to Malaga, Ted said to Ross,

"You know, we haven't really discussed the bathrooms. You chose the bath, loo, bidet and wash basin, decided to have the wooden floor that was suitable for bathrooms, but not once have you made any comment regarding the decoration. You decided to paint all the bedroom walls so they could be changed easily if you wanted to, but what about the bathroom walls?"

"You're right, Ted, I hadn't even given it a thought. We can look at some tiles while we are at the store. I don't even know what colour I want, so we'll have to look round and see if anything catches my eye."

"The salesman from the garden furnishings was the last thing I saw that caught your eye." said Ted with a laugh.

"Mmmm," said Ross. "He was rather dishy, but far too young for me and a man like that is sure to be married."

"Or gay!" said Ted. "Or even both." he added as an afterthought.

"You aren't supposed to say things like that Ted Hall, it's not politically correct."

"You know the answer to that, without me saying anything." he said as they pulled into the store's car park.

Over an hour later they emerged pulling a large trolley with a number of boxes of tiles in a nice warm oatmeal colour, enough to do all four bathrooms. Also on the trolley were seven ceiling lamps, four wall lamps, four table lamps, two florescent lights for the kitchen and four double ones for the corridor outside the bedrooms. Ted had also got some more bags of cement, enough, he thought hopefully, to finish the bathrooms and bedrooms and also to fill the grooves in the wall and ceiling that the electrician would be making.

By the end of the week, the electrician had finished his work, and the power was on to both blocks. Ross had also signed the electricity contract, and paid in advance for her meter. Although the lines were connected, the meter would be fitted at a later date by the electricity company, so for the time being, electricity was free! The plumber was finishing off the installation of the solar panels and all being well, he would be finished the following week. All that had to be done was find a way into the drain under the bedroom block. Ted thought they would have to drill through the concrete, but the plumber assured him the pipe would not be buried in concrete before any waste piping was fitted into it. They would work on that together on Monday or Tuesday of the following week.

The plumber had fitted all the pipe work through both of the bathrooms, so Ted decided to finish off the brick work so that they were hidden from sight. Both walls were finished by mid-afternoon and Ted borrowed the plumber's ladder so he could smooth out the grooves the electrician had left in the ceilings and walls. He used special white concrete so there would be no visible lines when it was dry and a second coat of paint on the ceiling would follow at a later date.

The plumber said he would not be working over the weekend, but hopefully everything would be completed by the middle of the following week.

On Saturday morning, Ted and Ross went to the house and had a look round, making notes of the things that had to be done. The hardest work was to finish off the living room and fit the kitchen out. Ted suggested they mix some concrete and finish skimming both bathroom walls, ready for sizing and tiling.

"Remember to be careful with the boards this time Ross, we don't want any more accidents."

"Don't remind me of that," she said, "it was cold and wet and the feeling as it slid off me.... well I can't describe it. Don't worry though, if it happens again, I won't ask you to wash it off me."

"Shame!" said Ted with a grin, "I would have been able to tell you if the forbidden fruit was ripening."

"Ted Hall!" said Ross with what seemed a catch in her voice, "we'll have none of that sort of talk if you don't mind."

Just after lunch time, both walls had been skimmed, and would be dry when they started work on Monday morning. There was quite a considerable amount of concrete left over and Ted was thinking where it could be used.

"Shall we measure the remaining area, divide it in two and lay the base of the last dividing wall? There is enough concrete to do at least the base line of the walls, and we can leave it ready to finish when we want."

Ross agreed with his idea, and two hours later they had finished. Ted pointed out that there were only about a dozen breeze blocks left in the bedroom area, and they would need more when the walls were ready to be finished.

"Aren't there some more on the pallets outside, as well as bricks and balustrades?"

"You are probably right, Ross, I've not paid much attention to the stuff outside, I've concentrated on emptying these pallets in here. It's looking a lot less junked up and there's certainly more room to move around in."

They finished tidying up and made sure everything was clean before locking up for the rest of the weekend.

"Where are you taking me tonight?" Ross asked as they got into the pickup.

"I hadn't got as far as thinking about tonight, Ross. Is

there anywhere you'd like to go?"

"Well we've been to Nerja and seen someone I didn't want to, so is there anything the other way?"

"Yes," Ted answered, "I know there are some smaller villages along the coast, with restaurants right by the sea. Would you like to try one of those?"

"Yes please," Ross answered, "I'd like to go somewhere different for a change. We can have a late siesta at the flat, and then get washed and changed for a night out. It's my treat tonight for the food, and you provide the wine, is that all right with you?"

Ted found a restaurant in one of the small villages which had a 'buffet libre' sign outside. He drove into the car park and asked Ross if she was hungry.

"I am very hungry, Ted. We seemed to have missed a meal today. Does this restaurant serve large portions?"

"The portions are as big as you want them. The sign, 'buffet libre' means 'free buffet'. We pay, I think it is ten or twelve Euros each, and we help ourselves to as much as we want from about thirty or more different dishes. There are salads, cold meats, hot meats, vegetables, potatoes and an abundance of sweet dishes. We pay extra for the drinks, but it's still good value for money."

Ted led Ross inside, and at the desk by the door, they were given a ticket.

"We take the ticket to the bar and they write the price of the drinks on it. When we've finished and ready to leave the restaurant, we hand the ticket in and pay for the food and drink together."

They found a table outside overlooking the sea, and sat down.

"I'll go for the drinks," Ted said, "do you want your usual red wine, or would you like to try something different?"

"Now there's a question to put to a married lady." said Ross, with a wide smile.

"I do try my best to behave while you are around," said Ted, "but it is getting harder…."

He was interrupted by a loud peal of laughter from Ross.

"I don't wish to know that." she said, almost crying from laughing.

Ted walked away and came back with two glasses of red wine. He sat down next to Ross, and she slipped her arm through his and gave him a hug.

"Please don't get upset Ted. I'm in a good mood, and would like to have a laugh. I've not been able to enjoy myself for far too long, and now I have the chance, I want to enjoy it. There are many things I would like to tell you, and I will, one day. Today is not the right time, because when I do tell you about my problems, I will need to be sure I'm doing it for the right reason. The summer is coming to an end, and very soon we'll have to finish work early when it goes dark and cold, so I could sit and tell you my misfortunes then. I know you'll listen to me anytime, but today is too nice to waste, so let's go and get some food, drink a glass or two of wine and have a walk later to digest what we've eaten."

As Ross finished speaking, she kissed Ted softly, and hugged him again.

Over an hour later, they were strolling arm in arm along the Paseo enjoying the last of the evening sunshine. Both had enjoyed their food, but as usual, like anyone who visits a 'buffet libre', they had eaten too much. Ross stopped walking, and made her way to a bench at the side of the Paseo. Ted sat next to her and Ross took hold of his hand.

"Thank you for bringing me here Ted," she said, "the food was quite nice and so was the wine. This little

Paseo is so quiet we could sit here for ages and not see anyone."

She paused, squeezed his hand, and rested her head on his shoulder.

"Ted, there are times when I wish I wasn't married, and today is one of them. I like being with you, and I wish we could have met under different circumstances, because I think you and I could have made a happy couple. Sadly though, I will stick to my marriage vows and remember that legally, I still have a husband."

Ross looked at him as she stopped speaking, leant towards him and gave him a lingering kiss. When she broke, she said in a low, sad voice,

"I don't think I should stay in your apartment anymore."

"Why?" he asked softly, "Because of what you've just said, are you afraid I'll try it on with you?"

"No, Ted," Ross answered, "I trust you, but I'm afraid it might be me who tried it on. The things I've said, Ted, I sincerely hope it won't spoil our friendship."

"No, Ross," Ted replied after a moment's thought, "I think it will strengthen it."

When they got back to the village, Ross collected her things from Ted's apartment and drove back to her own rented house.

Ted spent Sunday cleaning his apartment, doing anything to occupy his time, trying to fathom out what Ross really wanted of him. In his mind, he thought she was hinting she wanted a bit more than friendship, but Ted knew he would not make any move on her while she clung to her beliefs.

Just before seven o'clock, his phone rang. It was Ross asking him if he would like to take her to the Chinese restaurant on the Costa for a meal. Ted agreed, and Ross said she would be outside his apartment in half an hour.

The meal they had together was fine, but the topic of conversation was mostly about her house. On the drive home, Ross apologised for seeming to be distant, but hoped they would still be able to pull each other's legs when they were at work the next day.

Ross was waiting outside his apartment at eight o'clock the next morning, and as Ted got into the pickup, wished her a cheery 'good morning' and lent over and kissed her cheek.

"OK driver," he said, "as fast as you can to the house in the hills, there is work to be done."

Ross smiled at his comment, but didn't say a word during the drive. They went straight to the bedroom block to check the bathroom walls had dried out, ready for the size to be applied. Both had dried perfectly, so they got the sizing powder, mixed it with water, and divided it into two buckets. While it was left to completely hydrate, Ted turned to Ross and said,

"Come here young lady, I want a word with you."

Ross gave him a weak smile, but came to where he stood.

"Rosalinda whatever Smythe-Jones," Ted said, "there is no need to be like this with me. We are two grown up people working together to build you a home to be proud of. On Saturday, you made one or two comments about me and I feel flattered you should think of me that way. Under different circumstances, I would be proud to have you as my partner, but as I've said many times before, I respect your beliefs. We have had many a laugh and enjoyed some days and nights out, and I see no reason why that shouldn't continue. I am not about to leap on you and have my wicked way with you, so please, put your smile back on, and let's do some work. Secretly, I'll be glad when the plumber finishes his work, so I'll be able to see the forbidden fruit again."

Ross put her arms round him and gave him a hug.

"I thought I'd made a fool of myself on Saturday," Ross said, "and you wouldn't want to help me anymore. I was so nervous last night that I could hardly think of anything to say, but today you've put my mind at ease. Thank you Ted, you don't know how much I appreciate that."

They picked up the buckets took a bathroom each and began to cover the walls. Ted had nearly finished his bathroom, when his phone rang. It was the plumber, who was ringing to let them know he would be late because he had been called out on an emergency.

Once the bathroom walls were finished, Ross was wondering what they should do next.

"I think I'll dig the earth up by the door, and see where the waste drain comes from. We may be able to find out how we can get the pipe work fitted into it. While I'm digging, why don't you fold up the tarpaulin and finish the underlay in your room? Afterwards you could sweep the floor and make a start on the underlay in the second bedroom."

Ross agreed with him, and went into her bedroom to start work.

Ted started to dig alongside the wall and the doorway, roughly where the plan showed the drain pipe to be. He had dug down just about a metre when he came to the drain pipe and carefully removed the rock and soil from the top of it. Digging back towards the block wall, he came to the concrete foundations, and found the pipe was not totally buried in the concrete, but in a box like structure with only enough concrete at the bottom to hold the pipe firmly in place. The top cover was a wooden board with about five centimetres of concrete on top. As he was looking at it, Ross appeared in the doorway without her T shirt on.

He told her what he had found, and said how easy it would be to connect the waste pipes once the concrete had been removed. Ross said she was glad the waste pipe problem had been solved and paused for a moment before saying,

"All the work you've been doing Ted Hall has got rid of the belly you had when we started, and there is certainly more muscle on your body."

"Thank you Ross, I do feel a lot fitter then when I began working for you, but I can also return the complement, because I've noticed your little tummy has disappeared and there is firmness around the forbidden fruit."

"I thought you weren't going to keep looking at my breasts."

"I have the occasional peek, just to make sure they aren't getting sunburned." Ted answered.

"You'll say anything to cover up the fact you have been ogling me, I think I may have to sack you."

"Typical," Ted laughed, "I help you to build your house, and as soon as it's nearly finished, you get rid of me. By the way, from where I'm standing, I can see up the leg of your shorts."

"You'll go blind if you're not careful."

"I'll close one eye and wear glasses."

"That's an old joke Ted, and no longer funny. I think you should get out of that hole you've dug for yourself and come and help me with the underlay in the bedroom."

Ted climbed out of the hole and followed Ross inside. He put his arm round her shoulder, and said,

"I'm glad to see you back to your old self again."

"Less of the old, if you don't mind." Ross said, giving Ted a dig in the ribs.

Between them, they cut and fitted the underlay in the

main bedroom, and by the time they had finished, decided it was lunch time. Halfway through eating, Ted's telephone rang again. It was the plumber to tell them he would be with them in an hour, and would work a bit later to make up for what he missed that morning.

"Bang goes our siesta," grumbled Ross.

"Don't worry, Ross, think how much better you'll sleep tonight."

"I didn't sleep very well last night. I was too busy thinking I'd made a fool of myself."

Ted reached over and took hold of her hand.

"Ross, you have done nothing wrong, and as for making a fool of yourself, that is something a person like you cannot do. We've been through different stages of jokes and had many a laugh at ourselves and each other. I know you weren't joking on Saturday, but as we've already said, there is nothing going to happen between us while you stick to your beliefs, we agreed on that long ago. I don't want you to start worrying all over again, so let's continue being good companions."

By Wednesday night, the plumber had finished his work. There was hot and cold water throughout both blocks and the drainage system was working without a problem. One major task they had was to re-lay the concrete down the 'corridor' where they had removed it to fit the waste pipes into the drain.

The following morning, Ted and Ross poured several mixes of concrete into the trench, and levelled it. Once it had set, it would be ready for the tiles to be laid, but that would not be for two or three days.

"Let's sit down for a drink and have a think about what still needs to be done."

They made their way to the loungers and sat down with a bottle of water each.

"Have we anything else we need to buy, Ted?"

114

"Well," he said, "You need two bathroom doors and frames, two bedroom doors and frames, and if this was my house, I'd replace the old doors on the bedroom block with strong plastic or aluminium doors, the top half double glazed."

"You know Ted, I'd never even thought about doors. Let me write this down and we can go to Malaga to buy them and you can fit them at your leisure."

"The floors will have to be finished first," said Ted, "and then we can fit the doors to the correct height above them. I have an idea in my mind, so while we are in the store, I would like to look at some stone that can be used as steps. If I see what I'm looking for, I'll make you a sketch, and if you think it worthwhile, we can get them at the same time. If the floor levelling works as I hope, I think we should look at putting another door from the lounge area into the loo."

"Now that's good thinking. In my mind, I've built a covered pathway from the front door to the toilet. Just as a matter of interest, have you any thoughts about, for want of a better description, the garden area between the two blocks?"

"Not really Ross, because this isn't my house. If it were, there would be no grass area and very little in the way of flower beds. I think I would have a pool in the centre, and balustrades round the whole plot."

"There's no way I'm having grass in that area either, I'm more inclined to think of paving slabs and small stone, but that's not for today's thoughts. Is there anything else we need to be thinking about?"

"Building wise, I don't think so, but before long you will need to be thinking what you are going to put in the rooms in the way of furnishings."

"If you were in charge, how would you work?"

"Firstly I would fill in the hole outside the door. I

think the floors to each room should be laid next, but we can't fit the doors until the tiles are laid down the corridor. It will be two or three days before we can start that. After fitting the bedroom floors, we could make a start drilling out the concrete in the living area."

"Shall we lock up now, and go to Malaga to buy what we need. When have unloaded everything, I suggest, that just for a change, we finish work until Monday morning."

"Sounds good to me Ross. We can leave for Malaga anytime, after you've covered up of course."

"Pass me my T shirt then, I'm sure you're afraid of anyone else seeing your forbidden fruits."

"My forbidden fruits?" said Ted with a laugh.

"Well you know what I mean, it's you that calls them that. Come on, let's go to Malaga before there's any more confusion."

Ross drove the pickup to the store and after collecting a flatbed trolley, went to the section displaying all types of doors. The doors and frames for the bedrooms and bathrooms were relatively easy to choose, but the outer doors were more difficult. Ross eventually found a design she liked, white aluminium with a big square double glazed window.

"Shall we get one for the toilet, just in case you decide to put the doorway inside?" asked Ross.

"No need just now," said Ted, "we can sort that out when we are ready to fit it."

They made their way to a section that had coloured stone pieces that could be used as steps. Ted found some polished cream ones, and told Ross how he envisaged the floor and incorporating the stonework to form a step between the two rooms. Ross thought his idea was brilliant, and after measuring the pieces of stone, worked out how many they needed. He piled them on the trolley and they made for the checkout desks, where Ross used her card again to pay for their goods.

Between them, they carefully loaded the pickup, and once everything was secure, Ross drove back to her house. They off loaded the purchases into the bedroom block, and locked all the doors until Monday morning.

They spent the next three days on the beach lying on sun beds and shaded under a parasol. They ate out every day, and generally enjoyed their break.

SIX

Just after eight o'clock on Monday morning, they were back at the house ready to start work again, refreshed after their days of relaxation. They went into the bedroom block and checked the concrete was ready for them to start setting the tiles. Ted went to the store by the front door, and came back with a couple of boxes.

"Before we start in here, Ross, I need to measure the area accurately, and make sure we have enough tiles to do both the living area and the bedroom corridor. I'm sure there is, area wise, but a lot depends on how much cutting there is to do."

Ted spent quite some time making sure of the measurements of both sections, before he decided they had enough tiles to complete both jobs.

"It will be close," he told Ross, "but we will be able to finish both areas, providing we don't do anything stupid like dropping a box. I thought at one time there would be enough to tile one bedroom as well, but I can see now we haven't."

By late lunchtime, they had laid the tiles just over half way down the 'corridor'.

"We can grout them in a couple of days," Ted said as they made their way to the loungers for lunch and a siesta, "and by the end of the week, we will be able to walk on them."

"How are we going to get into the bedrooms to lay the floor?" asked Ross.

"I was going to open the patio doors to both bedrooms, but forget about it. We will have to wait now until the concrete is dry before we start in the bedrooms. Sorry Ross, that's my fault, put it down to old age and memory loss."

Ross laughed at him and told him he was forgiven,

but only this one time.

After their siesta, they went back to the bedroom block and finished tiling the rest of corridor. Before leaving that night, they decided their next job would be to make a start on the concrete floor in the living area.

Early the following morning, Ted re-measured the floor to make sure they knew exactly where they had to start drilling. Ted started the compressor, and both put ear protectors on to combat the noise. It proved to be hard going, and by their usual finishing time, had made very little progress. Some cracks had appeared, but because the concrete was so thick, it was only coming away in small pieces. Both of them were beginning to despair with the lack of progress, and the next morning, they were dreading having to spend another day without having anything to show for it. It was mid-morning when they started to make an impression, and start to drill out larger chunks of concrete. When the going got easier, Ross took over the drilling, while Ted concentrated on getting rid of the rubble. He put it in the barrow, wheeled it to the corner of the track, and tipped it on top of the old floor and wall tiles. The area was starting to fill nicely and it wouldn't be too long before they were able to make the corner wider.

By the time Ross decided it was time to finish for the day, quite a lot had been removed and a 'step' was clearly visible.

"Let's leave it for today, Ted. I've had enough of this drill, it sends vibrations through me and it has made my breasts sore. It may have been better if I'd worn a bra, but as you are well aware, I haven't worn one for months."

"I had noticed, but you sacked me last week, because you said I was staring at your breasts. When do I have to leave your half built house?"

119

"Didn't I tell you? I've decided to give you a two year trial, and if you repeat the offence too often, you will have to go."

"Thank you Ross, it saves me having to go and sign on while I look for another job."

"Who would employ an old man like you?" Ross asked him with a laugh.

"You!" was Ted's simple answer.

"I must be mad or something." Ross answered, as she locked the door to the house.

"You can get treatment for your form of madness." Ted said.

"What's the treatment for my madness, oh most talented doctor?" Ross asked him.

"Plenty of TLC, pure and simple. It may take a few years to show the results though, and if you stop the treatment, you could revert to the old symptoms again."

"I got no TLC from my husband, but as a companion, you are doing quite well. Do you think I'll be cured in a year or two?"

"Probably not if you stay with me, but while I'm still here, I'll do my best for you."

With that final remark, they got into the pickup and drove home.

It took them another three and a half days to clear and level the earth ready for a new base. For them to re-lay the floor would take many mixes of concrete, so with Ross's permission, Ted contacted a ready mix company and told them what he wanted to do. They suggested he buy some special flooring blocks from them and with the help of an experienced worker, lay metal strengthening over the top of them, and a wagon would then deliver the required amount of concrete, using a chute through the doorway. It should only take two days to complete, but it would take three or four days for the whole floor to set completely. They gave Ted a quote, and Ross accepted, saying if it would save them a lot of time, it would be worthwhile. The company said they could deliver the blocks on Thursday afternoon, and their workman, who would come with the blocks, could start setting the area up on Friday morning. If all went as it should, the concrete would be delivered on Saturday.

"I don't mind paying money for a big job like that," Ross said to Ted, "it would save having to bring everything over from the other block and mix it ourselves."

"I must admit," Ted said, "I hadn't thought about using blocks as the base, it isn't something that is done much in the UK."

As promised, the blocks arrived on Thursday afternoon, and the man who was to help them introduced himself as Juan. He spoke no English, but managed to explain to Ted what was going to happen.

They were at the house early on Friday, and with guidance from Juan, set the blocks and metal on the living room floor. By working steadily, the job was complete by the time they would normally have lunch. Before leaving, Juan said the concrete would be delivered no later than eight thirty the following morning.

They were all there when the wagon arrived, and spent the next two and a half hours doing the back breaking work of dragging concrete over the metal and blocks. They finished levelling the floor just after one o'clock, and Ted and Ross were glad to get back to the apartment and have a rest.

"Where shall we start on Monday?" asked Ross as they tucked into the meal that night.

"Grouting the floor tiles in the bedroom block." Ted answered immediately. "We let it dry out properly, and in the meantime we start the tiling in the living area."

"We are starting to see the light at the end of the tunnel, aren't we?" Ross asked. "It's taken less time than I thought, but I know there is no way I could have done this without your help. I would have had to get in builders, and they would have done it their way, not wanting to take instructions from a woman. The clocks go back at the end of October, so that means short days, and long cooler nights. I met you just after the clock went forward, so that's seven months of hard graft together. How much longer do you reckon now Ted?"

"Grout the bedroom area on Monday morning, and start the tiling in the living area when that's finished. It will take at least a week to complete, so I think in another four weeks, you could be ordering your furnishings. Do you want me to help you with the jungle between the two blocks?"

"Yes, please Ted, but let's concentrate on the next few days."

When they arrived at the house on Monday morning, the first thing they did was check the living area. The concrete had dried perfectly, and they could clearly see two tiers of level floor.

"This will look nice with the tiles down." said Ted, "A nice patterned fawn tile with a cream step dividing the two sections. Before we lay the tiles, I think a quick paint over the walls and ceiling would make a difference. The dust we made from the drilling has dulled it a bit. It won't take long if we both do it. I'll bet we could finish it in less than a day.

"That's a good idea Ted, we can go and buy some paint later when we've finish the grouting."

The grouting of the corridor took less time than they thought, so just before lunch, drove to the village and bought enough paint to do the lounge, and give the bedrooms two coats. As well as paint, they bought some brushes and two rollers with extending handles.

Back at the villa, they swept the window sills clear of dust, and when Ross said it was clean, they started on the ceiling. Ted was doing one half of the room, and Ross started on the other, and they had the ceiling and two walls painted when Ross decided it was lunch time. Sitting on the loungers while they ate, Ross said she thought it was getting near to the time for her to cover up for the winter, but promised she would reveal her assets again when she felt the sun was warm enough.

They ended the afternoon by finishing the walls in the lounge and giving the walls in the loo a once over.

On Tuesday morning, they made preparations to begin the floor tiling in the living area by bringing all the boxes of tiles inside. To check how much cutting there may be, Ted laid a single row of tiles across the wall that backed onto the kitchen. He completed the row, stood up and turned to Ross.

"Look at this" he fumed, pointing at the floor, "a bloody centimetre short. If we have to cut a centimetre off a tile to fill the gap, there's going to be a hell of a lot of waste."

He was stood by the wall, hands on hips, feeling extremely agitated. This was the one of the few problems they had come up against in the whole project.

"What's the alternative?" Ross asked him.

"Can I make a suggestion?" he asked.

"Yes please." Ross replied, slipping her arm through his.

Ted couldn't help but smile at the way she spoke, so he shook his head and said,

"If I made the suggestion you are inferring, you'd run a mile."

"I wouldn't! I'm not a very good runner, and I know

you would catch me after about fifteen metres, so to save energy, I wouldn't set off."

Ted laughed, kissed her on the forehead, and said,

"You are getting as daft as me, you know that."

Ross just smiled, and asked what suggestion he was going to make.

"I'm certain we could find a skirting tile that will match or complement the colour of floor tiles. I don't know if you've noticed, they are all round the walls in my apartment. They are one centimetre thick, so if I set the edge tiles half a centimetre in from the wall, when we put the skirting tile on, it will cover the gap."

"You aren't as daft as you pretend to be, are you? Perhaps it's a good job though. Nice thinking Ted, so let's get sorted. How are you going to measure half a centimetre from the wall?"

"We could buy a pack of plastic spacers and cut them to size. I can put a couple of pieces against the wall, and butt the tile to them. Two other spacers would fit in at the other side."

Ross thought it was a good idea, so they drove down to the tile shop in the village.

She bought two large packs of spacers, and had a look at the designs for the skirting tile. They had brought a tile with them to make sure they would match, and after much searching, Ross found the ones she wanted. She checked with Ted how many they would need.

"We need eight boxes for the living room and three for the corridor in the bedroom block."

He gave the shop owner the order, and Ross paid for it with her seemingly bottomless credit card.

They were told they would be at the shop the following week, and would be left outside the store with Ross's name on ready for them to pick up.

Back at the house, they worked together cutting the

spacers to the right size before making a start on the tiling. Ted tried a row without any adhesive, and as he put the last tile in place, turned to Ross, and said it worked a treat.

A bag of tile adhesive was mixed, and Ted was ready to start the first row. He had to spread the adhesive slightly thicker than normal to make sure the tiles were the same height through the door as the ones in the kitchen. They took turns in mixing, laying and levelling, but it was taking much longer to do than they anticipated. They had only laid four rows by lunch time, and Ross asked Ted why it seemed to be taking so long.

"Probably because we have to use thicker adhesive, and mix more than usual. It also takes longer to make sure all the tiles are level and square, but when we do the lower section, we won't need to use as much and therefore shouldn't take as long."

When they finished for the night, less than half of the top part was complete. Ross said she was happy with the results, and Ted got a kiss for his work. Both of them were starting to wonder when they would finish the renovations. The end was in sight, but the days seemed to be dragging on, and some jobs appeared to be no nearer finishing. Ross thought that part of the problem was that the days were shorter, and they had to finish before it got too dark to see what they were doing. The next morning they started again in the living room and by lunch time, they had almost reached the step.

They went outside into the sunshine, which was still warm enough for them to sit on the loungers without tops on. They set them up without the parasol and sat down together to eat. Half an hour later the food was gone and they lay back for a rest. Both had their eyes closed, neither asleep nor fully awake, when Ross, almost in a whisper, said,

"Ted?"

"I'm still here." he replied.

Ross didn't say anything else, so Ted turned his head to look at her. Their loungers were close to each other so he could see her very clearly. She still had her eyes closed, and looked slightly flushed. He was about to speak, but thought that if she wanted to say anything, she would do in her own time. He turned his head back, and as he did, glanced down her body. It was then he noticed her nipples. He had never seen them quite like that before. They were very swollen and extended, as though Ross was ready for sex. He turned away, still waiting for Ross to speak again.

A minute or so later, she said again,

"Ted?"

As she spoke, she reached over and ran her hand lightly along his arm.

"I've not moved away," answered Ted, turning his head towards her, "do you want to say something?"

"Yes, but I'm embarrassed to ask." she replied.

"You should know by now Ross, there's no need to be embarrassed when you talk to me."

Ross turned her head towards him, looked into his eyes and said, almost in a whisper,

"Ted.... you've never said anything about it, but.... but.... what *are* your feelings.... for me?"

"Ross," he replied slowly, "you are a married lady, and therefore I'm not allowed to have feelings for you."

Ted noticed a change in her expression as he said that, so quickly carried on by saying,

"But I can assure you that if you weren't married, I would have confessed my feelings weeks ago, especially with you lying next to me undressed like you are."

Ross smiled, and said,

"The feeling's mutual."

"Are you trying to tell me something?" he asked.

"Believe it or not, I'm feeling rather…. randy, and I can assure you I've not felt like this for many years. Like I said when we were at the 'buffet libre', if it wasn't for my belief of not committing adultery, I'd certainly be making a play for you."

Ted turned on his side facing Ross, and took hold of her hand.

"Now then, randy Ross," he said, "what's brought all this on then?"

"I'm not sure exactly why," Ross replied, "well I am sure, because as a woman with normal feelings, I've got to admit that I do rather fancy you, and have done for quite some time. Reluctantly though, I've to stuck to my beliefs."

Ted was still holding her hand, gave it a squeeze, smiled and said,

"Thank you for that bit of flattery, but as we've stated previously, if things were different, and we were both single, then I would be… err… how can I put it?"

"Wanting to give me more than just a good night kiss?" asked Ross with a smile

"I would definitely want to give you more than just a kiss Ross." Ted answered quietly.

He lifted her hand to his lips, kissed her fingers, and said,

"Ross, I think you are a lovely lady, and I do admire the way you admit your feelings, but still honour your belief regarding adultery. Do you mind if I ask you a question about your thoughts on adultery?"

"You can ask me anything you like." answered Ross, turning on her side to face Ted.

Now there were two people facing each other, holding hands and their faces only inches apart. Ted could not help himself, he leaned forwards and gave

Ross a gentle lingering kiss.

"Ross" he said quietly, "what is your understanding of adultery?"

"When two people have sex, and one or both are married to somebody else." was her immediate answer.

Ted nodded, and then asked,

"Have you used a dictionary to check on the definition of adultery?"

"No, I've just accepted the meaning the way others talk about it. I've never really needed to go into detail." Ross answered.

"If you look in the 'Collins Oxford Dictionary' for their definition, you would find it says, 'Voluntary sexual intercourse of married persons other than with their spouse'. If you then look for 'sexual intercourse', you will see it defined as 'insertion of a man's penis into a woman's vagina'."

Ross was silent for a moment, then said,

"I obviously understand what you're saying, but am I missing something?"

"A few minutes ago, you told me you were feeling randy." Ted said.

"Yes, and I still am." Ross replied.

Ted gave Ross another lingering kiss, and then said,

"I often feel like that as well, but to get rid of our feelings, do we need to have intercourse? I believe, using the definition from the dictionary, that if we lie here on these loungers, kissing and cuddling and then go on to give each other a screaming orgasm without me putting my penis into you, we are not committing adultery."

Ted gave her slightly longer kiss, looked into her eyes and said, huskily,

"Would you like a screaming orgasm?"

Ross hesitated for a moment, before taking his hand and placing it on her breast, making sure he was touching her nipple.

"Start there, and the way I'm feeling right now, I could have a screaming orgasm long before you get anywhere near me down there."

Ted started to stroke her nipples very lightly with the end of his fingers, and within minutes, Ross was moaning on to his shoulder and moving her body against his.

"Touch me down there, please Ted," Ross whispered urgently, pushing his hand downwards.

"I can't get to you if you have your shorts and briefs on." he said, reaching for the button and zip.

"I want you in my hand," Ross told him, "so let's both get naked."

They both took their shorts off, Ted removing his underpants with his shorts, but Ross still had her briefs on as Ted looked at her and said,

"You're only supposed to wear white to show purity."

"In that case," Ross answered, "I'll have to start wearing black ones, because at the moment, my thoughts are a long way from pure."

She stood up, slid her briefs down, sat back on the lounger and turned towards Ted. She reached out for him, pulled him closer to her body, and took him in her hand. She started to move her hand quickly on him, and Ted, with one hand on her breast, reached down to her open thighs and found she was more than ready for his touch. The rhythm he used matched Ross's movement on him, and very soon, Ted felt the old familiar build up inside him, a feeling that any man receiving this type of pleasure from a woman knows.

"If you keep doing it at that speed," he gasped, "you're going to get it all over your tummy."

"I don't care where I get it," Ross moaned, "as long

as I come as well. Don't you dare stop, Ted, I'm…"

Ross let out a long, low moan, and increased the speed of her hand.

Ted couldn't hold back any longer and cried out loud as he released himself. As soon as Ross felt it, she shuddered and pushed herself against him.

"Keep going," she gasped.

Ted did as he was asked, and seconds later, Ross cried,

"It's here…. it's here, ohh, ohh, Ted, Ted, ohh, Ted it's happened…. Ted…. Ted…. ooohh Ted…. I've come."

"You sound surprised." whispered Ted as she squeezed him closer to her.

Ross looked at him, and gasped,

"I am by the strength of it. I was certainly ready for that Ted. It's been a bloody long time, many years in fact, since I had an orgasm like that and I hope I won't have to wait as long for another one. Let's lie together, like we were before I seduced you."

Ted grinned, and said,

"I thought our seduction was by mutual agreement."

He sat up and handed Ross one of his old towels to wipe her tummy and thigh, and when she was cleaner, they lay down facing each other again, but this time their bodies were touching.

"I'd like a nice long, passionate after orgasm kiss." whispered Ross.

They put their arms around each other, and started to kiss, a long, passionate one, followed by short pecks, then more long ones. After a while, Ross started moving her lower body against him.

"Are you ready for starting again?" he whispered.

"Not really," Ross replied, "I just want to get as close as possible to you."

"Get any closer, and we will be committing adultery."

"I don't think I care now. After that little session, I'm ready for anything you offer."

"Tell me that again when you've had time to cool off." Ted answered.

"Do you think I'm going to forget what I had in my hand, and what happened? Are you telling me you didn't enjoy it, and you wouldn't want it again?"

"Ross, I enjoyed every second of it, and I'll be more than happy to enjoy it as often as you like, but think hard before you abandon your beliefs. Once broken, you can never go back."

"I know what you're saying to me," said Ross, "and I understand your concern, but are you going to lie there naked, and after what we just did, turn me down if I offered my body completely to you."

Ted looked Ross in the eye, and said, in a soft voice,

"If you were serious about it, there's no way I'd turn you down. You are a lovely lady, have a fantastic body, and I have a great deal of feeling for you. By making love to you would show how much I care, and I'd be a fool if I turned you down. At the same time, if you don't want to make love and we feel the need, we can satisfy each other the way we just have."

"Yes we can, but if I offered myself to you, I hope you wouldn't turn me down. I told you a few minutes ago I fancied you, and if I change my mind about adultery, you'd better watch out." Ross smiled as she spoke, then she turned serious, and said in a very quiet voice,

"Ted, the other Sunday, I said I wanted to tell you something. I've wanted to tell you for some time, but there hasn't really been a right moment, but I think it is the right moment now. Forget work for this afternoon,

131

let's lie here together, and let me talk to you. I want you to know who I am and some of the reasons I'm here in Spain. I need to tell you because I've expressed my feelings for you, and if we should decide to become more than work mates and good companions, I think you need to know some of my secret past."

Ross relaxed against Ted's body, and with her arm round his waist, started to tell him about her life before coming to Spain.

"As you know, my name is Rosalinda, but that's not half of it. Don't laugh please, because I'm going to reveal my worst nightmare. My full name is Rosalinda Abigail Penelope Delores. Until the age of eleven, my surname was Critchley. I was going on for nine when mum and dad divorced, but a year later, mum met another guy, and they got along famously, so decided to get married. My mum is a bit of a snob, because her parents were well off, and owned a huge publishing company. The man she wanted to marry was called 'Smith', but that was too common for her, and she told him, that if they were going to be married, he would have to change the 'Smith' into 'Smythe', making sure the 'y' sounded like 'aye' instead of an 'i'. To make things more complicated, she decided to hyphenate her name to 'Critchley-Smythe'. Sometime after they got married I was officially adopted and they changed my name as well, making me 'Rosalinda Abigail Penelope Delores Critchley-Smythe'. They were married for only five years, when my step-father suffered a heart attack after seeing a serious road accident while on his way home from work. Mum and I struggled on, but a month or so after his death, mum was contacted by an insurance company. Unknown to her, her husband had taken out a policy with them, and she was entitled to a monthly payment for the rest of her life. It helped us to continue a comfortable living.

Not long after my seventeenth birthday, I started to go out with a lad. Things were getting serious between us, and sex started to become a regular thing when we were together. I was a virgin, although I'd had some sexual experience. I'd, well, you know, done it with my hand to several lads, and most of them had their hands in my knickers as I did it. I had a few orgasms, generally enjoyed the pleasure, but had no real desire to go any further. He started to pester me to go all the way and eventually, after a lot of persuasion, I relented, and let him make love to me. I insisted he wear a condom, and left him in no doubt whatsoever that whenever we had sex he wore a condom, as I told him, 'no condom, no sex'. I don't know what I was expecting, but having sex... no... having intercourse with him left me feeling flat. The foreplay was quite good, but once he was inside me and started moving, I had very little sensation, just feeling short hard thing moving in and out of me. It didn't last long before he'd... you know.... had a climax and that was it. I was starting to think 'what's this big thing about..."

Ross stopped for a second, and said to Ted

"Do you mind if I call it 'shagging', it sounds less clinical?"

"If that's the word you want to use, it's all right with me." Ted replied.

"Good!" said Ross. "Now, what was I telling you?"

"Yes... shagging and no big deal. Brian was a persuasive person, and I fell for his charming words. Consequently I let him have sex with me more often than I really wanted to. On the occasions we didn't...

shag, and just played with each other, it was good, because at least I did have an org…. he made me come. We'd been together for well over a year, when we were invited to the wedding of one of his mates. It was in another town, some distance from where we lived and to avoid having to drive home, he booked two rooms at the hotel where the reception was being held. That night, we got pissed out of our minds, well I did anyway, and at the end of the party, I remember us going up to the bedrooms, and Brian holding me against the wall as he opened the door. He led me inside, sat me on the bed and I asked him to undo the zip at the back of my dress. He helped me to take the dress off and he actually hung it up in the wardrobe. I was still sat on the edge of the bed as he put it away, but then fell back, almost passing out. I felt him pull my tights off, then my thong, but couldn't believe it when a few seconds later I felt him open my legs wide and start to enter me. I could tell, even in my drunken state that he had no condom on. 'No, please Brian…' I managed to say, but he was doing it that fast there was no way he was going to stop. I don't remember any more until I awoke with a splitting headache, lying on the edge of the bed, feet on the floor and my legs spread wide open. I felt something down there and I knew immediately what it was, as the memory of the previous night came flooding back. The bastard had taken advantage of me being drunk and hadn't even the decency to put me into bed afterwards, just left me there, wearing only my bra. When I asked him about it later, he pretended not to remember if he did it, because he said he was drunk as well. To make matters worse, as I found out two months later, he'd got me pregnant.

Of course my mother was furious, and called him a callous gold digging prat, and he had done it on purpose so he could get hold of some of the families' money to help his ailing business. Looking back on what mother said, she was probably right. Of course, we had to get married, my mother insisting it was the right thing to do, so when it came to the final arrangements, mother took charge again. Brian's surname is Jones....'

"Don't you bloody laugh Ted Hall, it's not funny."

"Sorry Ross," laughed Ted, "it's just that there is no way I'm going to try and keep up with the Smith's and the Jones's."

Ross smiled at Ted's words, and then said,

"It is funny really isn't it, well it is now, but it wasn't at the time. Mother demanded the other names stayed, and a hyphenated Jones was tacked on at the end. So I became, and still am, Mrs Rosalinda Abigail Penelope Delores Critchley-Smythe-Jones. What a bloody handle!"

Ross stopped talking, moved closer to Ted and gave him a passionate kiss.

"Am I boring you?" she asked.

"Not in the slightest," he answered, "just don't think of asking me to marry you so you can have another name to add to your list. Just imagine, Rosalinda Abigail Penelope Delores Critchley-Smythe-Jones-Hall. That would be a handle to remember, or forget, as the case maybe."

"I don't think there is any way that you and I could ever be married." said Ross, with pure hatred her voice. "I know there's not a chance of me ever getting a divorce, so I'll never be free of him until the bastard snuffs it."

She reached out, and ran her hand down the side of Ted's face, and whispered,

"Ted, I need to tell you this, all of it, but I'm afraid

much of the next part is not pleasant. If you've heard enough, tell me and I'll stop, I don't want to bore or annoy you."

"Ross," said Ted "I want to know everything about you, good or bad. As long as you are not in Spain because you have committed murder, I'm with you all the way."

"I've not actually committed a murder," Ross whispered, "but I've thought about it many, many times. Let me continue with my story, and then you'll understand what I mean. Right, where was I?"

"Getting married." prompted Ted.

"We were married at the beginning of October, and the wedding day was a shambles! All of Brian's so called mates were there, and at the reception they had so much to drink they almost caused a riot and the hotel manager called the police because he was afraid they might cause some damage. The police managed to calm things down, but the party mood was gone and the other guests started to disappear quickly, leaving Brian and his mates trying to drink the hotel dry. Needless to say, Brian was so pissed he had to be carried to the hotel bedroom by the best man and his cousin.

Our marriage was not consummated that night!

He could only afford to take me on a short honeymoon, which wasn't due to start until Monday, so we spent Sunday night in my bedroom at home. He suffered a hangover all day Sunday, so we didn't have sex then either.

On Monday morning, he took me to some God forsaken, cold and windswept northern resort called Blackpool..."

"Watch it," Ted interrupted, "that's home territory,

136

and I'll have nothing said against it. Although I agree it often is God forsaken, and a cold and windswept place."

Ross nodded and smiled in agreement with him.

"Those five days were hell. It rained or blew a gale, and Brian didn't want to go out anywhere, he spent most of his time drinking pints of beer, while watching sport on the television. By the time we got back home at the end of the week, we'd had sex once. All the time we were 'courting' he wanted plenty of sex, now we were married he hardly seemed to want any. My grandparents live in an old mansion house, surrounded by a wall, and the only way into the estate is through some big iron gates. By the side of the gates, is 'the lodge', and they gave Brian and me the opportunity to set it up as our home. He'd jumped at the chance because it was what he referred to as a 'freebie' and it would save him money not having to save up and buy a house of our own. The weekend we returned from our honeymoon was spent shopping and sorting our new home out. On the Monday, Brian went back to his carpet fitting business, and I carried on working at the publishing house with my family. That week, Brian wanted a lot more sex than the previous one. If I remember rightly, we had sex on four of the seven nights, so he was happy. On Monday of the second week, Brian arrived home later than usual and smelled of beer. When I asked him about it, his answer was that he needed a drink after work, because carpet fitting was a dusty job, and the beer washed the dust away. He told me that before we were married, he went for a drink or two every night after he finished work, and being married was not going to stop him. It was then that I realized he was a habitual drinker. I'm not saying he was an alcoholic, but he certainly liked a few pints on a regular basis. When we were courting, Friday was his night out with the lads, and he made it perfectly clear that this was not going to stop either just because he had got married."

Ross stopped talking, sat up, and was staring into the distance, as though recalling those events. She sat still for a few minutes, lost in her own thoughts, and when she turned back to Ted, she was crying. She lay down by his side, put her arms round him, and let her tears flow. Ted held her close to him until he felt her tears subsiding. Ross was still in his arms, when she looked at him and smiled.

"Sorry about that." she sniffed.

"Nothing to be sorry about." Ted replied.

"Thank you, that's a nice thing to say." She whispered.

Her expression changed as she moved closer to Ted.

"Look after me, Ted." Ross asked softly.

"That's a strange thing to say." Ted answered. He looked into her eyes, and could see she was afraid of something.

"What is it?" he asked softly.

"Look after me, please." Ross repeated.

Ted took her tear streaked face in his hands, and whispered,

"Ross love, if that's what you want me to do, I'll look after you to the best of my ability for as long as I possibly can."

"Thank you Ted, that's what I wanted to hear you say."

Ross kissed him, and said,

"This is where things get a bit horrific."

"You don't have to carry on now, save it until tomorrow or the next day if you'd rather." he said.

"No", Ross said, "I've got to keep going for a bit

longer, let me get the next bits over with, then I'll stop for today. We can have part two another day."

"Are you sure?" he asked.

Ross nodded, took a deep breath, and carried on:

"We had been married for about two months, making me just over five months pregnant. One particular Friday night, Brian came home later and more drunk than usual. He staggered in through the door, and saw me watching the telly.

'Oi!' he shouted, 'where's my fucking tea. Don't sit watching that thing, get my tea made.' I told him he'd had his tea before he went out, but if he wanted something to eat, I'd make it for him. I got up to go to the kitchen, when he put his face right in front of me, and said, 'don't you come the smarty bitch with me. I've just finished work, had a few drinks, and now I want my fucking tea'. He was waving his arms around, and caught me on the breast as he stepped back. Being pregnant, that hurt more than it normally would. 'Careful,' I told him, 'that hurt.'

He turned back to me, and snarled 'don't you speak to me like that, who the fuck do you think you are. You are my wife, and you do as I tell you.' He slapped me on the top of my arm, and before I could say anything, he did it again on the other arm. I tried to turn away, but he grabbed my arm and shouted, 'don't you walk away from me when I'm talking to you.' He pulled me back towards him and gave me several hard slaps around my body. He stood looking at me, breathing heavily, and said,

'Bollocks to food, I'm going to bed.'

I was shaken..., no Ted..., I was terrified by what had just happened. We'd been married for two months without a problem, and suddenly out of the blue, Brian's

139

a different person.

Later, when I decided it was safe for me to go to bed, I was relieved to see Brian had managed to undress and get into the bed without any problem. He was snoring his head off, and an earthquake would not have fully woken him. I undressed, got into bed, gave him a nudge, and told him to turn over and stop snoring. He turned over, and as he moved, accidentally pushed his elbow into my stomach, muttering about self-righteous bitches not knowing their place. Eventually I managed to fall asleep, but was wakened sometime later with the most horrendous pain in my womb. I screamed at Brian to get a doctor, but he refused to wake up, no matter how hard I prodded him. He kept telling me to go back to sleep and leave him alone. I had another spasm, and then felt something between my legs. It was blood! I screamed again at Brian, but it was no use, he was dead to the world. I dragged myself out of bed and managed to crawl to the telephone, and call an ambulance. They were there quickly, and around fifteen minutes later, I was in the hospital. The doctors sent the police to the cottage to get Brian, but even they couldn't waken him. While the police were trying to wake my husband Ted, I lost my baby! The next night at visiting time, mum and my granddad came to see me, saying how sad they were at my loss, but strangely I felt relieved. Brian never came to the hospital once during the week I was there. They released me on a Friday afternoon and I had to make my own way home, finding the cottage cold and empty when I walked in. I realized that being Friday, Brian would already be out with his mates. He got back well after midnight, drunk as usual and when he saw me sitting by the fire, snarled 'Oh, you're fucking home at last are you.'

It was soon after that the beatings started again."

Ted put both his arms round Ross as she sobbed, pulled her gently to him and said,

"That's enough for today Ross, no more now, no more, you hear me?"

Ross nodded against his chest. They stayed like that for some time, until Ross looked up and said,

"There's a lot more to tell you, but as you say, not now."

Ted kissed her passionately then said,

"Ross, I know why you want me to look after you."

She smiled, and he could see the relief in her eyes.

"Let's go home," she said "I need a strong drink, some food, and then maybe a nice long cuddle."

They got dressed, tidied up the area where they had been working, locked all doors and got in the pickup. Ross drove to her little house first, and said,

"I'm nipping in for a change of clothes, and then we can go to your place to shower and dress ready for going out. I know you have a meal sorted for us, but as a special treat I'd like to take you for a meal at a nice restaurant of your choice."

She went into the house, and was back out a few minutes later carrying a large plastic shopping bag. As she got into the pickup, she put the plastic bag on Ted's knee, and with a smile, said,

"All my worldly goods I thee endow."

Ted looked at Ross, to see if he could tell if she was joking.

"I'm not kidding, well, almost not kidding," Ross said, "I'll explain in a minute when we get into your place."

A few minutes later, they were in Ted's apartment.

"Do you want a brew?" he asked.

"Not now," said Ross, "let's get showered and go out for some food. For some reason, I'm bloody starving."

"I don't know why that should be," said Ted, "you've done nothing all afternoon."

"If doing the nothing I did this afternoon affects me like this, I'm going to do the same nothing tomorrow." she laughed.

"What's this about worldly goods then?" Ted asked.

Ross turned to Ted, and put her arms round his waist. His immediate reaction was to put his arms round Ross, and hold her close.

"This is part of the story you haven't heard yet," said Ross, "but when I came over to Spain, I was in a desperate rush. All I brought with me is one dress, which is in that bag, three pairs of jeans, two T shirts, two bra's, two pairs of trainers, one pair of good shoes, the red shirt, my denim jacket and five pairs of briefs. Usually, when I get back home after our meal, I have a shower, dry myself on a spare sheet because I have no towels, and get dressed in the clothes I'm going to wear the next day. I wash my briefs and sometimes my bra while I'm in the shower, and hang them to dry on the towel rail. When I go to bed, I just take off my T shirt and jeans and sleep like that. I have no night clothes, and during the summer I shouldn't need any, but that house gets hardly any sun, and consequently can be quite chilly at night."

"We have been working together for nearly six months," Ted said, "and this is the first time you've said anything about your lack of clothes. Why didn't you say something sooner?"

"I was embarrassed to tell you about it." Ross replied. "I have plenty of money to buy things, but we've been so busy, I've just not got round to it."

"I think," mused Ted, "we should take all day off tomorrow. We tentatively agreed to go and look for your new bed tomorrow afternoon, but if we get away earlier, you could do some clothes shopping. If you have more things to wear, you can bring your clothes here whenever they need washing, and they can go in the machine with mine. You can take a couple of my towels with you when you go back, they'll be better than a sheet to dry yourself on."

"I'm all for shopping for clothes." replied Ross enthusiastically. "But, that's for tomorrow. Now I have an important question to ask you. Can we have a nice shower together?"

"It does save water," agreed Ted, "so why not, after all I made a mess on you, and the least I can do in return is clean it off."

Ross nodded, then in an almost shy, quiet voice, said,

"I've never had anyone wash me before, and I'd like you to wash me all over from head to toe. It will help me imagine you are washing away my past. Would you like to do that for me?"

"I would like very much to wash your troubles away," Ted replied, "but will you to promise to behave yourself."

"I'll only promise to behave in the shower, if you let me spend the night with you."

"That's blackmail," laughed Ted, "but I'll agree. Let me turn the shower on, and then we can make a start."

They spent a happy twenty minutes or so washing each other, having a laugh and now they were washed clean, and dressed ready for a night out at a restaurant that Ted knew served good food. Ross wore a light green dress which showed her figure off nicely. It had a square neck, and showed just enough cleavage to be interesting, and ended fractionally below her knees. When they had finished dressing, Ted took one look at Ross, and said,

"You look absolutely delicious. I'll be more than proud to be seen out with you tonight."

"Thank you," said Ross, and actually blushed. "I don't think I've ever been called delicious before. It's a long time since I had a complement paid to me, they have been a bit thin, no... barren for the past twenty odd years, and I'm not used to them."

"Shall we go? I'm taking you to a restaurant right on the beach, so after we've eaten, we can if you like, take a stroll along the shore in the moonlight."

"I'd love a moonlight walk with you, you old romantic," answered Ross, "Do you know I almost feel like a teenager out on her first date?"

"Well we're not teenagers anymore, but this is our first proper date," said Ted "the first of many, I hope."

Ross smiled, nodded, took his arm, and led him to the door. They drove down to the shore and found the restaurant was reasonably busy, but they were shown to a table within a few minutes of arriving. While they were looking at the menu, Ross told Ted he could choose what he wanted, and reminded him she was paying.

"I suggest we do our usual deal," said Ted, "You pay for the food and I'll pay for the wine. I've just read the wine list, and there's a reasonably priced Rioja on it."

"That sounds good to me." said Ross "Please excuse my ignorance, but what exactly is Rioja. I've heard people talking about it, but that is as much as I know."

"To many people," said Ted "Rioja is the best red wine in the world. To me, it certainly is one of the best Spanish reds. If you like it tonight, I may buy a few bottles to drink at home."

"Whose home?" laughed Ross.

"Both!" Ted replied firmly.

As they looked over the menu, trying to decide what they wanted, Ted quietly said to Ross,

"Did you mean what you said, about spending the night with me?"

"Of course! You're not trying to back out are you?"

"Not in the slightest," he replied, "it's just that I fancy Prawns Pil-Pil, and I wondered if you objected to the smell of garlic, that's all."

"I've no objections at all. There are things on this menu that sound rather strange, so I'll try them another day. I do like prawns, so what's the 'Pil-Pil' bit?"

"Prawns Pil-Pil," said Ted "is served in a round terra cotta dish, a flat base and about an inch deep. In it, there are prawns, pieces of garlic, green pepper, and chilli, all boiled together in olive oil. It's served sizzling hot with lots of bread to mop up the juice."

"It sound delicious," said Ross. "Is it a very strong garlic flavour?"

"Usually," answered Ted, "that's why I asked for your approval. It can also be quite hot, depending on the amount of chilli they use."

"Then that's for me as well." she said with conviction.

To follow their prawns, they both decided to have a steak for their main course, washed down with the excellent bottle of Rioja. Ross said she was surprised as to how nice the wine was, and said that even though she had drunk wine with her grand-parents and her mother, she could not remember enjoying one that good.

It took them over an hour and a half to finish their meal, and after paying the bill, they took the promised stroll along the beach. They didn't say much, just slowly walked with their arms round each other, enjoying the warm breeze off the sea.

They had been walking for quite some time, when they reached some rocks that prevented them going any further, so they turned round and headed back the way they had come. On the drive home Ross held Ted's hand, even while he was changing gear, and held it firmly until they got inside Ted's apartment. Ted asked Ross if she wanted a drink but she said 'no' and made her way to the bedroom, pulling Ted with her. She was undressed first and flopped on top of the bed.

"I'm shattered," she said, "I feel as if I could sleep for a week."

"Not a chance." answered Ted, "If we are going shopping tomorrow, I'll have the coffee made by six o'clock."

"You can have one at six if you want," Ross answered, getting under the sheet, "I'll wait until at least eight."

"Giving me orders already are you?"

"Yes. Now get into this bed, I need a few kisses before I get my beauty sleep."

Ted got into bed, switched off the light, turned on his side facing Ross and said,

"Thank you for taking me out tonight, I really enjoyed it. You looked like a million dollars, so good in fact I'm hoping I can take you out more often. I cannot believe my luck, only twelve hours ago we were laying tiles, and now here you are in my bed. I have to confess, I've thought of you many nights recently, wishing you were here with me."

"I've wished that as well." Ross said "I know I stayed when I wasn't well, but that wasn't the same as this. We've worked well together since the day we met and I showed you the house. I didn't think at the time you would spend so much time with me, but I'm glad I was wrong. I've grown to trust you, and now… well I feel as if we've been together for many years. I wish I could have met you twenty five years ago."

"I was married." answered Ted.

"We would have to have committed adultery then," joked Ross. "I think it's time we got some sleep, because

I'm feeling tired, but we can reminisce again tomorrow."

They spent the next few minutes kissing and cuddling each other, both thinking they had suddenly found happiness, and fell asleep still holding one another.

Next morning, Ted awoke before Ross, and as usual, the first thing he did was to switch on the coffee machine. He filled two large cups, and took them back to the bedroom. "Here you are," he said, "one cup of coffee just how you like it."

"What's all this, breakfast in bed." said Ross sitting up, "I could get used to this attention."

"You will, my love," he replied, handing her the coffee mug "you will."

Ted put his mug down on his side of the bed, and went into the bathroom. He filled the bowl with hot water, and started to shave.

"Are you getting washed and dressed?" Ross shouted to him.

"I'm having a shave," Ted answered, "you don't want to be kissed by a sheet of sandpaper, do you?"

"No thank you. I think I'll use the other bathroom, and then lie here on your bed, waiting in anticipation."

Ten minutes later they were testing the closeness of Ted's shave and Ross gave it a high rating. When they broke for some air, they took a few minutes to finish their now nearly cold coffee.

They lay back on the bed, and rolled into each other's arms again.

"I like this." whispered Ross.

"So do I." answered Ted.

"I can tell that." Ross said with a grin.

"It's your fault, lying there naked and looking so seductive." said Ted.

"Would you like me to give you a repeat performance?" Ross asked, moving her hand down towards him.

"Only if you want the same." he replied.

"I am a bit turned on, but not the way I felt yesterday."

"In that case, we'll wait." said Ted.

He pulled her closer to him, looked Ross in the eyes and said,

"I suggest that in a few minutes, we get dressed and wait for the bakery delivery van to arrive. I can buy a couple of crusty rolls for our breakfast, and after we have eaten, we take your empty suitcase..."

"I haven't got a suitcase." Ross interrupted.

"I know," said Ted, "but it sounds better than saying a plastic bag. As I was saying, we take the suitcase to your house. Into it we put, the rest of your worldly possessions, anything you have in the kitchen and refrigerator, lock your house and bring everything back here. That way I can look after you properly and personally. Later, we can take the keys back to the agent, get your deposit back, and change your address to this one."

"Are you sure about me moving in here? I mean, I don't want you to make a decision like that without thinking it through properly."

"I thought it through last night as I was going to sleep. Ted said. "It's up to you Ross. You've been saying for long enough you wanted to get out of that house, and it's not as if you haven't stayed here before."

"OK," Ross answered slowly, "I'm all for giving it a try. I do want to be with you, but I'm afraid that occasionally I might be forced to do some sexual things to you like I did yesterday."

"Is that a threat or a promise?" laughed Ted.

"Yes." was the obvious answer from Ross.

"You do know if you move in with me, you could be

in some danger." Ted said during a break from kissing.

"As far as I'm concerned, the only danger I'm in, is from that thick hard thing that is digging into my leg, and I would much rather it was digging elsewhere. I want that in me, Ted, I really do, but I'm still a bit unsure, you know. It will happen, I'm certain, but please give me time to make my mind up."

"Let's take one step at a time, Ross, there's no rush. Yesterday was the first step, and we can repeat step one as often as you like, then we move on when you feel ready."

Ross moved her hand down Ted's body, and reached for him.

"It's all right Ted I'm not going to start anything. I just want to hold it in my hand for a moment."

Ted moved slightly so that Ross could reach him.

"You remember yesterday," said Ross, "when I told you about Brian doing it to me the first time, I said it didn't do anything for me. I realized why that was when I was holding you during our siesta yesterday. I'm holding it now to clarify what I thought. Brian is nowhere near your length, and certainly not as thick as this. No bloody wonder I couldn't feel him inside me."

While she was talking, Ross was moving her hand gently on him. He put his hand over hers and said,

"Better not do that to me right now because there would be one hell of a mess in the bed. Let me explain something to you."

Ted put his arms round her and gently pulled her close to him. In a low voice, he said,

"Ross, what you just said about Brian and his size.... well maybe his length is short, but his thickness could be average. I have been told that mine is average length, but the thickness is much greater. I was once warned by a doctor to make sure my lady was ready for me before I entered her. Yesterday, when you did it with your hand, I had to hold it back a bit, because normally, I erupt like a fountain and there is a lot more of it than you got on your body."

"Why did you hold it back?" Ross asked him.

"I though it may put you off me, and I certainly didn't want that." he replied.

"Ted," Ross breathed, "never hold it back and don't change anything you would normally do. I enjoyed yesterday and would like to have the pleasure of my new awakening fairly regularly."

"I think," said Ted, "we should get dressed and do some shopping as we agreed because if we don't we'll be here all day."

"Yes we should, but just five more minutes, because I want to ask you something."

"Anything you want, just ask, and I'll do it willingly."

"Ted, just for once, I want you to be very serious, with no messing. I'm going to ask you a question, and I want a straight, immediate answer. Forget everything that's been said and done. OK?"

"Yes, Ross. I can be serious if it's necessary, so go ahead and ask me your question."

Ross hesitated for a minute, drew a breath, and said,

"Ted, if I offered you my body, right now, would you do it to me, you know, make love to me?"

"Yes, Ross, I would."

"Why?"

That question shook Ted, but he had enough courage to give Ross an answer.

"My belief is that the nicest way to show how much we feel for one another is by making love. Ross, I don't want a leg over, a shag, or a fuck. If we have sex eventually, I would like us to be making love to each other."

"That's a good answer Ted, and although I've told you I fancied you, I am not going to be here solely for *your* sexual pleasure. I've had enough of that in the past, and if I am going to renounce my belief, I need to know you are sincere. I think I'm falling for you, not just fancying, because I have a very strong attraction towards you, physically and sexually. I'm willing to move into this apartment with you, but remember, we still have work to do on the house, and that is a priority, for reasons I'll probably tell you about later. Before we get dressed, please can I have a kiss, the type of kiss that any man who is in love with his woman would give?"

That's exactly how they spent the next few minutes.

As they broke, Ross leaned back and looked into Ted's eyes, and said,

"I have been without satisfactory sex for too many years Ted, and you are managing to make me feel like a woman again. After you made me.... come yesterday, and we were having what I called our after sex kiss, I was getting more and more turned on. I wanted you to do it to me again, but for some reason, I couldn't tell you. I didn't want you to think I was sex mad."

"Ross, wanting more than one orgasm does not make you sex mad. While we are lying together, kissing and cuddling, as you know, I get hard. That is desire, not sex madness. I know your nipples get hard, and I'm sure you show other signs of desire. Those are not symptoms of sex madness. Please Ross, never be ashamed of showing me you need sex. What you did yesterday was highly satisfactory for me as well. No woman has done that to me for years, and to feel your hand round me was a sensation I can't describe. I like that being done to me, but I like making love even more."

"Ted, all this talk of sex is starting to turn me on, so

151

I'm getting out of this bed before I...."

Her voice tailed off as she reached for him.

Ted put his hand over hers, and said,

"Not now, Ross, let's save it for later."

"You just told me you liked it," said Ross, still trying to move her hand on him.

"I do," he answered, "but it's much better when we do it to each other at the same time. If we get back from shopping in time for a siesta, and we still feel the need, we can do it to each other then."

"Whatever time we get back," Ross answered forcefully, "we are having a siesta, a siesta like we had yesterday and without holding anything back."

Half an hour later, they were washed and dressed, ready to go shopping. They used Ted's car, because it was smaller and easier to park in the shopping centre. The first store they went into sold clothes as well as food and other household items. Ross spent quite some time picking out the type of clothing she wanted, and after a long walk round the ladies section, the shopping trolley was quite full of clothing and footwear. The final isle they walked down was displaying ladies underwear. Ross took hold of Ted's arm, and whispered,

"I want to find the coloured briefs. No more white for me, my thoughts are no longer pure. Very soon, I'm possibly going to lose my virginity again, so I want my undies to reflect my desires."

Ross searched the display to find what she wanted, then turned to Ted, and said,

"What do you think of these?"

Ross held two packets, one pack held patterned thongs, the other, multi coloured bikini briefs.

"Very sexy!" Ted answered, "I think any of those would turn me on, as long as you were in them of course."

"Which ones shall I have? You take your pick."

"I don't know." said Ted, feeling a bit embarrassed, "I've never been asked to choose ladies briefs before."

"I'll take both packs then." Ross said, laughing at his hesitation. Ross decided she had enough clothes for the time being, and asked Ted if he needed anything. He picked up a couple of packs of T shirts and two pairs of shorts that he could use when he wasn't working. Their shopping finished, they made their way to the checkouts, where Ross used a credit card to pay for her new wardrobe.

"What do I owe for my things?" Ted asked as they were walking back to the car.

"Nothing! That's my treat."

"Thank you, it's much appreciated."

"Show me your appreciation later" Ross said, squeezing his arm. "While we are here, let's go and look for beds and things. I saw a shop selling them as we went into the mall, so we can start there."

After putting their clothes into the car, they made their way back into the shopping mall and to the shop Ross had seen. They stopped outside, and looked into the window.

"They all look expensive in here" said Ted.

"Where beds are concerned," Ross said, "you get what you pay for. Buy a cheap one, and within a few years, it's worn out and you need another. I want a divan with storage space underneath, and a good firm mattress. Sometime soon I'm going to be entertaining a man in it, so the bed and the man will have to meet my needs. No more talking about it, let's go inside and test a few mattresses."

There wasn't a big selection in the store, and after a quick look round, decided there was nothing that met Ross's requirements. They didn't find any other bedding shops in the mall, so decided to go to one of the other stores nearer to the town centre.

"I've just remembered that the new IKEA store opened last week in Malaga. We can go and have a look round there if you like."

"I'm not that bothered, Ted. IKEA has a good range of furniture for every room, but you either like or don't like their range. I'm afraid I'm not keen, so I think we should start with the store by the roundabout, or the two we passed last week on the industrial estate."

The nearest store, by the roundabout, was large and amongst other things, had a huge selection of beds and bedroom furnishings. They spent a long time looking through the displays, because there were so many types of bed to choose from. There was a nice four poster, but Ross turned that down as pure showmanship. There was one which Ted thought different, having a fixed head board and foot.

"We could use that one for tying our hand and feet to the rails." Ted joked.

Ross grabbed hold of him and in a hard voice, said,

"Don't you *ever* say anything like that to me again".

She stalked away, leaving Ted wondering what he'd said to upset her so badly.

He walked after her, and tried to apologize as he caught her up, but Ross ignored him as she continued to look at the display. Ted followed slightly behind her, still trying to fathom out why his joke had upset her so much. After a long period of silence, Ross turned to Ted, buried her head in his chest, and said,

"I'm sorry Ted, I shouldn't take it out on you like this. I'll tell you the full story later, but I was tied to a bed once before, but it wasn't solely for sex. That's why I didn't think it funny when you said it. I know you meant it as a joke, but to me it was a reminder."

154

"I'm sorry Ross, I'm sorry. There is no way that I want to upset you, ever."

Ross smiled and said,

"Let's look for a bed we can use for sleeping and other enjoyable pastimes. I want to forget the past and enjoy the future."

They eventually found one that Ross liked. It had a large storage area underneath a lift up base, and the mattress was quite thick and firm, which Ross described as 'bouncing back on you'.

The price Ross paid included delivery, and the salesman said it should be at her house in the hills in a week or ten days' time, but they would ring to let her know which day. Ted and Ross made their way back to the display area to have another look at her bed.

"I'm looking forward to trying that out," she said, pressing the mattress with her hands

"We are supposed to be building a house." said Ted, pretending to be serious. "We have built your bedroom, and bought a bed. Now all you want to do is test it for firmness".

"I'm going to test you for the same thing," Ross answered, "frequently!"

"You are getting worse," Ted laughed.

"No love, I'm getting better. I keep telling you, with your help, I'm going to start enjoying my life once again. I'd like to go to the furnishings section now, and see what they have in the way of wardrobes, dressing tables and things like that. If they come in flat packs, maybe we can get a discount if I buy for the four bedrooms. I'm sure they can make some arrangement for four sets of furnishings and another three or four beds."

They found one of the salesmen who could speak some English, and asked him if they made any special deals for bulk buys. He showed them a brochure that gave prices for complete rooms for every part of a house. He told them that if the quality they wanted was better than the brochure showed, they would still be able to buy cheaper than if they bought a piece at a time. With the information and the brochure, they went back to the car.

"Late lunch time," said Ted, "how do you fancy a McDonalds?"

"Is there one here?" Ross asked in surprise.

"Yes, just down the road, near to where you bought your new clothes this morning."

A few minutes later they were pulling into the car park.

"Ted Hall, you need your eyes testing! This McDonalds is a Burger King."

"So it is. My eyesight must have deteriorated from ogling the forbidden fruit all summer. Never mind, they still do burgers, chips and a drink at a good price."

An hour later, they were on the Autopista heading home.

"I call that a profitable morning." Ross said.

"Profitable for the shops." Ted agreed.

"Profitable for us as well, Ted. Remember, profit is not only monetary, it also means beneficial, which is what I got by buying my essential clothing."

"I'm going to have to empty my wardrobe to make room for all your new stuff."

"Ted, love, if we are going to share our lives, we have to share everything. That means my share of the wardrobe is seventy five per cent."

"Typical woman." Ted said laughing.

"Chauvinist!" Ross replied, joining his laughter.

They arrived back at the apartment, and carried the morning's purchases to the bedroom.

"Leave the bags on the floor for now Ted, it's siesta time, and you know what I promised you this morning.

Ross never breaks her promises. Let me go to the loo first."

Ted got undressed before using the toilet himself and when he got back to the bedroom, Ross was stood waiting for him, wearing only her briefs. He put his arms around her waist while Ross put her arms round his neck.

"Ted," she whispered, "I'm almost bursting with anticipation. Why don't you take my briefs off, and give me the same pleasure as you did yesterday?"

Ted started to kiss her, and Ross responded by tightening her arms round his neck, and pushing her body firmly against his. He moved his hands down so that he could slowly slide her briefs down, and as they fell from her lower body, Ross started moving against him. She broke the kiss, put her head on his chest, and said,

"Ted, oh Ted, I want you. I want that thick hard thing of yours inside me. I want to feel it moving, Ted, I need you, but I'm frightened."

"Shall we lie down on the bed, and see what happens?" Ted said.

"I know what's going to happen, but it's not the same as what I want to happen." Ross whispered.

They lay side by side on the bed, and within seconds, Ross was moving against him again. Ted bent down and took one of her swollen nipples in his mouth and with the tip of his tongue, he licked the end. Ross put her head back, opened her mouth to pant.

"Ted, Ted, touch me, touch me down there, hurry, please hurry, Ted, now."

Ted slid his hand between their bodies and began stroking the spot she liked. Ross was so highly aroused that it only took a short time for her to reach her peak.

They lay together for a while, Ross winding down

from the sensation she had just received. Eventually, she opened her eyes, looked at Ted, and said,

"I think I'll let you take my briefs off more often. That was fantastic, especially when you kissed and stroked my nipple as you touched me down there. I have some more to learn about sex, and I'm starting to realize that lovemaking is completely different to shagging."

Ted smiled, it was the only answer he could think of.

They lay in each other's arms, and fell into a light and refreshing sleep.

Ted woke as Ross turned on her side. He opened his eyes, and looked at her. There was a smile on her lips as she woke, stretching languidly as she became fully conscious.

"Do you have to watch me like that?" she asked

"Yes. I think it's the best view in the village."

"Flattery may get you somewhere, but not right now, because I need a wee."

Ross got off the bed, and went to the bathroom. Ted went to the kitchen, and put the kettle on. He had the cups ready and the tea bags were in the teapot, when Ross walked into the kitchen, still naked.

"Go back to bed Ross and I'll bring your tea in."

"I like this. I have never felt so secure and relaxed in my life. You are a lovely man Ted Hall, and I'm so glad I met you."

She stood up on her toes, gave Ted a kiss, turned round and went back into the bedroom.

A few minutes later, Ted took their tea in, and after putting the cups on the bedside tables, lay down beside her on the bed.

She snuggled up to him, and in a soft voice said,

"I'm going to carry on with my story, from where I left off yesterday. Before you say anything, Ted, I have to tell you everything, it's important, in more ways than one. If you remember, yesterday, I got as far as the day I came home from the hospital, after losing my baby. I think I told you he started beating me again. That was not quite right. The first one or two weren't beatings, more like heavy slaps. Let me explain:

'The night I got back from the hospital, Brian arrived home well after midnight and drunk as usual.

'Oh you're fucking home at last are you? I've had some fucking peace while you've been away, nobody nagging at me for having a drink. From now on woman, if you make any more comments about me having a drink, or you answer me back in any way, I'll fucking near kill you. Don't ever think of trying to run away from me either, because I'll find you, no matter how long it fucking takes, and then I *will* kill you. Understand, you fucking bitch?'

I stood looking at Brian, too terrified to answer him.

'I fucking spoke to you, so answer me when I speak' he yelled at me.

He slapped me on my ribs with the back of his hand. It hurt, mainly because I wasn't ready for anything like that, and had no time to try and evade it. He staggered off towards the bedroom, but I stayed in the living room until I thought he would be asleep. Creeping to the bedroom, I looked through the gap in the door to see what state he was in. Thankfully, he was dead to the world, and I spent the rest of the weekend in a state of terror. I could not understand the sudden change in Brian's behaviour.

It was a week or so later that I got my next slap. It wasn't a Friday, but mid-week. He came home earlier than usual, in fact about half an hour after me. I was in the kitchen making the evening meal when he walked in, smelling of beer as usual.

'You're early tonight', I said to him.

'Why isn't my tea ready' he snarled, ignoring my comment.

'Because I've only just got home from work myself. It will be about half an hour, at the time you usually get home'.

Without any warning, he gave me two slaps, again with the back of each hand, on my ribs. The force of the blows knocked me on the floor, and I lay there panting. I had fallen on my back, and the skirt I was wearing had ridden up, showing my legs. He looked down at me, and in a sarcastic voice, said,

'Flashing your thong won't make any difference to me right now, and what have I told you about only wearing black ones.'

'I've no clean black ones', I sobbed, trying to get up.

'Well fucking buy some more', he said, giving me a kick on the thigh.

I scrambled to my feet, and carried on making the tea. When it was ready, I went to the living room to set the table and saw Brian asleep in his chair. I woke him up, by shouting that his tea was ready, and got another slap for waking him. I wanted to walk out of the house right then, but remembered his threat about finding me if I tried to get away. I was terrified, and that's just how Brian wanted me to be. I now had to think ahead, and it was like walking on egg shells. I hardly spoke to him and if he spoke to me I was very careful with my answers.

For some months, he never laid a finger on me, physically or sexually, which made me happy on both counts! I'd noticed on occasional Friday's when he came home drunk, he smelled of beer and perfume, but I never said a word to him about it, I was safer that way.

Over the next six or eight months, there were quite a

few more slaps, but one Friday he came home absolutely rat arsed. I don't even know how he got home from the pub. He staggered in through the door, straight past me and into the bedroom. I left him to it for a while, and then peered round the door. He had passed out on the bed, still fully dressed. I left him there, and made myself comfortable on the settee. I woke up at my usual time, and after washing and changing, made myself some breakfast. I didn't bother about Brian because he never had breakfast on a Saturday, rarely getting out of bed much before noon. That day was different though. I was drinking my coffee in the kitchen, when there was a shout from the bedroom.

'Dorothy, where are you'.

Dorothy, I thought, who the hell is she?

He shouted again for Dorothy, so I went to the bedroom and looked in. He saw me, and shouted,

'What the fuck are you doing here, where's Dorothy?'

'Dorothy who?' I asked him calmly.

He must have suddenly realized where he was, shut up for a second, and then without warning, jumped up off the bed and lunged towards me. He knocked the coffee mug out of my hand, and hit me at the top of my arm. The blow numbed it immediately, so I couldn't lift it to defend myself. He used his hands, front and back, to slap me over most of the front and sides of my body. I cried for him to stop, but he was in such a rage, it would have taken a strong man all his time to get him off me. I fell to the floor, and he started to kick at my hips. I had enough strength to stand up, but the next wave of slaps, knocked me on the bed. He stood over me, panting with exertion, his hands raised as if to hit me again.

'I've told you once, don't you ever question me. That was just a fucking start, so if you don't want anymore,

161

fucking do as I tell you. Don't try and be clever by telling people I slapped you, or you'll get double the fucking dose. Now, show me you take notice of my orders.'

While we were courting, and started having sex, he was turned on each time I wore a thong, especially black ones. He bought some for me just before we got married, with the instructions that I wore black thongs all the time. From time to time, he would demand I show him I was following his orders. On odd occasions, he had torn some as he pulled them off me when he wanted immediate sex, so when I had no clean ones, I wore another colour or a different type of underwear. That day, he wanted to see if my thong was black, and I'm glad it was. I lifted my skirt to show him, and suddenly realized he may want to have sex with me. He got hold of his crotch, and I shrank back, hoping he didn't want me, but he stepped away, and let me get up. I rushed into the bathroom, and threw up in the loo, then staggered back to the kitchen for another cup of coffee, although I felt I really needed something stronger to stop me shaking. I heard Brian in the shower, and a while later, he came into the kitchen fully dressed in his casuals. I shrank back against the cupboards, thinking I was in for more, but he just looked at me, and with a sneer, told me he was going out, and would be back at tea time. He walked out, and I stood there shaking all over. I'm ashamed to say it Ted, but I wet myself."

Ross stopped talking, sat up and drank her almost cold tea.

"Do you want another hot cup?" Ted asked her.

Ross shook her head.

"I'm OK Ted, for now. Later, when I've finished, I'll more than likely need something stronger."

162

Ross lay down again, and snuggled up to Ted. Putting her arm round him, said,

"You are my strength right now, so I'm going to continue for a bit longer."

"I stood in my puddle of wee, sobbing like I'd never done before. I hurt all over, and knew I couldn't do anything about the predicament I was in, so I would just have to take care in the future with everything I said or did. After mopping the kitchen floor, I went to the bathroom, had a shower and dressed in dry underwear and jeans. Not wanting anyone to see my wet clothing, I decided to do some washing. I took the clothes basket into the kitchen and started to load the washing machine. There were no whites, so everything went in on one wash. I was putting Brian's underpants in the machine, when I felt something on my hand. I looked at them, and there was a big wet stain at the front. The dirty, evil bastard had come in them while he was slapping me around.

I managed to get all the Saturday chores done, but the shopping at the local supermarket took longer than it should because I was sore, and it was painful walking at my usual pace. Everything was done, the lodge cleaned, washing dry ready for ironing, and Brian's tea well on the way. He came in at the time he said, and immediately asked where his tea was. I told him to sit down, and I would bring it to him in a few minutes. I dished up, and carried the plates to the living room.

'You're walking like I left it inside you' he said, 'what's the matter, can't you take a little fucking slap'?

I didn't reply, just put his food down, and sat to eat mine. He never said a word during the meal because he was too busy shovelling the food into his mouth. I asked what he wanted for afters, but he said he didn't want any, so I cleared the table, and started doing the washing up. He strolled into the kitchen just as I finished, and asked if there was any apple pie. It was on the tip of my tongue to tell him he'd just told me he didn't want anything else, but something at the back of my mind told me to answer him properly. I told him there was apple or rhubarb pie in the cupboard. He decided he wanted a slice of each, so I gave it to him without question, and he took it into the living room to eat. I stayed in the kitchen drying the pots, and when he had finished, he actually brought the plate to be washed. That must have been the first time he had done anything to help me in the house, and it certainly was the last. I washed and dried his plate, and went into the living room. He was sat in front of the telly, watching sport as usual, so I sat down in my chair, and picked up some work I'd brought home with me. After about half an hour, he turned the sound down on the television, and looked across at me. I stopped reading, instinct telling me to take notice of him.

'I'm going to get rid of my carpet fitting business,' he told me, 'it's not making enough money.'

It's not making any, I thought to myself, especially if you drink away any profit you *do* make.

'What are you going to do then?' I asked him.

'I've been talking to a bloke called Sidney Hitchen. He's the big cheese at the carpet supermarkets, and they have fitters attached to the stores. I can have a job with him, on the contract side. It means that sometimes I may have to work away from home for a week or so.'

That was the best news I'd heard in years!

'How does it compare to what you've been doing for yourself?'

'Instead of doing one room at a time in houses, I'll be re-carpeting offices, pubs, hotels, and motels over a wide area of the country. I'm not sure how much of the country yet, but I'll know next week.'

'What about your own business?'

'I'll return the complete rolls to the manufacturers, and what's left can be sold off cheap.'

'What about the shop?'

'What about it, it's rented, so I'll just stop paying the rent and leave it empty.'

'Aren't you supposed to give a months' notice?'

'Fuck 'em. I've paid enough over the years. If I'm not there, they can't charge me for it.'

'When do you start this new job?'

'Couple of weeks.'

'You've been thinking about this for some time, haven't you?' I asked.

Brian jumped off his chair, and stood over me with his fists clenched.

'What's it fucking got to do with you how long I've been thinking about it? Keep your big fat nose out of my affairs'.

'I haven't got a big fat nose' I couldn't help saying.

'You will have if you give me any more of your lip. You think you're such a fucking la-di-da lady, but you're not. I've shagged much better than you, you toffee nosed get, but I did the right thing for you when I got you in the club. You are my wife, and will be until you snuff it, so don't fucking try any clever stuff, like running away. I've told you what will happen if you do. Remember it! Talking of shagging, I've not had it from you for a while have I? Get those jeans off, now'.

Now I was worried. I did have a black thong on, but I didn't want the bastard anywhere near my… my… you know, down there. On the other hand, if I refused him, I was in for another good hiding. I unzipped my jeans, and let him see my thong. His trousers and underpants were already on the floor by this time, and he was hard and

165

waiting. He reached down and pulled the thong off.

'Spread 'em' he ordered, and reluctantly I did.

I knew from experience there would be no foreplay. He was going to put it in straight away, although I was unprepared for him. But Brian couldn't have cared less, he wanted his shag, and nothing was going to stop him. He forced his way into me, and I screamed out with pain and screamed the whole time he did it to me. I'm sure that turned him on even more, so thankfully, he only lasted a short time before he was finished. When he stood up, I could see there was blood on him, so I knew I must be torn inside. He left me sprawled in the chair, sobbing from the pain.

He went to the bathroom, where I suppose he washed himself, but I could hardly move, never mind wash. He was back minutes later, and as he walked through the living room said,

'Cover yourself up you tart, I've seen enough of it for today. I'm going out for a few pints, so don't wait up for me, I'll be late'.

'Going to see Dorothy, are you?' I thought. 'She's bloody welcome to you.'

I sat for a few minutes, until I felt I needed to go to the bathroom. I stood up, and quite literally staggered along the corridor and did something I had not done for a long time, I ran a bath. I gingerly stepped in, and slowly sank down. As the hot water reached my... I shrieked with pain. I lifted myself out, and then lowered myself very, very slowly back into the water. I slid down until I was almost submerged, just my mouth and nose above the water. I lay there for a few minutes thinking of what had just happened, and during those minutes, I very nearly put my nose and mouth under the water as well. I wanted to die!"

Ross was crying in Ted's arms, but as he drew a breath to speak, she anticipated him.

"Don't stop me yet Ted. I have to keep going for a bit longer, it's important to me. Not only am I telling you what I've had to put up with, I am getting rid of the memories. You are the only person who will know the whole truth. Two others know part of it, but I trust you enough to hear it all.

Ross managed to compose herself enough to carry on, but it took some time.

"The bath helped me to get rid of some of the pain and stiffness from my body, and I lay there thinking what I could do. The short answer at the time was nothing. I hoped he was telling me the truth about his new job, because the longer he was away, the safer I would feel. We had been married for just over two years at that time, and I could not even contemplate God knows how long with the vile Brian.

I haven't told you anything about my work before I came to Spain so I'll tell you now what I did. I've already mentioned that my granddad owned a publishing company, so when I left school, I went straight into the business to learn the trade. The company designs, prints, binds and distributes some monthly women's magazines, the local weekly newspaper, a couple of puzzle books, one very large catalogue for a national home shopping company, and quite a number of supermarket bargain sheets. There is a lot to learn, and the company is working flat out, occasionally seven days a week. My grandfather is a hard but fair man, and will not tolerate anyone who is not prepared to put his or her backbone into the job. Thankfully I'm a quick learner, and became competent in several of the sections. I am an only child, and I have no cousins, nephews or nieces, which made me the 'heir' to the company. It may seem stupid, but Brian had no interest whatsoever in my job or the position I was in, mainly because I neglected to tell him! He thought I was some sort of designer for magazine covers. I didn't want to put him right, especially at that stage of the relationship, because I could envisage him stopping work all together, and living off what I earned.

Fat chance!

From my birth, granddad had been paying into a trust fund to give me a nest egg on my twenty first birthday. I was approaching my birthday at the time Brian decided to give up his business, so I asked granddad not to let Brian know about the money, or the position I was in at the company. He agreed, and asked if everything was all right in the marriage. I could never lie to my granddad, and reluctantly, I told him there were problems, not mentioning what kind though. Being the man he is, he wanted to help, but I asked him to leave it for now, but if I needed help at any time, he would be the first I would ask. On my twenty first birthday, I was presented with a bank book and a number of 'shares' in the company, which made me the largest 'shareholder' after granddad. Grandma and my mother were the other shareholders, but sleeping partners. The 'shares' were not stock market shares, but a division of the company reflecting the capital they had initially put in. Granddad held the largest share, obviously but giving me part of his share meant that I really was now part of the company. That day really was a good one for me, especially because Brian was working away. He arrived back two days later, and saw the birthday cards on the mantelpiece. I'd left them there on purpose, just to see his reaction when he came in. Naturally, I hadn't got a card from him.

'Oh yea,' he said when he saw them, 'happy birthday. Suppose you got a rise in pay, it'll help with the housekeeping.

'Next month' I said, and left it at that

Over the next year or so, I got a few good beatings, mostly when he returned from working away. He also wanted sex on those occasions, and I got thumped when I tried to evade him. On one particular night, he had forced himself in me, and I was bleeding again, so after I cleaned myself, I tried to reason with him.

'Brian, ever since I lost the baby, you know I haven't been right down there. I'm dry, and whenever we have sex, you are doing damage to the inside of me. The more we do it, the more it hurts and as I'm your wife, I want sex with you, but not like this. There is some water based lubricant you can get from the chemists, and if you cover yourself with it, not only will it be easier for you to enter without hurting me, but it will make it more satisfactory for you as well.'

'If that's what you want to use, you can fucking buy it.' came his snarled reply. 'If it works like you say, we can have a lot more sex and you'll have no excuses then, will you.'

I hadn't thought about that, but if the lubricant worked as it was supposed to, I could lie back and let him get on with it. I had got used to the way Brian thought, well most of the time anyway, so the next day, on my way home from work, I called at a chemist, and got a large tube of the lubricant. As I passed the prescription counter, it suddenly occurred to me, that if we were going to have more sex, I needed some protection, and made a mental note to make an appointment with my doctor. I was right about his thoughts, because as soon as it was bed time, he asked if I'd got the 'stuff'. I handed him the tube, and he pushed me towards the bedroom, and ordered me to get ready for him. That meant being undressed except for the black

169

thong, and lying on my back waiting for him. He walked into the bedroom already hard, and proceeded to smother himself with the 'stuff'. There was no preliminaries, he looked at my body, pulled the thong off, and entered me. I have to admit there was no pain, but neither was there any sensation from him. I pretended to enjoy it, and for the first time, I faked an orgasm. I got very good at that over the next few years, though I still got the occasional battering for holding my mouth in the wrong position.

I can't think of all the happenings over the years, they just blur together into a nightmare. I was not in a marriage, as such, it was more like living in an institution. Granddad did keep his eye on me, and I'm sure he knew what was going on, although he said nothing to me, except to ask me frequently if I was still all right.

I'm going to jump ahead a few years, to the next significant part of my existence with Brian.

My grandmother had died, and a few days after the funeral, granddad took me into his office to tell me he wanted me to have grandma's shares in the business. That would put me almost on the same par as him, and he wanted to know if I had any problem with it. I told him I hadn't, but as far as I was concerned, he was the boss. I think he liked that! Some years previously, he had bought a villa here in Spain, and asked me if I would spend a few days with him sorting out grandma's things, and suggested we came over the next time Brian was working away. Brian had already told me he would be away for three weeks at the end of the month. The reason he gave was that he had a large hotel to carpet, but I thought he was taking a holiday from work, and going somewhere with Dorothy, or some other unfortunate woman. I'd got to the stage where I couldn't care less what he did, or who he did it to, just as long as it wasn't me. I told granddad the dates Brian would be away, and he booked flights for the two of us.

Two weeks later, Brian went off with his suitcase, supposedly to Norfolk, and the following day, I flew with granddad to Malaga. We picked up a hire car at the airport, and drove over this way. His villa was just outside Nerja, about twenty minutes by car to the town and the sea. I had never been to his villa, I'd seen photographs, but it was much better in real life. It is situated just outside the village of Frigiliana, and set in the hills on the road to Torrox. Apart from clearing grandma's clothes and giving the place a good clean we had a nice break. During the stay, granddad asked me point blank if Brian was mistreating me. I couldn't answer him directly, I was too afraid of Brian ever finding out, so I reluctantly nodded.

'I thought so' he told me, 'I've seen you on numerous occasions walking very slowly and stiff. I don't trust him, never have. Please be careful, and you know where I am if you need me.' He was silent for a while, and then in a hushed tone, said,

'Would you like to come and live in this villa?'

Reluctantly, I shook my head,

'No, granddad, but thank you for the offer. Brian knows about the villa, and if I ever went missing, this would be the first place he would look for me. If I was here, and he found me, I wouldn't get back to England. Well not alive anyway'.

He looked sharply at me, and asked if it was that bad. I told him it was, and if there ever came a day that I didn't turn up for work without me letting him know, he should send the emergency services to the lodge.

'I'm going to put the villa up for sale,' he told me, 'so if you need it any time before it's sold, just let me know'.

After we came back from Spain, I had two weeks of peace before Brian came home. On the night he arrived back, he showed me a photograph of a hotel, and another of him fitting a carpet on the stairs. I had been wrong, just for once, about his working away, but I was still not convinced he worked away for so many days in the week. It was then he proudly informed me, he was now on a two week holiday from work.

'Great,' I said, 'where are we going?'

'No fuckin' where,' he answered, 'we can't afford holidays.'

'But surely you're saving some of your wages, Brian. If we pool our spare cash, I'm sure we can spend a few days away.'

The moment I finished, I regretted opening my mouth. He pushed me on the shoulders, and I flew backwards on to the settee. He leaned over me and with hatred in his voice, said,

'How many more time have I to tell you to keep your nose out of my affairs. The money I earn is mine. I earn it, I keep it, so no more questions. If you've any spare cash, spend it on black thongs and making yourself look better.'

Talk about a smack in the face! I consider myself to be reasonably attractive, have a good figure, and dressed well. It was certainly all spoiled on him.

I tried to get up from the settee, but he leaned over me again, and said,

'Since you got that grease, I've been giving it to you regularly, and you're not in the club again. Have you been taking the pill?'

I nodded. That was fatal. He grabbed my hair and pulled me upright. He put his face right up to mine, and snarled,

'Where are they?'

'I… in… m… my b… bag.'

I got a slap on my side.

'Show me', he shouted, giving me another slap.

I got my handbag, and before I could open it, he snatched it from me, unzipped it, and emptied the contents on the floor. I bent down, picked up my pills and handed them to Brian. Before I could stand up, he gave me another slap, which sent me sprawling on the floor. The back of my head hit the solid leg of the big coffee table, and I saw stars. All I could think of was protecting myself, but I couldn't move, and I knew I was in for another rough time. He pulled me up again by my hair, and put the box in my hand.

'Down the toilet, every fucking one, and if I find you have taken one again, you'll regret it.'

He pushed me into the bathroom, and watched as I flushed them away. He got hold of the collar on my blouse, and twisted it until it was tight against my neck.

'Anything to say?' he demanded.

I knew I had to be careful now. I nodded and said,

'I'm sorry Brian. I won't take any more without your permission.'

'Now you're getting to be a smart girl at last.' He told me, patting my cheek with his hand. 'I'll let you decide your punishment. Which would you like, another slap or two, or a good shag?'

Neither, I thought to myself, and when have you ever given me a good anything?

'Well?' he asked, lifting his hand. 'If you don't answer me now, you'll fucking well get both.'

'Shag' I whispered.

'Good choice', he leered, letting go of my blouse collar.

'Off', he ordered, pointing to my blouse. This was another of his silly games, ordering me to undress article

173

by article when he told me to. I took off my blouse.

'Off' he said, pointing to my jeans. I removed them, and as I knew my thong would be the last item off, I started to remove my bra. Brian was already naked, but when he saw my hand touch the bra strap, his hand shot out and slapped my bare ribs.

'Who told you to take that off', he roared at me, giving me another slap. 'You never fucking learn, do you?'

In his rage, he got hold of the cups and pulled them apart at the front, tearing my bra in two. He ripped it from my body, threw it over his shoulder and it landed in the toilet basin. His hands shot out again, and he took hold of my nipples. He started squeezing them and at the same time, pushing me backwards.

'Bedroom!' he ordered.

I was screaming from the pain he was inflicting, but he ignored my cries, and pushed me backwards until my legs were at the side of the bed. He let go of my nipples, and pushed me over. He ripped my thong off, covered himself with the lubricant and pushed into me. I lay there and started to pant, closed my eyes, and pretended I was enjoying it. He suddenly slowed his stroke, and I knew it was time for one of my fictitious orgasms.

'That was better than a thumping, wasn't it?' he leered at me after he had finished. 'Behave from now on, and you can enjoy me much more'.

That's all I wanted! I don't think.

I was saved from further sex that week, because I started. Brian was not well pleased, but at least I was spared from his hands. The day after I finished, Brian started again."

Ross began to cry, and held onto Ted while the tears flowed. He held her as close as he could, because he knew there was something horrific to follow. In between the sobs, Ross managed to say,

"Just a few more minutes, Ted, and I'll stop for today." Ross paused, then with hatred in her voice cried,

"Ted, for the next three and a half months, Brian raped me every day, sometimes more than once. It was during this time that he tied me to the bed. It was a Saturday night, and for once, he said he didn't want to go out. He was watching the television, and I was reading a book. A short while later, I put the book down and went to the bathroom. On my way back to the living room, he confronted me in the hall way.

'Back to the bedroom' he ordered, 'and strip off, completely'

I had no option but to do as he ordered. I lay on the bed, dreading what was about to happen again. He'd already done it once that day, and I was in no mood for his stupid games.

He walked into the bedroom naked, carrying four pieces of fabric. It was much later that I found out they were four pieces of silk that he had cut from the hem of one of my best dresses. He tied my hands to the headboard, and my ankles to the feet at the bottom of the bed. I was spread eagled, like a living 'X', and I felt humiliated at being so exposed. I could hardly move, but then again, that's what he wanted. He spread himself with the lubricant, and did it to me. There is no way I can describe my feelings as he rammed himself repeatedly into me, only stopping when he came. He climbed off, went to the bathroom and washed himself. He came back into the bedroom, and calmly got dressed, looking at me all the time. I asked him to untie me, but he laughed, and said,

'No way. You'll be there ready for me when I get

back.'

I was left there until he arrived home, well after midnight, and he did it again. He went and slept on the settee and left me there all night. Ted, I was tied to that bed until Sunday lunch time. He didn't bring me any food, just the odd glass of water while he continued to rape me. He said he was only releasing me because he was hungry and wanted a cooked meal. I had been tied to that bed for about eighteen hours, no food, and no visits to the loo. I was desperate by the time he untied me. I could hardly move my arms and legs because they had been in the same immobile position for so long. That didn't worry Brian, he wanted some food before he started on me again.

During the three and a half months, he only stopped raping me when I was on, and he stopped completely the day I told him I was pregnant."

Ross could say no more. She lay in Ted's arms, and sobbed herself to sleep.

It was just coming daylight when Ross woke up. She looked at Ted, saw he was awake, and watching her.

"What time is it?" she asked.

"Just after seven," Ted replied.

"Have you been holding me all the time I slept?"

"I've not moved a muscle, I didn't want to wake you."

Ross reached up and gave him a lingering kiss.

"Thank you Ted, for looking after me."

"That's what I'm going to do, for as long as I can."

"What day is it?" asked Ross.

"I've lost track of the days, but I'm sure today is Sunday."

"If it is Sunday, we've no work to go to today. We are going to have a shower, get dressed in our Sunday best, and go out on the town. My treat and no arguments. You stay there and I'll make the coffee this morning."

Ross left the bedroom, went to the kitchen to make coffee and when she returned ten minutes later, Ted was fast asleep. He woke up sometime later, when Ross started blowing gently in his ear.

"Come on Rip van Winkle, time to rise and shine".

Ted slowly opened his eyes, and asked Ross the time.

"I asked you the same question three hours ago."

"Sorry sweetheart, I must have nodded off." Ted said, still trying to focus his eyes.

"Sweetheart? That's a new one. Come on, the shower's running, time for our ablutions."

"You make it sound as though we are in the army." Ted said groggily.

Ross dragged him from the bed, and into the shower, and it wasn't long before he felt ready to face the rest of the day. Ted decided he would give Ross a treat, and set off without telling her where they were going. He drove his car along the coast road, and into the next province.

"The scenery here is beautiful," said Ross as they drove along the coastline, "totally different than where we are."

"Granada province is much more mountainous and rugged. There is a section further on, where if there weren't cars on the road, you would swear you were in a prehistoric era, and you wouldn't be surprised if a dinosaur walked in front of you".

Ted drove into a small village where all the houses were in a single row facing the sea. He found a restaurant between two houses, and pulled up in front of it.

"I've never been here," Ted told her, "but a waiter I got to know in our village told me about it. He told me to tell the owner that Rolly had sent us."

They walked in, and found it surprisingly full. An elderly gentleman walked towards them, and in rapid Spanish, asked if they had booked a table. Ted replied with his limited vocabulary, saying they hadn't, but told him who had sent them. The man's eyes lit up, and he burst into loud laughter, asking how the 'old rascal' was. He pumped Ted's hand, then turned to Ross and enthusiastically kissed both her cheeks. He introduced himself as Antonio, the owner of the restaurant, and they were shown to a table for two by the window. There was no printed menu, just a verbal choice of starter, either Roasted Pepper Salad, or Grilled Prawns with Romesco Sauce. The main course offered was Austrians Casserole of Beans and Sausages, or Lamb braised with Sweet Peppers. Ted explained the dishes to Ross, who couldn't make up her mind which to have. Ted suggested they order one of each, and share the dishes. She was happy to agree to that. While they had been making their mind up, the table had been laid with a still hot, flat Spanish loaf, butter, a large carafe of red wine and a bottle of chilled water. Antonio seemed to know they would be sharing their meals, so brought two empty bowls with the prawns and the peppers, so they could each help themselves from the different foods. He brought extra plates with the main course as well. Ted and Ross took their time eating, and by the time they finished the main meal, were well and truly full, but knew they had to be polite, and have a sweet. They were offered 'Tocino de Cielo' which translated means 'Heavenly Bacon', but is really 'crème caramel', or they could have the very Spanish 'Arroz con Leche' which is cold rice pudding with cinnamon. They both opted for crème caramel.

During the time they had been eating, other diners had finished their meal, and before leaving, they came over to the table, and shook their hand. Ross said she felt like royalty. At last they finished eating, and Ted was about to ask for the bill, when they were given cups of coffee, and a glass of brandy each. Eventually, all the plates, cups and glasses were empty, so Ted and Ross stood up and walked over to the bar, where Antonio was sat watching television. He asked if they had enjoyed their meal, and they both agreed it was more than satisfactory, and would definitely be back to see him again. Ross gave Ted three, twenty Euro notes and made her way to the toilet, leaving him to pay the bill. When Ted saw the cost of the meal, he asked if it was right. Antonio said that was his standard charge for all his customers on a Sunday.

Ross came back into the dining room, as Antonio was telling Ted that he didn't get many English people in his restaurant, because he wouldn't serve 'roasted beef or lamb'. He laughed, and said one time, a couple of English wanted 'roasted meat', and were quite upset when he hadn't any, but rushed out of the premises when he offered to roast them some goat meat.

Ted translated for Ross, and she had a laugh at his joke.

Antonio shook hands with Ted, and kissed Ross again when they once more promised to come and see him again.

Outside, Ross turned to Ted, and said,

"That was a fantastic Spanish meal for Spanish people, served by a proud Spaniard. I was happy but humbled to be in their company. We will be back again, but not too often, or we'll get as fat as pigs. Are we going to have a walk to help digest our food?"

"I think we should walk along the Paseo, find an empty seat, then spend an hour in the sun, snoozing."

Ted held out his hand to give Ross her change.

"How much was it all together?" she said, putting it

into her pocket without checking what he had given her.

"Twenty six Euros." Ted answered.

"How much is that in daft money?"

"About eighteen pounds seventy five."

"Hey, that's not bad, eighteen pounds seventy five each for all that we've just eaten and drunk."

"Ross, the twenty six Euros was for both of us."

"You are joking, aren't you?"

"No. I asked Antonio if it was the right price, and he said it was, so I gave him thirty. He was very reluctant to take the extra, but I insisted."

"So, for all that food and drink, the actual cost was under ten pounds each. It's incredible, if we had eaten a meal like that in England, we wouldn't have had much change out of fifty quid."

They had been slowly walking hand in hand along the Paseo, when Ted led Ross down a ramp on to the beach. There were some loungers and sun shades between the Paseo and the sea, so they each sat down on one for a rest. Almost immediately, a man came out of a hut, and asked how long they wanted to stay. Ted said about two hours, and how much did he want. He told them it would normally be two Euros each for all afternoon, but if they only wanted a short siesta, they could lie there for free. Ted gave him four Euros anyway, and he went happily back to his hut.

"We should have brought our swimming things." Ted said, "We could have got a little sun on our bodies, and had a paddle as well."

"That's something I didn't buy yesterday, I forgot."

"You can always swim in your bra and briefs."

"Not in these new ones, the water could make it look as though I'd nothing on."

"That sounds good to me."

"Down boy! Anyway, I'm not showing the locals

everything I share with my new found love."

Ted sat up, and took his shirt off, and lay back on the lounger. Ross looked at him, and said,

"If you can, so can I." and proceeded to take off her blouse and bra.

Ted leaned over towards her, and pretended to kiss her nipples.

"Don't you bloody dare Ted Hall, or you may be sorry. Do you want to get me into trouble?"

"That's something *I* can't do, get you into trouble."

Ross half sat up, and leaned on her elbow.

"What do you mean?" she asked.

"I can't get you into trouble, you know, pregnant."

"Why not Ted?"

"I had a vasectomy some years ago, when I was still married. The old pistol only fires blanks nowadays."

"That's not a pistol Ted, it's more like a cannon. Do you remember yesterday's siesta, when I said I wanted you, but I was frightened? Ted, if you had got yourself anywhere near me, I would have let you make love to me because I was desperate for you. That's probably why I came so quickly. I told you I was afraid, because I don't want to get pregnant, that would be fatal."

Ross lay back down and took hold of his hand.

Although it was late in the year, there was enough heat in the sun for them to be able to relax, and drift off to sleep in its warmth.

Ted woke up about an hour later, and felt so comfortable, he lay there with his eyes closed, enjoying the sun through the shade.

He felt Ross stir from her nap, and without opening his eyes, asked,

"What's for tea?"

"Don't you dare mention food Ted Hall, I still feel bloated from our lunch. Are you really hungry?"

"Only for you".

"Later maybe, depending how I feel".

Neither of them moved or opened their eyes, still holding hands and relaxing.

"Can I spoil the party mood," asked Ross, "and continue with my tales of woe?"

"Not now, Ross. Later maybe, depending on how I feel."

There was silence for a moment, then Ross realized what Ted had said, and gave him a slap on his arm.

"Don't take the pi... mickey out of me Ted Hall or you will find yourself in trouble."

Ted opened his eyes and looked at Ross. She was smiling at him, a gleam in her eye.

Ted smiled back, then said to her,

"Ross, you can continue if you want, but I'd rather you waited until we were at home. If you cry, it would be a wee bit difficult me comforting you on these loungers."

Ross agreed with him, so they lay there for a while longer, but when the sun went behind some cloud, they decided it was time to make their way home. During the drive, Ross put her hand on Ted's arm, and said,

"I know I've been telling you for years .... oh, all right then, months, about wanting to get the house finished, and move into it as soon as I could. Well, now I'm living with you, and we are getting towards finishing the renovation, I think we should revue my earlier ideas. I suggest we work early morning until lunch and have a siesta if we feel like one. We carry on until we finish the bit we are working on, or we are too tired to keep going or the light is too bad for us to see what we are doing. If we work like that, Monday to Friday, we can keep the whole weekend free for us to relax and enjoy. I like driving around visiting places, and eating in restaurants

182

like the one we've just been to. That is what I wanted when I escaped over here, but then I met a man who's made me feel like living again. I hope that when the house is habitable, you will leave your apartment and move into it with me."

"Yes please Ross, there is nothing I'd like better, but you are aware that us living together at either home could cause major complications if Brian ever found out."

"If that problem crops up, then we can face it together." Ross answered. "That's settled then, we finish the house, move into it together and hopefully live happily ever after."

The rest of the journey was spent in silence, both thinking about what they had just agreed.

They arrived back at the village around nine thirty, and after parking the car, walked to the apartment. Neither wanted anything to eat, but settled for a large mug of tea each. Sitting down on the settee, Ross leaned her head on Ted's shoulder.

"I keep thanking you for looking after me, and how good you make me feel. There are times when I can't believe what I've missed being married to a bastard like Brian. Ted, I'm forty two, and been married to Brian since I was nineteen, twenty three years of misery. I think I've only had two birthday cards from him, definitely no valentine cards, and apart from the first few weeks, no money from him either. I've had to run the house on the money I earned. The money from my granddad is still in a high interest investment account at the bank earning me money. I've never used any of it, and re-invested it over the years. I'm not able to touch it for about another two years and by then I'll be a lot richer than I am now. Tonight, I'm going to bring my saga up to date, and when I finish, you'll know more about my life than anyone else.

If you remember, I told you about Brian raping me continually until I told him I was pregnant. He has not touched me sexually since that day.

I gave birth to a girl, and my mother had her say in naming her. The poor girl, like me, has a string of unusual names and is called, Samantha Amanda Yasmine Katrina Critchley-Smythe-Jones. The only name I wanted, 'Catherine' was altered to Katrina, and put at the end, so now you know why I sometimes feel as though nobody cares what I want."

"I do." Ted said, giving her a kiss.

"I know you do. It's a pity nobody else has the same outlook on life as we do, things would be so much better."

"How old is Samantha Amanda… err… who?"

Ross laughed, and said,

"It's a wonder that anyone remembers all the names of either of us."

"Rosalinda Abigail Penelope Delores Critchley-Smythe-Jones." Ted recited.

"All right clever clogs, what about my daughter, try that one again."

"Samantha Amanda… err, oh yes, Yasmine and of course Katrina."

"Well done. I hope you'll remember those names, because I would like my lovely daughter to come and live with me… us, when the house is finished. What do you think about that?"

"You are full of surprises, aren't you? Ross my love, I would actually look forward to having your daughter with us, but there's just one problem. What do I call her?"

"She will only answer to Sam or Sammy, but knowing you, you'll find another name for her."

Ted smiled, and said,

"Mandy, Yas, Katie, Kat …."

"Enough, you mad sod. Is that all you can think about?"

Ted looked at Ross, and in a serious voice said,

"I think about you."

"Idiot"

"I love you when you talk rude".

"We are supposed to be having a serious conversation here."

"Sorry sweetheart, I didn't mean to put you off."

"That's not the first time you've called me sweetheart."

"Is it a problem, me calling you that?" Ted asked.

"No… no… Ted, it's nice, but… it's just, I'm… not used… to anything… like that." Ross answered with a sob and a tear in her eye.

"We've got a lot of time for you to get used to it." he whispered.

"As far as I'm concerned Ted, we've got years if all goes according to plan, but let me get back to my story, and then we can have an early night, we've got work to do in the morning."

"Of course, I'm sorry to mess about and spoilt your concentration. For a change, I'll keep my gob shut."

"Good. Now let me get on with it."

'After Sammy's birth, nearly eleven years ago, I saw very little of him at the house. He would come home on a Friday, go out and get drunk, then spent the weekend slapping me around. I have a feeling he's living with someone else during the week, he could in fact be married to her. I know, I know, its speculation, but don't forget I know the bastard and how he works. I hope he has married someone else, because if he gets found out, I can have my freedom and he goes to jail for bigamy. As I said, I got slapped around most weekends, but as time went on, these were a lot more severe than they had been previously. He knew how and where to hit me, always on my body, where nobody could see the marks. I never had a mark on my face, below my elbows or my knees. He has broken or cracked some ribs, and I'm sure my collar bone was cracked one time, because it can be awkward to move my shoulder at times. He used his hands most of the time, but has used his fists, and more than once, a tightly rolled wet towel. Ted, that bloody hurts. I screamed my lungs out at the start, but he cured that by stuffing my underwear in my mouth, the underwear that I had before I was ordered to wear the black thongs. I've also had bites on my body, love bites only, that is, he never actually broke the skin I'm glad to say. At work, granddad and I ran the company between us. We were a good team, and sadly he always knew when Brian was at home. About three years ago, our company received the offer of a take-over. Granddad and I talked this over with the group who wanted our business, and after almost two years of discussions and two increases in the offer, we eventually agreed to sell. When the sale went through, granddad insisted I had a share of the sale price for all the hard work I had put into it. He had the largest amount, Mum was given a small percentage, and I had the balance. This is one of the reasons I've been able to pay for, renovate and furnish my house without any problems. I know there is a substantial amount of money left at the bank to cover us all for many years, plus my investment account. I'm not going to tell you how much I got from the business sale until I'm sure it's me you want and not my money. Granddad's villa had still not been sold so three months after we sold the business, my mum, Sammy and I came to granddad's villa, and stayed for two weeks. It was during those two weeks that I bought the house in the hills. Mum was happy to spend the days on the beach with Sam while I looked for a place I could escape to. I looked at a few projects, but the only one that I wanted was the one we are working on. Other properties I saw were very nice, but what I call 'clinical' and I wanted something that was individual. I chose this one because I could re-build it the way I wanted. During that holiday I told my mum some of the things about Brian and his behaviour. She was obviously shocked that it had been going on for so long without anyone knowing, but warned me that whatever future plans I had in mind, Sam was my responsibility, and those plans must include her. I agreed with her, and it was then that I told her about buying the house. She was a bit sceptical at first, but after seeing it and me describing my aims and future plans, she could see the reasoning and accepted what I had done. When we got home, Brian was waiting, and wanted to know where we'd been without asking him.

I don't need to tell you what happened!

For the next two months, he worked from home, going only on local jobs, and during those two months, there wasn't a day when I didn't suffer. What I don't understand, is why he didn't ask why I was not going to work each day. He allowed me to drive Sammy to school, and pick her up at night, and apart from shopping, I was confined to the house. One night, when Sammy was in bed, the phone rang. I literally limped across the room to answer it because I was in agony from his last session with me. It was his boss telling Brian he was needed for an urgent job in the Midlands. He had to be there early the next day, and the job would last for three or four weeks. He packed his suitcase, rang a hotel to book a room and half an hour after his phone call, Brian was off in his van to a new job in the Midlands. Before he left, I got the usual reminder. His last words before he left on any job were,

'If you're not here when I get back, you and that kid are dead meat'.

The next morning I took Sammy to school, and after I kissed her goodbye, I started to plan my escape. I was so desperate to get away, I couldn't think straight, and apart from knowing I was coming to granddad's villa and my house, nothing seemed to register in my brain. I left it until the following week, fearing that Brian would come home at the weekend, and check I was still there. He didn't come home or try to contact me, so the following Tuesday, instead of taking Sammy to school, I packed some clothes for her, grabbed a few things for myself, put them into a large shopping bag, and took Sammy to my granddad. I'd already told him of my plan and he agreed to look after Sam while I was away. While I had been thinking about my escape, I decided I needed to sell my car and buy something that would be more suitable for carrying building materials and driving on the tracks around my new home. I found my pickup advertised for sale at a garage some way from our home. It was a demonstration model and was cheaper than list price, but I also got another discount for paying for it in cash. They didn't give me much for my car, but that didn't worry me, I had something new to escape in. I had to wait until they registered and sorted it out at Swansea before I could pick it up. They phoned me one Monday afternoon and said I could pick up any time I wanted. After dropping Sam with granddad on the Tuesday morning, I went to the garage in my car, and half an hour later, drove away in my pickup, knowing that if Brian wanted to find me, he would give the police my car registration number and it could take months before he knew I had sold it. I caught a night train under the channel, and drove in easy stages to granddad's villa. The next day, I went to the estate agents to make sure everything was sorted and my house had been paid for in full. He gave me all the necessary legal papers proving I was the proud owner of the house and land.

I was aware that there had been several people viewing granddad's villa and one couple had agreed a price with him. He had warned me before I left that I would probably have to move out fairly quickly once they had signed the contract and handed over the money. I stayed locked in the villa for a nervous week, hoping that I wouldn't have a crazy visitor from England. At the end of the second week, the new owners called to see me. They knew I was staying at the villa and also who I was. They were very friendly, but asked me if I could move out at the end of the month. I had no option but to agree, and that's why I'm renting the house here in the village. I moved into the house here and a couple of days later went up to my house in the hills, measured the rooms and decided where I should make a real start on the renovations. As you know, I thought it best to start with the kitchen wall tiles. I knew there was the tile shop in the village, so I drove down and had a look at what they had. I made my choice, placed the order, and left a deposit. They told me the tiles would be at the shop in four days' time and I was looking forward to making a start. I knew the renovations would take a long time, but I was determined to do as much as I could without calling for professional help. I had to do all the decoration in our house, so I was looking forward to making a start on my new home. I was up at the house one day when my mobile rang. It was granddad, warning me Brian was on the warpath, and was threatening to come over to the villa looking for me. Brian only had a rough idea where the villa was, but he could not have come looking for me anyway, because I'm certain he doesn't have a passport.

Granddad suggested I left the area for a while, just in case he decided to send someone over and check if I was there. I drove back to the French coast, and when I got to Calais, phoned granddad and told him where I was. He told me to stay there, and he, my mum and Sammy would catch a train, and meet me at Calais railway terminus. We spent a week together, discussing and hopefully perfecting my escape from the dreaded Brian. I promised Sammy I would bring her to Spain once things were sorted out and the house was habitable for the two of us. They left me crying on the station platform as the train disappeared into the Channel Tunnel. I drove in stages back to my rented house, and when I got there, there was a letter waiting for me about my order for tiles. I drove down to the village to pick them up, and while I was there... I met this man..."

Ross looked up at Ted, and smiled.

Ted gave her a hug and a kiss, before saying,

"Nobody deserves to be treated the way you have been, especially a lovely person like you. You've had to put up with his abuse for all those years, yet you trust me. How do you know I'm not like him?"

"You, my love, showed me trust from the day we met. You did the work for me and with me. If you had been a bully, you certainly wouldn't have done any hard work, you would have left it all to me. Also, you've accepted I'm married, and haven't tried to 'move in on me'. You still don't, although you seem to know when I want sex, and you satisfy my need. You know how much I want you, but you are prepared to wait until I'm one hundred per cent sure about my feelings. That is not the mind of a bully, Ted. Enough talk about bullies for tonight, I'm shattered and would like a good night's sleep without any horrific dreams. Take me to bed, hold me, cuddle me, kiss me, and help me to wake up refreshed, ready for a days' work on our house in the hills."

The next morning, they were back at the house ready for some hard work and to make it fit for a new family.

Ross, Ted, and a young lady called Sam.

SEVEN

A couple of days later, they had delayed their lunch break to finish what they were doing in the kitchen. They had not finished the tiling in the lounge, Ross preferring to wait until the skirting tiles arrived before carrying on with the floor.

Now the days were shorter, they didn't always have a siesta, and this particular day after they had eaten their sandwiches, Ross asked Ted if there was anything urgent to do. He said there wasn't, so Ross suggested they finish for the day and go and do some shopping. The first stop was back to the apartment, where they had a wash and changed out of their work clothes. Later, they visited two of the local supermarkets and bought what they needed to feed them for a week. Ross had taken on the task of making the lunches, and Ted always made the other meals and drinks. This was a satisfactory arrangement so each knew what food they needed to buy whenever they shopped. Ross insisted the cost of the food was shared equally and they always sorted the money out at the end of each week. They drove home with many bags of food and had to carry it all from the car park to the apartment. Putting it away was usually a laugh, as they dodged around each other while putting things in cupboards, fridge or freezer. When everything was in its place, Ted looked at Ross, and said,

"After all that hard work, I think we deserve a drink."

"Good idea," Ross replied, "I'd like a large one."

As soon as she spoke, Ross knew she had put her foot in it, and burst into peals of laughter.

"Don't you say a bloody word, Ted Hall!" She gasped.

Ted laughed with her, and answered,

"Whatever you say, my love. Shall we go into the

Plaza and sit watching the world go by?"

"To the Plaza, rather than the Paseo?" asked Ross.

"I think so," Ted replied, "we can have more than one drink if we want to, not having to drive home afterwards."

"If we go to the little place in the middle of the square, I may be tempted to try their version of chilli con carne."

"OK, said Ted, "it's my turn to pay, so let's go mad. Chilli and a sweet with a nice bottle of wine to wash it all down."

"It's a date! Come and give me a kiss before we start smelling of garlic."

They stood in the middle of the kitchen, and started to kiss. Ted was the first to break, and with a sigh, said,

"Ross, if we start again, I assure you we will not be eating or drinking tonight."

"I'm hungry for you as well as food and drink," Ross whispered, "I think we had better go out now, before we decide to christen the kitchen floor."

Reluctantly, they separated, and made their way to the main square and restaurants.

They enjoyed their chilli, but agreed that it was not as nice as the one they had at the restaurant on the Paseo.

Later, back at the apartment, Ted made some coffee and they sat on the settee to drink it. Ross looked at the television guide, and discovered that the film 'Ghost' was showing, and although she had seen it once, she said she would like to see it again. Though the film finished at one thirty in the morning, much later than they usually went to bed, Ross said they didn't really have to be at work by eight o'clock, and could please themselves when they arrived. Ted agreed, and so they settled down to watch the film. By the time they had wiped their eyes from crying, and had another drink, it was well past two o'clock when they got into bed. They had the usual kiss and cuddle before turning over to sleep. Ted was almost asleep when he was roused by Ross moving around in the bed. He turned towards her, and asked,

"Are you all right?"

"Sorry Ted, have I wakened you?"

"Not really," Ted fibbed, "I was nodding off when I felt you moving around. Can't you sleep?"

"I thought I was tired, but for some stupid reason I can't fall asleep yet. I do need a wee though."

Ross got out of bed and went to the bathroom. There was no need for her to put any lights on, as the full moon was shining through the bedroom window. Ted watched Ross as she walked into the room in the moonlight, and as she got back into bed, he turned to her and said,

"Rosalinda Jones, I think you really are one bloody gorgeous lady."

"Th… thank you," she stammered, completely taken back by his sudden complement, "you're not so bad yourself."

"I wish you were my lady."

"I am your lady, aren't I?"

"I meant, my lady, as in my wife."

"Is that some kind of proposal?"

"If you were free, Ross, I would have proposed weeks ago."

"If I'd been free Ted, I would have accepted."

Ross turned on her side, facing Ted, and putting her arm round his shoulder, said,

"Would there be many changes to our life if we were married?"

"Only one major one." Ted answered.

"I know what major change that would be." declared Ross.

She gave Ted a soft lingering kiss, and whispered,

194

"What would you say, if I suggested we live the rest of our time together as though we were man and wife?"

"I'd say that nothing would give me greater pleasure." he whispered back.

"That's settled then! Now, please will you give your new wife a nice long passionate kiss?"

As she spoke, Ross snuggled up to him and put her arm further round his shoulders. They began to kiss, mildly passionate at first, but suddenly with more urgency. Ted started to get aroused, and Ross pushed her self gently against him.

"I love it when I feel you like that." Ross whispered, "It makes me feel good as well, knowing it is me that is making it happen."

Ted bent down and started kissing her nipple which became hard and extended as he gently washed the end with his tongue. He moved his lips away, and immediately started to touch the end with gentle strokes using his left hand. As he stroked her, he started kissing the other nipple and by this time, Ross was moving her body against him, and moaning with ecstasy as Ted stimulated her with both hands. When he moved one hand downwards, Ross opened herself to him and because she was so ready, it was easy for Ted to find the spot that gave her so much pleasure.

Meanwhile, Ross had taken Ted in her hand, but the grip was not as firm as usual, more of a gentle stroking action, matching the movement Ted was using on her. She cried out in passion as Ted's fingers and lips kept up their relentless movement on her body, Ross digging her fingers into Ted's shoulder, and crying out with bliss. Suddenly, her grip on him tightened, and she pulled him towards her and at the same time, opening her legs wide so that he could lie between them. She guided him towards her, and just as he touched, she gasped,

"Push Ted, Push!"

He started to push, but had only just entered when she lifted herself up, and with a cry of joy, took the whole of him into her. She started to move, and within seconds, they were moving together as though they had known that joy for years. It only took a few moments before Ross stiffened with an ecstatic cry, but Ted continued to move inside her, until a few seconds later, he reached his own climax.

They lay panting with the exertion of their lovemaking, slowly bringing their minds and bodies back to normal. Ross's eyes were still closed, as she slowly relaxed in his arms. He bent down and gave her a long and tender kiss, Ross tightening her arms round him.

"*Now* I'm your woman, Ted Hall," she whispered as they broke, and started to cry.

Ted stayed where he was, leaning on his elbows, inches from her face. He gently kissed her eyes, tasting the saltiness of the tears, and moved his lips slowly down her face until he reached her lips. He put his lips on hers, just touching and moving them very slowly from side to side. Ross's reaction was to tighten her arms around him, and pull his body down, so that he was completely on top of her. His erection had subsided, but Ross closed her legs round it, as though to hold it in place. She put her lips close to Ted's ear, and whispered,

"I love you Ted Hall, and you have just proven your love for me. I have never had sex like that before, but you can be assured I will want more. I hope you can stand the pace, because I've got a lot of catching up to do. Those tears were of joy, not sorrow, because I have no regret for allowing you into my body. Please, Ted, keep on looking after me the way you are doing, and I promise you will never regret it."

"I promise with all my heart to look after you." Ted answered "I'll keep you safe from anybody and anything, and defend you as much as an honest husband should. I love you Ross, and I'll never stop reminding you. I sincerely hope we have a long time together and I'd like to be able to make you happier than you have ever been before."

"I'm already happier, and if you can make me more happy, I'll look forward to it. Now, I'm afraid you'll have to get off me, because I need to go for a wash."

When Ross came back to the bed, they had a kiss, turned over, and both were asleep within minutes.

When they woke later that morning, it was raining. They drove up to their house and looked out over the wet landscape.

"It seems that the summer's over Ted." Ross said sadly. "From now on, if the weather is fine, we work from first light until dusk, but one rule Ted, we never work with any of the lights on. If it is too dull to see the job properly, we don't do it. At the moment the light isn't too bad, but if it carries on raining and gets any darker, we go home."

Inside the bedroom block, the grouting was completely dry and ready for rubbing off the tiles. They set to, polishing each tile until no loose grout was evident. It took all morning for the two of them to finish in the corridor, and when the job was complete, Ross decided it was time for something to eat. They walked hand in hand across the 'garden' to the living block where they had left their sandwiches. There had been no rain for months, and that morning's downpour had turned the dust into a muddy mess, and by the time they got to the kitchen door, their shoes were full of mud and they were wet and cold.

"We're going home," Ross told Ted firmly, "we can't

work in these conditions."

Ted made his way back to the bedroom block and locked the door, then trudged round to the front of the house where Ross was waiting. They took off their muddy shoes before getting into the pickup and Ross drove home barefoot.

Back at the apartment, Ted turned on the gas heater to warm them and the room up.

"Would you like some soup with our sandwiches?" he asked.

"Now that's a good idea." Ross said, "what varieties have you got?"

"I think there's tomato, asparagus, mushroom or chicken."

"Tomato, please Ted. Do you want a hand?"

Ted told her he could manage and went to the kitchen to heat the soup. Ross had made the sandwiches before they left for work, so all Ted had to do was put them on plates.

After they had eaten, they were sat relaxing in front of the gas fire, when Ross's telephone rang. She looked surprised as she took it out of her bag and looked at the screen.

"Granddad." she said softly to Ted.

"Hello granddad," she said as she left the room.

It was quite a few minutes before Ross came back into the living room, and in a worried voice said,

"I'm going to have to go back to the UK Ted, hopefully only for a few days. I'm sorry I have to rush off like this, but granddad seems to think Sam is being followed, and Brian has been sniffing around her at school, demanding to know where I am. I need to see Sam, and assure her I'm almost ready to bring her here. Shall we go down to the internet café and see when I can get a flight and then I can pack my smalls and get away."

They had to use the internet café in the village because there was no telephone line connected to Ted's apartment, so he could not go on line from his computer.

"Do you want to borrow my small suitcase?" Ted asked, "it's fairly light, and can be used as hand luggage. If you are only going to be away for a few days it will be OK, but I have a medium sized one as well if you prefer that."

"I'll borrow the medium sized one please," Ross said, "there are a few things I'd like to bring back with me if I get the chance."

While they were discussing these options, they were on their way to the internet café. When they got on line they checked for flights to London Gatwick, that being the nearest airport to her previous home. There was a flight leaving Malaga at eight fifty five that night, and there was room on the flight for her. Ross made the booking using her credit card, and within a few minutes, had the confirmation e-mail printed out.

Back in the apartment, Ted gave Ross the case, and left her to pack some clothes and get herself ready to leave. She came back to the living room and said,

"Here are the house keys Ted, so if the weather's fine, you can do what you think is necessary. I don't want you to come to the airport with me because I hate goodbye's, especially to you. I'll drive to the airport and leave my pickup there. I know parking is expensive, but if I'm only going to be a week, it won't be too bad."

"Why not take my car, it will be easier to park and I can go to work in the pickup."

"Thank you Ted, that's a good idea."

A couple of hours later, Ross was driving away after a tearful kiss and cuddle from Ted, reminding him she would keep in touch if she could. She had rung her granddad to tell him the flight number, and he was going to meet her at Gatwick.

Ted sat in his living room, dejected after all the rushing around in the last few hours. It was suddenly very quiet in his apartment and for the first time in the last seven or eight months, he felt very much alone.

He awoke next morning and remembered that his new love was not next to him. He lay there for a few minutes thinking about her and hoping that everything would turn out all right.

As he left the apartment that morning, Ted could see the boxes of skirting tiles outside the shop, so he loaded them into the pickup and drove off to the house. Now that he had the tiles, he decided his first job was to complete the living room floor.

It took him three days to finish the main floor and step and set the skirting tiles all the way round the room. When the adhesive was completely dry he would have to grout the whole room on his own, and knowing it would be hard work, he was not really looking forward to it.

He started to apply the grout, but had not got very far down the room, when it suddenly went very dark and started to rain again. He had to stop work, but by working in-between rain showers and the half dark they brought, it took him a further two days to complete the grouting and the polishing. He had to finish early each day because of the poor light, and thought later that he could possibly have hired a polishing machine to do the job he had just done by hand.

The day after finishing the living room floor, Ted started work in the kitchen. He built the remaining base cupboards and drawers and fitted them where Ross told him they had to go. The hole for the sink had already been cut out of the work top by the plumber, and had been placed loosely on top of the units, so Ted carefully measured and cut the work tops to size before securing them on the base cupboards. He finished by building the wall cupboards and measuring and marking the screw positions where he would fit them the next day. Before leaving for home, Ted had a look round to see what else needed doing in that block. He looked at the idea of making a doorway from the living area into the toilet, thought it was possible, and decided he would measure it up the first job next morning. After putting up the wall cupboards and making the toilet door, nothing else needed to be done in that block. The only big task was in the other building, where the floors needed laying in each bedroom and bathroom, and when the floors were laid, the doors had to be hung. It wasn't hard work, Ted thought, just time consuming.

The following day was fine and sunny when Ted left for the house in the hills. The warmth in the sun gave him incentive to get on with the work and he set to with a will. He measured the wall in the toilet, and then in the living room, and decided that a door would fit nicely, and would not look out of place as it would be partly screened by the edge of the fireplace. He measured and marked where the door would go, and scored round the mark with his cold chisel. The sheet of thick plastic was put on the floor to prevent any damage to the new tiles, and an hour later, he had knocked out the breeze block, cleared the rubble away and was all set to get it ready for the door frame. Mixing some white concrete in the wheelbarrow, and working from the toilet side, Ted set and squared off the edges. He made sure they were smooth and even before clearing everything away, leaving the concrete to dry thoroughly before he could fit the door frame. His use of the white concrete would lessen the need of painting the walls again when the door and its frame were fitted. He went into the kitchen, where he drilled and plugged the screw holes, and followed up by firmly screwing the cupboards on to the walls. Another morning's work finished, and as far as he could tell there was nothing else he could do in that block at the moment. His clock told him that it was nearly two thirty, and after eating his sandwiches, Ted decided to clear the rubble that had accumulated in the bedroom block. They had used all the breeze blocks that were on pallets inside, and all that remained were broken ones and the piles of chippings that were left when he had to break a block to fill a gap. Outside there was another two pallets of blocks, so after clearing the mess and sweeping up the dust inside, he loaded the wheelbarrow and restacked the blocks neatly where they could be reached when he needed them. The room was looking much tidier, but as the light was beginning to fade he decided to finish for the day. He had locked the doors and was on his way to the pickup, when his telephone rang. Thinking it would be Ross, he said a cheery 'hello' in English, without checking the number on the screen. He was answered by a Spaniard who told him he was ringing from the store where Ross had bought the bed, and they wanted to deliver it the following day. Ted said that would be fine, and gave them the directions to the house. When they had the deliveries of concrete, Ted had fixed a red painted board with a white arrow on it, by the turning up to the house. He asked if the driver could give him a ring as he approached, then he could show him where it had to go. His first task next morning would be to lay as much of the floor as he could before the bed was delivered.

The sun was shining as Ted arrived early at the house to start on the bedroom floor. Armed with his tape measure and a saw, he opened the first of many boxes of flooring and started work. The first row was easy to lay and only needed a short piece cutting to fit comfortably.

By alternating the cut pieces, Ted kept up a steady pace, and was just over half way along the room when his telephone rang. It was the driver with the bed and was by the red board awaiting instructions. Ted told him to come up the track, and he would meet him at the front door. The bed and its mattress were carried through the patio doors into the bedroom and fifteen minutes later the men were on their way back to the store, and Ted was hard at work again laying the floor. He finished the main floor as far as the corridor and then started in the bathroom. The wood to be fitted in the bathroom was specially treated and sealed to avoid warping from the water, and as there was only a small area to fit, Ted ate his sandwiches while he worked. When the floor had been laid to his satisfaction, Ted secured the toilet, bidet and washbasin bases to the wood. Another job successfully completed! He started fitting the door frame to the bathroom, but by the time he had cut the pieces to size, it was going dark. He tidied the room, put away his tools, closed the shutters and after checking everything was as it should be, decided to pack up for the day.

The next morning it was raining again and by the look of the cloud, it was set for the day. Ted knew there was no point in going to the house so sat and watched some daytime television, something he rarely did, especially over the past months. It rained all day, and the forecast for the next day, Saturday, was not much better. When he got up on Sunday morning it was still dull but at least it wasn't raining. It was almost eleven thirty when the weather brightened, so he got into the pickup and drove to the house. He went straight to the bedroom block, and opened the shutters in what would be Ross's and his bedroom. The flooring he had laid had settled nicely, and he was able to knock the wood to tighten it up. There was only a fraction to cut off the last piece, which he did using a plane, and fit it into the frame of the main doorway. When he was sure the floor was right, he put the new bed in place and removed the wrapping from the base.

He next went to the bathroom, fixed the door frame to the wall and did the same to the main door. All that remained to do in that room was to hang the doors. He measured the door frames carefully, screwed the hinges into them, lined up the doors, and fixed them to the hinges. Looking at the clock on his mobile phone he saw it was already mid-afternoon, and after a quick sandwich break, decided he would keep going as long as the light was suitable, but as soon as he went into the bathroom in the second bedroom, he realised there was no way he could lay the floor in that light even with a light on. He could hear Ross saying, 'If the light isn't strong enough for us to be accurate, we don't do the job.' Reluctantly, he closed the shutters, locked the doors and drove home.

Monday was much brighter, but as Ted drove to the house, the promised sunshine still hadn't appeared. He unlocked the door to the bedroom block and went to the second bedroom. As he opened the shutters, the sun broke through the cloud sending warmth into the room, and the whole area suddenly took on a bright light. Heartened by it, Ted set to and before long had got into a rhythm. The bathroom floor was soon finished, and the toilet and washbasin secured. He started the main floor by the patio doors, just as he had done in the other bedroom. In the warmth of the sun through the open doors, Ted soon got into the swing, and was making good progress. He did not want to stop for his lunch, so carried on laying the floor while he ate. By mid-afternoon he was about two thirds of the way up the room, when he heard footsteps coming along the corridor. Before he could ask who was there, he heard

Ross call out,

"Ted, are you in here?"

"Second bedroom love" Ted called, clicking another length of wood into place. At that moment, Ross appeared in the doorway, and holding her hand was a fair haired young lady with lovely blue eyes.

"Hello!" said Ted, "you must be the world famous Sammymantha."

The young lady smiled, and said,

"Mum said you would think of a daft name for me."

"Your mum told me about you, but she never said how pretty you were. Come and give me a hug and a kiss, then you can call me Ted."

Without any hesitation, Sammy came into the room and hugged him tightly. She pulled away and planted a big kiss on his lips.

"Has your mum showed you round yet?" Ted asked.

She shook her head, and said,

"We've only just got here, and all the other doors are locked, so we had to come here first."

Ted was still kneeling on the floor, so he got up and took hold of her hand.

"I've said hello to you, now is it all right if I give your mum a kiss of welcome?"

Sammy nodded her head, and with a smile said,

"Mum's been telling me all about you, and she said this morning she'd missed you and was looking forward to seeing you again."

Ted went over to Ross, gave her a gentle kiss, and said he was happy to see her again too.

Keeping hold of Sammy's hand, Ted looked round the room, and said,

"Can you imagine this room with a bed by that wall, and maybe a wardrobe here." As he spoke, Ted pointed to the places he envisaged the things he described.

"There could be a dressing table there, and maybe a chair or two and a table with a lamp on it. Over here," he carried on, turning to the bathroom, "is what's known as an 'en-suite' bathroom, with a bath and a shower over it, a wash basin and a loo. There is a door to go on it yet and another door to go in the gap that you came through a few minutes ago. When I fit that door, I could paint a square in the middle panel and write on it,

'Sammy's room, keep out'."

She looked at Ted and then at her mum, and in an amazed voice, said,

"Is this going to be my bedroom?"

Ross took hold of her other hand, and said,

"Yes Sam, as soon as Ted's finished it and we buy you a bed and some furniture, this will be your bedroom."

"Where are you going to sleep?" she asked her mum.

"This way, young lady," said Ted as he led her through the door and turned to the other room. "Open the door and go inside."

Sammy opened the door and stepped inside. She turned and said,

"This is like my room but the other way round, and you've got a bed."

"When was that delivered?" Ross asked Ted.

"Last Wednesday morning." he replied. "I've not been able to do much for a few days because of the rain and poor light, but all I have to do in this block, is finish Sammy's floor, and fit both doors. I have the two aluminium doors to replace at the ends, but I can do that when I've finished everything else."

"You've had a tidy up in here as well, haven't you?" Ross said.

Ted grinned and replied,

"Nothing gets past your eagle eye, does it? Come on,

let's go across to the other block and show Sammy where she's going to live."

Ted and Sammy were holding hands as they started out across the gap so Ross got hold of his other hand, and gave it a squeeze. They came to the back door, and Ted had to leave go of his ladies hands so he could get the keys from his pocket. He opened the door, and stood back to let them in.

"You've finished it!" cried Ross, as she stepped inside. "Oh, Ted that looks perfect. Thank you."

She turned round and gave him a nice kiss.

"I'll finish all the other rooms if I get rewarded like that." he said.

Ross had a good look round, and saw that he had set it up just how she had planned it. She opened the door into the living area, and slowly walked across the tiles towards the step.

"This room looks so warm now the tiles are polished. The step really divides the room as you thought. We can eat at the kitchen end and relax at the bottom.... what's the gap.... have you knocked through to the toilet? You have, you clever old sod. That's brilliant Ted, thank you."

For that, he got another kiss!

"I've still to change the door over and brick up the outside wall, but there's no big rush at the moment."

"Have you and mum built this house?" Sam asked.

"Not the main outside walls," Ross answered "but most of the rest. What do you think of it?"

"I think it's a fabulous house and the view to the sea is fantastic, but where's Ted going to sleep?"

"Would you mind if Ted slept in my bedroom?" Ross asked.

Sammy smiled and shook her head.

"Is Ted going to live with us then?"

"Would you have any objections if he did?"

"No," said Sammy, taking hold of Ted's hand again, "I think he's a nice man and I'd like him to look after us."

"I'll do my best for both of you," said Ted, "but what I'd like to know now is have you eaten or are you hungry?"

"We had a sandwich on the plane, so we're all right for now." Ross said. "What do you want to do?"

"Well, there's only the floor to finish in Sammy's room, but the sun will be setting in about half an hour, so I won't be able to finish it today. Shall we lock up and go back to the apartment? I can get changed and we can take this little lady to the Paseo to show her where the beach is."

Ted left them in the house while he went back to the other block and put his things away before closing the shutters and locking the outside doors. There was a lightness in his step as he walked back, having two ladies to look after was something he was looking forward to. He locked the back door behind him as he went into the kitchen, and as he went into the living room he saw the two ladies were still looking round, Ross telling Sammy how the room might look when they bought some furniture. Ted opened the front door, and they walked out to the sight of the sun starting to go down behind the hills.

"We can leave the pickup in the top car park tonight, go to the Paseo in my car and swap them over in the morning on our way to work." Ted said.

In convoy they drove to the village, left the pickup in the car park, and a few minutes later, Sammy was looking round Ted's apartment. She went to the bathroom, and told Ross she was going to the toilet and have a wash ready to go out.

While she was in there, Ross took hold of Ted's arm and said in a low voice.

"I'll tell you more later Ted, but Brian found me in the lodge and gave me a bloody good pasting. My body is black and blue and there are bites on me as well, so please don't hug me too tightly."

Ted was shocked at the news, and could hardly think of what to say.

"I'm sorry, Ross, I wish there was something I could do, but you can guarantee it will never happen again, because whenever you go back to the UK, I'm coming with you."

He gave her a soft kiss without a hug and asked if she needed any pain killers.

"I don't think so," Ross replied, "but you can look at the damage tonight and we can decide if anything needs to be done."

Sammy came out of the bathroom and Ross took her to the room where she was going to sleep until they moved into the other house, and started to unpack her clothes.

While Ross was with Sammy in the bedroom, Ted was having a good wash. It didn't take him long to get changed, and a few minutes later, they piled into the car and drove down to the Paseo. They took jackets with them, knowing that now the sun had set, the evening would be quite cool. Sammy was impressed with the Paseo in almost the same way that her mum had been all those months ago. She was also amazed by the number of food places, but when she heard about the 'chilli-con-carne restaurant', she wanted to try it straight away. They found the restaurant open, and went inside to eat. As Ted said, eating in the open air was for the summer and sun, but the winter months it was warmer eating inside.

They had a starter, and were sat waiting for the main meal, when Ross said,

"It seems a long time ago that you and I sat out there with the drawing pad." Ross turned to Sammy, and told her that Ted had drawn the outline of the bedroom block the first night they met. She said that the way he drew it made it look so simple, but building it had been very hard work at times.

"That hard work has paid off as you can see," Ross continued, "and we are almost ready to move in."

"When did you meet Ted?" Sam asked.

"Tuesday the twenty eighth of March at five minutes to ten." Ted answered.

"How can you remember it so exactly?" asked Ross.

"We'd put the clock forward on the Sunday, and I remember that was the twenty sixth. I know we met on the Tuesday after, as I was waiting for the ten o'clock bus to go shopping."

"When do the clock go back again?" Ross asked.

"This Sunday," Ted answered, "so we've been working together for seven months."

"And a very good seven months as well. We've done quite a lot in that time, haven't we?"

"We have Ross, and enjoyed every minute of it."

They were served with their chilli-con-carne, so there was a pause in conversation while they started to eat. Sammy said the chilli was nearly as good as her Mums, but she could manage to eat it because she was hungry. They enjoyed the meal as much as Ted and Ross had done on the first night they met, but the walk back to the car was much quicker than that night, because there was a cool breeze blowing in off the sea. They arrived back at the apartment and sat down in the lounge to have a cup of tea, but after about ten minutes, Ted carefully nudged Ross and nodded at Sammy.

She was sat on a chair, and her eyes were closing, then she would wake up with a jerk, only to nod off minutes later.

"Sam," Ross said in a soft voice, being careful not make her jump.

Sammy opened her eyes and gave a weak smile.

"Are you ready for bed?" Ross asked her.

Sam nodded, and got up from the chair. Ross went with her to her room and a few minutes later, Sam came back to the living room in her nightdress. She put her arms round Ted, kissed him and said good night. A few minutes later, Ross came back to the living room.

"How are you feeling?" Ted asked her.

"I'm tired, but I can wait for a bit longer before going to bed. Is it all right if I have another talk to you? I'd like to tell you about what happened, and then when we go to bed, you can see for yourself what the bastard did.

"I wish I'd been able to come with you Ross, because I can assure you that your husband, or ex-husband would not have got anywhere near you."

"He's a big man, Ted and would have had a go at you too."

"Possibly, but don't forget he's a bully, and bullies don't like people who stand up to them, no matter how big they are."

"That's true, but let me tell you what happened."

'I arrived at Gatwick, and granddad was waiting for me with Sammy and my mum. We had our usual tearful reunion and we were all glad to see each other again. Because Sam was still living at granddads', mum had temporally moved in as well, so it was obvious that I would stay with them. After a sandwich and a drink, I went to bed telling them we would catch up with the news the next day. I slept well that night, and after breakfast we sat down to talk. I told them about you, how we met, and what we had done together on the house and how we enjoyed our leisure time. I promised Sammy it would not be long before she could come over to live with us, but I wasn't certain that I would be bringing her back with me on this trip. But when granddad told me about Brian harassing her, I had to think carefully before making a decision. I asked granddad and mum if they knew where Brian was, but neither could be certain. I wanted to go to the lodge and get some personal things and some of the clothes I'd left behind on the day I escaped his clutches. From the house, you can see the lodge so I kept watch from eight o'clock the next morning, and never saw anything of him. I kept a lookout for another couple of days, just wanting to make sure he wasn't keeping out of sight, but on the Wednesday evening, I saw him go into the lodge with a woman in tow. That didn't worry me one bit, but wondered how long she was staying, because it could stop me from going there for the things I wanted. She stayed for the rest of the week, but left the lodge with him on Saturday morning. He was carrying a suitcase, and I thought my luck was in and he was going away on a job. I left it until around one o'clock and decided I would go down there, get what I wanted, and out again as quickly as possible. I told granddad what I was going to do, and although he suggested he came with me, I said I'd like to spend some time sorting out what I wanted, but if I wasn't back at the house within three quarters of an hour, he should come looking for me. I nervously walked down the drive towards the lodge, and had a good look round. I neither heard or saw anybody, so put my key in the lock and went inside. I had been there for perhaps half an hour or so and got quite a few things I wanted in a pile on the living room table. Then I heard a sound that I had been dreading. Brian came in through the front door, and obviously knew that someone was in the lodge because of the pile of my clothes on the table. He came straight to the bedroom and saw me with more clothes in my hands. He rushed across the room and punched me in the stomach which obviously knocked me down. He started kicking me around the body, and in between the kicks said,

"What did I fucking tell you, bitch? If you ran away I would fucking kill you and that pretty little kid. Who shagged you to give you a blonde you dirty whore? She certainly isn't mine and I'd never give you a penny for another tart like you."

By this time Ted, I was curled up in a ball trying to ward off the kicks, but the bastard grabbed my hair, pulled me to my feet and forced my head backwards. With his free hand, he tore my blouse down the front, and then ripped it off me completely. I dreaded what he was going to do, and started to scream. He gave me another punch to my stomach, which shut me up immediately. He took a pair of my briefs off the bed, pushed them into my mouth and started punching me again. My bra was torn off, followed by my skirt and briefs, so there I was, naked with a gag in my mouth at the mercy of an evil, short tempered bullying bastard.'

At this point, Ross was sobbing, and tears were pouring down her face at the memory. Ted knew there was no point in trying to stop her talking, so held her as tightly as he dared while she continued.

'I was certain I was going to be raped, and although I would fight it, in the end I knew it was inevitable. He continued to slap my body, but much harder than he'd been doing for years, and all I could do was scream into the gag. I was fighting back with everything I had, but he is much stronger than me and my fight was in vain. He pushed me back onto the bed, and I thought, 'this is it' as he took off his trousers and underpants. He was already hard, as he bent over me and snarled,

"I'm going to give you the best shagging of your life, and then I'm going to kill you. You knew the consequences when you left, so you'll fucking well pay for it now and I'll get the kid later."

He bent down and bit me on my right breast. There was no attempt to break the skin as he applied pressure, in effect, giving me a 'love bite'. He was sucking the skin and he kept it going and going and going. He stopped for a second, and moved to the other breast, but underneath this time. The pain was excruciating and he kept up the relentless pressure and I was still screaming into the gag and made a hopeless gesture of hitting him on his back with my fists. Next to suffer was my pubes. He put his mouth onto my flesh and bit, this time I could feel the flesh break. I was kicking out with my legs, but the position he was in, none of the kicks landed. There is no way I can describe the pain I was going through and I was slowly beginning to pass out. I was almost unconscious when I felt him jump up. He stood over me, and I felt the dirty bastard let it go onto my stomach. I felt so humiliated as he stood looking down on me and started to smear it all over the front of my body. Then the slaps and punches started again. Somehow I managed to roll over, so that the blows were now on my back and occasionally my bottom. I was exhausted with screaming and the beating I was getting, and again I was nearly passing out from the pain. Suddenly he stopped punching, and through the darkness I heard a voice. In my fuddled brain, it was you I could hear calling for me, but I knew you were in Spain, and decided it was wishful thinking or I was hallucinating. But help was at hand! The voice I heard was granddads'. He had come to the lodge looking for me because I had not gone back to his house within the time we agreed. He shouted for me again, and Brian gave me one last punch, pushed past granddad and ran out of the lodge wearing just a shirt, his trousers and underpants in his hand.

Granddad came into the bedroom, saw me sprawled naked across the bed and without thinking, wrapped the throw-over round me. Of course, he didn't see the bite marks on the front of my body, but he realised there was something in my mouth. He gently pulled the briefs out, allowing me to breath properly again. He held me in his arms while I sobbed on his shoulder, but then I had to rush to the loo. I sat down and let everything go, shaking like a jelly as it happened. As I stood up, I turned and threw up into the bowl. I was still shaking all over, as I went back towards the bedroom. I could hear granddad in the kitchen, putting the kettle on, and when he heard me, called to say that the police were on their way. I told him I didn't want to see them, but he insisted, and I had no option but to wait for their arrival. I got dressed into some clothes that I'd put on the bed, leaving the torn ones on the floor to show the police. I knew I could have him put away, but that would only provoke more problems, so I decided to see what the police advised.

When they arrived at the lodge, it was granddad who spoke to them first, telling them what he had seen. They took his statement and then while granddad was out of the room, asked me to describe in as much detail as I could what had happened. I told them, exactly the same way as I'm telling you now. I unbuttoned my blouse, showed them the marks on my body and one of them actually winced when he saw what Brian had done. It was only after he had finished writing the report that one of the policemen said,

"We answered a call last week from a lady called Dorothy, who complained that she had been beaten up by the same person. We have been looking for him all week, but he's very elusive. However when we do find him, we can add your assault to the charge with the other lady's."

After they left, granddad helped me with the clothes I'd collected, and he locked the door behind us.

"I'll have the locks changed first thing on Monday," he told me, "so if he wants anything, he will have to come and see me first."

"I don't somehow think that will happen." I told him, "but keep an eye open for broken windows, he'll more than likely get in that way."

Granddad just nodded as we walked slowly back to his house. I took my clothes to the bedroom, then went to the bathroom and got under the shower to rid myself of the dirt he'd left on me. You don't know how good it felt to be washed clean and into fresh clothes after the ordeal I'd just gone through.

Later that night, I showed my mum my midriff, sides and back, but not the bites. I knew if she saw them, I would have been shipped off to the hospital, and would probably have had to stay there for a day or two. All I wanted to do was pack suitcases for Sammy and me and get back here to Spain as soon as we possibly could. I talked to you in bed that night, and because you weren't there to answer me, I cried myself to sleep thinking of you.

The following morning I felt like hell but stubbornly refused to let anyone know just how bad. I was in granddad's study getting the computer set up to look for a flight, when Sam came into the room. Very gently she put her arms round me, and said,

"Has daddy beaten you up again, mum?"

I could only nod at her, and then I asked quietly,

"How do you know what happened?"

"I guessed, because I've seen you before, walking very stiffly after daddy has hit you. I've seen him do it to you, but I've not said anything because I was too afraid of it happening to me. I've known for a long time that he likes to hit and bully you, so I knew when you left me with granddad you were running away from him. I was glad for you, but at first I was worried you wouldn't come back for me. Thank you for all the telephone calls you made from Spain, it was always good to hear your voice. I could hardly believe it when granddad told me you were flying over especially to see me."

I hugged Sam as closely as I dared, and made up my mind that we were coming back to our house as soon as we could. I was worried about taking her from school before the end of the term, but decided her safety was more important at that moment. I let her sit beside me as I went on line and almost immediately found a flight that left Gatwick at ten past eight this morning.

Was I glad to get back here, not just to the house, but to you Ted. I missed you more than anything and as you said earlier, next time I go back, you are coming with me. Mum, granddad and of course, Sammy know how much I want to be with you and granddad has promised to ring me if the police catch Brian and if I need to go to court for any reason. I hope my nightmare is over, the only worry I have are the bites on my body. Please, when we go to bed, have a good look at them and make sure they are not going septic."

Ross stopped speaking for a moment, wiped the tears from her eyes, and put her arms round Ted.

"I love you Ted Hall, and I want us to be together for

a long time. Ted, please keep protecting me, and help me look after Sam, because all I want from now on is a happy and peaceful life, the three of us together."

"That's something we are going to have, peace. I told you some time ago I would look after you to the best of my ability and that promise still stands, and is extended to include your lovely daughter."

"Thank you Ted." Ross said with relief in her voice. "Let's go to bed, then I can flash my naked body at you while you examine my wounds. I'll tell you something that may surprise you, it certainly surprised me. I've only been away from you for ten days, but one night before Brian found me, I was thinking about you and started to feel a desire for sex. That's something that never happened before I met you."

When they got to the bedroom, Ross undressed and lay on the bed and Ted sat on the edge beside her. She showed him the bruises on her body, and Ted had to admit that he had never ever seen anything so brutal. The bite mark on her right breast was easy to see, and although it was badly bruised, the skin wasn't broken. The bite underneath her left breast was badly bruised as well, but even though he could see teeth marks, the skin on that one wasn't broken either. The bite in her pubes was different though. It was very badly discoloured and in three or four places the skin was broken and looked slightly inflamed.

"Ross," he told her, "the skin is broken, and really I should remove the hair round it, but I have nothing that will shave it closely without removing the whole lot. I'll clean it up with soap and water first and then put some antiseptic on it."

When he was satisfied it was clean, he found some antiseptic and gently bathed the area. Ross jumped slightly as he started, but got used to the sting and lay still until he finished.

"I don't think there will be a problem, Ross, but it's best we keep an eye on it for a while."

"You'll tell me anything to see me undressed." Ross said to him with a smile.

"I see you undressed every night when we go to bed, and partly undressed nearly every day at work, enjoying the sight of the forbidden fruit."

"They're not forbidden fruit any more Ted, neither is any other part of my body, so why don't you get undressed, get into bed and carefully remind me of the pleasure I've been missing for the last twenty five years."

The careful reminder was a joy for both of them, and when they eventually got their breath back, Ross whispered,

"Ted Hall, I've said it before, and I'll repeat it now, I wish I'd met you when I was a teenager, I'd have been happy to have spent my life with you. I love you very much, and as I said earlier, I want the three of us to enjoy the chance of a new life together."

Within minutes, Ross was asleep in Ted's arms.

Ted woke to following morning, to find Ross looking at him and smiling.

"This is a nice way to wake up," he said, "a gorgeous lady lying next to me and smiling. How would you like a kiss and a gentle cuddle?"

"I can hardly wait," she said pushing herself close. They hugged and kissed for several minutes, happy to be in each other's arms again.

"What are we going to do today?" asked Ross, still cuddled up to Ted.

"We could go to a furniture shop to look for and order the things we need for the house. They probably won't be delivered for a few weeks, and that will give me time to finish the bedrooms. We need bedding as well and I suggest a heater for each room for this winter. It will be all right next winter though, the house will have absorbed the summer heat, and will retain it longer."

"It's a good job I have money to buy it all, isn't it."

"Can I give you some of my money?" Ted asked her, "I mean, you've paid for everything that's in the house, and now you want me to live with you, I feel as though I should contribute something."

"Your contribution had been to plan and build our home, and as I've said before, I could not have done it without you. You are mine and Sam's bodyguard and that is worth something beyond payment. Let's not think about money Ted because without being funny, I don't need any more, I have enough for the three of us for many years. If you want to make a contribution to something, you can keep me satisfied on a regular basis."

As she spoke, Ross was moving suggestively against him, then whispered,

"Step one will be enough for now."

Before Ted could oblige his wonderful lady, there was a tap on the bedroom door.

"Is it safe for me to come in?" Sammy shouted.

Ross said that it was perfectly safe.

"Later!" Ross whispered to him, as Sammy got onto the bed beside her.

"Did you sleep all right?" Ross asked Sam.

"Yes, thanks Mum. When I woke up, it took me a moment or two to remember where I was. I feel wide awake now because I have a lot to look forward to with both of you."

The three of them had a cuddle before deciding it was time to get dressed.

Ted was first out of bed, and being as discrete as he could, picked up his underpants off the chair and put them on.

"Do both of you always sleep with nothing on?" Sammy asked.

"We do," he answered, "I hope you won't be embarrassed if you see us without clothes."

Sammy shook her head and told them she had seen her dad without clothes when he got dressed in a morning. Eventually they were all washed and dressed, and in the kitchen eating breakfast. While they were at the table, Ross told Sammy they were going to get her a bed, and she could have whatever she wanted, and could choose the furniture as well.

"We'll need some more food," Ted said, "now we've got an extra mouth to feed."

"What kind of food do you eat?" asked Sammy.

"We usually have our main meal at night, and Ted prepares a mean salad, which we have with meat, and potatoes."

"Ted does the cooking?" asked Sammy in surprise.

"Yes he does," Ross answered, "and makes a good job of it. We'll never go hungry while this man's about."

"Do you love Ted?" Sammy asked directly.

"Yes I do Sam. He's helped me with the house, and acted like a true gentleman. He never once tried to get romantic with me, although I knew that he liked me very much. We have been to many places together, seen plenty of things and enjoyed being together. It's only recently we have told each other how much we care, because I've been afraid your dad would try and find me. You know what would happen if he did, but now I have Ted to look after me, and you of course. I've never had anyone to look after me before, your dad looked after himself and nobody else, but Ted is different, he puts me first and makes me feel important. That's why I can say to everyone, I love Ted Hall."

Ross stopped speaking, and Ted could see she was close to tears.

"I'm happy for you mum," said Sam, "and if you say Ted's the best, I'll accept what you say, and what I've seen so far I agree with you."

"Enough," said Ted, "you'll have me blushing if you keep on like that."

"That'll be the day when you blush, Ted Hall." Ross said.

"Come on ladies," Ted said, standing up, "let's get the breakfast pots washed, and go and look for a bed for our Sam."

"Our Sam! Now that sounds nice, I've never been called that before. Now I know why you love him.

EIGHT

By mid-morning, they were in a furniture store. Sammy was walking around on her own so she could pick what she wanted without influence from anyone, while Ted and Ross were looking at different bedroom furnishings, trying to decide which type of wood they would like. Ted had brought a piece of flooring so they could see which colour complemented the floor. They had made a decision, when Sammy came over to them, and said,

"Did you mean it when you said I could have anything I liked for my bedroom?"

"Yes love, of course I meant it." Ross said, "Why?"

"I've just seen a complete bedroom set up that I think is fabulous. Can you come and look at it and see if you think it's suitable for me."

Sammy led them to the display she wanted, and it turned out to be a typical teenager's room. The furniture was white with soft pink trimming and the three quarter size bed was at set up at right angles to a double wardrobe. There was a table beside the bed that had two small drawers, and included in the price, there was a dressing table and mirror plus a chest of drawers.

"Are you sure this is what you want Sam?" Ross asked.

"I'm certain," she answered, "it's light and clean and the bed is comfortable. I know it is because I've just bounced on it."

Ross had a good look at the suite, and said that it seemed good quality. On the side table, there was a brochure showing the suite in different colours, but Sam insisted it was the white one she wanted.

Ross went to the customer service desk to order it, plus some furnishings for their bedroom as well. Ted enquired about a discount if they ordered another two units as well, but was turned down.

"Tell them it's their loss," she said to Ted, "we will go elsewhere for our furniture."

Ted translated Ross's words to the salesman, who realised that he was about to lose a sale. He asked them to wait a moment while he rushed off towards an office at the rear of the store. He was gone for a while, and Ross was almost on the verge of walking out when he returned. In Spanish, he asked if the other two suites were to be the same quality as the one they had asked about.

Ted translated to Ross, who asked Ted to make it clear that they wanted good quality furniture in their bedrooms, and if they wanted this order and another order for living room furniture, all paid for in cash, they had better start to review their discount scheme.

The salesman shrugged his shoulders, and begrudgingly offered Ross a meagre two and a half per cent discount on whatever she ordered.

Ross shook her head, and turned towards the door.

"Tell him I'm going somewhere else for my furnishings. If he can turn down an order for several thousand Euros, his prices are too high."

Ted told the salesman what Ross had said, and once again he shrugged his shoulders.

"My boss says that two and a half per cent is the best he can do."

"We have been in this store three times recently, and there have been no other customers here on each visit, so I assume you will not be trading here very long."

Ted turned away and the three of them walked out.

Sammy looked a bit down at the prospect of not having the bedroom she wanted, but Ross said there were a few more stores up the road, and one of them was bound to have the same suite. It was in the third store they visited they found what she wanted. Sammy's eyes lit up with delight when she saw the same layout she had seen in the first store. They found a salesman who spoke reasonable English, and told him what they were looking for, including furnishings for the living area. After a lot of looking through books and brochures, Ross made up her mind and asked him to add it all together, and then give them a price for cash using her card.

This salesman was no idiot. He recognised the value of these customers and offered a fifteen per cent discount if they ordered and paid for everything together.

Ross was happy with the agreement, and she was promised the bedroom furniture by the middle of the following week. The living room furniture would take three to four weeks before it was delivered though, because it had to be ordered from the manufacturer.

She gave him her card, and after checking the amount, entered her PIN in the machine, and the transaction was complete.

"It's after two o'clock," said Ross as they left the shop, "and time for a late lunch. Are we anywhere near the place where we can eat as much as we want Ted?"

"Not far," Ted answered, "about ten minutes up the road. I'm not sure they have the buffet libre at lunch time though, but there definitely will be something to eat."

As Ted promised, they were at the restaurant ten minutes later, and as luck would have it, a small buffet was being served until mid-afternoon.

After their meal, they took a walk along the Paseo, enjoying the sun, but aware that Sammy wasn't used to the warmth, even at that time of the year. Sitting down on a bench Ross explained to Sammy about siestas and suggested they go back to Ted's apartment for a rest. She said there was plenty of time to look around the area but at the same time, she and Ted had some unfinished business to attend to.

Later, when Ted and Ross were lying naked on the bed having their pre sleep kiss, Ross reached down for him and said,

"Now, where were we this morning before someone interrupted us?"

"If Sammy had knocked five minutes later, she would have seen the white fountain. I think we are going to have to be a bit more careful if we do it in a morning. Afterwards you would normally go to the bathroom and wash yourself and I would follow on, but that is going to be a bit awkward now especially if Sammy leaves her door slightly open. I think we should invest in a big box of strong tissues or better still, a pack of baby wipes, which we can use for cleaning ourselves, and throw in the bin later."

"That's a good idea, Ted." said Ross, "but what's going to happen now?"

"Who cares?" gasped Ted as he felt his body prepare for the satisfying pleasure that was almost upon him.

Ross pushed herself to him, and whispered urgently,

"Touch me Ted, touch me…. hurry."

Ted did as she asked, and they both reached the satisfaction they wanted almost at the same time.

Ted found an old handkerchief to temporarily clean themselves, and then settled down for a relaxed sleep.

They were sat having a refreshing drink after their siesta, Ted deep in thought about what still needed doing at the house and running a plan through his mind. He was brought back to reality when he heard Ross calling his name. He looked at her and said,

"Sorry love, I was miles away. What did you say?"

"I asked you what you were thinking about."

Ted smiled, and said,

"I may have been thinking about you!"

"If you were," said Sammy, "it must have been a rude thought, because we spoke to you twice and you never heard us."

"What do you know about rude thoughts?" asked Ross.

Sammy smiled and said,

"You'd be surprised at what some of us girls talk about at school."

"I'm not sure I would be surprised Sam, and I'm certain you have seen and heard a lot more in our other house than you are letting on about."

Sammy nodded head, slowly and sadly.

"Mum, I know how dad hurt you, especially at night. I've heard you shouting and crying in pain, while he laughed at you. Tell you the truth mum, I've nearly run away a few times, but I knew what dad would do to you, and me as well, if I did. Did he do those bites on your boobs as well as all those bruises on your body?"

All Ross could do was nod. She was nearly in tears at the comments her young daughter had made.

Sam turned to Ted and asked,

"Would you like to kill my dad?"

"I think killing is going a bit too far Sam, but if I got the chance I would want to give him a taste of his own medicine, preferably over twenty three years, the same length of time he had been abusing your lovely mum."

Sam swivelled back to face Ross, and said,

"Twenty three years? Mum, it's no wonder you came over here. Why didn't you come sooner though?"

"Your dad threatened to do more harm to me and to you if I ran away or told anyone what he was doing to me, but in the end I was so desperate, I had to risk it. I am so glad I did, because I would never have met this man who idolises me and makes me feel good in every

227

way."

"Every way?" asked Sam, with a huge grin.

Ross decided to let her know the truth, so answered,

"Yes Sam, in every way, including sex. If you hear me crying out any time while I'm in bed, it will be with pure joy, because he satisfies me in a way that I've never experienced before. Now, enough of my private life, and let's get back to what we asked Ted half an hour ago."

"I was thinking how much work I have to do at the house. As well as finishing Sam's bedroom, I would like to build up the walls for the other two bedrooms, and get the patio doors fitted. Once we've done all of that, we can clear the whole area of building materials, and keep the tools in one of the un-used rooms until we find a more permanent home for them. There is no need to lay the floors, or fit the doors, but I still have to fit the doors at each end of the passage. The bedroom furnishings will be delivered next Thursday, and that will keep us busy for a day or two. I can manage quite a lot on my own if you want to give Sam a tour of the area, but there are a couple of jobs that I'll need a hand with, your favourite being one of them."

"I haven't really got a favourite job," said Ross, "which one are you thinking of?"

"Skimming the walls." Ted answered with a smile.

"Ugh! Don't remind me of that one." Ross said.

She told Sam how and where she got covered in concrete as they skimmed the wall in her bedroom.

"You were working without anything on?" asked Sammy.

"I did have my shorts on." laughed Ross. "Don't look so shocked, the temperature inside that room during the heat of the summer was so high that our shirts would have been wet through and sticking to our bodies, making it uncomfortable to work. Ted had no shirt on, I trusted him, and so I worked all summer topless, and got a good sun tan as well."

"It's possibly a bit too cold for either of us working topless all day," Ted said, "but there is only the one bedroom wall and the shower rooms to build. You and I can do the building, Sammy can mix the concrete and bring it to us in the wheelbarrow."

Sammy looked at Ted, and saw in his face he was joking.

"Is there really anything I can help with?" she asked.

"I can't think of anything offhand but when we start work I'm sure we can find something. In the morning, we start work at eight thirty and not a moment later. I need a lot of light to be able to finish the floor and fit the doors, so those are the first jobs to do."

The following morning, three people dressed in their 'working' clothes walked to the car park, got into the pickup and drove to their nearly completed home.

"I'm going to miss all this building work," said Ted, "It's a long time since I've been this fit, and the problem I have hasn't bothered me one little bit. Well it has, but not enough to stop me from working."

"What problem?" Ross asked him. "You told me you had to finish work on medical grounds, but you've never said what it was."

"I didn't want to worry you, because if you knew exactly what the problem was, you wouldn't have let me do half of the work I've done."

They had reached the house by this time, and made straight to the bedroom block. Ted still had the keys and opened the main door.

"Open the shutters in your room." Ted said to Ross as they went in.

"Our room." corrected Ross as she went into the bedroom.

She raised the shutters, and opened the patio door to let in some fresh air. Ted was doing the same in Sam's room, the conversation they were having regarding Ted's disability was now forgotten.

It didn't take him long to finish the floor, and after inspecting it carefully, said he was happy with it.

Ross and Sammy had gone into the next room and under shouted instructions from Ted, drew the outline on the wall where the patio doors were to be fitted. Once the outline was drawn, Ted checked it for them and they started to knock out the concrete.

Meanwhile, Ted started fitting the door frames to Sammy's room and had almost finished them by lunch time. He decided to carry on while there was enough light for him to see what he was doing.

Ted ate some sandwiches while he worked, and finished the doors at the same time the ladies finished their lunch.

"We have about three hours of reasonable daylight to work on these walls." he told them. "If I can get three or four rows done this afternoon, I could finish building tomorrow and it should be ready for skimming the day after."

He went to the end of the building where the generator and mixer were, and got a mix underway.

While the concrete was mixing, Ted got the wheelbarrow and everything else ready to start building immediately the mix was ready. He was in the bedroom area setting things up when Ross came to him and said,

"I think the mix is ready Ted, would you like me to tip it into the barrow and start another one?"

"Yes please," Ted answered, "I think there is enough sand for about two more mixes, so we will need some more to do the skimming."

"You aren't going to skim the walls today though, are

you?"

"No love, I'll probably do everything over the next three or four days," Ted said, "and then we can get the electrician to fit the lights and plugs. The patio doors can be fitted to both rooms and in theory that will be the end of the building work inside."

Ted took off his shirt, and started to build.

"I can see now why both of you were not wearing T shirts while you were building," said Sam a few minutes later, "it is warm in here, and the way Ted is lifting those blocks is enough to make anyone sweat."

"Look at my shirt," said Ross, "it's almost see through. While I'm helping Ted, I'm going to do the same."

Without a seconds pause, off came her shirt and bra and Ross started another mix of concrete.

The next day, they had a large bag of sand and five bags of cement delivered, enough to finish inside the bedroom block, with possibly enough left over to start outside in the spring.

It took a week for Ted to finish the brickwork and fit the patio doors to the two smaller bedrooms, and as a last minute decision, Ted decided to fit the shower units, and place the washbasins and toilets on leftover pieces of flooring.

The building work was almost complete.

Ross arranged for the electrician to come the following week to complete the tasks in the bedrooms and the plumber would be there the week after to fit the pipe work. On his previous visit, he had been able to fit the waste pipes to the main drain, thus there was no need for any of the tiles on the corridor to be taken up. The day after the plumber left, Ted started work in the small bedrooms firstly by skimming and later on tiling both shower rooms.

While Ted was working on the shower rooms, Ross and Sam had started painting the walls in each bedroom.

After he finished the shower rooms, Ted examined each other room carefully, checking for any unfinished building work. He found that everything was as it should be, and told Ross that all that remained for him to do was fit the new doors at each end of the corridor and at a later date, lay the flooring and hang the doors in the small bedrooms.

On the day the bedroom furnishings were to arrive, Ted, Ross and Sammy were at the house early. The floors were swept and mopped and the patio doors left open to allow the floors to dry. Ross suggested the flat packs should be carried straight into the bedrooms, then they could start building whenever they were ready.

It was mid-morning when Ted's telephone rang. The van driver was at the bottom of the drive, and wanted to know if it was all right for their van to come up to the house. Ted assured him there was plenty of room, and went out to meet them.

Because of the rough ground between the two buildings, they had to carry everything from the van instead of using a trolley, and consequently it took longer to unload than had been anticipated. The van eventually left the house, leaving the three of them looking at all the boxes in each bedroom.

"There's a lot of work there," said Ross, "and I don't want the job rushed. The furniture for the living quarters won't be delivered for another two or three weeks at least, so we are in no hurry to move in. If the day is dull, like it is now, we are not going to work on anything that requires accuracy. Now that we have laid down the ground rules, let's lock up and go shopping. We need a washing machine, a fridge freezer and anything else electrical that takes my eye."

"We don't really need a dish washer," said Ted, "we have Sammy."

"But you make such a good job of it," Sammy replied sweetly, "I should hate to deprive you of the pleasure."

Ross and Ted smiled, and Ted realised Sam had her mother's sense of humour.

They spent the rest of the day and the following morning buying the essentials needed for the house. It had been decided that as a temporary measure they would use the pans, crockery and cutlery from Ted's apartment when they moved into the house permanently. Ross said she wanted her own kitchen things when they could find time to get them from the lodge in the UK.

Ross had carefully chosen curtains for the whole house, and rails for them to hang on, which would be ready to pick up from the shop in a few days' time. The bedrooms would have net curtains as well as cotton ones and would cover the whole width of each patio door.

As they were driving to work the next day, Ted turned to Ross and said,

"I had another thought about the house last night."

"What have you come up with this time?" she asked in amusement.

"We are going to have to make a pathway from the house to the bedrooms. We can't be walking across the bare earth every night to go to bed especially in winter, or if it's raining."

"That's true, so what have you got in mind?"

Ted paused for a moment, and then began to outline his plans.

"How about making a doorway in the end wall beside the fireplace? It would open outwards and onto a pathway leading to the door of the bedroom block. We could also make one from the kitchen door to the opposite side, but if you look at it logically, we don't really need a door at both ends. We could block the kitchen end doorway off and just have the one entrance to the bedrooms from the lounge end."

"What about the door we've bought for that end of the bedroom block?" Ross asked.

"We use it for the exit from the lounge."

"I'll think about that one, but the pathway sounds an excellent idea. What will we need for that?"

"We could either lay paving stones or we could mix concrete in a colour and lay it over stone chips, then when it's almost dry, use a special mat to make a design."

As Ted was explaining his theory, they had arrived at the house. They went through the front door and over to the wall where Ted showed Ross where the door would go.

"That's a good idea Ted, and I agree to making a doorway here. I would rather have a door that matches the others in the room though, not the one we bought for the other block. Let me think about the bedroom block for a day or so, but we can go ahead with a doorway here."

"How about using the loo door here?" Ted said. "It's an outside door and fairly easy to change over. We could take the white door back to the store and exchange it for one that matches the other interior door, which I use for the loo, unless you still want two doors to the bedrooms block."

"What you are saying makes sense Ted, but let me think it over and I'll decide before we go home tonight. Show me where you think the pathway should go, it will give me a better idea."

They went to the rear of the house, and Ted said,

"We can lay a pathway here between the two blocks and later on we could erect something like a loggia along

234

the sides and make a cover above it. It will keep any rain off us when we are going to bed. Would you rather have the path in paving stone or concrete?"

"I'm not sure." Ross replied, "what's your opinion?"

"If we do it in concrete, we can mix and lay it ourselves. There is a dye we can use to make the pathway coloured, anything from grey, to red, or black, and I know there's an orangey one that would match the tiles on the roof. We can hire some mats to press on the top which makes a pattern of bricks or squares. I think there are several designs that you can choose from."

Ross looked up at the roof tiles, nodded and said,

"That looks good, though I don't want the path too bright."

"We could always make it luminescent orange then we could see our way in the dark." Sam told them.

Ross turned to Sam and with an almost straight face, said,

"Any more comments like that young lady and you are on the next plane back to granddads."

Sam looked at the ground, thinking she was being told off, but she glanced sideways at Ted and saw he was smiling at her. She broke into a smile, looked at her mum and said,

"I'd rather stay with you and Ted."

"In that case, don't come out with any more 'Ted' comments. It's bad enough having to listen to him all the time. Right, what's today's programme?"

"Before we rush off, I'd like to finish telling you my idea about the pathway."

"Sorry Ted, I was distracted by somebody talking about luminescent paths. What's the alternative to concrete?"

"Paving stones could be a better solution. We need about thirty square metres of slabs, and we would only need a nominal base layer of concrete. When we were in Malaga the other day, I saw some paving stones on special offer. There were different colours, but I think alternating maroon and grey would look nice down here."

"I think they would Ted. We've laid enough tiles inside, let's go for paving stones out here, and I'll have a look at them if we take the door back. Now then, for the second time, what's today's programme?"

"For me," Ted answered, "it's the doorways here. If I knock the wall out, can you two take the loo door off?"

"Do I just unscrew the hinges? Ross asked. "I've done this before at our house, but it was an inside door."

"Same method," Ted said, "wedge the bottom, and undo the screws. Just be careful when the last screw comes out that the door doesn't fall. Being an outside door, it is heavier than an interior one. When you've got the door off, I'll show you how to remove the frame. It's a lengthy job, but if you do it slowly and carefully you won't split it along the grain. Obviously I can't fit the door today, we will have to wait for the concrete to dry. Once you have the door and frame off, I can fit some breeze block into the gap and skim both sides."

By late afternoon the doorway into the house was squared off and new breeze block had been built into the toilet wall where the door had been. Unfortunately, Ross had not been able to take the door frame off the toilet wall without splitting two pieces, so they would have to buy a complete new frame. The new doorway was covered by a sheet of wood, and they finished work for the day. Later that evening, they were sat with a drink, relaxing before bed, when Ross told Ted she had decided that only one door was necessary on the bedroom block.

As soon as it was light enough the next morning, they were up at the house. Ted took the old door off the 'kitchen' end of the bedroom block and the gap was filled in and skimmed over. While the momentum was going, he fitted the new door at the opposite end. That afternoon, they drove to the store in Malaga, taking the white door back to exchange for an interior door for the toilet, and to buy a new frame for the outer door. Ross looked at the paving stones that were on offer and decided she liked Ted's idea and bought enough to make the pathway. By the time everything had been off-loaded at the house, it was starting to go dark, which signalled the end of another busy day.

Next day, they drove to the shop that had made up the curtains. They had been packed into several boxes and were put onto the pickup along with the rails. Back at the house, Ross and Sam unloaded the boxes, while Ted started to fit the frame and door in the end wall. Once he was satisfied the doorway was right, he went into the bedrooms area and drilled and plugged the walls and then screwed the rails on to the wall above the patio doors. As soon as he finished in one room, Ross and Sam followed him in and gave it a thorough cleaning. When Ross said the rooms were clean, the three of them began to hang the curtains. When all the curtains in the bedroom block had been hung and Ross was happy, she said that it was time to start on the bedroom furniture. Working only when the weather allowed, it took them five days to put everything together and complete both rooms. With everything in place as Ross wanted, she looked around their room, put her arm round Ted, and in a hushed voice, said,

"I don't believe we are nearly ready to use these bedrooms. All we have to do is put some sheets, pillows and a duvet on each bed, and we're ready to sleep in them. We could actually come to bed for a siesta during the cooler days."

Ted gave Ross a hug.

"I'll look forward to that," he said, "but may I suggest that we bring radiators into both bedrooms and while the electricity is free, we leave them on all day and night to warm the rooms up, and air the beds and bedding."

"I agree with both suggestions! We can plug them in tonight before we go home, and leave them until the rooms feel warm and comfortable. The furniture for the other block should be delivered towards the end of next week, and once we have that set up, we're almost ready to move house."

The next few days were cold, windy and wet, so the three of them stayed in the apartment, discussed the future and started to pack non-essential things that belonged to Ted. They had just finished lunch on one of those days, when Ross's telephone rang.

"Answer that please Sam," Ross said, "you're nearer to it than I am."

Sam took the telephone out of her mum's bag, glanced at the screen, and her eyes lit up.

"Hello grandma," she said, "it's Sam speaking."

She had a brief conversation, and after a couple of minutes, Sam said,

"Yes, mum's here, I'll put her on."

She handed the phone to Ross, who answered in a bright and cheery voice,

"Hello mum, how are you?"

Ted decided to go to the kitchen, put the kettle on and make a pot of tea while Ross kept her family up to date with the progress on the house. He had the tea brewed and was about to pour it into the mugs when Ross walked into the kitchen, still talking to her mum.

"Yes mum, Sam and I are living in Teds' apartment permanently, and as far as we are concerned, we won't be going anywhere without him, ever."

Ross smiled at Ted, and blew him a kiss while her mother asked more questions.

"I don't know mum, I'll ask him." Ross said.

She took the telephone from her ear and said,

"Have you anything planned for Christmas?"

"Nothing special," Ted answered, "I haven't had time to think about it just yet. Why?"

"Mum and granddad would like the three of us to spend Christmas and New Year with them."

With a smile, Ted took the telephone from Ross's hand and lifted it to his ear.

"Hello mum," he said in a happy voice, "thank you very much for the invitation. I will be happy to join you at Christmas, and I'm looking forward to meeting you all. I'll hand you back to Ross and she can make the arrangements. Bye for now."

Ross took the phone back and smiled as her mother said something, to which Ross replied,

"I know, he's like that sometimes, and it's because of his good natured attitude that I think so much of him."

Ross was walking back to the lounge, still talking, and Ted followed her with the tea.

After a few more pleasantries, Ross ended the call.

"You are honoured," she said, "an invitation to spend Christmas and New Year with my family. Except for the first Christmas, Brian never got invited to any do that my family gave."

"They only want to see what the 'new man' is like." Ted said, "If they don't approve of me, we won't get another invite."

"They'll approve Ted," said Sam, "so you have nothing to worry about there."

"I'll second that," Ross said, "there's nothing for them to disapprove of. We had better have a think about how we are going to sort our time out."

"It's six weeks to Christmas." Ted said. "I can't do any more building until the weather improves, and the living room furniture is due at the end of the week. We want time to set it out and we need to put some heat into the room as well. We can't leave the heating on while we are away, so we will have to warm the house up when we get back. The question is, how long do you want to stay in the UK?"

"I have no idea, Ted," Ross replied, "two weeks at least. I can see that brain of yours is working overtime, so tell me what you are thinking about."

"I'm thinking about this apartment as well as the house." he said. "I have to give two months' notice to leave, so if I give notice at the beginning of December, we would have to be out of here at the end of January. All my non-essential things could be boxed and moved out of here to the house before we fly to the UK for Christmas. I suggest that we get everything sorted out at your house......."

"Our house!" Ross interrupted.

Ted smiled, and carried on,

"I suggest we get everything sorted out at our house, and fly to the UK somewhere around the eighteenth. We spend Christmas and New Year with your mum and granddad, and if you like, we could go and visit my parents. I don't see much of them, but when I do call, I'm made very welcome. My brother sadly won't be there though. He and his family emigrated to New Zealand several years ago."

"You've never once mentioned your family all the time we've been together." Ross said in a surprised voice.

"I've never really had to. Mum and dad know where I am, but dad is strictly a Brit. He won't travel anywhere abroad and when they go on holiday, it's touring round so he can see as much as possible in the two weeks they are away. Dad is a nice old guy, but his thinking is sometimes a bit weird. Many years ago, they bought a two bedroom bungalow. It had a small lounge/diner, too small for his liking, so he made the smallest bedroom into a dining room. Stupid part about it, it's hardly ever used, and if they have any visitors, there is nowhere for them to sleep. Everyone has to use a nearby hotel if they need to stay longer than a day. I've gone completely off the subject; we were talking about our travel arrangements. If we fly back to Spain, shall we say the fourth or fifth, we can celebrate the Spanish Christmas on the sixth. Doing it that way will give us three weeks to warm the house and get all the remaining stuff out of here."

"I wish my mind was as organised." Ross said, "You seem to be able to think and work things out weeks in advance."

"Probably because of the work I used to do. With a number of 'sub-companies' belonging to the main business, I had to be able to look well forward if a new project started. I have to brag a bit now," Ted said, slightly embarrassed, "because I was not just an accountant as I told you, I was a financial advisor as well. I had to price jobs up and be able to allocate other companies to work to the price I set."

"Were you a director of the company?" Ross asked.

"I was one of four," Ted told her, "but I was the senior one."

"A responsible job then. Why did you leave? Or is this the company you had to leave for medical reasons?"

"I had a serious accident which stopped me from working for several months. When I returned, I was unable work full time, so they pensioned me off."

"What kind of serious accident, Ted." Ross asked in a worried tone.

Ted shook his head, before saying,

"Not today, Ross. If you like, I'll tell you all about it while we are at your granddads over Christmas."

Ross looked at Ted with a worried frown. In a quavering voice, she asked him,

"It's not…. well…. you're not going to….?"

Ted laughed,

"No my love, I assure you it's not life threatening. You can't lose me because of my accident."

Ross put her arms round Ted and said,

"Thank God for that! You have me worried now, though. Have you been doing things you shouldn't have while you and I have been working on our house?"

"I have, but as I told you a few weeks ago, it hasn't affected me much. Don't worry Ross, with so little left to do on the house, there is nothing that can aggravate the problem anymore. Subject closed until I give you the full story while we are away."

"We seem to have strayed from the subject again," Ross said, "we were sorting out the travel arrangements. I'm with you on the dates to and from the UK, but we will have to get the flights booked soon."

"We can do that in the morning before going to the house. We need to put the heating on from now until we go away, and I can tidy up any odds and ends that need to be done. The loo door has to be fitted for a start, but that is not a big job though. The remaining curtains need fitting in the lounge, and the blinds for the kitchen need sorting out and fitting. If we start taking out things that we don't need here, it will save time when we get back."

The plans they made worked very well.

The living room furniture was delivered on the day it was promised, and the three of them spent the following day unwrapping it, giving it a polish and arranging it to their liking.

When all the furniture was in place, two of Ted's heaters were switched on to take the cold chill off the room and warm the furniture, while two heaters were in the bedrooms doing the same thing.

Most of Ted's things were now in the villa, including most of his clothes. Ross had brought nearly all hers and Sam's as well, and everything was put away in the proper place.

"There is a place for everything, and everything has its place" Ross told them. "I'm not an obsessive, but I like things tidy. That means you, young lady. No clothes thrown on chairs and no dirty knicks on the floor."

Ted looked up and smiled.

Ross saw him look up and asked him what it was he was smiling at.

"Knicks," he answered, "the daughter of a very close friend of mine calls her knickers, 'knicks'."

Ross smiled back at him.

"Yes," she said, "I do remember saying that. I nearly let it slip that I had a daughter. That was before I told you all about me, my family and my problems."

Sam was glancing from her mum to Ted and back again with an amused look on her face.

"I hope you both know what you are talking about, because I don't."

"It's all right Sam," Ross said, "some months ago, before I knew Ted properly, I made a comment, and suddenly had to change it as I spoke. Of all the things I've told him over the months, he has to remember a gaffe I made."

Their house was almost ready to move into. Ted had fitted the loo door, and given the walls another coat of paint, Ross preferring paint to tiles.

On the day before they flew back to the UK, all the heaters were switched off and the house secured. Any more work would have to wait until the following year.

NINE

Their arrival at Gatwick Airport went without a hitch. Their luggage was almost first off the carousel and Ted had found a trolley to put it on, more than could be said for many of their fellow passengers.

On their way through to the arrivals area, Sam skipped ahead, saw 'granddad', rushed over and gave him a hug and a kiss. Ross followed Sam and she too gave her granddad a hug and kiss. She half turned to Ted and said,

"Granddad, this is Ted, the man who has helped me build a house to be proud of."

Both men put out their hands and greeted each other with a firm handshake.

"It's very nice to meet you Ted," he said, "Ross has told me so much about you, I feel as though I know you already."

"It is very nice to meet you as well, Mr…. I'm sorry I don't know your name." Ted replied.

"Call me granddad," he said with a laugh, "everyone else does."

They all made their way outside to a car that he had hired, complete with a driver. The suitcases were put in the boot and they drove off to granddads' manor house. Granddad explained that now he was in his eighties, he thought it better to let someone younger do the driving, especially at night.

Ross's mum was waiting at the old manor when they arrived, and Sam ran ahead to kiss and hug her grandma. Ross did the same, while Ted and granddad got the cases out of the car boot. Ted turned to pick up two of the cases and found Ross had brought her mother over to the car.

"Mum," she said, "this is Ted."

Ted took her hand, then kissed her cheek.

"Hello again," he said, "it's nice to meet you. Will it be all right if I call you mum as well?"

She looked a bit startled for a moment, then broke into a big smile, and said,

"I am pleased to meet you as well, Ted, and I think it a splendid idea that you call me mum."

The introductions over, they made their way inside, and after cups of tea and sandwiches, went upstairs to bed.

The next morning, after breakfast, Ross asked her granddad if anything had been seen of Brian.

He said he hadn't actually seen him, but she had been right about the window. He had broken in one night and taken all his clothes, but the things he had left behind had been boxed and removed, and stored in one of the out buildings behind the manor. The lodge had been boarded up and made secure and only he had a key for the door. Ross told him that she and Ted would go through the things in the out buildings before returning to Spain, and anything they didn't want could be given to charity. The things they wanted would be shipped over to their new house.

"So the lodge is empty again, is it?" Ross said, sadly. "It has a lot of very bad memories, but it was my home, and I was proud of what I put into it."

"I can tell you are proud of your homemaking by the way you've worked on and set up our new house." Ted said.

"That's the first time I've heard you call it our house without being prompted." Ross said in surprise.

"Shows I've been listening to you, doesn't it." Ted said with a grin.

"You may listen to me but you don't always take any notice." Ross replied.

"I do take notice of you. The only time I don't is when you nag me."

"Ted Hall," said Ross, "when have I nagged you?"

Ted pretended to think, and after a moment or two said,

"Well there was that one time several months ago when you wanted me to work faster to get the house finished."

Ross smiled, and said,

"I have never had to nag you about anything to do with the work on the house."

"No love, that's true." Ted answered. "OK, I give up, when have you nagged me?"

"Ted Hall, you get worse." She turned to her granddad, and said,

"I have to put up with this all the time at home. Some of the things he says exasperate me at times, but because I think so much of him, I just groan inwardly and get on with what I'm doing."

Granddad smiled, and said,

"There's no shyness about Ted, and I like the way he treats us, as if he's met us before. I also like the way he has the ability to play on words. You must have been well liked when you were working Ted, what exactly did you do?"

"It's quite a long story, but if you'd like to hear about my working life prior to meeting your lovely granddaughter, I'm happy to tell you."

"Why not wait until mum gets here," Ross said, "that way you won't have to repeat yourself."

"Pardon?" Ted said,

"I said, why don't you.... Ted Hall, I'll slap you if you try any more tricks like that, and don't you encourage him granddad."

Granddad had been chuckling as Ross fell for Ted's

little joke.

"Sometimes he comes out with these one line jokes that drive me mad." Ross said. "Come on Ted, quick joke."

Ted thought for a second, turned to Ross and said,

"A cowboy walked into a German car showroom and said, 'Audi'."

Granddad chuckled, Ross groaned, and then said,

"Go on, one more and that's it until we get back home."

Ted grinned, paused, and then said,

"I went into a pet shop and asked 'can I buy a goldfish?'

The owner said, 'of course you can, do you want an aquarium?'

I told him I didn't care what star sign it was."

They were saved from any more of Ted's awful jokes as Ross's mum came into the room.

"Good morning all," she said, "I can see everyone is happy and smiling this morning."

"We're smiling at Ted's rotten jokes." Sam told her.

"I'll have to hear some of them later then." Mum said.

"You won't," said Ross, "I've banned him from telling any more while he's here. He doesn't need encouraging, so please spare us the agony."

"You seem to be very happy Ross, and you've put some weight on, in the right places of course, and for a change you are completely relaxed."

"It's my new lifestyle mum, and obviously the way I'm treated nowadays. I've told Ted on many occasions that I wish I had met him when I was a teenager. I didn't but I now have to be thankful I won't be living the rest of my life in fear or sorrow. I am more than happy with Ted, and so is Sam, so granddad, mum, please accept

Ted as my partner and allow us to live together without any animosity."

"Of course we will Ross. You are old enough to know your own mind, and I have this in built feeling that Ted will look after you and Sam. I blame myself for the problems you had with that psycho. If only I hadn't insisted…. "

"Mum," Ross interrupted, "it's over and done with, and there is no need to rake up my past. Ted knows everything, and I do mean everything, that happened in my marriage to Brian. He is my protector and Sam's as well. He makes me happy, despite his rotten jokes, and in the last nine months has treated me like a lady and given me something to live for. We will continue to live together in Spain, and as soon as we find her a place, Sam will be going to school there. It seems funny, but over the past few months, I have told Ted my life story since I was about sixteen, and I only found out last week about his parents, and that he has a brother in New Zealand. He was about to tell us about his work prior to going to Spain, but I asked him to wait so you could hear as well."

"Thank you dear that was thoughtful of you. Shall we all have coffee before we start?"

Mum went out and was back minutes later, saying that Laura would bring it though in five minutes. Laura was granddads' house keeper, and her husband was the gardener. They lived in the manor, and between them kept it running smoothly. The coffee arrived on a silver tray. There was a matching china coffee set made up of coffee pot, cups, saucers, sugar bowl and cream jug. Granddad poured two cups out, and then turned to Ted, and asked,

"Café con leche Ted?"

Without any hesitation, Ted said,

"No, no, café solo per favor y grande si posible."

Granddad looked at him and smiled.

"That was automatic, wasn't it?"

Ted nodded ruefully, a little bit embarrassed at being caught out so easily without thinking.

"Do you speak any other languages?" asked mum.

Ted felt more embarrassment because he thought he was being put on a spot to prove his suitability for Ross.

"Well," he replied, "I speak reasonably good Spanish, fairly good French, a smattering of Italian, and some rude swear words in Russian."

"We don't want to hear those, thank you very much." Mum said in a haughty voice.

"If I used them, you wouldn't know if they were rude or swear words, they sound just as obscure as the rest of the Russian language."

"Do you know any swear words in Spanish?" asked Sam, with a grin.

"If I did young lady, I certainly wouldn't tell you. I'm sure you will pick them up yourself when you start school, so if I hear you using them, watch out."

Mum nodded in agreement, and then went and sat down next to Sam on a settee.

"Are you going to tell us about your work?" asked Ross, "or do we have to sit and question you?"

Ted smiled and said,

"I'll tell you about my work, and my accident...."

"Accident? What sort of accident?" Mum interrupted.

"I repeat, I'll tell you about my work and my accident, as long as there are no frequent interruptions. I'll let you know about some of my private life as it happened, but I'm not going to tell you anything that is not relevant to my work."

"That's fair enough." said granddad.

"I agree as well." Ross added.

They looked at mum, who looked a bit put out, almost as though she wanted to ask questions, but she agreed to keep quiet while Ted told his story.

"I'm not going to start with my early life, because that has nothing to do with my work, but I will admit to being very good with figures throughout my school days. From the age of eleven, I went to a good school, a private grammar school in fact, but sadly it is now co-educational. In my final year there, as well as doing 'A' levels, I was going to night classes twice a week at the local technical college taking a book keeping course. When I eventually left school, I had 'O' and 'A' levels and a book keepers certificate which gave me a fast track to an accountancy course, which I passed after two years of hard work."

Ted paused for breath, and to drink some of his coffee, but before he could continue, Ross asked,

"How many 'O' levels, how many 'A' levels, and how did you do with the other examinations?"

Ted looked at Ross, and said,

"I know you want to know more about me Ross, but to answer questions like that makes me sound as though I'm blowing my own trumpet, and I don't really like doing that. However, for you, I'll make an exception and brag just a little bit. I have ten 'O' levels with good grades and five 'A' levels, again with good grades. I got a 'B plus' for my book keeping certificate, and straight 'A's' in my accountants' exam. Now that's enough bragging, let me tell you about my work, otherwise we could be here all week."

"After passing my accountancy examination, I started work in the accounts section of a local building firm. It was a medium sized company and a subsidiary of the huge and well known 'Ashley Lee Group'. After a year

251

or so, they recognised my ability with figures, and I spent time in another section of the company, working with someone else and helping him with the costing of projects. I was doing this as well as my own job, and found it relatively easy to do both.

I had been with the company for just over four years when the person I had been working with went into hospital. I can remember it quite well, because it was two days after my birthday. I'd celebrated quite well over the weekend, and was a bit on the rough side when I went into work the following Monday. After lunch, my head was a bit clearer, and I was well into my weekly update of accounts, when the phone on my desk rang. It was the general manager wanting to see me in his office. I was a bit worried because he had never asked me to his office before. He had spoken to me many times, but it was usually in my office, and being asked to go 'upstairs' was usually for a roasting for doing something wrong, or the sack. I knocked on his office door. He shouted 'enter', and as I went in, I guess the look on my face showed I was worried. He told me I had nothing to worry about, he wanted to talk about work. I was very relieved and sat down at his desk. He told me that Frank Jolly was out of hospital, but was going to be off work for a week or two longer. He wanted to know if I thought I was capable of doing some of his work that had built up in his absence, or should he send it to head office. A major project had come to the company for a quotation and the general manager had decided it was worth costing out and sending in a tender. There was a smaller project to be worked on as well, and he wanted to know if I could cost them out and send them to head office for evaluation. I said I would give it my best shot, and he told me I should start work on it as soon as possible, as there was a deadline to keep to. I finished the accounts update the following morning, and set to with the costing's. I followed all the guide lines, worked the way I had been shown and had final figures sorted out three days later. I double checked what I had done, put it all into the computer and made a print of each. I sent the costing to head office, and went back to my own work. The following week, I got another call to go to the general manager's office. When I got there, another gentleman was sitting with him, and he was introduced to me. His name was Mr Lee, the chairman and owner of the group. He congratulated me on having a costing sent to the head office within a few days of it being received, and then said he thought the final figure was a bit high, and did I want to reconsider it. I shook my head and said I stood by the figures and would not reduce them just so the company could get the contract. The quotation I gave would make a profit, reducing it just to get the contract could lose the company money. The general manager was looking at me with his mouth open, not believing I had dared to speak in such a manner to the chairman. But Mr Lee thought differently, and said he would submit it as it stood, and if 'Ashley Lee Group' got the project, it was down to me.

The general manager then asked me if I had allocated a gang to the other project. I said the quotation had not been confirmed and planning permission had not been given.

'A mere formality,' I was assured.

'There's no such thing,' I said. 'When I see both on paper, I will allocate a gang.'

He wasn't pleased at what I said, and made it clear.

'Frank Jolly will be back next Monday, we'll have to wait and see what he advises'.

I left the office feeling let down. I had been asked to do a job, I had done it to the best of my ability and there was the top man and my own general manager pulling my work to pieces. I vowed I would do no more work for the company other than my own accounts. The following day, the manager came to my office, and demanded I allocate a gang to the job. I told him I was too busy with my own work, and if a gang was needed Frank could do it when he returned on Monday. He slammed the door on his way out but I knew he couldn't do anything, because it wasn't my job in the first place. On Monday morning, Frank didn't turn in to work, and by mid-morning, the general manager was panicking because there was nobody standing by to start a job he was certain the company had got. At lunchtime I went into town, first to the bank and afterwards went to a sandwich bar for my lunch. I was on my way back to work, when I saw something that made me stop, and I almost laughed out loud. I bought something, and when I got back to work, I made sure the boss was in his office, before going into mine. I made a telephone call, and when I finished, went upstairs to the office. I knocked, and when he shouted for me to enter, I went straight to his desk.

'What do you want' he said, 'I'm busy, trying to sort out a job that you wouldn't do.'

I opened the local evening newspaper out and placed it directly in front of him. The headlines screamed out:

Planning Officer Arrested for Accepting Bribes.

'The local council planning officer was arrested this morning suspected of accepting money in exchange for assuring planning permission, and looking favourably on certain companies bids for work put out to local tender. A number of others were arrested at the same time and will be charged accordingly. All planning submissions presented in the last month will be put on hold, and no further applications are being accepted until the investigation is complete.

Arrested for questioning in conjunction with the scandal were the following:

There followed a list of five names, and the piece concluded with:

Further arrests are not ruled out'

I took the newspaper back, and said,

'Planning permission is a certainty is it? I think I know why. I see our Mr Jolly is one of those arrested, so where has he been getting the money from to pay the planning officer?'

The general manager had suddenly gone very quiet.

I turned to leave the office, when the phone rang. I heard him talking to Mr Lee as I closed the door behind me.

Back in my office I was settling down to work, when I had a sudden thought. If the general manager and Jolly had been working hand in hand, would I be implicated because of my involvement with some of the costing's. Was my job in jeopardy I wondered? There was a knock on my door and a secretary came in. She gave me an envelope, and with a smile, said,

'Tomorrow morning, you are booked on the six thirty train to Manchester Airport and on the ten oh five BA flight to Gatwick. You will be met and taken to head office because Mr Lee wants to see you. Your train tickets are in the envelope, and the flight tickets are waiting for you at the airport'

She gave me another smile, and said,

'Good luck Mr Hall, you deserve it.'

The following morning, I was met at Gatwick Airport by a gentleman holding a piece of cardboard, on which was hand written,

'Mr E M Hall'.

I smiled at him and said,

'Where did you get my Sunday name from?'

The man smiled back, and said,

'The boss knows everybody's proper name, and insists on using it in all forms of communication. If you are with him formally, he will call you by the name everyone uses. When you meet him later, he will call you Ted'

Ted paused at that moment, because he saw Mum take a breath as though ready to ask him a question.

Before she could speak, Ted said,

"It's Edwin, Mum, shortened firstly to Eddy and then to Ted. The M is for Michael."

Mum smiled at him, nodded her thanks, and sat back so he could continue his story.

"I was driven to the head office and taken straight to meet Mr Ashley Lee again. There was another man in the office with him, well built, short haircut and looked every inch a policeman. Mr Lee stood up, and shook my hand in welcome.

'Nice to see you again Ted, and thank you for the telephone call yesterday. Did you bring the newspaper with you?'

I handed it to him, and he looked it over, nodded, and gave it to the other gentleman.

After he had read it, he put it on the desk, and said his name was DI Royston, from the fraud squad. He was investigating this sort of fraud throughout the whole country, and thanked me for bringing this particular one to Mr Lee's attention.

They both questioned me about any involvement I had with the costing's, but seemed satisfied I was not in any way implicated in the fraud.

'As the accountant of that firm,' said Mr Lee, 'has nothing occurred to you that made you in any way suspicious?'

I shook my head, and told him I always queried anything that looked out of place. I said that if he gave me some time to look through the books, I would double check to see if I could find any money being paid out through the company.

'Have you any ideas where you'll start?' asked Mr Lee.

I thought for a moment, and then said,

'I could start in wages and casual labour payments. I'd check payments against names and make sure they were on our payroll.'

DI Royston looked at me and said,

'You have a sharp mind, Mr Hall; you could have been a policeman.'

He left a few minutes later, and Mr Lee and I went out for lunch. Over the meal, he told me that the project costing I had refused to alter had been awarded to the Group, but would have to wait until a new planning officer was appointed. I looked surprised and he told me that it was for a new school in my own town, where the scandal was.

I left head office to catch the evening flight back home, and as I shook Mr Lee's hand, his parting words were,

'I'm sure you and I are going to see quite a lot of each other in the future Ted'

At the time, I didn't realise the implication of that remark, but I would find out the following weeks.

A few days later, two plain clothed and two uniformed policemen arrived at the yard. As the senior person at the time, I had to take charge and speak to them. One of them introduced himself as CID, and said he wanted to speak to the general manager. He was not at his home, so they had come to his place of work. I told them that his car wasn't here, so presumably he wasn't in his office either. He asked me if I knew where he was, and when I had last seen him. I told them I didn't know where he was that day, but I had seen him the previous night as he left for home.

The detective asked me if I would show them where his office was. I took them upstairs and found the door was unlocked, which was unusual when he was not at the yard. They went inside, asked me to go back to my office, and said they would come and see me when they had finished the search.

Meanwhile, I had got a list of all personnel on our payroll, and was checking to see if there was anyone listed who shouldn't be. I had gone through the list for the last three months but couldn't find anything out of the ordinary. I was beginning to think I was wrong about the payroll. There is a system called 'ghost payrolling', where somebody with the ability can add a fictitious name to the list and have money paid regularly into his or her bank account. This is what I thought was happening, but could find no trace of anything like that. Many of the employees, especially the plasterers, are paid on a piece work rate plus bonus, and therefore their wage differed from week to week. Was there an employee on the books whose wage was the same every week, I thought?

Before I had time to start the search, the police came back to my office. They were taking papers and files for checking, and his computer for deeper examination.

They gave me a receipt for everything they had taken, and left. The chief foreman of the yard came to my office when he saw them leave and asked what was going on. I told him what I thought, but he hadn't to take what I said as gospel truth. He wanted to know who was in charge now, and who did he have to report to with problems. I said I would find out for him and he left me to it. I telephoned head office, hoping to speak to the boss, but he was in a conference and couldn't be disturbed. I was put through to his secretary, and I told her of the happenings that morning. She said she would tell Mr Lee as soon as he was free, and asked if I would take charge until I heard from them again.

Me, in charge? I was an accountant, not a builder and didn't really want the responsibility, but had to agree so that it could be seen that there was a senior person on site.

I got back to the payroll and started my search. It took me a while, but I eventually found an employee who was seen to be earning the same amount every week. He was listed as a labourer, and one hundred and ninety five pounds was going into his bank account. All I had was a name, no other details, not even a check number. I phoned head office again, and spoke to the personnel section. I told them I had the name of a labourer on my books with no clock number, so could they give me the number so I could keep my records straight. After a lengthy search, they told me they had no record of anyone by that name, and was I sure the name was right. I told them it was, and asked to be put through to Mr Lee's secretary. She told me that Mr Lee was still in conference, so I asked her to tell him that I knew where the money was coming from.

It was about an hour later when Mr Lee called me back. The first thing I told him was about the general manager and the police looking for him. I wanted to know who was in charge at the yard and what was happening in the future. I then told him about the ghost labourer and the money that was being paid into a bank account. I said we would have some difficulty tracing who set it up, but the police possibly could do it now they had the general manager's computer.

He was quiet for a moment or two, and then said he would send a temporary manager to the yard the following morning to keep it running until a solution could be found. He asked me to find out the name of the police officer in charge of the case, and give him all the details I had found regarding the payroll. There was another moment of silence, before he asked me if I would show the new man around when he arrived and get him settled in. The day after, he wanted to see me back in his office, and asked me to get the same train and flight as last time, and I would be met at Gatwick.

Two days later, I arrived at head office, and was welcomed like a long lost relative. I sat and chatted with Mr Lee over coffee, and then he took me to the board room. He introduced me to four men who were sat waiting for us. One was from the architect's section, two were from the planning department and the other, an elderly gentleman, was the company accountant and a finance advisor. We all talked business for quite some time. I was questioned as to how I worked the costings out, how much I allowed for inflation over long term projects and how much I allowed for profit. By mid-afternoon, we had covered many subjects pertaining to the building industry in general, but Mr Lee had not joined in or said a word during the discussions. He called a halt, and questioningly looked at the other men. They all nodded at him.

'Ted,' he said, turning to me, 'the five of us here all

agree that you know what you are talking about, and I know from personal experience, that you are not afraid of sticking to your findings and your principles. We would like you to come and work for us at head office. You would work with Trevor in the auditing section until he retires in September, and then you would take over his job. I will offer you a substantial raise in salary, and if you need to, we can allocate you one of the many homes we own. You will have to pay a small rent, but all other outgoings for the house will be your responsibility. I don't want an answer right now, have a talk with your fiancée, see what she thinks, and then get back to me.

Now then, what about the yard where you are now? I suppose that when local people find out about the scandal at Sam Miller and Son, the company could start to be shunned. I think we may have to try to sell it.'

'Might I make a suggestion?' I asked.

All five of them looked at me expectantly.

'Why not let me tell our local newspaper that because of the scandal, the business has to be put up for sale and if a buyer isn't found, all the employees would lose their jobs. Some weeks later, it can be announced that the Ashley Lee Group has acquired it, we change the name board outside the yard, and carry on as normal.'

There was a moment's silence, and then Neil from the planning department stood up, leaned over the table, and said,

'Welcome to Head Office, Ted.' and shook my hand. The others did the same, and left me with Mr Lee. We chatted for a while before I said that I would have to leave to catch my flight home. Although it was getting late when I arrived back, I went straight to see my fiancée Tina. I wanted to tell her the good news about my promotion and pay rise.

But Tina was far from happy! She didn't want to live

in London, she wanted to stay where she was with all her friends. I was genuinely upset at Tina's attitude. I was so pleased with my promotion and the trust I had been given, I never thought that Tina would want to put her friends before her soon to be husband, and a much better standard of living that my promotion would bring.

'If I don't go to London, where would you suggest I work?' I asked her.

'Where you are now.' she replied.

I told her that because of the scandal, the yard was for sale and I could be out of work with the rest of the staff. She wasn't impressed with that news either, so begrudgingly said she would think about moving to London with me.

I said she had to think hard and fast, because whether she liked it or not, I was going to work at the head office. If she didn't want to come with me, she had to tell me, and we would call the wedding off. I left for home feeling quite deflated after being on such a high all day."

Ted stopped talking, looked at the others, who were listening intently to him, and said,

"I have a feeling it's our lunch time. Shall we go and eat and if you like, I'll continue afterwards."

They made their way to the dining room, where Laura had laid out a buffet for them, complemented with wine, beer or soft drinks. Without hesitation, Ted and Ross made for the red wine.

During lunch, granddad said to Ted,

"I'm not going to ask you anything about your work Ted, but the Ashley Lee Group rings a bell. I've seen boards all over the place in London, shouting out what they are doing."

"They are renovating old apartment blocks and warehouses along the river." Ted said, "That's where you will see many of the signs now."

"I'm thinking quite a few years back," granddad said, "didn't the group have something to do with work on the South Bank?"

Ted smiled, and nodded his head.

Seeing the look on Ted's face, Ross asked,

"Did you have something to do with it?"

Ted nodded again and said,

"I was one of a number that worked on it."

"But you were the chief one, weren't you?" Ross persisted.

Ted didn't answer directly, but said,

"I got a very good bonus for that."

"I'll wager you've had many good bonuses haven't you?" asked granddad.

Ted just smiled and nodded, not wanting to appear to be showing off.

Mum had disappeared from the room, and when she returned, she was carrying a book. It was a year book, a commercial version of the book, 'who's who.'

"The Ashley Lee Group," she announced, "is the largest building company in the British Isles. It has also quite a number of smaller subsidiaries. The owner of the group is Sir Ashley Lee KGB, and Knighted for his services to the building industry. Also recognized for their services was their chief architect, Mr David Holmes, and the chief financial advisor Mr Edwin 'Ted' Hall, both receiving the OBE. There is a list of other employees, but I don't need to read any more, do I?"

Mum closed the book and looked at Ted with admiration. So did granddad, Ross and Sam.

"You've never mentioned that." Ross said quietly.

Ted was clearly embarrassed at them finding out about his award.

"I didn't want you to think I was someone

important." Ted replied. "I wasn't the only one to work on those projects, but it was me that did a lot of work with the government. When our bid was accepted, it was Mr Lee that shouted my name from the roof tops. I'm proud of my OBE but I'll never use it to get attention."

A little while later, they all made their way back to the lounge, so that Ted could continue his story.

They sat in the same places as they were before lunch, all looking expectantly at Ted. He remembered the point he had ended on, and took it up from there.

"The morning after my visit to head office, I went to work as usual, and during the morning, made a phone call to the local daily newspaper. I knew one or two of the people there, and asked for one person in particular. When she answered, I said,

'This is a spokesperson for 'Sam Miller and Son'.'

There was a pause, a laugh, and then she said,

'Hello Ted, how are you?'

She knew me because she is the wife of one of my cousins, and obviously knew where I worked.

I gave her the news that the yard was up for sale because of the scandal involving two of the managers, and gave her as much information as necessary at that stage. She thanked me for the report, and promised not to use my name.

I continued with my work, but at the back of my mind was the threat that Tina was making, and I started to think that I was being selfish by asking her to move to London. Things didn't change much between us over the next week or so. I usually saw Tina once or twice in the evening during the week, and all afternoon and evening at the weekend. No matter how I tried, I could not change Tina's mind about moving to London when we got married. After a week or two of stalemate I decided things had to be sorted out once and for all. We were talking with her Dad one night, when I suddenly said,

'Have you made your mind up yet, Tina?'

Her Dad looked at me sharply and said,

'Made her mind up about what?'

I told him of my promotion and the salary increase, plus the cheap rented house, but that Tina had so far refused to come with me. He turned to his daughter and asked why she hadn't mentioned any of this to him or asked for his advice. Tina pulled her face, and said that she didn't think it had anything to do with him. After a comment like that, her Dad was less than pleased with her and told her she had to start thinking about other people instead of just herself. I stood up, ready to go home, but before I left, I told Tina and her father that I would not change my mind about the promotion, and said I would not be coming to the house again until she decided what she wanted to do. As far as I was concerned, I said, all wedding plans were on hold until she made up her mind.

It was two weeks later when Tina's dad rang me at work. He had seen in the paper that the yard had been 'sold' to the Group, and he wanted to know if I was staying in the area.

I told him that there would be no managerial staff at the yard, and all financial matters would be dealt with through me at head office.

Once again I felt as though I was being pressured to forget my promotion and find an accountancy job nearby. There was no way that was going to happen, because I had made my mind up that I was going to London, and although there was another five weeks before I left, I was resigned to the fact that if it meant leaving Tina behind, so be it. We had been engaged for five years, and prior to all this upset, had been looking forward to married life. Now I was having my doubts. Two weeks before I left, Tina got in touch with me and asked if I would go and talk to her about our marriage and my job. I agreed, and she asked me to come to her dad's apartment on Saturday afternoon when both her parents would be there. We sat down and started to discuss things properly. I asked her again why she didn't want to live and work in London. She gave me the same excuse, she would miss all of her friends. I asked which ones she would miss the most and she named two, two that she hardly saw, one of whom was married and living twenty miles away. Her Mother broke into the discussion, and told Tina that she was being stupid and bloody minded, to which Tina took a funny. She yelled and shouted at the three of us in turn, and stormed out of the room. I stood up, shook hands with her mum and dad and said,

'I leave here a week on Monday, and if Tina wants to talk at any time, she can ring me at the head office. As far as I'm concerned, the wedding is off. I'm sorry about the money you have paid out, but if Tina can't accept that I have worked dammed hard for the past five years to give us a good living when we got married, there is nothing more I can do to convince her."

I left them and made my way home, seemingly without a care, but when I went to my room later that night, that's when I broke down and cried.

Two weeks later, I was working at head office.

I put a lot of effort into my job, and it started paying dividends within a couple of months.

What it all involved doesn't matter, because it is not part of the storyline.

One Friday night, just as I was finishing work, I took a phone call in the office. It was Tina. She had come down to London and was at Victoria Coach Station. I gave her directions how to get to the station nearest to the office, and I said I would meet her there. We spent the weekend together in the apartment I was renting, and had a good talk. I showed her two houses that we could rent and she seemed pleased with a three bedroom semi on the outskirts of Romford.

Cutting a long story short, we did eventually get married, but I was sure that Tina's change of heart was more to do with the pressure from her parents, rather than love for me. Tina told me when we got engaged that she wanted to start a family as soon as we were married, which gave her a reason not to get a job with any prospects.

I'm going to cut the story short again, for obvious reasons.

Over the next five years, Tina had eight miscarriages, all in the early stages. After the last one, the gynaecologist warned us that to continue trying for children was dangerous to Tina's health, and she should consider sterilization. Of course she would not hear of it, so I said I would have a vasectomy to avoid any more problems. It avoided the pregnancy problems, but sadly started some personal ones. Tina started going out with a couple of her friends from work, and began drinking fairly heavily. She wasn't an alcoholic, quite, but three or four night each week she was out. One night she came home quite the worse for wear, and when I tried to help her to take her coat off, she got loud and abusive. At first, I just put it down to the drink, and let her get on with it, but when it got personal, I tried to calm her down. The worst bit came when she told me that because I couldn't get her or any other woman pregnant, I was only half a man. She was also adamant that it was my fault that she had miscarried eight times. To hear all that coming from my drunken wife hit me very hard, and from that night onwards, I slept in the spare bedroom, and avoided Tina if I possibly could. Her drinking got worse and it had got to her being out most nights. The odd night she didn't go out was spent in silence, and as far as I was concerned, our marriage was over. She went out one Friday night, and didn't come home until around mid-day on Saturday, when she almost fell out of a taxi. I didn't even ask where she had been as she staggered past me and went upstairs to bed. That night, she was off out again, so I packed all her belongings, of which there weren't many, left a suitcase and a holdall outside the front door, and locked it as I went back inside. I sat in the dark, waiting to see what would happen when she saw her bags. In the early hours of the next morning, a car pulled up outside the house. Tina got out and staggered towards the door. I waited for the screaming to start, but was most surprised when she walked back to the car, spoke to the driver, came back to pick up her bags and threw them in the car. A few moments later it drove away and I haven't seen her since. I don't know where she went or with whom, but I knew there would be no second or even third chance for her.

It took a couple of years of searching by my solicitor, but eventually she was found and given my divorce papers. She didn't contest it, or try to claim any maintenance from me. Tina had been my girlfriend, fiancée and wife for a total of thirteen years, and now I was free of her for ever. I carried on with my life, and threw everything I could into my work.

Over the years, my involvement in senior management increased, and as you are now aware, I was the head accountant and the chief financial advisor for the Ashley Lee Group, and was making more money than I could ever have dreamed of. Part of my work was travelling around the subsidiaries and make sure they were working to Group instructions. One day I was rushing around the area in my usual way, and had just finished a meeting at one of the large yards. I left the building, and started down a metal staircase outside the offices. There were a number of steps, then a square landing before more steps. I had gone down two flights and, as I stepped onto the landing, stood on a metal rod. What it was doing there, or who left it there, nobody has yet found out. Before I stepped on it, I was looking down on the yard, next I saw the sky, then nothing until I came round in hospital. I was on a board, strapped tightly so I couldn't move. When the doctor saw that I was conscious, he asked me if I could feel anything. I told him I had a splitting headache, and he said he wasn't surprised as I had banged it on the metal step and it was badly cut. It would have to be stitched later after they had done some x-rays to make sure if there were any broken bones. He then ran something down my feet, testing the reaction. It tickled! He asked me if I would move my toes, feet, fingers and then my wrists and arms. I was feeling a little worried by now, and asked why he was doing these tests. His answer shook me. He thought my back was broken."

Ted paused for a moment, as the revelation of a broken back brought gasps from everyone. He waited to see if anyone wanted to ask a question, but as nobody spoke, he carried on.

"'Apparently', the doctor said, 'as my head hit one of the metal steps, my back hit one of the lower ones, and he had to wait until I became conscious before he could test my reactions'.

I was wheeled off to the x-ray department, and it was while they were moving me around to take the photos, that the pain set in. I was in agony in my lower back, but nothing could be done to relieve the pain until I was back in A and E. It turned out I had broken two of my vertebrae, displaced a disc and the bone below it.

They took me to a side ward, and took off the straps that were holding me rigid. I was warned not to make any sudden movements in case I did more damage before they operated.

Before they could operate on my back, they had to shave me, front and back, mid-chest to mid-thigh. I was carefully rolled onto my side so they could do my back and as one nurse shaved my body, another stitched and bandaged my head.

When I came round from the anaesthetic, I was in a plaster cast from my chest to my thigh, but a gap had been left for my genitals. Because I was unable to sit, the bed I was in could be raised up from the top so that I wasn't flat on my back all the time, but my body had to be kept rigid. The surgeons had opened me just above the end of my spine, and had been able to wire and pin the two broken bones together. The disc and the displaced bone were manipulated back into place before they sewed me up and wrapped me in the plaster cast. I was in that cast for just over two months, and had many visitors from work, all saying they wanted to see me back at the office, then signing my cast before they left. It was full of names, drawings and so called humorous comments by the time it was removed. I still have that cast somewhere! One of the secretaries wrote a humorous comment on it, but as there are ladies present, I am not going to tell you what it said. Mr Lee came to see me while I was in hospital, and I asked him if he could send some work in for me to do, because I was going mad with frustration at not being able to move or do anything. He wouldn't though, and I had to lie there and endure two months of boredom.

When they took the cast off, I had to learn to walk again. I was given two elbow crutches to help me, but even with those, I was in quite a bit of pain. All together I was off work for eight months. I went back to head office and tried to get back into the old routine, but because of the pain, I couldn't run around visiting the subsidiaries like I used to. I spent much more time sitting at my desk, and because of that, the pain in my back became acute, and I started having to take time off to recover.

Eighteen months after my accident, Mr Lee called me to his office. We sat and chatted and between us came to the conclusion that I was not as mobile as I used to be, and the problem was affecting my work. I was still capable of doing the job, but it was taking me much longer to do things, and I was slipping behind my own meticulous schedule.

Mr Lee said that the Group accepted full responsibility for my injuries, and through their insurance company, I was being compensated for the accident. When he told me the figure, I nearly fell off the chair! He was silent for a moment or two, and he was almost in tears as he softly said,

'Ted, this is the saddest thing I have ever had to do. You are by far the best employee that has ever worked for me, but as a result of the accident, you are not able to work in the way you once did, and some of your work has had to be passed on to others. I am not dismissing you Ted, rather asking if you would accept retirement from the company on medical grounds. If you do, I will offer the following package. I, that is the company will take one third of your previous year's salary, and pay it monthly into your bank. From time to time, I will send you some work from our major projects to check over and comment on them. We can call this work 'consultancy' and your monthly payments will be known as a retainer. In time, if we reduce the amount of work we send you, your retainer will be reduced as well, but whatever happens you will receive some money from the company, which will in effect, keep you on our books as an employee. Your company pension plan will be held until your sixty fifth birthday, and you will be notified in advance of its value and paid accordingly. If you need time to think about all of this, Ted, it's no problem.'

I sat for a few minutes in silence. I was almost in tears at the prospect of not working for the company anymore, but at the same time, I knew that I was much slower because of the pain. I looked again at the figures he had put on paper, and could see that if the worst came to the worst, I would still have enough money to live on.

'I don't need time to think,' I told him, 'I know my limitations, and sadly have to accept I'm not as fit as I used to be, but I will be happy to work from home as a consultant to the Ashley Lee Group.'

Mr Lee stood up and grasped my hand, once again apologizing for having to let me go.

'Can you finish all you are doing by the end of next month?' he asked.

I went back to my office and carried on with my work as though nothing had happened. Two days later everybody knew, and my office was like Piccadilly Circus with well-wishers. The secretary that had written on my plaster cast actually cried on my shoulder, telling me how much she would miss me. I did all the work I could, and the last few days were a bit of a bore because I had so little to do. My final day started out quite well. I spent my time talking and giving advice to some of my colleagues. At lunch time, I was escorted into the dining room, where a huge buffet had been set up and there

272

were free drinks as well. I stuck to my usual glass of red wine, and enjoyed the food. It wasn't easy holding a glass, eating food and walking with my elbow crutches, but somehow I managed.

The speeches began, and I was suitably embarrassed by some of the comments. For my services to the company, I received a gold, engraved Cartier watch, presented by Mr Lee. From the work force….."

Ted paused his story, as tears welled in his eyes, and it took a few moments for him to compose himself before carrying on.

"…. from the work force I got a silver tray with the company logo on it, and engraved with over one hundred signatures and messages from the staff I had worked with over the years. I left the building that night with great sorrow, helped to my taxi by the senior secretary, who kissed my cheek as I got in, and left the head office for good.

That was it! I was thirty nine, out of full time work and unable to do any more if my back continued to give me trouble. I went to physiotherapy classes, but that made the pain worse, so I had to keep using the crutches for walking until the muscles strengthened. It was five long years before I could finally dispense with those crutches. During those years, I received quite a few project costing to check, but as time passed, they became fewer, and eventually dried up. I still receive a small consultancy fee, or as Sir Ashley calls it, my retainer. I'd not had a project to check for nearly a year, when I decided to come over to Spain, where I could allow the sun to warm my back and hopefully relieve the pain. I'm pleased to say that it has, and although Ross has said to me many times that I have given her a new lease of life, she and Sam have done the same for me. I am so glad I met Ross, because not only have I found a lady I want to spent the rest of my life with, but helping her with the house in the hills, has allowed me to re-live my glory days and bring out my skills again. That is all I can tell you about my fairly short working career, but I can assure you Ross, there is still some life in the old builder yet."

There was silence as Ted stopped speaking, and then suddenly everyone wanted to ask questions.

Mum was the first.

"Ted, you went from a humble start to great heights and suddenly down to rock bottom again in such a short time. How long was it in total?"

"Nineteen years and a few months, start to finish." Ted answered.

Mum shook her head, possibly not believing such a thing could happen.

Granddad asked Ted how old he was now.

Ted smiled, and was about to say that even Ross didn't know his age, when she interrupted.

"He's forty eight on the fourteenth of February." She turned to Ted, and with a smile, said,

"I have your passport in my bag, and as I put it away, sneaked a look at your birth date."

Ross took hold of his hand, and with a serious look, asked Ted if he really had been doing things he shouldn't have done while working on the house.

Ted answered by saying,

"I don't really know Ross. Nobody can really say what I can or can't do, or even should or shouldn't do. Four years ago I could not have done much wall building at the speed I have done over the last nine months. I have had no serious adverse effects, but if I felt the slightest twinge, I stopped what I was doing and moved to something less strenuous."

"How long have you been able to walk without crutches?" Mum asked.

Ted thought for a moment, then said,

"I used two crutches for about two years, and for the next year and a half, I managed with one. I have only been walking unaided for about five and a half years.

"Both crutches are in his car boot." Ross told them.

"Just in case." Ted answered.

"Ted," said Sam, "what would happen if you broke your back again?"

"I don't think I would break it again very easily, but if I did, you would have to push me around in a wheel chair. Just think, if you accidentally let go of the chair at the top of the drive, I would rush down the slope to the track and down the hill again until the rise just before the main road. You would have to run after me and then push me all the way back up to the villa."

Sam grinned, and said,

"I'd go and get mum, who would follow you down in the pickup, and then drive you back home."

They laughed at Sam's answer, which gave granddad the excuse to stop the questioning.

"I'm sure we all have more we'd like to ask Ted, but I think it's time for a cup of tea and a walk round the garden."

Granddad took a stroll round his garden most afternoons if the weather was fine. They all joined him, mum walking alongside her father, Sam skipping ahead, and Ross walking beside Ted, holding his arm very tightly.

Granddad was a meticulous man in all things. He insisted that everyone was in bed by ten thirty, and up the following morning between seven thirty and eight

275

o'clock. Neither Ross nor Ted were ready for sleep at ten thirty, so that night when Ted came back from the bathroom and got into bed with Ross, she put her arms around him, held him tight and said that she thought he was a very brave man.

"What makes you say that?" he asked in surprise.

"Your life has been like a rollercoaster ride, highs and lows with no flat bits in between. High when you first started work and met Tina, even higher when you started at head office and the rewards it gave you. Then the downward plunge into your marriage problem, but like the man you are, you went higher and higher and at the peak of your career with a fabulous future ahead, you were cruelly sent down again by your accident. Yet you are still cheerful, and as you've proved to me, willing to help others. It cannot have been easy re-living your problems and telling us all that you went through. I am proud of you Ted Hall and I think we are going to be able to comfort each other for many years to come."

Ross gave Ted a soft, lingering and loving kiss.

They were still cuddling, when Ross asked if she could ask him a question.

"You mean the one that goes, 'what did the secretary write on your plaster cast, that you couldn't tell us because there were ladies present'."

"How did you know what I was going to ask?"

"Intuition." Ted answered.

"Was it rude?"

"Not really," Ted replied, "but with Sam and your Mum listening, I thought it better not to say anything. The secretary's name was Sandra, but was always known as Sandy. She was a nice lady, a few years older than me, and married to a computer programmer who never knew what day it was. I had known for a long time that she, shall we say, fancied me but apart from some flirting at work, that's as far as it went. When she visited me in hospital, she read some of the comments others had written on the plaster, and asked me if there was somewhere she could write a message, without it being too visible to anyone else. She settled for a gap that could be covered by my arm, and in red ink, wrote, 'Ted Hall, this is just where I want you. In bed, hard all over and unable to move. Wish I could take advantage. Love, Sandy.'

"Did she love you?" Ross asked Ted.

"I'm not sure about love," Ted answered, "but as I said a moment ago, I knew for certain she fancied me sexually. One of the other secretaries apparently once asked her if she'd like to get Ted Hall into bed, and Sandy replied 'it didn't have to be in bed'. The remark was overheard by one of my young accountants, and he had great delight in rushing to my office to give me the news. You aren't jealous are you?"

Ross shook her head against his chest, kissed one of his nipples, and replied,

"Don't be silly! It's like me asking you if you were jealous of Brian. If I asked, could you name all the ladies you have had any sexual contact with?"

"Yes, probably. Could you name your men?"

"I doubt it! I was a randy little bugger when I was fifteen and sixteen. I told you some time ago that I've had a few hands in my knickers and given them a hand job at the same time. Brian was the first to have intercourse with me, and you are the only other. I'm glad I was able to save the best 'till last."

"Thank you Ross. I have noticed that since we decided we should live together as man and wife, you have been getting more and more passionate, so I must be doing something right."

"You are, my love. I enjoy having sex with you

because you satisfy me and don't stop until you know I am. To me that is love of your partner and not just thinking just about your own needs. It's still early for us to be in bed, so why don't you tell me the names of those ladies you have had sex with."

Ted looked at Ross, not really knowing if she was joking or not. Ross lifted her head, and whispered,

"Go on, it's all right, I'm just curious that's all. I don't care how many lovers you've had in the past, so why don't you tell me the intimate details of your early sexual encounters."

"Are you sure Ross?"

She nodded again, and whispered,

"You tell me all the details, and you never know, it may give me a greater appetite for this."

As she spoke, she moved her hand down, and took hold of him. She kissed him, put her hand back on his shoulder, and said,

"I'm listening!"

"Well," said Ted, "if you remember when we first met, and you came to my apartment for your evening meal, I gave you a quick guide then. I had been out with two or three young ladies, just to the pictures and that sort of thing. We'd snogged in the dark, and on a few occasions I had a feel of a breast through their clothing. Later, I started going out with a girl called Anne, who I thought was a bit special, and after a few weeks, tried it on with her. She slapped my face, and brought her knee up, missing my conkers by inches. After that, she didn't want to see me again as her boyfriend, although we did speak to one another if we met at any time. Her reaction to my touch put me off, and it was quite a while before I went out with anyone else. I met a girl called Louise and we went out together for a while. She let me inside her bra quite frequently, and I managed to get my hand up her skirt, but never into her knickers. She did it to me on a few occasions though, while I stroked her clitoral area through her knickers. Then Anne started to take interest in me again, and after a couple of months, she invited me round to her house one Saturday night because her parents were away. We got into a pretty steamy kissing session, and before long we were both naked. I made love to her, the first time for both of us, but certainly not the last. We lasted for just over a year and it only finished when her parents decided to move to another town. There was another girl I met called Carol, but she only lasted a few months. I had sex with her maybe three or four times, before she decided to go back to the boy she finished with before she met me. It was then that I met Tina. She was sex mad and couldn't get enough of it. For me, I suppose having sex with her on such a regular basis was just what a randy old teenager wanted. When we started the arguments about her coming to London with me, sex between us became almost non-existent. I wondered then, and still do, if she was seeing someone else when she wasn't with me. When we got married sex between us got back to the very regular sessions, mostly, I think, because she wanted children. I didn't have any sex with her for several months before she left and I was a good boy for a long time afterwards. After my accident, to keep myself active, I started to get out a bit to do my own shopping. It was a struggle with two crutches, but I managed somehow. One Saturday morning, I was in a supermarket and walking up an aisle looking for the spaghetti. Stood in front of the packs was a lady that I knew. She was looking at different types of pasta, I suppose making up her mind which one to take. I stopped beside her, and said,

'Pass me a pack of spaghetti, please.'

She picked one up, handed it to me and went back to

looking at the other things. Suddenly she swung back to face me, broke into a smile and threw her arms round me. It was Sandy.

She wanted to talk, so we arranged to meet in the cafeteria half an hour later. We had a coffee and she partly brought me up to date with what was going on at work. We had been sat chatting for a while, when I said I was sorry, but I would have to leave to catch my bus home. She told me there was no need to rush off, she would drive me home in her car. We stayed for a bit longer, and then we drove back to my place. She insisted in carrying my shopping into the apartment, and when it was all put away, I asked if she would like a sandwich, because I was going to make one for myself. She agreed, and we sat in lounge and ate them with another cup of coffee. A little while later, she said she should to be thinking of getting home. We carried our lunch things to the kitchen and she washed them up for me. She turned from the sink, and said,

'I miss you at work, Ted, there's nobody to flirt with anymore.'

'I've missed you as well, Sandy, especially in a morning when you brought the mail into my office, bent down, and allowed me to see right down your low cut blouses. That always gave me a good start to the day.'

Sandy smiled at my remark.

'You did it on purpose though, didn't you?' I asked.

Sandy smiled even wider, and said,

'You enjoyed it, didn't you?'

'I sure did,' I told her, 'I've often wondered what you would have done if I put my hand down there.'

'Dragged you into the room where the files were kept and let you do what I wanted you to do to me.'

'Now you tell me!" I said, "I've not seen down your blouse for ages and today you are wearing a jumper that hides everything from view.'

Sandy laughed at the comment, then without another word, took her jumper off.

'Today you can see the real things.'

Sandy was undoing her bra as she spoke, and threw it on the floor with her jumper.

Seconds later, we were kissing and I had both hands on her breasts. I don't remember who took each other's clothes off, but I do remember pushing her thong down. As soon as she kicked it to one side, I knew what was going to happen. We made love on the settee because I couldn't make it to the bedroom. That was the start of a very passionate and very sexual affair. Sandy would come round to my flat, and more often than not, we would go straight to bed. We didn't always have full sex because of my back, but when we did, Sandy would be on top. After about three months of regular sexual activity, I asked her if she would like to come and live with me. I'm not sure she expected me to ask her that, but she said she would think about it. Some weeks later, we were in bed, winding down after a pretty steamy session, when she started to cry. I asked her what was wrong, and after a moment's silence, she said,

'That was the last time we'll make love Ted. The reason isn't because I don't love you or don't want sex with you again, but it was confirmed yesterday that I am pregnant. We know it can't be yours, and I have had sex with Phil occasionally, he is my husband after all. If I hadn't got pregnant, I would probably have come and lived with you but at this time of my life, my place now is with my husband. I love you Ted, but sadly, from now on, there must be no more sex between us.'

She left later that day, and I have only seen her once since then."

"Do you think she really did love you?" Ross asked.

"I think she did, Ross." Ted replied, "I thought at the time that I loved her, but looking back, I think I just loved the frequent sex."

"Is there anymore?" Ross asked, "It's nearly midnight, although I'm not really tired. Do you want to carry on for a bit longer?"

"There's not much more to tell you," Ted answered, "so I may as well confess all tonight. Sometime after Sandy and I parted, I saw an advert for a new social club that was opening in a nearby town. I didn't go to the opening day, but waited for a while until it was established. They were offering four weeks free, and if you decided to join after that, then you had to pay for each visit, so I decided to go along and see what was on offer. It was an absolutely brilliant club, but the 'committee' that ran it had no idea of what people wanted. All they had to offer each week was half an hour with a coffee and a chat to the other members, then there was the quiz. Then it was time for another coffee and chat, before everyone sat down for.... bingo. That was it, quiz and bingo, with a monthly coach trip to one of the big hypermarkets to stock up on cheaper goods. When you added the cost of the coach to your purchases, it was probably cheaper to shop locally. I'd made two visits to the club, and halfway through the third, decided I'd had enough. At the end of the coffee break, instead of going back to play bingo, I went to the door. There was a man sat there who had been taking names and the money from people as they came in, and a lady stood in front of him. As I approached, I heard her say that it shouldn't be called a social club, but a pensioners club. I stopped beside them, and said I agreed. I said that I was on a pension, but mine was a disability pension, not an old age one. The man didn't like the idea of anyone leaving halfway through a meeting, but he could see we were determined to leave and let us out. The lady rushed away, and I shuffled along on my crutches to the bus stop. She was still waiting there when I arrived and we got chatting. We sat next to each other on the bus to the shopping centre, and when we got off found we were going in different directions. I asked her if she was going to the club the following week, and she said she wasn't, because that day's visit had been her fourth, and if she went again, would have to pay. I offered to meet her at the shopping centre the following week and we could have a social gathering of our own. She agreed, and that was the start of a very strange relationship.

We had been out together for a couple of weeks, when she invited me to her home for an evening meal. Afterwards, we had a talk, watched some television, and at the end of one programme, shared a kiss. The kiss led to another, then another and finally she took my hand and helped me to her bedroom. From then on, it was almost clinical. We undressed ourselves and got into bed. Facing each other we began to kiss, when she suddenly grabbed hold of me and started moving her hand fairly quickly. Of course it had an almost immediate effect, and when she felt it rise, she climbed on top of me, and as she started to move, the moaning started. Boy was she loud! I'm sure the neighbours could hear as she had her orgasm. Seconds later, she stopped moving, making it clear that sex for her was over for the night. I lay on my back as she grabbed a handful of toilet paper and wedged it between her legs, what for I have no idea.

'What about me?' I asked her.

It was with some reluctance that she put a piece of toilet paper in one hand, and did it to me with the other. She told me I had to let it go onto the paper, and not get any on the bedclothes. You know how much there is

283

normally when I let it go…."

"A white fountain, and gallons of it." Ross agreed.

"Well I was that put off, there wasn't as much as usual because I'd purposely held it back. It was late by then and I had missed the last bus home, so I stayed with her all night. There was no more sex, just a kiss goodnight. The following morning, we woke almost together. She smiled and said good morning, and then gave me a kiss that was soft and passionate. I responded by tickling her nipple, which was hard almost immediately.

"Don't do that Ted," she said, pushing my hand away, "I don't have sex in a morning, only at night."

"Sex is good anytime," I said, moving my hand downwards. As soon as I got over her pubes, I felt the toilet paper still wedged between her legs, covering the place I wanted to touch. Talk about an instant turn off! We both got out of bed, and got washed and dressed. She gave me a cup of tea and a piece of toast, and after agreeing to meet her the following week, I caught the bus home. Over the next week or so the same thing happened. There was never any foreplay, it was always straight in and move until she stopped. I never tried it on in the morning again though, once had been enough. I noticed after a few weeks, it was taking her longer to reach her climax, and the sex was lasting a bit longer, although she was always finished before me. I was getting tired of the way it went, oh so precise every time. One day when I was at home, thinking about the ritual, I found myself thinking of it as 'shagging by numbers'."

Ross started to laugh at Ted's comment, and it turned into her having a fit of giggles that took some time to stop. She gave him a long passionate kiss, and asked if he had nearly finished.

Ted told her there wasn't much more before he was

up to date.

"One night I had managed to be the one on top, and she was just at the peak of her noisy climax, when I felt mine arriving. I kept on moving when she told me she had finished, and I gasped, 'in a minute, just a minute.'

'Don't let it go up there.' she shouted, but it was too late, I gave a groan and let the white fountain go. You would have thought the world had ended! She pushed me off, grabbed the usual toilet paper, stuffed a huge wad between her legs, and then put her knickers on. That's when the row started. Needless to say, I didn't stay the night, but rang for a taxi and went home.

She was on the phone a couple of weeks later, begging me to go and see her. The ritual lasted a few weeks before we rowed again, and I didn't see her again for about six months. I was at the checkout in the supermarket one day, when I felt a tap on my shoulder. It was her! The Dreaded Dragon! She asked me to wait for her after we had paid for our things, and as we were walking out of the store, asked me if I would go home with her. She promised there would be no more arguments as long as I.... and these are the words she used.... promised not to fill her to overflowing again. We started our strange relationship again, but I cannot for the life of me explain why. Some weeks later, we were in bed, and she had enjoyed her noisy orgasm and was doing it to me. I had always held myself back when she did it, and she knew the small amount that came would go into the paper she held. This one day, just for a change, she was kissing me as she did it, and fairly passionately. I started feeling her breast again, and her passion increased, so I slid my hand lower. As I reached her, the speed of her hand increased. I knew the rules when she was doing this, I had to tell her when I was ready, and she would put the paper up to me. I was stroking her nipple and down there at the same speed as she was doing it to me, and there was no way I had time to warn her I was coming. Her sudden found passion had got to me, and I knew there was no way I could hold it back. I let it go, and it was seconds later that she realized what I had done. She pushed me violently away, and leapt out of bed, shouting and calling me a disgusting, filthy, depraved animal who was quite happy let his seed go into places it shouldn't. She rushed to the bathroom and got under the shower. By the time she had finished, I was gone, never to be seen again. It was a quite few years before I met another lady. She was extremely attractive, had very beautiful eyes and the rest of her was exciting as well. We didn't have a close relationship for some months, but I knew I was falling in love with her. I'm not sure she knew of my feelings at the time, but I wished I could tell her how I felt. Each time I looked at her, I fell deeper and deeper in love, and even now cannot properly express how deep I have fallen. She makes me feel special, and if she can ever get rid of her husband, I will ask her to marry me. I don't know what she'll say, but I'll ask anyway."

At this point, Ted was holding Ross tightly in his arms.

Ross was kissing his neck, and whispered,

"Are you crying, Ted Hall?"

He nodded his head, unable to speak for a moment.

Ross kissed his neck again, and whispered,

"Make love to me Ted, make love to me like you have been doing for all the months we have been enjoying it. Make love to me like you would to your real wife, the one you will have if I can get rid of my husband."

They made love to each other, bringing each other to a peak, and slowing down just before they went over the

286

top. The earth really shook by the time they felt it time to end it for that night.

"That was wonderful, my darling Ted. We get better and better each time we do it."

Ted was still panting from the exertion, but had enough breath to say,

"I felt as though I couldn't stop and I'm certain when I roll off you'll leak like a tap."

"That's all right," Ross said, "I'll shove some toilet paper between my legs."

They both started giggling together, and by the time they stopped, both were weary from laughing and their love making.

It was no surprise when they fell asleep in each other's arms, and almost didn't make the eight o'clock breakfast deadline.

TEN

Later that morning, Ted and Ross were in one of the out buildings where Ross's possessions from the lodge were stored. They started by sifting through boxes of clothing, most of which Ross put back, saying she didn't need that sort of clothing in Spain. Partway down one of the boxes, she found some underwear. She picked out a silky and lacy pale blue pair of short French knickers, held them up to show Ted, and said,

"There are quite a few pairs of these in this box. I used to wear them all the time before Brian and I got married, but I had to put these to one side when he demanded I wore the black thongs."

Ted was looking at them as she spoke, and then said,

"Those are very sexy Ross, and if you were wearing them they definitely would turn me on. I don't often talk about ladies underwear, but personally, I like to see my ladies in different coloured undies, it makes things more interesting. If they were the same colour day after day, it becomes boring, and less exciting."

Ross didn't say anything, just picked up all her coloureds and put them firmly in one of the 'send to Spain' boxes. There were boxes of Sam's clothes, of which Ross thought the majority were either too small for her or not needed in Spain, so they were put in a box with Ross's unwanted things. At the bottom of one of the boxes, she found an un-opened cellophane package. She looked carefully at it, turned to Ted and said,

"I'm saving this for my wedding night."

It was a beautiful black lace nightdress and negligee. She put it in the 'send to Spain' box, went over to Ted and kissed him.

"I will wear that for you, that's a promise." she said.

A few minutes later, mum came to the out building to

see what they were doing. She saw that there were plenty of clothes in a box that Ross said were not going to Spain.

"I'll get rid of those, dear," she said, "I can take them to one of the shops in town who deal with this type of thing."

She went to a box that had not been sorted, and opened the flaps.

"Are you going to keep this?" she asked, holding up a photograph frame.

Ross glanced at what her mother was holding and said,

"You can throw that in the deepest pit you can find,"

Ross took the photograph off her mother, handed it to Ted, and said,

"That is the lovely Brian."

Ted glanced at the picture, and said,

"Ugly bugger isn't he?"

Ross was about to put the picture back in the box, when Ted turned back to her, and said,

"Hang on, let me see that picture again."

Ross handed the picture back to him, and he looked closely at it. In a low voice, Ted said,

"That's not Brian Jones!"

"Of course it is Brian Jones." Mum almost shouted, "Do you think I don't know my daughter's husband?"

"Mum," Ross said, "there's no need to speak to Ted like that."

"Well coming out with such a comment," yelled mum, "it's almost like calling us liars"

At that moment, granddad came in with Sam.

"What's all the shouting for?" he asked.

"It's Ted," mum cried, "he has the audacity to say that isn't a photograph of Brian Jones.

"Mum, that isn't….." Ross started to say, but was

interrupted again by her mum.

"I might have known you'd defend him. I know what I heard him say."

"Stop it Beth!" Granddad said to his daughter. "Let me hear from Ted what he said."

He turned to Ted and Ted took the cue.

"I did actually say that it wasn't Brian Jones….."

"See, I told you." Mum interrupted.

Exasperated, Ted looked at her, and said,

"Mum, will you get down off your high horse and listen to what I have to say."

Ted turned back to granddad and said.

"Sorry, I didn't mean to be rude, but mum won't let me finish what I am trying to tell you."

Mum drew a breath to interrupt again, but Granddad looked at her with an expression that told her to keep quiet.

"I did say, 'that's not Brian Jones', but what I should have added was, 'or it wasn't Brian Jones that I knew him as.'"

There was silence as Ted started to pace up and down, something he often did if he was thinking deeply about something.

"He should be on the stage." Mum said in a frustrated voice.

"Quiet, mum," Ross said. "Ted's thinking."

Ted stopped in mid stride with his eyes closed. He lifted his hand, and pointing with his finger, said,

"Ross, when you were telling me all about Brian and his antics, you mentioned at one point about him going away to work for three weeks, and at the time you were sure he was going away on holiday with a woman."

"That's right," Ross answered, "it was when he came back he was on holiday. He showed me a photograph of him working at the hotel."

Ted nodded, paused, and said in a low voice,

"The Royal Palace Hotel."

Ross gasped, and said,

"That's right, how on earth did you know."

Ted opened his eyes, smiled, and said,

"That was one of my projects."

They were all staring at Ted as he spoke. Ross was the first to recover.

"Are you saying that Brian has worked for you?"

Ted nodded and said,

"I rarely forget a face of any of my workforce. I can't always remember their names immediately, but it will come to me eventually. There is something odd about this episode as well, so if you'll give me a little time to unscramble my brain, I'll try and remember what it was."

"Coffee time!" said granddad, "why don't we go back to the house and relax for a while."

Once inside, Ted and granddad went to the den, where Ted slowly paced the floor, thinking back several years to the refurbishment of the hotel.

Granddad was sat at his computer, while mum, Ross and Sam were in the kitchen talking to Laura.

When Ross came into the den a few minutes later, Ted was still pacing, but had remembered one or two things, and was still trying to piece it all together.

"Relax love," Ross said, "I'm sure what you are trying to remember isn't all that important."

"Oh it is my love, believe me, it's very important." Ted answered.

Ross looked at the expression on his face, and said,

"Have you remembered something about him?"

Ted put both arms round Ross, kissed her and was about to say something, when mum walked into the room carrying the coffee things.

"Can't you two leave that until you are in bed at night?" she said in a superior voice.

Ted continued to look into Ross's eyes, and said,

"I think you are confusing the two words love and lust. Love is something people feel twenty four hours a day, seven days a week and fifty two weeks of the year, not for ten minutes in bed. Also, lust, if that's the name you would like me to use, is not just for bed and not just at night. Like the Martini advert said, 'any time, any place, anywhere.' I love your daughter Mrs Critchley-Smythe, and I'm not ashamed to show the world how much. Sometime after we met, Ross told me all about her life from the age of seventeen, and I do mean all. I have cried with her when she told me of the horrific things that Brian had done to her, things that she hasn't told you or anybody else. Do you recall the last time Ross was here? She went to the lodge to get some of her belongings, and Brian found her there. Do you remember what he did to her?"

"Yes, of course I remember, I saw the marks on her body. He gave her a few slaps and punches."

"No, Mrs Critchley-Smythe, he didn't give her a few slaps and punches, he gave her many, many slaps and punches, front and back plus three bites on her body, the teeth marks of two of those bites are still visible. Those punches were hard, very hard, and it was Brian's intention to kill this lady for daring to leave him. If granddad had not gone to the lodge looking for Ross, she would not be in my arms today. Granddad actually saved her life that afternoon. I will do all that I can to nail that bastard, and I think I know how I'm going to do it."

Ted held Ross in his arms, looking at her the whole time he spoke. Ross was looking back at Ted with tears rolling down her cheeks.

"One of these days," Ted continued, "I am going to

marry this wonderful lady, and we are going to spend the rest of our lives together in peace and harmony, looking after each other, and bringing Sam up in the knowledge that she will not have to put up the things that she saw her mother going through."

"Rosalinda is already married." was the haughty reply.

Ted smiled at Ross, kissed her, and said,

"I'm not so sure about that."

"Oh, we're back to talking rubbish again, are we?" said mum. "I went to the ceremony, so I know for certain she was married."

Ted shook his head sadly, looked at her and said,

"Mrs Critchley-Smythe, I don't want to fall out with you. You have been very kind to invite me to spend Christmas here, but after we saw the photograph of Brian, you have been defending him since I said I knew him as someone else. Have you heard the word 'alias' before?"

"Of course," she said, sniffing with displeasure, "it's something criminals use."

"Exactly!" Ted replied.

"Have you remembered something about him working at the hotel?" Granddad asked, handing Ted and Ross a cup of coffee.

"Yes, I have." Ted answered, "He used a foreign sounding name, that's why it took so long for me to remember it. Now I don't want to say anything at this point, but if I may use your phone, I have an idea how we could solve some mysteries."

"Help yourself Ted, we'll go out and leave you to it."

"No, please granddad, I want you all to hear the conversation. I see your phone has a speaker connected so you'll be able to hear both sides of the conversation. It may be rather long, because the persons I'll speak to

293

haven't heard from me for many years. Let me drink this coffee, and then I can try unravelling the past."

"Do you need a telephone directory?" asked granddad.

"No thank you, unless the number has been changed, it's stored in my long term memory."

Ted drank his coffee, and then after re-filling his cup, sat down at the desk, wrote something on a piece of paper and folded it in half. He handed it to granddad, and said,

"Please keep that folded, and don't look at what I have written until I ask you."

Granddad took the paper and sat down next to Ross.

Ted pulled the phone towards him and dialled a number. Everyone heard the number start to ring, and leaned forward so they would be able to catch every word.

Ted was smiling as the call was picked up.

"Good morning, this is Sir Ashley Lee's residence. How may I help you?"

In a bright and cheery voice, Ted answered him.

"Good morning Thomas, how are you today?"

There was a moment's pause, and then, in a very friendly voice, Thomas said,

"Good morning to you Mr Hall Sir. How very nice to hear your voice again. Are you still having problems with your back or has it cleared up at last?"

"My back is a lot better thank you Thomas. If Sir Ashley had been able to wait another five years until I was fit again, I would still be with him."

"I don't doubt that for one moment, Sir. You were like a son to him, and it hit him very hard when you had to leave. If you had been able to stay, I know for certain you would be at the top today and running the company on his behalf."

"Thank you Thomas, but it's no good thinking of what might have been, we have got to think of what we have got and make the best of it."

"Very true Sir, very true. Would you like to speak to Sir Ashley, I know he will be extremely pleased to hear from you. If you hold the line, I'll put you through."

There was a few moments silence, and then a quiet voice said,

"Ted Hall? Is that really you Ted, after all these years?"

"Hello Sir Ashley. Yes it is me, in the flesh, so to speak. How are you keeping?"

"I'm not too bad. I had a slight stroke last year which left me with a limp in my left leg, but apart from that I'm fine now. Have you got rid of those crutches yet?"

"Yes I have. I've been without them for about five years, and I've very little pain from my back now."

"Then you can come back and work for me." Sir Ashley said with a laugh. "I heard on the grapevine that you are living in Spain now."

"I'm living in Spain permanently now, so if I came back to work for you, it would be a long commute each day. I am in the UK at the moment, staying with a lady and her relatives. We have just come across a problem that needs sorting out and although I have most of the answers, I would like to confirm them with you, if you don't mind."

"That's no problem Ted, anything to help a friend."

"I have the telephone on speakers so they can hear the answers to some questions I'd like to ask you. Have you any objections to that Sir Ashley?"

"None at all Ted. Fire away and I'll help as much as I can."

"Before I start though, I'm staying not too far away from you. Would it be all right if I came to see you and brought the lady and her daughter with me?"

"That would make my day Ted. I'm not planning on going anywhere, so just give me a couple of days' notice before you come. Now what are these questions you'd like to ask?"

"Do you remember the refurbishment of the Royal Palace Hotel?"

"The Royal Palace," Sir Ashley repeated and a few seconds later said, "Yes, I do remember it. One of your projects that gave me a handsome profit. Mind you, all of your projects did that. We were doing another refurbishment in Glasgow at the same time, weren't we?"

"Edinburgh," Ted prompted.

"That's right, and there was a problem there with the carpets not being delivered on time."

"That was one of the questions I was going to ask. Now then, because of that late delivery, what did we have to do?"

"We needed someone to fit all the carpets in the Royal Palace so it could re-open. I had a word with the boss of our normal fitters, and he said he could get someone for us. We both visited the site that weekend, and on the Sunday evening, a chap with a foreign sounding name turned up and we had to put him up at the hotel next door."

"Can you remember his name? I can, but I'd rather hear it from you."

There was a few seconds pause, and in a low voice they heard Sir Ashley say,

"Robbi, no not Robbi, Rolli? No, no. Rossi, that's it, Rossi. Now then, what was his Christian name?"

There was a few more seconds of silence before Sir Ashley said,

"No Ted, it's gone, you'll have to remind me."

"Before I rung you, I wrote his name on a piece of paper, folded it so nobody could see, and gave it to a gentleman who is sat beside me. I'm going to ask him to read that name to you."

Granddad opened up the paper, and in a clear voice, said,

"Ted has written, 'Cervello' as the Christian name."

"That's right," Sir Ashley cried, "Cervello Rossi. A bloody good carpet fitter he was as well, but there was something about him I didn't trust. Does this help, Ted?"

"It does indeed help. I'm sorry to keep asking questions, but I am trying to sort out a situation that at the moment is rather delicate. Can you recall the end of his first week when you and I were discussing weekend working with him and the site foreman?"

After a pause, Sir Ashley hesitantly said,

"Are you referring to the Rossi chap? He told us he couldn't work that Saturday because he was getting married….."

Sir Ashley paused as he heard a collective gasp from Ross, her mum and granddad.

"Have I said the wrong thing Ted?"

"No Sir you have not." said granddad, "I would be most grateful if you can tell us anything else you know about this wedding."

"Well, I recall Ted and I having a meal on the Saturday night, when Rossi walked into the dining room with a woman. She was displaying the biggest pair of….. sorry, I forgot there are ladies present. She had the British version of the silicon valley and most of it was on view. He asked me if he could have the honeymoon suite for him and his bride until the job was finished. I was a wee bit wary of the way he leered at the woman, so I told him the honeymoon suite was only for genuine newlyweds. He then proceeded to show me a certificate proving he had been married that morning at the Lambeth registry office. Does all this help you?"

"More than you will ever know." Ted answered. "That man was married to someone else at the time, so now I'll have to do some more searching to find out how he managed it. Just as a matter of interest Sir Ashley, the name he used was a clever alias. His proper name is Brian Jones, and the lady he was first married to is known as Ross. I know some Italian, and realized that his so called Christian name, Cervello is Italian for brain, a twist on his real name, Brian. His wife's name, Ross, add an 'i' and we have a clever name change. Thank you for your time Sir Ashley; I'll explain this in more detail when we come to see you after Christmas."

"It's been great talking to you again Ted, and when you bring the lady and her daughter to see me, you forget the 'Sir'. I really am looking forward to seeing you again Ted."

Both men said goodbye and hung up their phones. Ted sat back with a weary sigh.

"You are something amazing, my lovely Ted." Ross said with pride.

"He is indeed," said granddad, "and so is Sir Ashley. Both of them remembering so clearly something that happened years ago. This sheds a different light on things, don't you think."

"Mum?" Ross said, turning to her mother.

But mum remained stoically quiet.

Ted was not the sort of person who held a grudge or easily lost his temper, but mum's attitude was getting to him. He didn't know if he had said or done anything wrong, but he wanted to get to the bottom of the problem. He could see the stubbornness and decided to confront her.

"Mrs Critchley-Smythe," Ted said, "I don't know

what I've done today to upset you so much, but I'm afraid I cannot accept the indifferent attitude you have towards me. When we met the day before yesterday, you were all smiles and wanted me to call you 'mum'. Since I mentioned marriage to Ross, your manner has changed. If you no longer want me to stay, please say so now, then I can make other arrangements. Alternatively, why don't you explain to all of us what the problem is."

Mum looked at Ted, and sniffed, a sniff of disapproval.

Ted could take no more of it, so he stood up, turned to Granddad and said,

"Granddad, thank you so much for your hospitality, but I feel I am intruding on your family. I'll go and pack a bag and get out of the way so you can celebrate Christmas without me."

There was a moments silence as Ted started to walk from the room. Ross jumped up and called,

"Ted, where are you going? If you are leaving, then I'm coming with you and so is Sam."

"That's it, you harlot," yelled her mum, "go with him and spend the rest of your life in sin."

Everyone turned and looked at her as she started ranting again.

"You are a married woman, and have no right sleeping and fornicating with anyone other than your legal husband. You should seriously think about returning to him and sort your marriage problems out together, not throwing yourself into the bed of the first man that makes a pass at you."

"Return to her husband?" Ted said in horror, "do you really want to see your daughter killed? Have you so little regard for Ross and Sam that you will push them both into certain torture? Have you forgotten what you have just heard about Brian? He is married to someone else, so is he not sleeping and fornicating with another woman? Or is your attitude 'it's all right if a man does it, but a woman should be at home cooking, washing and scrubbing, always ready for her man when he demands it'? Does it matter to you if his demands are sex or violence, or even both? Does it matter to you that your granddaughter has seen her mother repeatedly beaten because her dad was drunk and felt like asserting his power over Ross? Or are you happy to turn a blind eye and pretend nothing is wrong and Ross and Sam are making it all up? If that is the case, Mrs Critchley-Smythe, you are as sick as Brian."

Ted was panting with the effort he put into his words, and he was starting to sweat as his fury at mum's narrow minded opinion took hold of him.

"How dare you speak to me like that?" she shouted. "I think you should leave this house immediately, and take that harlot with you, but you are not taking Samantha, she can go and live with her father."

"Ted, Ross and Sam are not leaving this house," granddad said calmly, "if anyone is to leave it's you. I don't know where you got these stupid ideas from, but you can forget about them, immediately."

Ted suddenly confronted mum.

"You have been talking to Brian, haven't you?"

She made no move to answer, and when Ross asked her the question again, she nodded her head.

"Did you tell him that Ross and Sam would be here over Christmas?" asked granddad.

She nodded again.

"I don't understand you, mum." said Ross furiously. "Yesterday morning you said you were sorry you insisted I had to marry him and called him a psycho. Now you are talking as if the sun shines out of his arse. Have you conveniently forgotten that he killed your first grandchild?"

"How can he have done that, you stupid woman," Mum retorted. "You fell down the stairs at work, so are you trying to say he pushed you?"

There was silence for a moment, as Ted, Ross and granddad looked at her. Sam was holding tightly onto Ted's arm and crying as she saw, but couldn't believe, what was going on.

"That's what happened, isn't it? Brian told me that was what had happened." mum said in a hushed voice.

Ross turned to Ted, took hold of his hand, and said,

"Do you remember me telling you about that night? The first time he hit me? I told you that he gave me several hard slaps around my body before he staggered off to bed. Because of the strength of those slaps, he caused damage to my womb, so as far as I am concerned, he murdered my baby that night."

Ted put his arm round Ross and held her to him as she cried.

"What are we going to do?" she asked him.

"I'm not sure," Ted answered, "we can't get back home before Christmas day, so we will have to stick to our plans and fly back on the fifth. We could go and see my folks on Boxing Day, and stay up there. We can come back and see Ashley and then go straight to the airport afterwards."

Granddad was annoyed at what his daughter had done, but couldn't think of any way he would be able to keep Brian away from his house.

"I'm going to phone the police," he said, "and report that he has threatened to come to the manor and take revenge on you for leaving him months ago."

Granddad left the room and Ted, Ross and Sam followed him, leaving mum sulking on her own.

The three of them went back to the out building and

started looking through the only large box that was left. Ross took out a pile of clothes and quickly started to go through them. She decided they weren't needed, all went into the charity box, and she took out another pile.

"Oh, look," she said with a laugh, "my wedding dress."

"Are you going to save it for when you marry Ted?" asked Sam.

Ross laughed again at her daughter's question.

"No way am I using this dress again. It brought me nothing but bad luck, and from now on, there is no such thing as bad luck for any of us."

As Ross was talking to Sam, Ted had looked into the almost empty box. He saw a fairly thick A4 file right at the bottom and took it out. He started flicking through the papers, and suddenly his eyes lit up. He skimmed through more of the papers and had almost got to the end when Ross said,

"That's it Ted. All this lot can go to charity, and these three boxes can be shipped over to our house. You seem very engrossed in that file, what is it?"

"Do you mind if I don't tell you just yet? I would like to go back to the house and see if your mum is still there, because I have found something I would very much like her and everyone else to see."

Ross gave him a funny look, but agreed to his request. They made their way back to the house and into the den. Mum was still sat in the same place, and granddad was just about to sit down at his computer.

"All finished in there?" he asked them.

"Yes thank you granddad," Ross replied, "there are three boxes that we can tape up later, and make arrangements for them to be shipped to Spain, to our house where Ted, Sam and I are going to live together in perfect peace."

"If you go to Spain and live in sin with Ted," shouted her mother, "I never want to see you again, and I'll do all I can to see that Samantha is returned to her father."

Ted stepped forward and stood in front of her,

"Mrs Critchley-Smythe, I am not going to ask you those questions again, because I see you are determined to have your own way at any cost. I would like to ask you one question, and I hope you will answer it honestly. If Ross wasn't married to Brian, and was a free person, would you still object to me marrying her?"

"She will never get a divorce from Brian so my answer is irrelevant, but if she was a free person, I would have no objection to her marrying you."

"Thank you! So your objection is a moral issue, and the fact that you have been 'got at' by a habitual drunk, a liar, a bully, and a bigamist."

Mum looked down at the floor, but refused to answer Ted's question.

Ted turned to granddad and said,

"I have just found something very interesting in one of those boxes. I haven't had time to read it all, but I would like to read the file properly, make a few notes and after lunch, read you my findings. I think we could all be happy at the outcome.

"The day we met, Ted Hall," said Ross, "you called me a 'mysterious maiden', Now I can return the complement, and call you my 'man of mystery'. Whatever you are up to must be worthwhile, otherwise you wouldn't be pursuing it."

"If I'm right, it will make our Christmas and probably our new year as well. Just one question Ross, where was Brian's shop?"

"Mill Lane, off the High Street. Why?"

Ted nodded, smiled and said,

"All will be revealed after lunch." He pointedly

looked at mum before saying, "I hope everybody will stay and listen to what I have to say."

Ted moved to a table with the file, worked steadily and was almost finished, when he said,

"Ross, do you know anyone called Michael Entwistle?"

Ross thought for a moment, and replied,

"I don't know him personally, but I'm sure he is one of Brian's drinking pals. I've heard the name, but can't say I've met him. Is it important?"

Ted just smiled and repeated,

"All will be revealed after lunch."

They went to the dining room to eat, and afterwards took their coffee back to the den, where they all sat round the table, Ted at the head. He looked round at them, and said,

"This reminds me of the board room meetings I occasionally chaired, worried faces staring at me, each one worried they were in for a rollicking for something. However, today is different, much different...."

"Oh for God's sake, get on with it." mum interrupted.

"I see the wine hasn't mellowed your mouth." Granddad said. "Why do you have to be so impatient? There is no rush, we aren't going anywhere, so sit back, relax and allow Ted to tell us what he has found in the file."

Mum waved her hand dismissively and sat back scowling.

Ted glanced round the table, and started to speak.

"It won't take too long to tell you what I have found. I'll ask a question or two, but they will be directed at Ross, so please allow her to answer me before anyone else butts in. Ross, before lunch, I asked you about Brian's shop. Now this may seem like a silly question, but, did you ever live there?"

"No Ted, nobody could live there, it's just a lock up shop with a store room and office at the rear."

"The file I found in the box contains quite a number of letters addressed to you at Mill Lane, all of which have been opened and replied to. There are copies of those replies with your signature on them, well I say your signature, but I know your hand writing, and the signature on the letters is not yours. I have the letters in order but I'm not going to read out all of them just now, just summarize them. Ross, you told me earlier you didn't know Michael Entwistle."

Ross nodded her agreement.

"Well," Ted said, "it seems that about four years ago, Mrs Rosalinda Abigail Penelope Delores Critchley-Smythe-Jones, of eleven Mill Lane, sometime between the first of March and the thirtieth of July, committed adultery a number of times with Michael Entwistle at the said address."

Ted looked up from his notes at Ross's horrified face.

"Ted, I swear......" she started.

"It's OK sweetheart," Ted interrupted, "I don't believe it, I'm only reading what's written on the papers. There are a number of legal letters addressed to you and to Brian, at number eleven Mill Lane. There are two different styles of handwriting, so I presume one set is Brian's and the other his accomplice. There is a summons for you to attend court on the eighteenth of October, three years ago, and then there is a letter dated the nineteenth of October, saying that because you did not attend court the previous day to answer the charges and defend yourself, proceedings went ahead and the decision went against you."

Ted looked up from his notes to look at Ross. She was staring open mouthed at him as he read from his notes. Ted gave her a smile, and said,

"There are some more legal papers here, but the last one is the most important. It tells me that you, my lovely lady, have not been married to Brian Jones for almost three years. He had falsified evidence, got someone to forge your signature, and because you didn't answer your summons, a decree nisi was issued. Because there was no reconciliation, the decree absolute was applied for six weeks later. It was sent to you at the shop and put in the file with all the other papers. I have it here in my hand."

Ted held the paper up, and then slid it across the table to Ross.

She picked it up in disbelief and sat staring at it, unable to speak. There was silence in the room, all waiting for her response. With tears pouring down her face, Ross asked,

"I…. Is this legal, I mean this…. document…. I mean it's not a copy or forgery or something?"

"I don't think so love, but I can check on line through the courts register of births, marriages, deaths and divorces. In the light of all this, I think your mother owes you an apology for the names and accusations she made against you."

Four pairs of eyes turned to mum. She was looking down at the table, a tear running down her cheek. She wiped it away brusquely with her hand, and then said,

"I don't like to be proved wrong. I usually look deep into things before I say anything, but when I was in the supermarket yesterday, I bumped into Brian. He never said anything about a divorce, but convinced me that he truly wanted Ross and Sam back again so he could sort things out. After listening to Ted, I can see just how he would sort things out. I am sorry Ross, but until Ted just showed us how devious he is, I thought I was doing the right thing."

"That's OK mum, I'll accept what you say. I know Brian can lie through his teeth and make it sound convincing. I think you owe Ted a bigger apology though. He has only been here for a few days, and you made him feel so unwelcome that he was prepared to go home by himself. We are only staying for a short time, so tell him you are sorry, and we can start enjoying our Christmas. Just as a matter of interest, the comment you made about jumping into bed, etc., Ted didn't make a pass at me, I made the pass at Ted. He had treated me so well, knowing I was, no… thinking I was married, and therefore behaved like a gentleman at all times, so it was me that made the first move."

Mum smiled at her daughter, reached across the table and took hold of Ross's hand.

"I can see how much you both care for each other, and Sam spends more time with Ted than I ever saw her do with Brian. I apologize wholeheartedly to the three of you, and wish you all the luck in the world in your new home. When you get settled, I would love to come out with your granddad to see how you have built it and enjoy spending some time with you. Before you leave, will you give me your address then I can keep in touch with you?"

Ross looked over to Ted, and said,

"What is our address, Ted, do you know?"

"The only address for our home is on the licence. It is 'parcela número cuatro, polígono número dos, Rio Guadalminó, two nine seven seven etc. We will have to rent a post box when we get back, because there is no postal delivery to any home out in the campo. When we get sorted mum, we will send you the full address."

"Ted, I've just had a horrible thought." Ross cried. "Does this mean that Brian and I have been living together when we were actually divorced?"

Ted nodded and said,

"It looks like that Ross, but what we need to do is tie up any dates from the records. I'll go on line and see what I can find, while I leave you to read the letters that are in the file."

Ted passed the file down the table, so that granddad, Ross and mum could read in full all that Ted had just outlined. Meanwhile, Ted went on line to the records office to authenticate the divorce, and once he had verified it, made a print out, and went searching again. A few minutes later, he burst out laughing, and the others turned to look at him.

"What have you found that's so funny?" Ross asked,

"I'll make a print out of this for you." Ted said, "I started a search for his name in the records, and the first one I found is the one I'm laughing at. While that lovely man was still married to you, he was cited as the co-respondent in the divorce case between Malcolm and Dorothy Rutter. Would that be the Dorothy you told me about?"

"It could well be," Ross replied, "I think he was seeing her for quite some time. Is there any more dirt in there?"

"I'm going to do some more searching and I'll make a copy of anything that I find."

A short while later, Ted switched off the computer and went to join the others at the table.

Ross saw the look on his face and with a big smile, asked,

"Found anything juicy?"

Ted held out some papers, and said,

"Brian's been a busy boy; he's been puttin' it about a bit, as they say. He has been cited as co-respondent in two other divorce cases, and he has had two divorces himself. He must think he's God's gift to women."

"He may be to them, until they find out what he is really like." Ross said.

"According to the dates I've found," Ted told Ross, "he was still married to you when he married someone called Lynda. That was at the time he worked for me. Then came his divorce from you, and a year later, the divorce from Lynda. He immediately married Stephanie who had a son six months after the wedding. He may still have been living with you when he divorced Lynda and married Stephanie. I've had a search round, but there are no records of him locally. Maybe it was a coincidence that mum saw him in the supermarket."

"Ted," mum said cautiously, "this divorce thing that we're reading, it can't be legal, surely."

"The way it was done is highly illegal, but the court record show the marriage was dissolved and that cannot be reversed. I suppose if we went to the police and reported it, eventually he would be prosecuted, and in the meantime he would spend his time terrorizing you and granddad. In my opinion, we just let it go, get on with our lives and forget Brian ever existed."

Sam came round the table and sat on Ted's knee.

"Ted," she said, "are you and mum really going to get married?"

"I hope so, Sam. I haven't asked her for about an hour, but as far as I know, we still are."

"Does that mean I could be a bridesmaid?"

"I don't know love, that will be your Mum's decision, not mine. With a name like Sam though, maybe you should be the best man."

Sam beamed at him, and in a charming voice, said,

"For your wedding day only, I'll let everyone call me Samantha."

They all laughed at her words, and went back to reading the letters.

309

"When you and Mum are married," Sam asked Ted, "will you become my dad and will I have to call you dad instead of Ted?"

"No Sam," Ted answered, "I will be known as your step dad, but that is really a legal term, so to you, I will always be Ted."

"I'm glad about that," Sam said, cuddling up to Ted and resting her head on his chest. Five minutes later she was asleep.

ELEVEN

Christmas day was a happy one for all of them. Ted and Ross had bought presents for mum and granddad, and they were thrilled with the Spanish things they received. They in turn had not really known what to buy for Ted and Ross, so between them they had bought a number of cut glass ornaments for their new home.

Ross said they were a very nice present, but would have to go in one of the boxes in the outhouse.

"They are too heavy to go in our suitcases," Ross explained, "we would probably have to pay extra for the added weight."

"I never thought of that," said granddad, "we'll have to be careful what we buy for you in the future."

Sam got clothes from her grandma and money from granddad. Ted had explained to Sam before they left home, that the children in Spain exchanged gifts on the sixth of January, and because they would be home on the fifth, she could have her presents when they got back. She was delighted when Ted gave her a small digital camera, just to keep her happy until they got home. Ross was quite surprised, because she knew nothing of Ted's present. He got a kiss though for his generosity and thoughtfulness.

The following days passed quickly and on the thirtieth of December, Ted, Ross and Sam used mum's car and drove north to see Ted's parents. They spent a very good day, talking about the things that had happened since the last time they were together. Ted found out his brother was one of the top men in a research laboratory in Auckland, attached to a brand new hospital. His mum gave Ted his brothers new email address so he could get in touch with him and keep him up to date with his life in Spain. Ted's parents were happy about their intended marriage, but said they wouldn't be able to attend if the ceremony was going to be in Spain.

Tea was served at six o'clock in accordance with his dad's wishes, and by seven thirty, they were on their way back to granddads'.

The next morning, Ted rang Sir Ashley and arranged for them to visit him in the afternoon of the third of January.

They all saw the New Year in together, toasting it with an old Malt Whiskey that granddad kept for special occasions.

"I hope the next toast I give will be on your wedding day." he told Ted and Ross.

Being New Year's Day, they were allowed an extra hour in bed, but even though Ted and Ross were down by eight thirty, Granddad was up and about before them.

Later that morning, Ted was in the den sat on a settee in front of a log fire and reading a book. He was engrossed in the plot, and didn't know Ross had come into the room until she stood in front of him.

"Hello Mrs Rosalinda Critchley-Smythe-Jones." he said, looking up from his book. "What are you going to call yourself when we get married?"

Ross sat on Ted's knee and cuddled up to him.

"I want to be Mrs Hall, plain and simple." she said. "When a lady gets married, she usually changes her surname. My three named hyphenated one will go, and I will be proud to be your wife Mr Hall."

"I've been doing a bit of thinking Ross." Ted said. "and I'd like to make a suggestion."

"Yes please! But you'd better hurry before anyone comes in and catches us."

"When I have sex with you my love, there is no such thing as hurrying. We take our time and enjoy it, so if we

312

haven't the time, we don't do it."

"Pity, I'm feeling a bit randy this morning."

"All the more reason to wait until you are feeling a lot randy, you'll enjoy it more. Now, before you corrupt the conversation again, I was going to suggest going to the local register office before we fly back home, and see if we can set a wedding date for later on in the year."

"You mean come over to the UK to get married?" Ross asked in surprise.

"Why not?" asked Ted, "We can invite more people to join us here than if we get married in Spain. What do you think? We can see what dates are available, make a decision, and only when we have a fixed date do we tell everyone."

"That's a good idea Ted. We'll have to do that as soon as we can, then we can think of whom to invite, and give them plenty of notice as well. With an idea like that, Ted Hall, I may reward you tonight."

Ted was about to reply, when they heard mum and Sam talking as they approached the door. Ross stood up, determined not to allow her mother the chance to make any more snide remarks about showing her feelings for Ted.

Mum told them she had arranged for someone to pick up the boxes of unwanted clothes the following morning, and asked Ted if he would move the other three boxes so they wouldn't mistakenly be taken with the rest.

Their visit to see Sir Ashley Lee turned out to be a day to remember. They arrived at his home at two thirty as arranged, and as soon as the door opened, Thomas welcomed Ted, dropping his usual reserve, and giving him a hug.

"I never thought I would see this day, Mr Hall. When you had to leave, it was like the driving force had been taken away from this house and the company."

Thomas turned to Ross, and said,

"The day Mr Hall left, Sir Ashley came home in tears. He told me that he knew the company would never be the same again because one vital element was missing, and could never be replaced."

Thomas asked them to follow him to the sitting room. He knocked on the door, and put his head inside.

"Mr Hall is here with his two ladies." he said, and stood aside to let Ted in.

Ted walked into the room and almost stopped as he saw a number of people stood there. They burst into applause as Sir Ashley greeted him with a hug of welcome, and said,

"I couldn't let this opportunity go without inviting some of your former colleagues."

There was Neil and Brendan, two of the company's chief planning officers with their wives, his old sparring partner David Holmes and his wife, and to make up the party, his very good friend Sandy, with her husband Phil and a young boy who they introduced as Michael.

Ted introduced Ross and Sam to everyone, and they were treated in the same affectionate way as Ted.

It turned into a very lively and enjoyable afternoon, particularly when Ross started to tell them about the house they had built. When she had brought them up to date, Sir Ashley said,

"That proves that Ted has lost none of his skills."

He turned to Ross before carrying on,

"He had been at head office for maybe a couple of months, and asked if he could spend some time with a gang so he could learn something about their work. He told me that he couldn't expect someone to take orders from him if he didn't know what he was talking about. I allowed him the time, and he proved himself to be a very capable person. At the end of his time on site, there wasn't a man who didn't respect him for what he had done, and word quickly spread to the other gangs about his ability. Nobody argued with Ted Hall's decisions when he was on a site inspection."

"Did Ted tell you about our award?" David asked Ross.

"Yes.... no..., no he didn't tell me, I found out when my mother found the details in a year book. He said he hadn't told me because he didn't want me to think of him as someone important."

"In that case, he won't have told you about him turning down a Knighthood." said David. "When Ashley was offered the honour as chairman of the group, Ted was also offered one as the vice chairman. He turned it down because he thought it too higher an award for just doing his job. He took the OBE instead. Everyone thought he should have taken the honour, but he stood by his convictions."

Everyone was now looking at Ted, waiting for him to say something.

"I still stand by what I said at the time." said Ted. "I wasn't the only one doing important work."

Ross turned to Ashley and said,

"He never told me that he was vice chairman of the company either."

"Did he not?" Ashley said. "I took a month off work to take my wife on a cruise. She had a terminal illness, and wanted to see some of the world before she died. I promoted Ted and left him in charge while I was away. When I got back, I found a happy and contented workforce beavering away without any sign of anyone skiving. I started taking more time off to be with my wife, knowing my company was in safe hands. I was away from work for quite some time, and during those months my wife died. Ted organised a tribute to her, and every person from head office was given the day off to attend her funeral. When eventually I returned to work, I found he had been to meetings with Government officials, tendered many quotations for jobs, and had only lost out on two. Sandy also told me that his dictation made more sense than mine. He ran my company on his own for well over a year, and it was for all that hard work he was offered the Knighthood. He turned it down because he thought he was only doing his job. I wish I'd been able to keep him working Ross, because he would now be in my office running the Ashley Lee Group on my behalf, and I'm sure everyone will back me up when I say the Group would be making a hell of a lot more profit than it is doing now."

Everyone was looking at Ted again, waiting for a reply, but he was actually feeling very uncomfortable because of the way Ashley was talking about him. He was saved any further embarrassment by Thomas coming into the room, saying that afternoon tea was served in the dining room.

While the adults had been talking, Sam and Michael had been in a room across the hall, where there were many playthings left by Ashley's children before they grew up. Thomas brought them both to the dining room to join the adults and Sam sat with Ross and Ted telling them what she had been doing.

Afternoon tea was informal, nobody sitting down for long, just walking around chatting while eating sandwiches and drinking cups of tea.

Soon after they had finished, David and Brendan said they should be on their way, and after wishing Ross and Ted all the best for their marriage, thanked Ashley for inviting them to what they regarded as a long overdue reunion.

Not long afterwards, Neil said it was time he and his

wife left, and Sandy had to leave as well because she and Phil had come in the car with them.

Ashley, Ted and Ross were walking from the front door back to the sitting room, when Ted heard a voice. He turned to Ross and Ashley, putting a finger to his lips as he did. He beckoned them to follow him to the playroom door and they heard Sam talking. One at a time, they looked round the door to see Sam sat in front of a huge doll's house, talking to a row of dolls.

They crept back to the sitting room where Ted and Ashley spent another hour telling Ross of some of the happenings during Ted's time at head office.

Sam came into the room as they were deciding it was time to go home, and Ashley asked her if she had enjoyed playing with the doll's house. Sam told him she had enjoyed it very much, had put all the dolls to bed, and had to come out of the room so she would not disturb them.

They wished each other goodbye and Ross promised to send Ashley an invitation to their wedding. Thomas came to the door to see them off, and even his wife came as well. The three of them stood on the door step and waved until the car was well down the driveway.

During the drive home, nothing was said about the day's events, but when they got home, and granddad asked how the day had gone, Ross told him all that had been said about her man. When she finished telling him everything, Ross spoke with pride, saying,

"I was proud of Ted before we went to visit Sir Ashley, but now, I'm in awe at his talents. I thought I had a good man before today, but now I am certain of it, and I am going to make sure I never let him down in any way."

When they got to bed that night, Ross cuddled up to Ted and after kissing him said,

"I don't know what to say to you Ted Hall. The obvious thing is that I love you, and the more I find out about you, the more I realise how lucky I am that we met. The things I found out about you today! Events you hadn't told me about, or your more important work, and the way you insisted you were only doing your job. That to me is such modesty that cannot be understood. You have a brilliant brain, and it's such a pity that you can't put it to good use."

"I'm using it to build our house." Ted answered.

"Yes you are," she said, "and I now know why we finished it so quickly. It was your expertise, and as for working out how long certain jobs would take, that was second nature, wasn't it?"

Ted nodded his head, again clearly embarrassed by the way Ross was praising his ability.

"The people who were at Ashley's house today were the pick of his team, and listening to the things that were said, you were top of the tree. Your accident robbed the building trade of a brilliant man, and it's such a pity that you couldn't have gone back to work to prove it."

"If I had gone back to work, I would not have fallen deeply in love with a lady that I want to spend the rest of my life with, or her lovely daughter that I will treat as my own. I am proud of my achievements and everything else that happened while I worked for the group, but I will stand by what I have said, I was only doing my job. OK, I did it better than most, but my reward for that hard work, was getting my pay check each month and my bonuses for successful projects. I did not look for or want rewards other than that, especially a Knighthood. I am Ted Hall and would like to be Ted Hall all my life. I cannot imagine ever being Sir Edwin Michael Hall, and if I had accepted it, I have no doubt that I would have been Sir Ted to everyone, and that would have made a mockery of the honour."

"I think I would have liked to have been a Lady." Ross said quietly.

"Mmmm." said Ted, "can you imagine us going to one of the posh dinners that Knights of the realm are invited to. We arrive at the door, a man looks at our invitation and shouts out, 'Sir Edwin Michael Hall and Lady Rosalinda Abigail Penelope Dolores Hall'."

"I see what you mean," Ross agreed, "it is a bit of a mouthful, isn't it?"

"If you remember," said Ted, "a few months ago I said I wished you were my lady. Now you are my lady and will be for as long as I live. If you want me to, I'll call you Lady Ross occasionally, as long as I'm never Sir Edwin."

"I had a chat with Sandy at tea time," Ross said, changing the subject. "The way she spoke about your work and your attitude, she clearly did love you, and I could see she still had feelings for you. I let her know that you had told me about the affair. At first looked a bit shocked, and then she smiled, and said, 'That is typical of Ted Hall. Most men would have bragged to their friends, but not their partner. Ted tells his partner and nobody else.' She told more about you, but what she said is between her and me. I can see why you had a fling with her though, she is very attractive and a nice person to talk to. Just as a matter of interest Ted, how old is Sandy?"

Ted thought for a moment, and then said,

"I will be forty eight next month, so Sandy will be either fifty five or fifty six in September."

"Really? She certainly carries her age well. How come they have such a young child?"

"I don't know Ross, but I would imagine she was one of the unlucky ladies who got caught when approaching

319

the change."

"If you were still with the group, and I was fortunate enough to have met you, I would be very jealous of Sandy."

"Ross," Ted said in a serious voice, "I am strictly a one woman man. I never have, and never would, cheat on my lady. I know what you are going to say about Sandy and me, but I was not with anyone at the time. Sandy could have stopped me if she had wanted to, and we both went into the affair with our eyes wide open. Tomorrow, you and I are going to the register office to arrange out wedding date and I promise you faithfully that I will look after you and Sam for as long as I am able. Before you lost your virginity to me, I described you as 'one gorgeous woman' and 'wished you were my woman'. Well you still are 'one gorgeous woman' and when we are married, you will become my wife, lover, companion and my best friend. In other words, you are going to have to put up with me for ever, rotten jokes and all."

"I'm not so sure about the last bit, maybe I should have a re-think….. I just have, and I still want to marry you. What month should we aim for?"

"I think that July would be best, because if we get Sam into a school, she would finish for the summer at the end of June. She would not go back until September, so we have a wide choice without her missing anything."

"You mean I have to wait for another seven months before I can be Mrs Hall?"

"If you are that desperate, we could try for the end of March or the beginning of April and then we could have our wedding anniversary around the date we first met."

"That's not a bad idea," Ross said, "I think it better if we wait until we see what options we have."

Ted was silent for a moment, and Ross asked what he

was thinking about.

"I've just had a horrible thought, Ross. I'm not sure we can arrange a date because I haven't got all the necessary details. I think I need proof that I am divorced from Tina and that is in the house in Spain. We can ask if they can get a copy though; let's wait until tomorrow and listen to what they say. We can't get married yet anyway, because the three boxes in the outhouse have to get over to Spain first, and then you will have to find your sexy nightdress for our first night."

"We've already had our first night, and that was one to remember, as are all the other first nights we have. I like having 'first nights' with you and I also like having our 'step one' and I would like to think we can enjoy each other sexually for many more years to come. Not tonight though, I'm feeling a bit off, must be all the long days meeting your family and old workmates. Let's have a kiss and cuddle, a nice sleep, and wake up ready to fix our wedding day."

Next morning, they drove into the town and made their way to the register office. The receptionist filled in a form with all their details and when it came to proof of Ted's divorce, went on line to confirm what he had told her. She came back a few minutes later and said everything was in order and she would accept the booking, provided that Ted sent her his copy of the decree absolute. Then came the time to set a date. They couldn't have the end of March or the first two weeks in April, because that was Easter time and they were totally booked up. In the end, they settled for Saturday the fourteenth of July at two o'clock. Ted paid the necessary fees, and they left the office in a state of bliss. Over a late lunch, Ross told mum, granddad and Sam where they had been that morning, and what date and time they had chosen. Mum was glad they were getting married in the UK, and immediately took charge of the guest list. Granddad said he was happy for them and offered them the use of his Manor for the reception.

Ted left Ross and her mum talking weddings while he went to telephone a company that transported household goods to Spain. He arranged for the three boxes to be picked up the following week, and gave them the details of his credit card for payment. By mid-afternoon, Ted, Ross and Sam were packing their suitcases ready for an early start the next morning. They had to be at the airport by six o'clock so would have to leave the house around four thirty to make sure they were in good time for the check in.

After their evening meal, Ross, Sam and Ted said good-bye to mum. She said it was far too early for her to be making a trip to the airport, but would look forward to their next visit. She wished them a good flight, and asked them to keep in touch. Before they went to bed, granddad and Ted swapped email addresses so they could keep up to date with the wedding plans.

They reached the airport with time to spare, but granddad didn't stop to see them off, he wanted to get home before the rush hour started. Before he left, he hugged Ross and Sam and shook hands with Ted.

"Have a good flight, and a very nice day tomorrow. Look after each other, and I'll look forward to seeing you for your wedding in July."

The check in was not busy and once security had been cleared, they went to one of the cafeteria's and had some breakfast to put them on until they got home. Their flight left Gatwick on time and arrived in Malaga ten minutes early. After picking up their luggage, they made their way outside where the car park bus was waiting to take them to the compound. Ted paid the fee, and minutes later, they were on their way home. He stopped at one of the supermarkets to buy fresh food, and back at the village, laden with bags and suitcases, made their way to Ted's apartment. Although they were tired from the early start and the flight, all three wanted to go straight to their house in the hills, to remind themselves where they would be living in just three short weeks. It was exactly as they left it. Ross opened the door and Sam and Ted followed her inside. She looked around the room, put one arm round Ted and the other round Sam, and said,

"Ours, our own home lovingly build by us. See Ted, I did say you would get your reward for the time you spent on it. Let's switch the heating on in both blocks and go back to the apartment. We must have an early night to refresh ourselves ready to prepare this house for its new family."

On the evening before the sixth, Ted took Ross and Sam to the main square to await the procession of the three Kings through the village. They passed slowly by, throwing sweets into the crowd of cheering people. Sam was as enthusiastic as the other youngsters, and even joined in the friendly pushing and shoving to pick up the sweets off the street. Her face at the end of the procession was a picture of delight because she had never seen anything like it before. Ross and Ted smiled with joy as one of the village children walked up to her and said,

"Hey rubia, que tal?" (Hey blondie, how are you?)

Ted explained to him that her name was Sam and she had only just arrived from the UK and didn't understand him.

The lad put his hand out for Sam to shake, and said,

"Bienvenida Señorita Sam." (Welcome, Miss Sam)

Ted translated what the boy had said, and once again, Sam's face lit up with delight.

Later that night, Ross and Ted gave Sam her Christmas present. It was something she had been telling them about for the last couple of months. A games console and controllers they could all use on the computer or the television, and a couple of game discs to get her started. Sam was absolutely delighted and thanked them over and over again, though she was a little disappointed when Ross told her she must wait until the following morning before playing on it.

Later, when Sam had gone to bed, Ted and Ross were sat drinking a cup of tea. Ross took hold of Ted's hand, and said,

"I have never seen Sam so happy and contented as she was tonight. I think we are going to see a huge change in her in the months to come. When we were with Brian, he took no notice of her, and Sam seemed to plod along without any real interest in anything. I think this new found happiness is all down to contentment and a father figure showing her some love."

"I'll do anything I can to keep my two ladies happy," said Ted, "and to prove it…." he paused and put his hand in his pocket. He took out a box, and gave it to Ross.

"Happy Christmas you gorgeous lady."

Ross opened it to find a diamond ring, one she had seen in a shop some weeks back. She told Ted at the time that it was a beautiful ring, but thought it a little bit expensive. Ross sat looking at it, almost afraid to take it out of the box.

Ted took the ring, lifted her hand to place it on her finger, and said,

"Darling Ross, please will you marry me?"

"Yes Ted Hall I will marry you, and I will be the happiest lady alive when I do."

Ted put the ring on her finger, but unfortunately it turned out to be slightly too big.

"We can take it back to the shop to be altered," Ted said, "I arranged that when I bought it."

Ross gave him a kiss, a very long and loving one. When they broke, Ross said,

"I have a present for you my love, but it hasn't been delivered yet, though I have been promised delivery here before the end of the month."

They spent the next few days packing and moving what few belongings Ted had in the apartment, and making sure the new house was keeping warm because there was only a couple of weeks before they were to move in completely.

A week before they moved, a package arrived at the apartment addressed to Ted.

Ross was by his side as he opened it. Inside a well packed box was a wooden plaque with a coat of arms on the top, and an inscription under the shield which read:

EDWIN MICHAEL HALL. OBE
has been elected to the ranks of the Guild of Master Craftsmen and has been awarded the title of
MASTER BUILDER

He is hereby entitled to use the designation:
Member of the Guild of Master Craftsmen (MGMC)

Ted was speechless. He stared at the plaque with his mouth open, before managing to whisper,

"How on earth did you manage to get this?"

"Ashley helped me. He showed me a brochure while you were talking to Brendan and Neil. Ashley signed the proposal form and I filled in the details and my credit card number to pay for it."

"Ross love, this is something I will cherish for ever."

"I think it should go in a display cabinet in the living

room." said Ross. "It can go on a shelf with your engraved tray and your OBE. The shelf of Ted Hall's claim to fame."

Ted was still staring at the plaque as though it might disappear if he looked away.

He turned to Ross, and with tears in his eyes, thanked her for such a special present.

They went to bed and celebrated Christmas again!

Ted and Ross took Sam to the local school to see if it was possible for her to start there. Luckily there were two other girls in the same position, so the head teacher said he would allow her to start when the new term began. He would put her in a special class until she could prove she could mix with the others, academically and lingually.

Ted marked out the pathway from the living block to the bedroom block and laid a concrete base, but said he wouldn't put the paving stones down until the weather was warmer. He would renew his building when spring showed itself.

Everything was moved out of Ted's apartment before the end of the month, and after a final tidy up and an inspection by the owner, Ted, Ross and Sam moved into their new home.

TWELVE

February turned out to be a cold and rather wet month, but the living area was kept warm by burning logs in the fireplace, and the bedrooms by using the electric heaters.

It was the second week in March before Ted felt it warm enough to start work outside. The first things he checked were the outer walls of both blocks, making sure they had weathered the cold and wet winter. Although there were no signs of the paint flaking, Ted talked it over with Ross, and decided that later on in the year they would get a professional to come and spray the walls with silicone based paint. Using that product, the advert said, they would not have to think about repainting the walls again for another five years.

Ted and Ross worked together again, and laid the footpath from the main house to the bedroom block. They agreed it certainly was better being in two colours, and the maroon and grey looked well together.

Ted knew that one of the biggest jobs that had to be done was the building of the balustrade walls all the way round the plot. He would need to dig a trench about eight centimetres deep, fill it with concrete, and allow for a brick post every so often. Digging out the trench would be a very hard task, because he knew there would be a problem with his back long before he finished it. Digging a trench of such a length was much different to building walls and he really was dreading it. He had already made up his mind that if the task got too much for him, he would hire a tractor with a small excavator shovel to do the job. He was ready to make a start at the edge of the plot near to the bedroom block, and tested the top soil for depth. He was surprised when the spade sank easily to about six centimetres and then hit rock. Using the bottom of the spade, Ted scraped away the top soil with ease. He scratched his head, wondering how he was going to be able to lay a base of concrete in such thin soil. His only option would be to lay lengths of timber and fill the trench slightly above ground level. The problem was, how to get down to bed rock when the top soil was in fact just dust and would not be easy to remove. If he could remove it, where was he going to put it? One solution, he thought was the corner of the track, where they had dumped all the building rubbish. His thoughts were broken when Ross came out of the house to see what he was doing.

"You won't get any work done by standing and looking at it." she told him.

Ted explained the problem, and asked if she had any ideas of how they could shift the dust.

"You could use a sweeping brush to make a line, then use the spade in the way you would if you were shifting snow." Ross said.

"That's not a bad idea," Ted answered, "I'll give it a try. One problem that I can see for the future is how are we going to get through the rock to build a swimming pool? It may mean us hiring a JCB with a man to dig the rock out and that could prove to be very costly."

"We will have to think about that one. A pool would be nice though, we could swim in the nude during the summer, there's nobody about to see us."

"There was nobody about last year when you were flashing the forbidden fruit at me, then sacking me for daring to look at them. What's going to happen when I start admiring your naked body?"

"You are still on trial for ogling me last year. I review the case every so often, and extend the time if I think you deserve it. At the moment your trial is well into the future, many years, in fact. Every time you stare at my body, time is taken off, but whenever you touch it, time

328

is added on. If I enjoy it, which I always do, the time is doubled."

"I could get the sack again for what I'm thinking right now." Ted said with a laugh.

"Well keep on thinking about it while you remove that soil and prepare the ground for the wall. You are starting to get greedy, Ted Hall, you have already had sex once this month."

"You aren't starting to ration me before we are married are you?"

Ross smiled and shook her head.

"The way you touch me, there is no such thing as rationing, quite the opposite in fact. I've said this before, I wish I had met you many years ago. I think we would be surrounded by children of all ages by now. I do wish we had been able to have children of our own Ted, it would have made our lives complete."

"It's a bit late for that now, my lovely Ross, but I hope we can enjoy the practice for a long time yet."

"I think we had better get some work done," she replied, "otherwise I'll be dragging you back to bed."

Ross got a sweeping brush and swept a channel so Ted could use the shovel at rock level.

It was a long, hard and dirty job, and just to clear half of the area took them two days.

Just before Ted was ready to lay the outline, he had a sudden thought.

"Ross, while we are doing this, why don't we build a storage shed and attach it to the end wall of the bedroom block, near to where the old door was."

"Now that's a good idea," Ross replied, "we can put the mixer and the generator in there, and generally clear everything we don't need out of the block. We may have to finish the bedrooms off soon if mum and granddad want to come and see us."

"You think she'll approve of the way we built the house?" Ted asked.

"She'd better!" Ross answered, "There is nothing for her to disapprove of, although as soon as she sees the interior, she will say something like, 'if this was my house, I would not have put that there.', she just has to object to something, no matter how trivial."

Between them, they build the storage shed onto the bedroom block, and hired some shuttering to make a solid concrete roof. Ted damp treated the bare concrete, ready for tiling it at a later date.

Meanwhile, he had laid some timber lengths, and marked out the foundation for the balustrade bases and the brick posts. The first post was built onto the new shed, and when the concrete base had been poured and set, the bricks were lined up to see if they could build the wall in a curve, following the natural contour of the plot. It was easier than they thought, laying short lengths of bases and then a square post in facing brick. Ted found it slow going because of the weight of the bases he had to lift onto the brick, but in the warmth of the sun they soon got back into the routine they had the previous year. Ted took off his shirt and Ross quickly followed suit.

"These need ripening again." she said, "The colour has faded during the winter cover up."

"They look ripe enough to me," Ted answered, "but I'll check them later just to make sure."

"You could have checked them now if we had time, but sadly one of us has to go and pick Sam up from the village in half an hour."

"It should be your turn today, but can I go instead? My back is playing up a bit, and I think it prudent we don't lay any more bases until I feel better."

His back did not suffer any long lasting effect and two days later was able to carry on with building the wall. It was much easier to secure the balustrades to the bases, because they had a guide rod top and bottom. A small amount of concrete was put in the hole, the rod fed into it, and then left to dry before the top stone was fitted to them.

It took ten days to complete the balustrade wall half way round the property. Ted decided the other half could wait for a while because he was starting to feel some strain in his back.

"Are you doing too much Ted," asked Ross.

"Not really too much Ross, it's just there is more weight in those bases than in anything we used in the bedrooms. What is concerning me though, is how we are going to remove all of this dust so we can make an area for laying out a garden. I know we don't want flower beds or a lawn, but we can't lay paving stones on top of dust."

"We aren't going to concrete the whole area just to lay paving stones are we?" Ross asked.

"No," Ted replied, "but we'll need a foundation where the paving stones are to go, just to keep them firm."

"We will just have to take our time using a brush and shovel." Ross said, "We can do it in stages, and Sam can help at weekends."

The following Saturday, they discussed how to lay out the ground in between the two blocks.

Sam wanted lots of flower beds and flowers, Ross didn't want any flower beds. Ted suggested they compromise and have flower boxes and pots standing on the ground or fixed to the wall.

They all wanted a pool, but as Ted had already said, it could be an expensive one if they had to hire a man and machine to drill the area out. Ted had seen an advert in one of the magazines that sold ready-made pre-formed pools that could stand on the ground, rather than in it. Ross thought that a structure six feet above the ground would be a little daunting, but agreed to have a look in the showroom when a decision had to be made.

Ross wanted paving stones in front of the patio doors from the bedrooms to join a pathway running around the whole of the area between the two blocks, and all agreed that an outdoor eating area with a barbeque was essential.

Ted suggested that before they started any more work, they should move all the remaining building materials from the middle of the 'garden', to an area the other side of the pathway that ran from the house to the bedroom block. There was a spare pallet which Ted put down where the materials were going, and bit by bit, they emptied one pallet. The empty pallet was then moved next to the full one and they started over again. They had emptied the third pallet, and Ted was walking back to get the empty one when he tripped over something hard. He felt a pain in his back, and he screamed out in agony as he hit the ground and slid head first into a pile of bricks. He was stunned for a moment, but heard Ross and Sam urgently calling his name. Ross was knelt at one side of him and Sam on the other. Ross got hold of his shoulder, and said,

"Ted, are you all right?"

"I don't know," Ted replied, "but that fuckin' hurt."

"There is a cut on your head, and it's pouring blood." Ross told him.

"Have I broken any of the bricks?" Ted asked.

"Ted Hall, you are an idiot! There is blood pouring down your face, and all you can do is joke. You screamed as you hit the ground, so have you hurt yourself anywhere else?"

Ted nodded, and said in a low voice,

"I've twisted my back. I'm not sure if there is any major damage but we will find that out in a few minutes. Sam, please will you go to the kitchen, get a clean tea towel from the drawer and wet it with cold water. Wring it out, but leave some water in it. We can put it on the cut until I can stand up."

Sam went off to get the towel, and Ross asked Ted if he wanted her to help him up.

"You are going to have to roll me over first," he told her, "then we will carefully and slowly stretch my back to see if there is any damage. Once I feel it's all right, then we can think about me standing up."

Sam came back with the wet towel which Ross used to wipe Ted's cut and the blood off the rest of his face.

Ted was still lying face down on the ground, so he told Ross how she had to turn him over.

"Kneel down near the centre of my spine. Put one hand on my shoulder, and the other on my hip."

Ross nervously followed his instructions.

"Lean over me, and lift my shoulder and hip off the ground. Stop when I'm on my side, or I scream out in agony."

With a little bit of help from Sam, Ross managed to roll him onto his side without much trouble.

"Put your hands under my shoulder and on my bottom, and slowly roll me over until I'm on my knees."

Very carefully, Ross and Sam did as Ted asked.

He told Ross how to check if the bone had displaced, and if it had, explained how she was going to have to push on it until it moved back in the right position. Without needing to touch him, Ross said she could see the bone was out. Ted flexed his body, stretching his spine so that Ross could start pressing the way Ted had told her, but it wasn't long before the pain started. Through clenched teeth, he urged her to push harder, but she was reluctant to hurt him.

"Oh, fuckin' hell, this is all I bloody need!"

Ted cried out, thinking he may have to go to the hospital to have it put back under anaesthetic. He clenched this teeth when Ross pushed harder because the pain was almost unbearable and he was ready to stop her. She gave another push, and Ted almost blacked out with the pain, when he felt the bone click back into place. He collapsed sideways and brought his knees up towards his chest and took several deep breaths. He was sweating from the pain and as he opened his eyes, he saw Ross's anxious face looking at him.

He gave a weak grin, and said,

"Panic over, the bone has gone back in."

It took a while, but with help from Ross and Sam, Ted gradually got back on his feet.

He put his arm round Ross's shoulder and the other arm on Sam's and gave them both a hug.

"I'm sorry about using bad language Sam," he said, "I shouldn't say things like that in front of you."

"It's all right," Sam said, "I heard my dad talking like that all the time."

"I was using those words because I was in agony; your dad used those words because he thought it was clever." Ted told her.

Ted stood up as straight as he could, and tentatively took a step forward. He felt a mild pain as he moved, but he was able to walk very slowly.

"Let's have a look for what I fell over," he said, "whatever it was felt very solid."

They walked back about three paces and saw a mark in the dust where he had tripped. Using his foot to feel what it was, he touched something solid and straight. Not wanting to put pressure on his back by bending down, he asked Sam to nip over to the other pile of bricks and bring the sweeping brush over. Very slowly, Ted brushed away the dust, and to his amazement, saw the edge of a paving stone. He brushed further along the edge for a few metres where it stopped, so he turned round and cleared the dust in the other direction.

Looking round at Ross, he said,

"There is a length of paving stone under all this, and to find out what they are for, we are going to have to brush it all away."

"Not today, were not," said Ross firmly. "You've just fallen, hurt your back and cut your head. We are going inside the house to clean you up and nobody is coming outside again today. Ross has spoken, so inside the pair of you."

They put their arms round each other and slowly made their way into the house.

Ross cleaned the cut on Ted's head and washed all the blood off him that had dried in the sun. She covered the cut with an Elastoplast dressing, and made him sit down and relax for the rest of the day, telling him that unless they had burglars overnight, the paving stones would still be there the following morning.

Despite his eagerness to find out more about the paving stones, Ted could hardly move the following morning and spent the next two days doing nothing. It was a rarity for him, because recently he had been used to getting up in a morning ready to start work. The pain in his back prevented him from moving freely and he had to sit and rest, occasionally walking slowly round the room to relax the muscles. At the back of his mind was the reminder of his accident at work, and the use of the elbow crutches to help him walk. If the pain carried on, he told Ross, he could use the crutches that were in his car boot. On the third day, he was able to move without as much pain, and Ross allowed him to walk round the 'garden' area but holding on to her arm. She said she thought he was fit to do some light work, but he wouldn't be able to start until the afternoon because they needed to go shopping.

Ted was so eager to get started again, that he decided not to have a siesta that day. Ross said she was coming out to help him, because she was as curious as Ted to find out what it was that he had fallen over.

Ted carefully swept the area around where the paving stone was, and then moved forwards. After a few minutes of sweeping, Ted felt his back hurting again, so Ross took over the dust removal. She came to what looked like a piece of canvas, so Ted asked her to concentrate on the edge, and slowly sweep along the canvas. She came to a leather strap that was fixed onto a metal stud, and as soon as Ted saw it, he had an idea what it was.

"Stay here for a moment." He told Ross as he slowly walked forward five or six paces. He turned and asked Ross to come and join him and when she stood in front of him, Ted put his arms round her waist.

"Put your arms round my neck," he told her.

Ross did as he asked, and a few seconds later, Ted flexed his knees as though he was on a trampoline and they felt a slight give in the ground. Ross asked Ted what had just happened.

"The earth's just moved," he told her, "and we are still fully dressed."

Ross laughed, tightened her arms round him and said,

"Undress me then and see if we can get a better reaction."

"Don't get greedy, Mrs Critchley-Smythe-Jones you've already had sex once this month."

Ross had to smile, knowing he was getting his own back for the comment she made a few days ago.

336

"What Ted?" Ross asked. "What does all this mean?"

"I have got a funny feeling our dreams may, and I stress may, be about to come true."

Ross was looking at him, getting frustrated at his infuriating way of saying something, but saying nothing at all.

"Are you going to tell me what this is all about, or am I going to have to resort to violence?" Ross asked him.

"I have a feeling there is a pool or part of a pool under here. I think the canvas is a pool cover and attached to the paving stones with a special hook, but we are going to have to finish moving all the building bricks and pallets before we can check it out. There may be a hole a couple of inches deep, or there may be a complete pool or anything in between."

"Are you sure about this?"

Ted shook his head, and said,

"I can't be sure about anything to do with this finca, but just consider this: The two blocks are built, they have all the materials to complete the interior, but dig out a pool first. No wonder they went bust."

Ross was still a bit stunned by Ted's words.

"This wasn't mentioned when I was being shown round the place before I bought it. First there was the complete kitchen and work surfaces, now the possibility of a pool. Is there anything else we could find?"

"I'm not sure we want anything else. Don't get your hopes up too high about the pool just yet, as I said before, we don't know what's underneath the canvas. It will take a day or two to shift all these bricks and balustrade bits, then we have to get rid of the top soil. It will be at least a week before we are ready to take the canvas off."

They worked steadily through the afternoon carrying small amounts of building materials in the wheelbarrow.

By the time Ross picked Sam up from school, they had cleared half of the area, and could see a slight sag in the canvas. It looked as though the pallets had been placed round the canvas to keep it taught. It took them the whole of the next day to clear all of the building materials, but they would have to wait until the day after before they could start the boring work of sweeping the dust off the canvas.

Taking it in turns, they plodded the length of the paving stones, covering the same area two or three times to clear the fine dust. Sam helped them when she came home from school, but by the time they could see all the canvas and the straps that held it firmly, another day was almost over. There was a huge pile of dust at each end, and Ted was adamant that it had to be cleared away before the canvas was removed.

"Can't we just have a peek?" pleaded Sam.

"No," said Ted, "That dust could very easily get blown into whatever is underneath the canvas and would have to be brushed out again. Tomorrow, after your mum and I have done the shopping, we may make a start on moving it. If it is clear by the time you come home from school, you can help with the unveiling."

It took Ross and Ted most of the afternoon to clear the dusty top soil and dump it on the corner of the track. It was that fine, it sank through the tiles and other rubbish, or got blown away by the breeze. Ross picked Sam up from the village and before she went to get changed, came rushing round to the garden to check if the dust had been cleared. The look on her face showed her delight when she saw the canvas cover was ready to be removed.

"Don't start until I get changed," she cried, "I want to help discover what's underneath."

Ted put a length of wood through the straps at the end

and using some old washing line, rigged up a link so that he could pull the canvas along when the side straps were undone. He explained that if the canvas wasn't kept reasonably tight, it would fold in two along the centre and drop into the pool, and because of its weight, would be difficult to lift out.

Sam came running out of the patio doors of her bedroom, eager to help Ted and her mum. Ted shouted to her in Spanish, telling her to stop running and to remember what happened to him a few days ago. She stopped immediately, and walked to where Ted and Ross were waiting. Ted grinned at her, and said,

"Good girl! Good for doing as I asked, and good for understanding my Spanish."

Sam grinned back at him, and said,

"I think Spanish most of the time now, and have to reorganize my brain when I come home."

Ted asked Sam if she was enjoying being at a Spanish school, and without any hesitation, said she was.

"The lessons don't seem as hard as when I was in England, but we seem to learn more in a shorter period of time. Some of the work I've already done in England, but I didn't understand all of it. I do now though."

By talking to her, Ted had calmed Sam down and now they were ready to remove the canvas. He showed them how to unhook a strap along one end, and let them undo the others. Ted pulled on the rope until the canvas doubled back on itself and move to the first set of straps along the side. Ross was on one side and Sam on the other, and Ted was holding on to the rope at the end. When he told them to, they each undid the strap, Ted pulled the rope, and canvas folded back on itself to the next strap. They undid two straps before looking into what they had uncovered.

It was the shallow end they had started at, three steps

from one corner proving it. There was only rough concrete along the sides and bottom and plenty of the dust they had removed from the ground above it.

"The sides and bottom look as though they have been prepared for tiling," said Ted, "so we can't leave the pool uncovered in the sun without any water in it, or the concrete will crack. We can take the canvas off until we reach the far end, just so we can see the depth of the pool and more importantly, see if there are any pipes fitted and if there are, where are they leading to."

They pulled the canvas as far as the last strap, which was roughly one metre from the end. The depth at that end was one and three quarter metres, it was written in pencil on the side wall.

Alongside the end wall there was a plastic 'box', and inside it, loosely packed, was the filter and the electrical connections. In front of the box were a number of lengths of plastic pipes taped together.

The three of them got into the pool and examined their find. Ted looked in the box and said,

"At least we know everything seems to be here. We will have to find a pool fitting company and ask them to come and see us so they can suggest what to do to finish it off."

"There is an address on the box," said Ross, "and the same address on this roll of pipes. I'll contact them and see if they know what the plans were for this pool, and how much it will cost to finish it off."

They got out of the pool, pulled the canvas back and secured the straps in the hooks.

It was starting to go dark by the time they had it secured, and after putting everything away in the store, went inside to make their evening meal.

The following day, Ted rested his back while Ross made contact with the company whose name was on the pool fittings. They told her that they had started the job, but had to stop when the owners left the site. They arranged to come out to see Ross and establish what was needed to complete the work.

Ted told Ross that if and when the pool was finished, they would have to buy some tanker loads of fresh water to fill it.

"If we start pumping our well water into the pool, we could deplete the water stock." He said. "We have no idea how deep our well is, or how big the water table actually is, so we should only use the well water for personal needs."

"I never thought about anything like that," she said, "In the past I've always been able to turn on a tap and have clean drinkable water flowing out of it."

"One of the problems of living in the campo is the uncertainty of thing we take for granted in the towns and cities." Ted acknowledged.

A couple of days later, Ross and Ted sat in the sun talking to the owner of the pool company.

He told them that the original quotation for the building of the pool included total installation, and they had been paid in full before the job started.

"The price we quoted was four years ago," he said, "so I will have to evaluate what has to be done and price it according to the present building rates."

He added that he would have to hire a builder at extra cost to make the base and wall for the casing.

"There's no need for that," Ross told him, "we have a master builder here on site."

The man looked at Ted, and echoed Ross's words.

"You are a Master Builder?"

Ted nodded, and said,

"I am, and believe it or not, you and I have met before. You used to work for Yates and Ambrose as a water and sewage consultant on large new housing estates."

The man looked at Ted and said,

"I vaguely recognise you but I'm sorry I can't recall your name."

Before Ted could answer, Ross butted in and said,

"Vice chairman of the Ashley Lee Group."

There was silence for a moment and then he said,

"You are Ted Hall?"

Ted nodded, then replied,

"I am, but I left the company several years ago."

"You had a serious accident, didn't you?"

"I broke two bones in my back, which slowed me down so much I could no longer keep pace with the work."

"In that case, I can give you the plan for the base and you can build it whenever you like. Once it is done, we can come and complete the pipe work."

"Is the box going to be partly underground, or totally at ground level?" Ted asked.

"It will be partly underground. This box is deep enough to hold everything and enable maintenance to be carried out without having to work almost flat on your stomach. It will be at the height of an average persons' waist. I would suggest that the electrical control box and circuit is housed in a waterproof case and secured to the house wall."

"Can Ted build the base wherever he wants?" Ross asked.

The man shook his head, and said,

"We should have made a channel for the pipes, and made a hole where the box will go. I'll have a look in a minute, and if everything is in the correct place, the base can be built there. I'm going to ask for three hundred Euros to complete all the necessary work, with your husband doing the brickwork, and lending us a hand if it is needed."

"That suits me fine." said Ross, "When will you be able to start?"

"I'll give you a ring on Monday to give a definite starting date, but probably Wednesday of the following week. I can't be certain until I get back to the office. I have some tile samples in my car, and a brochure showing pictures of pool tile designs that we have done. Most of the tiles we have in stock, those that need ordering are marked with a star in the brochure."

He went to his car, took out two boxes and showed them there was a number of squares of tiles for them to choose from. He examined the pool edges and eventually found the channel for the pipes and the hole for the base. They had been covered over with wood, and the dust had blown over them, hiding their existence.

"That's everything sorted," he said, "so your husband can start building the base whenever he wants, and we will carry on from there."

He shook their hands, climbed into his car and left.

"When did we get married?" asked Ted.

"The afternoon we cuddled on the loungers and brought each other to a glorious climax." Ross replied. "We've been working together as a man and wife ever since that afternoon, but the best part was when I lost my virginity to you. I started to fancy you after we'd been working together for a few months. You took me out and showed me you were a person who could be trusted, and that is what I wanted in a man. Many nights I've been in bed thinking of you, wishing you were next to me. Do you remember a remark I made about 'doing it myself', those are the times I wanted to do it."

"Do we need to go back to the UK and get married?" Ted asked with a laugh.

"Of course we do! I want to be Mrs Hall, legally."

"There is something I'd like to ask you Ross….."

"We haven't time for that, I've got to go for Sam."

"In that case, I'll wait until you don't have to rush off before I ask you a very serious question."

Ross looked at Ted, and saw the expression on his face. She clearly had upset him and his train of thought.

"I'm sorry Ted, I didn't mean to upset you, I could see you were going to say something serious, but I just came out with the silly remark."

"It's OK Ross, there's plenty of time for us to talk about what I was going to ask."

"Sorry Ted." Ross said again as she gave him a kiss. "I'll be back in twenty minutes."

While Ross was out, Ted looked at the plans for the brick base. He saw that it was a simple square over a concrete base, with holes at each corner leading to a soak away for any water getting in. There was a sixteen brick standard wall on each side of the square, involving very little skill to complete, and Ted wondered why the boss of the company had made such a big deal of it. He put the plan to one side, knowing it would be three or four days before he needed to read it again. He looked at the paving stones round the pool, and thought they may have to build a thicker concrete base to lay another row of them. That was something he didn't want. His back was not getting any better, and the idea of mixing load after load of concrete was making his back ache at the mere thought of it.

Three days later, Ted had built the wall for the filter box, and by Friday of the following week, the pipe work had been laid and fitted, and an electrician had connected all the wiring from the pump to a control box on the wall. The tile work was to have been started at the same time, but the person supposed to do it had recently gone back to the UK for a holiday. He had not returned on the day he was supposed to, and as the other tilers were other jobs, Ted and Ross would have to wait. Ross asked Ted if he could do it and save some time, but he said he had no experience laying tiles for pools. It was a specialist job, he said, and he would rather leave it to the experts.

Five weeks later, their pool was complete.

Ted had decided not to put another row of paving stones level with those round the pool, but two rows alongside, and slightly lower. The paving and the making of areas for stones was coming along slowly, Ted preferring to take his time and not put too much strain on his back.

Ross had contacted a company that could fill their pool with water, and on the day the first delivery was to be made, Ted had got everything ready for when it arrived. He went over to the loungers, where Ross was sunning herself, topless as usual, and sat down beside her.

"I'm going to get the sack." he said.

"Are you letching after my breasts again?"

"They are very nice and firm, or they were the last time I touched them." Ted answered.

"Not bad for a woman my age, are they?"

"No they…. that's a good point, a woman of your age. Ross we have been together for over a year, and we haven't celebrated your birthday. When is it you secretive woman?"

Ross smiled and said that her last birthday she had celebrated while working in the bedroom block. She said she hadn't told him because they had not been working together for very long and at the time, it was of no consequence.

"So Rosalinda, you are forty three this year, but what

date?" Ted asked her.

"May the eighteenth." Ross answered.

"That date's stored away in my memory, and will never be forgotten. We were saying that these weren't bad for a woman of your age, I think they are remarkably firm, and I hope they continue that way for many years to come."

"They will if you keep on handling them like that, and if you keep touching my nipples I'm going to have a..... bloody hell Ted, I love you kissing them like that.... put your hand down my shorts....."

Minutes later Ross was digging her nails into Ted's shoulders as she reached her peak.

"You are getting greedy Rosalinda Smythe-Jones, that's the second one this month." Ted told her with a laugh.

"It could be the sixth or the seventh," Ross gasped, "and today is only the twelfth."

Ted was about to answer when his phone rang. The tanker driver was on his way up the hill and needed Ted's help to guide him into the property.

"Time for my famous cover up." Ross said, getting up from the lounger.

Ted directed the tanker up the drive, and there was enough room for him to park by the open store. A line of hose was run from the tanker pump to the pool, and filling began.

It took two days and five tanker loads to fill the pool, and only then could the filter pump be switched on to clear any debris.

Sam wanted to get into the pool immediately she came home from school, but Ted warned her that the sun had not warmed the water sufficiently just yet, but if she wanted to try it at the weekend, she was more than welcome. He did however say that on no account must she jump or dive into the water, but walk slowly down the steps.

The pool had been suitably filtered by Saturday, so Sam put her bikini on ready to see if the water had warmed up enough. Ross and Ted were beside her as she started down the steps, and she had only got to the second one when she paused, and said,

"I don't think I can go any further, it's too cold for me. I'm going to try and sit down on the step so at least I'll get my bottom wet."

Sam slowly sank into the water, and just as her bottom touched it, she jumped up with a shriek and leaped out onto the side. Ross had been holding a towel and as soon as Sam was out, she threw it round her and started to dry her legs.

"Sorry I doubted your word Ted." Sam said, shivering. "It really is cold, and if I had jumped in I could easily have drowned. How long do you think it will be before we can swim in it without dying of hypothingamy, what's the word?"

"You mean hypothermia?" Ross said with a laugh.

"Yes, that's the word." Sam answered.

"Well it is only the end of April," Ted said, "and there isn't quite enough power in the sun yet. What warmth gets to the water is lost because the nights are still quite chilly."

The answer satisfied Sam, and she said she would have to wait impatiently until Ted told her the water would be warm enough for her to try again.

A few nights later, Ted and Ross were in bed, having a kiss and cuddle before going to sleep, when Ted said,

"The eighteen is getting closer, so what would you like for your birthday?"

"Now there's a question to ask a woman in love."

"I thought you would corrupt the conversation when I

asked you something like that." Ted said.

"Well you did encourage me twelve months ago, so don't start blaming me for being suggestive."

"I thought they were biscuits."

"You are impossible, Ted Hall. What was it you wanted to say to me the other week when I had to rush off to pick Sam up?"

"I'm not sure that this is the right place to discuss what I want to say."

"That sounds serious, Ted. There isn't a problem of any kind, is there?"

"It is serious, but there isn't a problem, well not really."

"Would you please explain yourself, Ted Hall? You are in the nicest place for a man and a woman to talk to one another, so put your arm round me, give me a kiss and tell me what's going through your mind."

Ted did as Ross asked, and then said,

"I love you my lovely Lady Ross, and would do anything for you, you know that. I am so happy you want to spend your life with me as Mrs Hall, but what I want to ask you is possibly a bit delicate. I have been thinking about this since New Year when we set our wedding date. Ross, when we're married, how would you feel if I said I would like to legally adopt Sam so she would be my daughter?"

There was silence for a moment or two, as Ross digested what Ted had just said. She tightened her grip on him as she started to cry against his chest.

When the tears stopped, Ross gave him a kiss with a great deal of feeling.

"Ted Hall," she said, with a sob, "you really are the most thoughtful person I know. I would be so proud for my…. our daughter to have the same surname as yours. I have never had the privilege of thoughtfulness before and when you come up with ideas like that, I can't describe the feeling. I'll let you tell Sam and see what she says."

"No sweetheart," he said, "I'll ask Sam. She may only be young, but she has the right to make her mind up about things like that. It won't please your mum though, will it?"

"She has had enough say in names to last a lifetime, and this is one time she won't have her own way." Ross said forcefully.

"We may have a problem if the authorities need Brian's permission." Ted said.

"Do they need his permission?" Ross asked.

"I think so for adoption," Ted replied, "but if he refuses, or there is any other sort of problem, we change her name by deed poll. If Brian does refuse, we could always blackmail him and threaten to expose his divorce scam."

"I don't think it will come to that," said Ross, "but whatever happens, with Sam's consent, we can change her name to Hall."

"That's what I hope for. It's as good as having a daughter of my own, something I have never had the pleasure of having."

Ross gave him an affectionate squeeze, and then whispered,

"I've said it before Ted, I dearly wish that you and I could have had children, or at least a child, that would have made me a very happy woman."

"Yes, I agree it would have been something special for both of us." Ted answered softly.

"I seem to have forgotten how to make babies, would you like to remind me?"

"Well," he said, "you usually start off like this......"

THIRTEEN

Ross, Ted and Sam were starting to get things together ready to fly back to the UK for their wedding. They had booked the mid-morning flight on the fifth of July, giving them plenty of time to get up to date with the arrangements that had been made. Granddad had organised the manor, Laura had taken charge of the catering, and emails had been going backwards and forwards for some time. The guest list was complete, although there were a few people on it that neither Ted nor Ross knew. They were some of mum's long lost relatives and she insisted they be included.

One morning, Ted returned from the village, where he had collected the mail, and there was a large, thick envelope addressed to him. On the bottom corner of the label was something he recognised. AL/SG – Ashley Lee / Sandy Gorton. In the past when Ashley had sent him work to check out it was never as thick as this one. He went into the kitchen where Ross was making sandwiches for their lunch, so putting the mail on the work top, he kissed her neck and put his arms round her from behind.

"Mrs Critchley-Smythe-Jones," he whispered in her ear, "I fancy you like crazy, but I'm sorry to tell you that I am getting married very soon and afterwards I will only be making love to my wife. Would you like me to do it to you right now while we have the chance?"

Ross made no reply, just gently pushed herself backwards into Ted's body. He reached down, undid the zip of her shorts and pushed them down with her briefs. Bending down, he took them off completely, and as he stood up, removed his own shorts. Ross hadn't moved so he gently pulled her backwards and took her from behind.

Later, when they had got their breath back, Ross kissed Ted very passionately, and said,

"You had better do that to me again before you do it with your wife. Now are you going to dress me before we have our lunch, or would you like me for afters?"

"Under normal circumstances, having you for afters could end up with you getting very fat."

"Yes they could, and I would have liked to get fat on that type of afters, but I can't, so unless we are going to have an encore, please would you pass me my briefs and shorts so I may resist temptation."

Ted did as Ross asked, and got dressed himself.

"Not much in the mail today," Ted said, "the quote for the solar heating for the pool, a letter from Kevin and Mary in New Zealand, and a big thick envelope from Ashley. By the looks of it, he wants me to work extra hard for the retainer he's paying me."

"He's not sent you anything for a while, has he? Maybe this is something he wants you to do before we fly over to the UK for the wedding."

"I'll have a look after lunch," said Ted, "the lunch I stopped you from making a little while ago."

"Will you stop me from doing other jobs like that?"

"Now don't get too ambitious," he said with a laugh, "remember I've got a bad back."

"It doesn't seem to bother you when you fancy a bit on the side. Will you tell your wife you can't manage it because of your back?"

"No, I'll let her be the one on top, and then I won't have to move, just lie there and think of England."

"You're crazy; you do know that, don't you?"

"Has it taken you over twelve months to realise it?"

While they were having their bit of fun, they carried the sandwiches out to where they had recently made a tiled concrete terrace. Ted was in the middle of building a brick barbeque and already they had set up a table and chairs, with a parasol to keep the sun off them while they ate. This was to be their summer eating place, and when the meal was over, they could move to the loungers by the pool to rest and enjoy the warmth of the sun.

Ross and Ted were relaxing on the loungers after their sandwiches, when Ross asked,

"What has your brother got to say in his letter?"

"I'd forgotten about the letters," Ted answered, "I had other things on my mind at the time. I'll go and get them now."

Minutes later he sat down to read. He opened his Brother's letter first and as he read it, broke into a huge smile.

"Kevin, Mary and Jane are coming over for the wedding." he announced. "I'm very pleased at that, because now there will be no problem as to who can be my best man."

"How old is Jane?" Ross asked.

"Oh, she will be…. I'm not sure off hand whether she will be nine or ten this August."

"In that case," said Ross, "maybe she can be a bridesmaid with Sam. I'll send a picture of the dress, and if Mary sends me some measurements, we can get a dress made up, and any alterations can be done when they arrive."

Ted handed the letter to Ross so that she could read all the other news.

Ted opened the thick envelope from Ashley, and found another envelope inside with a smaller one attached. There was a note on it which said, 'Read this letter first', and was signed 'Ashley'.

Ted started to read Ashley's letter, and halfway through, he sat up and started to take more notice and read a bit slower.

Ross saw him sit up and asked if there was a problem.

"It looks a bit like it," Ted answered, "Ashley thinks there is some underhand work going on. They have lost out on a number of contracts recently, all to the same company. He wants me to look the quotes over and see if I can find anything wrong with them."

"Then what?" Ross asked.

"I've no idea love. That is a matter for him to deal with."

Ted lay back again and started to check through the sheets of paper covered in figures. He was soon back in his old role, and very quickly found a pattern starting to emerge. He took the papers over to the table, and set them out so that he could refer to the contracts lost and by how much, and the same for the ones they had won.

A little while later, Ross came to the table, put her arm round Ted's shoulder and said,

"You miss all this, don't you?"

Ted smiled ruefully, and answered,

"I've been out of it for too long to say I miss it."

"I've been watching you go through those papers, and the way you do it is second nature. If there is a problem, I'll bet that Ted Hall finds it."

"There is a problem, and I think I've found it. I am sure it's down to collusion between the two who submit the costing for each job. The quoted figure from each company is similar in difference. For example, this one was won by the Group, and the difference between the winning bid and the losing one is nineteen thousand pounds. Another one that was won by our rival, the difference is eighteen thousand seven hundred and fifty pounds. Others are similar. If I were a betting man, I'd say both men contact each other, give the figures they have worked out, and agree to split the bonus when it is paid. That way, either companies win or lose the job, the persons doing the costing know their jobs are safe and they are earning bonuses twice as quickly."

"And you've worked all that out just by reading those notes and checking the figures?"

Ted nodded, and answered,

"There are subtle differences in the costing for certain sections which are not within the usual guidelines."

"What are you going to do now, Sir Ted?"

"Sir Edwin to you, Lady Ross! I'm going to write back to Ashley and tell him my findings. I'll also suggest that the person concerned is followed to see if he does meet up with his counterpart in the other company, but what happens after that is down to him."

"Is that it now? Have you done what he asked?"

"I have Ross, and this evening I'll get on my computer and send him my findings. Have I time for a quick siesta before going for Sam?"

"You had your siesta before lunch." Ross told him.

"You are supposed to have a sleep during a siesta." Ted said.

"Now you tell me." Ross replied with a laugh.

Later that afternoon, Ted decided to ring Ashley at home. Expensive it may be, but Ted was being paid enough to cover the bill. He told Thomas he was on a Spanish phone, and was swiftly put through to Ashley. Ted read out his findings, gave his recommendations and said he would confirm it by email that night. Ashley said he would deal with it first thing the next day, and thanked Ted for his prompt action. He took Ted's telephone number and said he would call if there was any news.

Ted and Ross were sat outside, relaxing in the sun after eating their evening meal. Sam was doing her homework, and had asked her mum if she knew the answer to a question. Before Ross could reply, Ted gave her a silly answer.

Sam slapped her pen down on the table, and came out with one word,

"Dad!"

Immediately, she put her hand over her mouth and looked at Ted.

"Sorry Ted," she whispered, "I didn't mean to be rude."

Ted stood up, held his arms out and said,

"Come here a moment Sam."

Sam walked slowly towards him, thinking he was going to tell her off, but when she stood in front of him, he put both arms round her and gave her a hug of delight. He still held her close, and said,

"Do you really think of me as your dad?"

"You have been more of a dad to me than the real one ever was," she answered, "and I call you my dad when I'm with my friends at school."

"Thank you Sam, that makes me feel very proud. A couple of days ago, I was telling your mum about something I'd like to do. She thought it a great idea, but said I should be the one to ask you if you would like to be my daughter, legally, and called Sam Hall."

Sam burst into tears, and through the sobs, said,

"That would be the nicest thing you could do for me. Thank you for wanting me to be your daughter, and I promise I'll do my best never to let you down."

Sam gave him a big hug and a kiss, went to her mum, thanked her as well and gave her a hug and kiss also.

Ted was pleased at Sam's reaction and vowed that he would work as hard as possible to get the process started as soon as he got to the UK.

Ross, Ted and Sam flew out of Malaga Airport on the fifth of July, looking forward to the wedding and the reunion of many friends. They had booked a return flight one month later, allowing them time to relax and enjoy themselves in the UK.

Some weeks prior to leaving Spain, Ross had said,

"You aren't taking me to Blackpool for our honeymoon, Ted Hall, home territory or not."

"I wouldn't dream of inflicting that on you again," he replied. "I have got something sorted out, but it's a surprise."

Despite questioning him, Ted would not tell Ross or Sam where he was taking them.

The wedding ceremony at the register office was a small family affair, but when they returned to the manor an hour after they were pronounced man and wife, they were met by many more people.

It turned into an extremely enjoyable day, the party going on into the small hours of the next morning.

During the early part of the evening, Ashley had made a point of speaking to Ted while Ross could hear what he had to say. He asked Ross if he could 'borrow' Ted for a day to sort out the problem he had discovered. Ross agreed, saying that if her husband was still on the payroll, he had to work for his money. Ashley arranged for both of them to go and see him the following Monday, when they could decide how the interview was going to be held.

They arrived at Ashley's home, and were taken into the library, where apparently Ashley now did most of his work. They sat down and chatted as Thomas brought in the coffee and an orange juice for Sam. They made more small talk while they drank, and as soon as Sam finished her drink, asked Ashley if she could go and play with the doll's house. Ashley told her she could play with it anytime, and Sam went across the hall, leaving the three adults to their work.

Sir Ashley had hired a private investigator to keep watch on the two suspects and they had come up with some positive results. With those results, and the costings he had checked, Ted made his suggestion as to how Ashley question the person they suspected of disloyalty. Ashley agreed with the idea, and then surprised them by asking if Ted would carry out the interview.

"You are the one who saw through their game," he explained, "and I would like you to administer the punishment it deserves."

Ted was taken aback by the suggestion, but at the same time felt some pride in Ashley's faith in him. Ted glanced at Ross, and he could tell by the look on her face that he had to do it. He suggested Ashley told nobody of his involvement, and he would go to the head office early the next morning, and conduct the interview in the chairman's office the same afternoon. Ashley agreed with Ted's idea and passed him the keys to the chairman's office. He picked up and opened a file that was on his desk, took out a letterhead and passed it over to Ted.

"What do you think of our provisional new stationary?" he asked.

Ted looked it over, and saw a revised logo at the top. It was the wording underneath that hit Ted immediately. He looked over at Ashley, and said,

"Is this for real?"

"I hope so," Ashley answered, "show it to your wife and see what she thinks."

Ted passed the paper to Ross and watched as she read the title. Her face lit up when she saw that her husband's name had been added with the title of 'Vice-chairman and Company Consultant'.

Ross nodded her head several times as she re-read the

wording.

"What would this mean to us and the company?" Ross asked.

"To you Ross, it will mean your husband will be running my company, and being paid a proper salary instead of a retainer. To the company, it will mean that once again, the right man is running it on my behalf. I would like Ted to make major decisions regarding the type and style of work we do. He would only need to be in the office two or three days a week and all travelling expenses will be paid by the company."

Ashley turned back to Ted, and asked what he thought of the proposal.

Ted in turn looked at Ross and he could see by the look on her face exactly what she thought of it.

Ted paused for a moment, then answered,

"It looks like Ted Hall is working for the Ashley Lee group once again."

When they got back to granddad's that night, and Ross told him and her mum what had happened, they reacted with pride. Mum was more than made up, because being a bit of a snob, she could go about telling all her friends that her new son-in-law was in charge of the biggest building company in the UK.

The following morning, Ted took an early train and was at the head office by seven o'clock. He went to his new office and brewed a cup of coffee. He thought it was terrible, but drank it anyway because he needed the caffeine! Next he set out the paperwork and everything he needed to interview the suspect. He wasn't really a suspect, because Ted and Ashley knew he was guilty, all Ted had to do was get him to admit to what he had done. His colleague in the other Company did not yet know they had been caught, but would find out while Ted was interviewing his opposite number. Ted had everything sorted and ready, and decided it was time to let certain people know that he was in the office, and why. He had opted for three senior members of staff, a union representative, and Sandy to take notes and observe what was happening. He would need to see each of them and let them know of his involvement now and of his future role in the company. He picked up the internal telephone, and dialled a number.

"Secretarial Office, Sandy Gorton speaking."

"Good morning Mrs Gorton," Ted said, "and how are you this lovely Tuesday morning?"

"Ted?" Sandy whispered, after a moment's pause.

"It is indeed, but please do not shout out my name, or come rushing from your office. Please take your time, and come up to see me in the Chairman's office." He put the phone down and sat back to wait for her arrival.

A few moments later, there was a knock on the office door, and Ted called for her to come in.

Sandy came into the office and saw Ted sat at the desk. She looked round, saw nobody else in the office and looked faintly puzzled.

"Come on in and close the door behind you." Ted said, standing up. He walked round his desk, put his arms out, and said,

"Come and give me a hug of welcome."

Sandy walked across the office and into his arms. She hugged him back, and as he stepped back, he saw her warm smile of friendship.

"What on earth are you doing here Ted Hall?" She asked, laughing as she spoke.

"Sit down, please, and I'll tell you what is going on. Sandy, today I have to interview someone who has been colluding with a rival Company. I am doing this with the authority of Sir Ashley, and I have a written letter of authorisation if anyone queries it."

Sandy looked in horror at Ted's remark.

"Why has he asked you to do the interview though?" she asked.

"Because it was me that found out about it, and Ashley wants me to question the person and deal with it accordingly."

Ted took a sheet of paper from the desk and handed it to Sandy.

"The new Company Letterhead." he said.

Sandy saw his name, and with a huge smile, said,

"Welcome back Mr Hall and it will be my pleasure to give you as much help as I did in the years when you were here before your accident."

She got up from the chair, went over to Ted and kissed him on each cheek.

Ted turned serious, and said,

"I need to ask you something though. Please, give me an honest answer and not the one you think is right. Before my accident and our affair, we worked together without any problem. I knew not long after I started at head office that Sandy Gorton fancied Ted Hall, and because I knew, we could flirt with each other and it made life a bit easier to cope with. If I was here in this office on a reasonably regular basis, could you and I work together in the same way as we used to, without you ripping your thong off every time you came through the door?"

Sandy laughed, and answered,

"I'm sure I could resist doing that, but it wouldn't mean I wouldn't want to."

Ted tried not to laugh as she spoke.

"I haven't really thought out how I am going to work yet, but I will need you as my main go between when I'm not here, and will need you to be with me continuously while I'm in the office. You will have to

360

make sure there is someone covering your duties on those days. Ross has suggested that I make you my Personal Assistant while I'm here. How does that sound to you?"

"That sounds perfect Ted," Sandy replied, "and I will give all of your work my undivided attention."

"I will give you my telephone number in Spain, but it is for your eyes only. I do not want anyone else, except Ashley, ringing me there. As I said, it was Ross's idea to make you my PA, so do not be afraid of talking to her if she answers the phone. She has encouraged me to take this job and as you know, she knows everything about our affair, including the invitation I gave you to live with me. So let's flirt like we did before, have a laugh, and on a serious note, get the company back on the right track."

"Is there anything you would like me to do before the meeting?" Sandy asked.

"Yes please Sandy," Ted said, "will you get rid of that terrible coffee that's by the machine. If necessary, I'll bring some from home on my next trip and we can use that. I am going to take a walk in a few minutes because I need to see Brendan, David and Neil to let them know the score. I also need to see Vic Borski and let him know about the meeting. It will be in here at two o'clock and will be recorded and the interview will be held under caution. That means we will have to be very careful of what we say. I'll see you later, and before we go back to Spain, Ross would like you and Phil to spend a day with us."

Sandy thanked Ted for the invitation, and said she would be in her office until he needed her.

Ted walked into the passageway and down a corridor. The first office he came to was Brendan's, and Ted could see him talking on the telephone. As he put the phone down, he glanced towards the door, and saw Ted smiling at him through the glass. He waved his hand enthusiastically, indicating Ted to come in.

They met in the middle of the office, hands clasped and hugging each other in the joy of meeting once again. The first question was inevitable.

"What on earth is Ted Hall doing in this building?"

Ted said he would tell him everything, but he needed to see David and Neil as well. He explained that Sandy was the only other person who knew he was in the building, and he would, for the moment, like his presence kept quiet. Ted asked Brendan if he would go for the other two, and bring them to the chairman's office without mentioning him.

Brendan agreed, went for the others, and Ted made his way back to his new office.

A few minutes later, there was a knock on the door and Ted called out for them to come in. Brendan opened the door, and then stood aside so David and Neil could see Ted sat at the desk. They broke into smiles of welcome, and hurried over to greet their friend and old workmate.

When the greetings were over, Ted asked them to sit down. He told them first of all the reason he was there and were understandably shaken when they realised one of their colleagues could do such a thing. Ted told them he would only reveal the person's name just before the meeting started.

The explanation over with, there was a pause, and then Ted said,

"Some years ago, we were the top four in this company. We worked together and made Ashley Lee a name to remember. We shared our successes and drowned our sorrows if there were any failures. Then I had to go and have an accident, which left the company one man short. You carried on regardless and as I can see, the company is still able to make a profit. I therefore hope that you will be pleased to learn that as of two o'clock yesterday afternoon, we are the top four once again."

There was silence for a moment or two as Ted's words sunk in. Then they all wanted to speak at once. They shook his hand again and made comments about Ted being in the place he should be, and they would be proud to be working with a man of his calibre.

They left his office later, promising not to mention his promotion, or his presence at head office before the meeting that afternoon.

His next call was to Vic Borski, a man he knew from his days working with a gang, and a man whom he respected for his views as a union official. Vic was not in his office, so he rang Sandy and asked her if she would find him and bring him to the office. He also asked if she could find him a decent cup of coffee sometime soon. She said she would do her best, and Ted sat back, thinking about the afternoon and his future in that office.

It took half an hour for Sandy to find Vic and bring him to meet Ted. She knocked and entered when told to, bringing Vic with her. As soon as Vic saw Ted, just like everyone else that day, he beamed with the joy of seeing his friend again. Sandy left, telling Ted the coffees would be served in a few minutes. Vic, who was of Russian descent, shook Ted's hand as though it were the handle on a water pump. He was laughing and welcoming Ted in his native tongue, a few choice words of which he had taught Ted many years ago while he was working with him. They sat down across the desk from each other, and Ted was about to explain his presence when Sandy brought a mug of coffee for each of them.

Ted once more explained the reason for being at head office, and when he had finished, the first thing Vic asked was if the person was a member of a union. Ted said he didn't think so, but wanted Vic to know about the interview just the same.

Vic said he appreciated being informed, but under these circumstances, would not represent the person, but would, with Ted's permission, sit in on the proceedings. Ted said that would be quite in order and told him how he would conduct the interview. When Vic left the office, he said he would be back at one forty five to join the others.

Ted sat in the quiet of the office, and ate a couple of sandwiches that Ross had made for him. He was still a bit uncertain of his role at head office, although he knew, as Ashley had told him, in effect he was running the company on his behalf.

Ross had told him the previous evening that she was sure he would be very happy working at head office, and now that their house was almost complete, it would keep him busy and his mind occupied in the future. He was still thinking it over when there was a knock on the door. He glanced at his watch and saw that it was almost time for the meeting to start.

He asked them in and they sat round his desk waiting to be told who the traitor was. He put them out of their misery, and said to Brendan,

"Please will you bring Roy Harold to this office."

They looked at each other, hardly believing what Ted had just said. Roy Harold was the senior cost manager, in his forties and had worked his way through different departments of the company over the past fifteen years, and had been promoted to his present position not long after Ted left.

Minutes later, Brendan returned with Roy Harold.

Ted stood up as Roy came to the desk, and said,

"Roy Harold, I am Ted Hall, vice-chairman of the Ashley Lee Group. I am here to ask you some serious questions, and because of their nature, I am going to caution you.

'Roy Harold, you have the right to remain silent and you are not obliged to answer any of the questions I or anyone else asks you. Anything you do say will be recorded and written down and may be given in evidence if necessary in a court of law.'

Do you understand what I have just said?"

"Yes, of course I understand, but why am I being cautioned?"

"Before I answer that question, I have to ask if, after that caution, you feel the need for union representation or any other person who may give you help or advice."

"No, I don't think so, I can speak for myself."

"As well as the meeting being held under caution, the proceedings will also be recorded, and you will be given a copy of the tape if you feel you need it. Have you any objection to what I have just said?"

Roy Harold shook his head.

"Right," said Ted, sitting down again, "shall we proceed? I have already introduced myself as the vice chairman of the company, and assisting me with the enquiry are …."

At this point, everyone gave their names and the position they held within the company.

Ted opened a box file and took out the costing sheets he had examined in Spain. He passed some of them towards Roy Harold, and said,

"Do you recognise these costings?"

"They seem to be in my writing, so I must have done them." he replied.

"And these?" asked Ted, pushing some more towards

365

him.

He nodded, and asked if this was about some of the projects the company had failed to win.

"What makes you say that?" Ted asked.

"Those in that pile we won, the others we lost. It's like that in this game, some you win, some you lose."

"Offering tenders is not a game, Mr Harold, and in this company, we don't play to lose. Let me ask you something else regarding your costings. Do you submit them for checking or do you sent them straight to the company asking for the quotation?"

"I send it in without anyone checking. I've been doing this job long enough to know there is no need for anyone to question my figures."

"I'm questioning your figures Mr Harold, and in front of witnesses. The major cost of projects for this company is the price per square metre of brick walling. That is a set price, and has to be used on all calculations. On some of these costings, they vary by as much as five pounds a square metre. How do you account for that?"

There was silence as Roy Harold stared at Ted.

"Are you refusing to answer?" Ted asked.

Again there was no reply.

Ted asked him about other costs that varied throughout his quotations, but once again, he refused to answer.

Ted asked the others if they had any questions, but as nobody had, he carried on.

"If you do not want to answer any more questions about the costings Mr Harold, I am going to ask you about something else. Do you know or have you associated with anyone named Steven Royle?"

"Never heard of him." came the sullen reply.

"That's funny," Ted said, "I have a photograph of you and Mr Royle together in a pub, and another, taken two weeks later, of you both in a restaurant."

Ted passed them to the others in the room, but Roy Harold refused to look at them.

Just at that moment, the telephone rang. Ted reached out, picked it up, and said,

"Ted Hall."

He listened for a moment, and then said,

"He has? Right Richard, thank you for letting me know"

There was something said by the other person, and then Ted replied,

"Not yet, but I'm sure it won't be long. Thanks again for your co-operation, and I'll let you know the outcome here."

Ted put the phone down and looked at Roy Harold.

"That was the chairman of Matra Enterprises. Mr Royle has just admitted his part in a plot to defraud Matra and Ashley Lee, and has implicated you as his partner. Have you anything to say to that?"

Mr Harold remained silent.

Ted looked round at the others and said,

"Would anyone like to ask Mr Harold any other questions?"

Sandy and Vic remained silent, but it was Brendan who angrily asked what he had hoped to achieve by deliberately undermining the good name of the company.

Roy Harold sat in his chair not saying a word, he knew he had been rumbled and if he said anything, it would make matters worse. There were no more questions so Ted gave Sandy a nod. She went to the door, and let two plain clothed policemen into the office.

Ted stood up, and said,

"Roy Harold, I am making an accusation that from April last year and up to the present date, you and an accomplice, known as Steven Royle, set out to defraud the two companies you work for. Both companies have undeniable evidence that connect you and Mr Royle to the crime and you are to be prosecuted in accordance with the law. You are dismissed from the Ashley Lee Group with immediate effect, and you will lose all rights and privileges the company offered. The two policemen will escort you to your office, where you may collect only your personal clothing, and the office will be locked prior to being searched for further evidence. Have you anything you would like to say in your defence before you are arrested and charged?"

Roy Harold shook his head and without another word, stood up and walked to the policemen, who led him out of the office.

There was stunned silence as everyone reflected on what had happened and what it would have meant if Roy Harold had not been caught.

Ted was the first to speak.

"Sandy, Gentlemen, thank you for your assistance in a situation I never want to see again. I don't know how you all feel, but I am still shaking inside. I would like to suggest that if you have nothing of importance to do right now, we all go home early."

They all nodded in agreement, and stood up ready to leave. Vic came to the desk, put his hand out and said,

"Mr Hall, you handled that interview admirably. As a union official, I congratulate you, and as your friend, I welcome you back to the company. The group is going to be better than ever with you at the helm."

Everyone else agreed with him, and they all went out of the office, leaving him with Sandy.

Ted looked at her and said,

"That is the worst thing I have ever had to do in my life, and on the first day in my new job. I am going home in a few minutes, and you have my permission to do the same if you want to. I would like the interview typed up from the tape, but not today. It will take a while for you to do, and I don't want you rushing to get it finished by tomorrow either. There is plenty of time before this goes to court, but please make sure it is ready when our legal team need it. I understand that now I am 'top dog' there is a car at my disposal to take me anywhere I want."

Sandy said there was, and would contact the pool for one of the drivers to come and see him.

Ted was suddenly alone in a quiet office, and after such a hectic day, was glad of the peace.

Ten minutes later, a driver came to the office, the same driver who had picked Ted up at the airport years ago when he was first asked to come to the head office.

"Word has got around Mr Hall that you are working for the company again. May I personally welcome you back, and as the senior driver in the pool, I will be available for you should you need to travel anywhere. If you need picking up any morning, let me know the day before and I'll arrange everything."

"Thank you Joe. I have a bit of tidying up to do, and I'm ready to go home. Shall we say fifteen minutes at the main door?"

Joe left, and Ted gathered all the days' paperwork together. He put it in a box file and was ready to go home. He phoned Sandy, told her he was on his way, but would be back at the office later in the week. He met Joe at the main door, and was driven back to granddad's home to be greeted by his wife and step-daughter. He was given a glass of red wine, and had to sit and tell them what had happened that day. He was glad when the evening meal was ready, because for some reason, he was absolutely starving.

In bed that night, a place where he and Ross did most

of their personal talking when they were at granddads, Ross asked,

"How did Sandy react when you asked her to come to the chairman's office?"

Ted told Ross exactly what he had said, and what Sandy's reaction had been.

"You didn't say that about her thong, did you?" Ross asked in horror.

Ted told her he had, and that she took it as a joke.

Ross laughed, and said she would have to apologise to Sandy next time she saw her.

Ted told Ross he now had a driver to take him anywhere and to pick him up whenever he wanted, which meant they could be taken to or picked up from the airport without having to bother granddad.

"Do you feel it worthwhile going back to work?" Ross asked.

"I think it will be in the long run. I am glad it's with your approval though, I would not have considered it if you hadn't encouraged me."

"It does a happy wife good to have a happy husband and daughter. And I am happy Ted, happy for us and for you as well. I can see you are shattered, so I'll not make any demands on your body tonight, but I'll let you recharge you batteries ready for tomorrow."

They had a kiss, turned over and Ted was asleep in minutes.

FOURTEEN

On Friday morning, Ted and Ross were driven to the head office. Ted had invited Ross to come with him so he could show her round and give her some idea what his work consisted of.

They were in the office before anyone else arrived. Ted did not want his colleagues to know they were there because he was sure they would act differently if they knew in advance, and Ted did not want that. As soon as he went to his desk, he noticed a new pack of coffee beside the machine. He smiled, and told Ross what he had said to Sandy about the coffee and she had made sure the right brand was ready for Ted's use. He brewed a pot, and he and Ross drank it while he showed her some of the plans the company was bidding for. Just after eight thirty, the normal starting time for many of the staff, Ted dialled a number on the internal phone. When it was answered, Ted said,

"Morning Sandy, can you come up to my office?" he was about to put the phone down, when he added,

"Oh, Sandy, better keep your thong on this morning, Ross is in the office with me."

"Ted!" Ross gasped in horror, but at the same time she could hear Sandy laughing.

Two minutes later, Sandy was in his office. She went straight to Ross, kissed her cheek and hugged her.

"Can't you keep your husband under control." she asked in amusement.

"I don't think anyone can keep Ted under control," Ross replied, "he has a mind of his own."

"That is one thing I know for certain." Sandy said. "When he first started here at head office, he was a 'go getter', and because of his attitude, most people could have a laugh and a joke with him. Then he started to get

371

cheeky, and I realised that he and I had the same warped sense of humour, which is one reason why we worked so well together. Only Ted Hall could get away with talking to me about thongs because I knew he wasn't being serious. Anyone else but Ted would have got a mouthful of abuse."

"I think I'll have to teach him a few manners," Ross replied, "it sounds to me that he is taking the interpretation of 'vice chairman' the wrong way."

They all had a laugh, and then Sandy passed a huge stack of mail over to him. While he started to read through it, Sandy and Ross sat and discussed their visit the following Sunday.

Ted sorted the mail into piles, destined for the sections or departments he thought it had to go. There was a large pile in front of him which would have gone to Roy Harold's desk, but since he was still in custody and his office had not yet been cleared, there was nobody to do his work. It should have been passed to a junior, but his work would have to be sent to Ted in Spain before it could be submitted. Ted decided the best plan at the moment was to take the major projects back with him, and he could work on them at home.

"Are there any more project enquiries anywhere Sandy." Ted asked.

"Not that I know of." she answered.

"What about Roy Harold's office?"

"There could be, would you like me to have a look?"

"If you don't mind please. I'm going to have to take these to Spain to sort out and I'll have to do them all until we employ a new person. We'd better get an advert sorted out and then Ashley can interview them and make a decision."

"I rather think that Ted Hall is going to be the one doing that." Sandy told him with a smile. "You are in charge of the company now."

"That's going to take some getting used to." He answered.

Sandy left the room and came back a few minutes later with a small stack of papers.

"These were on his desk, all waiting to be looked at." She put them on top of the others and said they would keep him out of mischief for a while.

Ted turned to Ross, and asked,

"When we were moving things into the house, did you see my brief case? It is grey leather with my name under the handle."

"No Ted," Ross answered, "I didn't see anything like that. Do you think you've left it somewhere?"

"I must have." he replied, "I know it was in my office before the accident. Maybe I had it with me at the yard and lost it when I fell."

Sandy left the office again while they were talking and returned minutes later carrying Ted's briefcase.

"I remember you putting it in the cupboard in the file room a few days before you left. There is nobody in your old office anymore, it's used as a store. The case was where you left it, top shelf of the section where all your projects were filed."

Ted thanked her for remembering where it was, and put all the papers into it.

Ted sorted all he had to do that day, and told Sandy he would be back next Thursday or Friday to tidy up before flying back to Spain.

"I know you and Phil are coming over on Sunday, but we will not be talking shop. It is a day of rest, and I regard the weekend for leisure and pleasure. I'll let you know next week about the future trips and how we will have to work. It may be a little strange at first, but I'm sure we'll get it right eventually."

When Sandy left the office, Ted phoned Sir Ashley and let him know what he had made a start on and brought him up to date with other matters. He mentioned Sandy's visit at the weekend, and said that Ross would like him to come over as well if that was possible.

Ashley declined the invitation, but told Ted to thank Ross for thinking of him.

Half an hour later, Ted and Ross were on their way back to granddad's home.

Ross told her granddad that she was impressed with what the company was doing, and was more than interested in the projects that needed costing and submitting. She told Ted she would take notice of the costings he did, and if he won, she would be proud to say that her husband had a hand in it.

"Where have Sam and mum got to?" Ted asked.

"It's Beth's day at the hairdressers and Sam went with her. Sam said something about having her hair trimmed. I hope that's all right."

"Yes granddad," Ross answered, "we said the other day that it needed tidying up. She knows what to have done without asking me."

As they were talking, they heard mum's car pull up outside, and moments later, Sam came running into the room with a new hair style.

"Wow!" said Ted, "Who is this young lady? Sam that is a very nice haircut you've had, it makes you look older as well. Anyone could take you for at least twelve."

"I am twelve." Sam said indignantly.

"See, I said it would work."

Ted put his arms round Sam and gave her a hug.

"Joking apart Sam, it looks smashing."

"I agree with Ted," said Ross. "It is nice and short, just right for the hot days when we get back home."

Mum said she wasn't sure, saying the hair should have more body in it, and maybe back-combing would help.

Ross ignored her mother's comments, knowing that it was her way of having a say, right or wrong.

On Saturday, Ted, Ross and Sam spent a day with Ted's Brother, his wife and daughter, who would be flying out of Heathrow the following day. Ted was glad he had been able to see him again after all the years, and said they hoped they could visit New Zealand in the near future for a holiday. They both promised to keep in touch with each other on a regular basis via email.

On the Sunday morning of Sandy's visit, Ted and Ross were in the garden setting up the barbeque and hoping the day would continue to be warm enough for them to eat outside. They were walking towards the house, when a van pulled up outside the front door. The driver got out and said he was looking for a Miss Samantha. Ross said she was Sam's Mother, and what was it he wanted.

"I have a package in the van," he said, "addressed to her, and my instructions are that if it was possible, I should deliver it to her in person."

Ross looked a bit sceptical, but went inside to find Sam. They came out to the van, and the driver opened the doors. There was a large box inside and a big label on the side with Sam's name on it. The driver and Ted pulled it to the doors and lifted it down to the ground. The driver asked Sam if she would sign his bit of paper so that everyone knew she had received it. Sam hurriedly wrote her name on the pad, and turned back to the box when the van disappeared down the drive. Sam was able to reach the top and pulled back one of the flaps. She looked inside, and her eyes lit up.

"Mum, dad," she shouted, "look, it's the doll's house

from Mr Lees' house."

Ted and Ross looked at each other, and then went to the box. Sure enough, there was the doll's house and several dolls as well. Sam was so excited she could hardly keep still, dancing around and asking Ted to take the house out of the box.

"Wait until we get it inside," Ted told her, "then we can put it somewhere where it won't get broken."

Ted and Ross carefully lifted the box and carried it into the den, where granddad suggested it went in the alcove near the fireplace. It was lifted out and placed with great care so nothing could get damaged. The dolls were taken out of the box as well, and Sam immediately wanted to play.

"First of all young lady," said Ross, "you are going to ring Sir Ashley and thank him for such a generous present and you can play with it to your hearts delight afterwards. Ted will dial the number for you."

Sam was very polite when she spoke to Sir Ashley, even calling herself Samantha as she thanked him for the very generous gift.

The afternoon was as warm as they hoped, the sun shining so they could have the barbeque in the garden. Granddad proved to be a dab hand with the grilling of the meats, while Ross and Ted made up the salad and baked potatoes. Everyone enjoyed the food and drink, especially Phil, who normally was quiet and reserved but opened up and held a good discussion with granddad and Ted about the future of computers in business. Phil and Sandy left after the sun had set and the remnants of the party were left until the next day for clearing away.

The next few days were very busy for Ross and Ted as they prepared themselves for the flight back to their home in Spain. Ted had to tie up his work at the office and Ross had to make sure everything was clean, ready for packing.

The afternoon they left the manor, they said their goodbyes to granddad and mum before being driven to the airport by Joe in the company car.

They were all glad to get back to their house and the guarantee of warm sunshine. The pool had been covered while they were away so had barely suffered any loss of water. Ted had to put some chemicals into the water to clear the slight cloudiness that had formed, before topping the water up from the well so that they could have a swim.

Before leaving the UK, Ted had arranged with Sandy that he would be at the head office on Wednesday and Thursday of the next week, but not the following two weeks as he would be on his belated honeymoon.

In the days that followed, Ross and Sam tried their best to find out where Ted was taking them, but he still refused to tell them.

The day finally came when Mr and Mrs Hall with their daughter Sam left the house to go on honeymoon. Ted drove towards Malaga, but before reaching the centre, turned off in the direction of the docks. He drove through the gates towards the cruise liner terminal and pulled up alongside the check in office. It was only when they got out of the car that he told them they were going on a cruise round the Mediterranean. He had booked a two roomed suite, Sam having her own bedroom next door to Ted and Ross. The cruise was a great success, and ten days later when they arrived back in Malaga, Ross and Sam declared it to be one of Ted's better ideas.

Three weeks after the cruise, Sam was back in school, Ted was flying to London and the head office, and Ross said she was glad of the peace.

Some weeks later, Ross and Ted were in bed, and as usual, started to talk.

"Do you remember some months ago," Ross said, "when I asked you about your previous girlfriends?"

"You mean when you wanted to know the intimate details of my sexual encounters?" Ted asked.

"Do you remember what happened after you finished telling me?"

"We had fantastic sex." Ted replied.

"We certainly did." Ross said, reaching down for him. "Talk to me again," she whispered, "Tell me about one of the times you had sex with someone, Tina maybe."

Ted looked at his wife with some amusement.

"Are you telling me, that if I describe in detail my movements with a woman, it turns you on?"

"More than you will ever know, Ted." Ross breathed. "Tell me about the first time with Tina. I want to stroke you like this as you speak, but don't touch me unless I ask you to. Will you do it for me? For some reason, I can imagine you doing what you are describing, and it gets me going big time, and if you put it in afterwards, I'll nearly explode with pleasure."

Ted was a little unsure of what Ross was doing, but thought he would tell her a couple of episodes of his time with Tina to see what Ross's reaction would be.

"We had been seeing each other for about three weeks when I had my first glimpse of Tina's sexual appetite. After leaving the dance hall, we went to the car park at the rear. It was dark and my car was parked in one corner out of the way. Once inside, we started kissing, but it wasn't long before I had my hand inside her dress top feeling her rock hard nipple. I wasted no time in running down the zip and undoing her bra so I could get both hands on her. I could only have been touching her for a couple of minutes when she took one hand off her breast and pushed it up her skirt. Her legs

378

were wide open and as soon as I got inside her briefs, she had my trousers open and was going mad with her hand. I moved my hand at the same speed as hers, and within minutes, I told her I was reaching my peak and let it go on her legs. She calmly reached inside her handbag, took out a pack of tissues, wiped her legs and told me she had managed it twice. Five minutes later she was dressed again and I drove her home. The following week, we were once again in the dance hall, stood in one corner kissing. Her kisses were very passionate, and as we broke, she said,

"Have you got any rubbers with you?"

"Yes." I replied, my hopes rising as well as something else.

She took hold of my hand and almost dragged me outside. Tina only lived about a hundred yards from the hall, and we were almost running in that direction. She opened the back door and rushed inside the house, which was in darkness except for a light on top of the television set.

"My parents are out and won't be back until late." she said. As she was speaking, she took her dress off and told me to hurry up and get undressed. She was naked before I got my trousers off, and was lying on the floor as I put the rubber on. There were no preliminaries that night, I was straight in and moving. I didn't take long for either of us to finish, and about half an hour after leaving the dance hall, we were back again."

Ted paused, and in a strained voice, said,

"If you keep that speed up on me Ross, you will get a white fountain any minute now."

Ross pulled Ted on top of her, and minutes later they both enjoyed the result.

It took some time for them to get their breath back, and it was Ross who spoke first.

"That was good! You can tell me more stories of your exploits occasionally if they all end like that."

Ross snuggled herself up against Ted and kissed him.

"Ted," Ross asked, "have you ever told me a lie since we have been together?"

"No darling," Ted replied, "I've always told you the truth. I've never needed to lie anyway."

"Have you been with any other woman since we've been together?" Ross asked.

"No!" said Ted in a shocked voice.

"I'm not accusing you Ted. I'm sure that you would tell me if you had. Have you wanted to have another woman?"

"Never Ross that I swear to you." Ted answered. He was starting to worry as to where these questions were going.

"What about Sandy?" Ross asked him.

"What about Sandy? We had an affair several years ago, and as far as I'm concerned, it finished when she found out she was pregnant. I've moved on and met and married a fantastic lady who I adore. She loves having sex with me, and I enjoy making love to her as well. I have no need for sex with anyone else. Sandy has dropped a few subtle hints that Phil is still not keeping her satisfied but there is no way I want to start another affair with her. Why all these questions Ross? Have I done or not done something to you?"

"It's nothing like that at all, Ted. I've seen the way Sandy looks at you, and I'm sure that if you dropped a hint, she would be all over you."

"I don't want her all over me Ross. Why have you started this conversation? Has Sandy said something to you? Is that what this is all about? If an accusation has been made, I'm packing the job in right now."

Ted was so annoyed, he got out of bed and left the

bedroom. Still naked, he made his way over to the house, and went straight to the computer desk. He switched it on and was waiting for it to warm up when Ross came into the house. She saw him start to type and went over and stood beside him.

"What are you doing?" she asked in a worried voice.

"Resigning." Ted answered simply. "As soon as I send this, I will move out of your house then I can't be questioned about something that is furthest from my mind. I love you with everything I have Ross, but I will not be accused of having sex with another woman."

Ross reached down and switched the computer off.

"What the...." Ted started to say.

"Will you stop being so bloody minded, and listen to what I have to say. I am not accusing you of anything, I merely asked you a question about Sandy. She has been dropping hints to me as well Ted, saying the same about Phil not keeping her happy. What I was going to suggest was that if you wanted to, I would have no objection to you putting your hand in her briefs, but I would want you to tell me all about it. A full and intimate description of how she reacted, what she was wearing and the colour."

"What's wrong with you Ross? I've not seen you like this before. Since we started our lives together we have known when we wanted sex and you have not needed me to turn you on by talking. Are you saying that I don't turn you on anymore and you need some extra stimulation? If that is the case, I *am* leaving, and right now."

Ted stood up and was about to take a step forward, when Ross pushed him firmly back in the chair.

"Sit there Edwin Hall, and don't move or open your mouth again until I have finished speaking."

Ted was so surprised at Ross's action that he sat and

looked at her, his mouth open.

"I am not making any accusations against you. You told me a few minutes ago that you had not told me a lie since we've been together. I believe that without a shadow of a doubt. You also told me that you had not touched another woman since we began our life together. Any woman who cares about her man would instinctively know if he had. I know for certain that you haven't. What I am telling you, is that I would have no objection to you helping Sandy to some relief occasionally. By that, I mean with your hand and only with your hand."

Ted had calmed down slightly, but was still worried by his wife's change. He stood up and wrapped both his arms round her, holding her naked body tightly against his. He kissed her on her neck and felt her respond by pressing her body even tighter against him. Ted felt her reaction, and despite the short length of time since their love making, Ted felt himself getting aroused.

"My dearest wonderful wife," Ted whispered in her ear, "is this all something to do with the change, and you don't want as much sex with me?"

"No Ted! It may have something to do with the change, but I swear to you that the feeling for sex has not diminished. If anything it has increased."

Ted moved his head so that he was looking into her eyes.

"Lady Ross Hall, I love you much more than I can ever express and standing here holding your naked body makes me feel so calm. Have we ever had sex twice in one night?"

Ross shook her head.

Ted took hold of her hand and led her to the bottom of the room. He took two cushions off the settee, and placed them on the rug in front of the fireplace. Without another word, they lay down and spent a long, long time making love.

When they got their breath back, Ross and Ted, still naked, walked slowly along the path with their arms round each other, back to their bedroom. No further mention was made about the words that had been said that night, there was no need, both understood what had been said and why.

About two weeks later, on a night Ted got back from London, Ross could tell that he had something on his mind. She waited until they were cuddled up in bed, and asked,

"What's wrong Ted?"

Ted was silent for a minute, and in a low voice said,

"Sandy is getting extremely suggestive. It's got to the point that she is all but asking me for sex."

"I said the other week that it would be all right….."

"No, Ross, it isn't all right." Ted interrupted. "The way that she is coming over is almost a demand. I'm sure she thinks she has a hold on me because of our affair, and I'm afraid that she could let it slip to the wrong person, and I would be out of work again with a big stain on my character."

"I don't think for one minute Sandy would do that to you Ted, because it would stir up trouble for her as well. Please, take my advice love, give her some relief. A couple of good orgasms may keep her happy for a while and help keep her mind on her job as your PA."

"I'm not happy with that Ross. You tell me I can do it as long as I tell you and then we can have fantastic sex. I could easily tell you I have done it to her when I haven't."

"Yes you could Ted, but that is not the way you do things. I know you better than that. Why not let her think she has won by giving her some relief."

"I'm more worried about the next one, and the next one and the one after that. If I do it once, she could want it every time I'm in the office, and wanting to do it to me as well."

"I don't blame her, I want to do it to you as well."

As Ross spoke, she reached down for him, and a few minutes later, they were snuggled together getting their breath back.

"You are getting greedy Mrs Hall." Ted said.

"It's your fault, you shouldn't be so good at it." Ross replied. "The more I have, the more I want and the more I want the more I enjoy it. For quite a while now, I've started feeling very randy when I'm alone with you, so I think you had better start working a full week, or I may wear you out."

"I hope there's many years before that happens, my wonderful wife"

"Me too dearest Ted. I think we had better get some sleep because there is the final load of stone for the patio area being delivered tomorrow, and then we have the balustrades to finish. I think we should have some kind of gate at the beginning of the track, keeping our house safe from unwanted visitors."

They gave each other another kiss before turning over. Ted did not fall asleep immediately because the things Ross had said were still going through his mind. Should he really do to Sandy what Ross had suggested? Ted thought it a bad idea, but at the same time he knew Sandy would continue to hound him if he didn't.

This was the one thing that spoiled his return to work with the Ashley Lee Group, and his main worry was if the situation would somehow distract him from his job. He could not afford that, knowing that he was now in a position of trust. He must be able to put all his skills together for the sake of the company.

Ted fell asleep, now wondering if his return to work was such a good thing.

If you enjoyed reading 'A House in the Hills', look out for the sequel. It is simply called 'Ted's Return' and will be available soon.

.

www.ingramcontent.com/pod-product-compliance
Lightning Source LLC
Chambersburg PA
CBHW030916050726
47498CB00003BA/769